THE ORGAN
LOFT MURDERS

DAVID BAKER

authorHOUSE®

AuthorHouse™ UK
1663 Liberty Drive
Bloomington, IN 47403 USA
www.authorhouse.co.uk
Phone: UK TFN: 0800 0148641 (Toll Free inside the UK)
UK Local: (02) 0369 56322 (+44 20 3695 6322 from outside the UK)

This is a work of fiction. All of the characters, names, incidents, organizations, and dialogue in this novel are either the products of the author's imagination or are used fictitiously.

Published by AuthorHouse 03/22/2022

ISBN: 978-1-6655-9760-9 (sc)
ISBN: 978-1-6655-9761-6 (hc)
ISBN: 978-1-6655-9759-3 (e)

Print information available on the last page.

This book is printed on acid-free paper.

ACKNOWLEDGEMENTS

I am grateful to Mary Auckland, Jennifer Baker, Dani Dolan, Anne Kilbey, Joan Letocha, Julie Taylor, and Francis Vaughan for all their help with this novel, whether it was assisting with the background research or reading and commenting on the various drafts. Especial thanks go to James Taylor for the cover illustration.

CHAPTER 1

A GREAT MUSICIAN IS NO MORE

Thomas Augustus Burchill, Doctor of Music (Yorbridge), Fellow of the College of Organists, Associate of the Philharmonic Society of London, was different; special; unique. 'TAB', 'the good Doctor', Tommy (to his best friends only), was the heart and soul of Hartleydale. There had never been a musician like 'our Yorkshire Choirmaster'. Queen Victoria had written to TAB personally after his singers' Command Performance at Windsor Castle in late 1878. Hartley Parish Church Choir was widely regarded as the best in the country. Burchill wanted it to be the best in the world.

Fame and celebrity status had not come easily. Burchill was a singular man; all were agreed on that. Choir members had been sacked; musical assistants had walked out; vicars and church authorities had railed against his antics. However, nobody, but nobody, could take away from TAB's achievements since being appointed Organist and Choirmaster; the singers had gone from a rough and rustic mob of musicians to the most heavenly choir on earth.

The dream was shattered in a mere 24 hours. 29th September 1879: Hartley was in shock; nobody could believe it. Monday morning's *Gazette and Argus* had lauded Burchill's immaculate conducting at one of his glorious choral concerts; that same day's late-night-final edition announced his death, sudden and unexplained.

The evening of Sunday, 28th September: TAB had locked the organ loft, made sure the hydraulic blowing apparatus that raised the wind was switched off, exchanged pleasantries with the Vicar, the Reverend Dr

1

Percy G. Banks, said goodnight to the verger, lit a cigar and walked up the road to his house on New Station Street. Unusually, Burchill had not stopped for refreshment at *The Station Hotel*. Instead, he persuaded Ernest Snelgrove, lead tenor in the Parish Church choir, to let him into the latter's sweet shop. TAB was in excellent form, according to Snelgrove, lashing out on a bar of his favourite chocolate as a reward to himself for 'the evening's excellent entertainment'. Snelgrove had offered the great doctor a discount on his purchase, given the awe, reverence, respect, and no little amount of fear in which he held the great choirmaster.

Martha Burchill had found TAB in good spirits on his arrival home, and, over a supper of cold ham and bread, followed by cake and preserved fruit, he had regaled his daughter with a report of the evening's concert, a 'stunning performance' (according to the conductor) of Charleton Mann's *David and Goliath*. 'If only May Eliz' had been alive to hear t'performance. Thiv nowt ont' choir at 'Artley; none of 'em anywhere! We's bound ta be a cathedral afore long'. The good doctor had looked at the large photograph hanging over the living room fireplace; five long years since Mary Elizabeth Burchill had died. TAB went to bed at midnight, slept soundly and snored loudly, much to Martha's consternation. Annie, the live-in maid, was well insulated from the noise, ensconced as she was in her minuscule attic accommodation.

The following morning, 29th September 1879, Burchill had breakfasted, as usual, on bacon, eggs, devilled kidneys (his absolute favourite) and bread. Martha had unlocked the side door to the house to let in the first of his piano students at half past nine precisely. He had left home at noon to do his daily organ practice. Once at St Martin's, he handed the music list to Assistant Organist Charles Verney. Verney had gone to the printers post-haste so that the details of the next services could be distributed in time for the following Sunday's worship. Scholars at the nearby charity school heard the sound of TAB practising his voluntaries until approximately two thirty. After that, there was silence, only broken by the sound of ladies dusting, tidying, and mopping up after the previous evening's performance. The church had been packed: some 400 singers from all over Hartleydale, in addition to the 70 men and boys in the Parish Church choir itself and over 600 in the audience. The cleaners' work was significantly more onerous than usual in consequence.

Martha had begun to worry when her father did not return for dinner at three thirty. Burchill was regular as clockwork, priding himself on being on time for everything: service; lesson; practice; food, and especially dinner. Any later than his customary dining hour and he would be hard pressed to eat, sleep and prepare for the Monday evening rehearsal with the men of the church choir. As the clock struck four, Martha told Annie to go down to the Parish Church and find out what had happened and when her father would be home for his food. Perhaps he had lost himself in his organ playing, or encountered a problem with the instrument, for he had recently been complaining about the unpredictability of the hydraulic engines, given the erratic water pressure in Hartley. Could he have been accosted by a troublesome student, or an errant choirman? Had a fellow Freemason tried to inveigle TAB into yet another land purchase? Burchill already owned fields and cottages to the north of Hartley and, as a 'reputable gentleman' was known to have his sights on more acquisitions before the town council got there first. Had the good doctor forgotten to tell his daughter he had a musical engagement elsewhere in Yorkshire and would not therefore be home until the evening?

None of these excuses for TAB's disappearance rang true, and Martha knew it. Thomas Burchill was meticulous in his arrangements, both personal and professional; he just did not miss an appointment of any kind. Her fears were confirmed when a breathless Annie returned from the Parish Church to report that Dr Burchill was nowhere to be found and had not been seen or heard since finishing his practice more than an hour previously. Upon hearing this news, Martha dispatched the maid once more; this time to locate Charles Verney. Verney and Annie searched both church (no sign of him) and various watering holes in which Burchill might have taken refuge (albeit for no obvious reason). There was neither sight nor sound in any of the locations visited.

By five o'clock, news of TAB's disappearance had begun to spread round the town. As a keen member of the Hartley Choral Society (conducted by TAB) Detective Chief Inspector Wright Watson, Head of the local CID, began to take an interest in the disappearance upon his return from Leeds. Alighting the train at Hartley Central Station, he was met by Detective Sergeant Harry Makepeace, who appraised him of the situation. Watson urged calm but also ordered a thorough inspection of central Hartley, based on Burchill's last known whereabouts.

A second search of the Parish Church, conducted this time by police constables, yielded nothing, until Charles Verney noticed that the blower switch at the organ console was in the 'on' position and yet no wind was getting through to the bellows. Verney, accompanied by two policemen, took the long and tortuous route down into the crypt, where the huge water engines and their supply tanks were located. Gas had never been installed in this subterranean space and the candle light was less than adequate for the three men to complete a proper search. As they neared the machinery, however, a large figure appeared. Verney recognised the frame immediately; he had observed that back over many years. It had been easy to do so from his vantage point in the choirstalls opposite the Parish Church's four-manual organ recently completely renewed and further enlarged by Ishmael Monkhill & Sons, organ builders of Leeds. Of course, TAB must have got absorbed attempting to repair a problem with those troublesome hydraulics! The good Doctor had been here all the time!

Verney's sense of relief was short lived. As he placed his hand on TAB's shoulder, Dr Thomas Burchill, Mus Doc, FCO, Associate of the Philharmonic Society of London, slumped forward, face down into the water tank. He was quite dead.

CHAPTER 2

JOURNEYING BACK TO HELL

The Reverend Canon Percy George Banks MA, DD (Hibernia) was worried; more than he had ever been. The meeting at Lambeth Palace had been a disaster; so bad, in fact, that he cancelled his room at The Athenaeum for the evening of 29th September. There would be no celebratory dinner with fellow clergy. There was nothing to celebrate. He determined to return home forthwith. The Archbishop of Canterbury had not been persuaded that Hartley's case for cathedral status was yet strong enough to take further at this stage. How could Tait not see the advantages of Hartley over Halifax and Wakefield? Or had Eboracum put him up to it? The Archbishop of York had been prejudiced against Hartley Parish Church ever since that prestigious party of American organists had visited. Banks smiled as he remembered how their leader, Hiram H Morton III, had said Burchill's choir was far superior to those of Yorbridge, York, London, and Canterbury Cathedrals, all put together. The moment of glory had been short lived, and Hartley Parish now had more enemies than friends in the upper echelons of the Church of England and, just as worryingly, the Houses of Parliament.

As the train left King's Cross, Banks wondered if his dream would ever be realised. Should I leave Yorkshire? I have never been accepted and my children and wife all hate it; Hartley is a cruel place for one not born there; 'God's Own County', they call it. I have never understood the people of the West Riding. I have tried so hard to fight the good fight. But I am no St Paul. I fear that I cannot win the race, even if I am able to keep the faith. Or at least not in the hellhole that is my present parish.

5

The Vicar of Hartley stopped writing in his diary and looked out of the carriage window. It was still light enough for him to see the north London suburbs. Banks thought he saw the spire of his old church in the distance. I was happier then and there, living on £75 a year, than I am at Hartley on £2,000! Those two years of curacy were the happiest days of my life! Engine smoke clouded his view and the glimpse of earlier joy was gone.

'Time to inspect the accounts!' Banks said loudly to his empty carriage. 'Perhaps looking at our finances will take my mind off today's debacle!'

He opened his briefcase and took out the papers for the next meeting of the Organ Trustees.

'It is good that I am alone. The last thing I want to do is to have to talk to people. As soon as someone sees my dog collar, they are off on their hobby horses: church, state, politics, Methodism! That is why I will never use this new-fangled dining car; I would rather go hungry than have to talk to strangers over dinner!'

The Vicar of Hartley pored over his Treasurer's neat copperplate then laughed out loud. 'The Parish and district of Hartleydale will never go bankrupt as long as Arnold Entwistle is in charge, I know it!'

The express train to Wakefield was steaming ahead at full speed. Banks smiled at the sense of power and rapidity that was emanating from the front of the train. It reminded him of his youth and the days when he went riding with his brothers on the family estate.

'But that is not the point, is it?' Banks looked around the compartment, as if expecting support from his invisible fellow travellers. 'If Hartley Parish Church is to become a cathedral, then we have to spend more: on the building, the staff, the school, the music!'

None of Banks's shadowy companions thought to reply.

'Then there's the bloody organ. We still haven't had Monkhill's last bill. I should never have agreed to all that work!' Banks found himself standing, his fists clenched. He looked at himself in the mirror above the seats on the other side of his compartment. 'Look at me! Just look at me! I am only 40, but I look more like 60!'

Banks noticed that the train had slowed; looking to his right, he saw that he was being observed from the carriage on the next track. The two vehicles bobbed up and down in response to each other as the stiff carriage suspension failed to cope with the junction into Doncaster. A group of children laughed and pointed at him. He smiled weakly, then pulled down the blind and returned to his accounts.

'I cannot agree to what goes on with that pipe organ! I am the Vicar! I am in charge. There is no other authority but me. I will get rid of these Organ Trustees! Who do they think they are? What right do they have to tell me, the incumbent, how the instrument should be built and located and managed? Why are the accounts kept secret from me? I swear that I will have done with them once and for all before I have finished.'

Banks put his head in his hands. 'Perhaps I should go back to Austria. I felt so much better after I had taken the waters at Bad Ischl.'

'What will Rose think if I do? I have hardly seen her or the children these past few months. I promised more time with my wife once the church had been rebuilt, but this bid for cathedral status is taking more of my time than anything else I have ever done. It will not do! I have six curates supposed to be helping; then four churchwardens and a Vestry Committee, to boot. None of them gives me the support I need – and deserve! Not one!'

'At least the Organist and Choirmaster is on my side, as far as he is on anybody's side.' Banks thought of Burchill and his stunning performance of Mendelssohn's *Elijah* in the Town Hall the previous April. 'What does the prophet sing? "And I, even I, only am left. And they seek my life, to take it away!"'

'And there are times when I really believe that!' Banks whispered, looking round the empty carriage and even out of the window, as if to make sure that no-one – no-one but God that is – was listening.

The train pulled into Wakefield. Banks snorted, in the knowledge that he had to alight there for the train to Hartley. He had always thought this to be the ultimate insult to 'his' town's aspirations. Wakefield had a direct train link to London; Hartley did not. Even Halifax had better connections!

Banks looked across at the spire of All Saints Church, Wakefield as he muttered to himself. 'Is that to be the home of the new diocese? Never! Never! Never! Not even if I have to commit murder to stop it happening!'

He wondered if anyone on the platform could tell what he was thinking. If they had looked into his eyes, they would have been able to read his every wicked thought, each piece of vengeance to be wreaked, one-and-all of his underhand and murderous plans. Banks calmed himself down with the realisation that he still held the trump card to end all trump cards: something that neither Halifax nor Wakefield would ever possess; an advantage that no other cathedral or abbey in the land had. 'World without end, Amen! As long as I have you, Thomas Augustus Burchill, I will prevail!'

The porter looked oddly at Banks as he carried the Vicar's luggage into his compartment. The extra tip meant that, once more, the space was empty, with not a potential fellow traveller in sight. The Vicar of Hartley smiled silently as the door was slammed shut behind him. The whistle blew and the train departed. He laughed as he glimpsed one more time at the spire pointing aggressively and threateningly into the night sky. As it disappeared ever more rapidly into both distance and darkness Banks calmed down and conjured up a glorious image of TAB in his red and gold DMus robes conducting the Choral Festival in Hartley Parish Church.

'Ee – a wor' in mi pomp an all'. Banks mimicked the Organist and Choirmaster's broad Yorkshire accent. 'Even the standing up and sitting down has to be practised to perfection when the good doctor is in charge!' The Vicar of Hartley's cares fell away knowing his greatest asset was making such a difference to the cause. Banks nodded and smirked at the thought of the extra salary he paid Burchill from his own pocket, and the pockets of his fellow Freemasons, though he wondered what his Organist and Choirmaster was also being paid by the Organ Trustees.

'Money well spent, that'.

Banks took out his pocket watch and calculated he had at least thirty minutes left. He put his business documents away and opened a secret pocket inside his case. He unwrapped the plain brown paper parcel and took out a series of cards. There was just enough opportunity to look at the photographs.

For once, the train from Wakefield to Hartley drew into its final destination on time. As the Parish Church clock struck midnight, the Reverend Dr Percy Banks walked wearily up the steps to where he expected his carriage and driver to be waiting for him. That was not the case on the evening of 29th September 1879.

'Detective Chief Inspector Watson! What are you doing here?'

'I am very sorry, Vicar. I have some bad news for you. And I believe that foul play may be involved'.

CHAPTER 3

AN IDENTITY IS CONFIRMED

Once arrangements had been made for the Vicar of Hartley's luggage to be returned to his house, Banks and Watson wound their way through the narrow streets leading from Hartley Central railway station over to the Parish Church. Much to the Vicar's frustration, the Detective Chief Inspector refused to give any detail as to what had happened at St Martin's, other than there had been a fatality in suspicious circumstances. The two men knew each other, though they rarely came into contact or conversed. Watson was a Methodist and (Banks suspected) a Liberal. TAB had attempted to recruit the Detective Chief Inspector to the Parish Church choir, given the policeman's fine bass voice. Watson would have none of it, preferring to spend his free evenings singing in the men-only Hartley Glee Union or the Choral Society, away from the demands of 'the missus' and five 'nippers', with a sixth on the way.

As detective and cleric neared the church, they were accosted by two beggarmen, stinking of ale. Banks shooed them away, resolving as he did so to renew his plea to the town council to have the hovels that detracted from St Martin's demolished, and their occupants dispersed to some far-flung out township. Banks had Holme Hill in mind. The more able and less work-shy amongst this detritus of humanity might even find gainful employment in Ernest Riddles's new factory there.

As the uniformed constable on guard at the entrance to the Parish Church moved the beggars on, they cursed and swore, spat, gesticulated, and grimaced at Banks and Watson. The Vicar looked disparagingly at the Head of Hartley CID; Wright Watson merely nodded in reply.

Banks looked up at his glorious church, freshly restored under the direction of the celebrated architect Sir Winston English. This was a cathedral in waiting, if ever there was one! And the interior was even more spectacular than the exterior! Each and every vestige of the old furnishings had been removed: pews, galleries, gravestones, monuments. In their place was a high altar, chancel choirstalls, a gargantuan organ (the largest and the finest in the land, according to Dr Burchill) and the best, all-male robed choir in England.

'Where are we going, Watson? Will you not tell me what has happened?'

'All in good time, sir. Walls have ears and, at this stage, I do not want the news of our discovery to leak out. There may still be a chance of catching the criminal almost red-handed'.

'Criminal? Red-handed? I wish you would tell me what has been going on here. Foul play in my church? That cannot be, surely!'

'All in good time, sir. We are nearly there.'

The Detective Chief Inspector led the Reverend Banks into the building, along the long, high-arched nave, up the chancel steps and past the far side of the organ. Charles Verney was standing at the instrument's console explaining the workings of the instrument to a constable. The Vicar grimaced as he noted that the bobby was still wearing his helmet in the House of God! Banks looked at Verney, who merely shook his head; never had the Vicar of Hartley seen the Assistant Organist so pale faced.

'Surely not down there, Watson? What on earth possesses you to make me visit the blowing chamber?'

'I think you ought to see, sir. Before we move the body.'

'Who is it, Detective Chief Inspector?' The Vicar of Hartley rubbed his tired eyes.

'All in good time, sir. We need you to identify the victim.'

Banks had of course encountered dead bodies many times before. He had performed the last rites as his parishioners lay dying often enough in his twenty years as a clergyman. No doubt he would see many more before he was done. Banks remembered the first time he had seen a person pass over. He had been a curate for barely a week when he was called to the home of a wealthy widow who had taken to the new priest as soon as she had set eyes on him. The Vicar of Hartley had benefited from her death in more ways than one as a result. It had shocked him: the moment when life ended and the soul departed. But where to?

'Mind your step, sir! A pity that you don't have proper lighting down here.'

'It was not thought necessary, Watson. Do you know how much the new gas installation cost us, and on top of everything else that we did to beautify this church?'

'I can imagine, sir.'

Banks followed Watson down the spiral stone staircase into the blowing chamber. The candles that they were holding flickered in the draught that was emanating from the far end of the cavernous space.

'This used to be a crypt, Watson. Over there you can see the old family vaults; on this side is the store where all the gravestones are kept.' Banks pointed vaguely to the surrounding walls.

'Gravestones, Vicar?'

'Before the church was restored, there were graves all across the floor of the nave. They were so shallow you could reach down and touch the skeletons below your pew seat. The place stank to high heaven with those rotting corpses. I had it all swept away, every skull and every bone. The slabs had to be moved as well. Either that or be broken up. Most families chose the former option.'

'And the other families?'

'They took their stones and their bones and had them placed in other churches,' Banks said haughtily.

Wright Watson scratched his head. 'I imagine you were none too popular with some of the good folk of Hartley over that, were you, sir?'

'Needs must, Inspector. I did not come to Hartley to be popular. I came to do my – God's – work.'

The Detective Chief Inspector took the Vicar of Hartley by the arm and led him towards the enormous water tanks that fed the organ's hydraulic blower. Banks recoiled as he saw a body leaning over the side of one of the metal containers, face down.

'We think the man must have drowned, sir. It seems to me that his head was held under until there was no more breath left in him. We will know more after the post-mortem.'

'Is that allowed, Detective Inspector?'

'It is if I say so, sir. It is possible that the man died of natural causes and just slumped over into the tank. On the other hand, the marks on his neck and the colour of his face suggest otherwise. Will you now take a look at him, sir?'

Banks nodded. Wright Watson ordered the two police constables standing guard by the corpse to turn the body over so the Vicar could look at the man's face. As they did so, Banks cried out in horror.

'Good Lord! It's him! It's my choirmaster. TAB – poor, poor TAB!'

'You confirm that it is Dr Thomas Burchill, then, sir?'

Banks took out a handkerchief to wipe away his tears and hide his emotions. He could only nod in answer to the policeman's question.

'Thank you, sir. I thought so, but I needed to be sure. A great man has been lost tonight.' Watson shook his head.

'He has indeed. And my plans have all gone awry.'

'Plans, sir?'

'For the music of this church, and much, much more.'

'Sorry to hear that, sir. Just one more thing, Dr Banks. Why is Burchill wearing this strange garb?'

Banks laughed, hysterically. 'That is not strange garb at all, Inspector. That is my Organist and Choirmaster's Doctor of Music gown and hood!'

'Bit strange to be wearing it down in this old crypt, though, isn't it, sir?'

Outside St Martin's Parish Church, the two beggars looked at the lights glowing and flickering in the church and watched the comings and goings at the porch and in the grounds. Two police constables appeared carrying a stretcher on which there was a body covered in blankets.

The beggars nudged each other and cackled quietly.

'Burchill's on his way, good and proper. Now who's next?'

CHAPTER 4

THE KING IS DEAD; LONG LIVE THE KING

Martha Burchill gazed down at her father. He looked asleep, content, at peace. She had seen that look on his face many times before, notably when he had finished a spectacular performance with one of his choirs, or yet another of his choristers had landed a prestigious post in a cathedral. She stroked his black wavy hair, then tugged his beard like she had done as a child.

'How did he die, Inspector?'

'We believe he was murdered, Miss Burchill. He was held face down in the water tank underneath the organ until he stopped breathing.'

'Murdered? My father? Who would do such a thing?'

'That's what I need to ask you. But first, shall we go to my office? This is not the ideal location to have a conversation.' Watson shook his head gently.

Martha Burchill nodded. She looked around the mortuary room and shuddered. An attendant had drawn the white sheet over her father's face. *This is the last place I should be. My father cannot be dead. I thought him to be immortal. He ought not to be lying here on a cold slab. He should be standing tall in front of his choir, barking instructions. What will I do? What will we all do?*

Wright Watson ushered Martha Burchill out of the mortuary room, down a long, tiled corridor, up a narrow staircase and onto the ground floor of Hartley Police Station. From there, they headed towards the

Detective Chief Inspector's office, where Watson introduced Martha to Detective Sergeant Harry Makepeace.

'Pleased to meet you, Miss Burchill. I was so very sorry to hear of your father's death. Dr Burchill was a great man. My mother used to sing in the choir when your father first came to Hartley. That was in the old days, when they were just a few gallery singers. Not like now, with all their fame and glory. No room for females in the choir anymore!'

'You are right, Sergeant. My father never liked women's voices in church. It had to be boy sopranos and male altos or nothing. The young lads all love – loved - him. I remember him saying how he caught some of them one evening. They changed the words of an oratorio they were rehearsing and went home after practice singing "we have no king but Burchill: crucify him!" Fether thought it so amusing, Detective Sergeant. He came into the house, flung his hat on the hat stand and shouted, "The king is dead; long live the king!"' Martha Burchill burst into tears and collapsed in Watson's arms. Makepeace fetched a chair. She sank into it, weeping.

'Fetch Miss Burchill a cup of tea, Makepeace.' Watson barked sternly.

'Yes, sir; at once, sir.'

Watson looked down at the victim's daughter. She was so small and frail in comparison to her father. How dainty and petite she is! Not like that bear of a man. What is she? 4'10"? What was he? At least 6'4" – taller than me, certainly; much taller! The Detective Chief Inspector could not help but notice the slimness of Martha Burchill's waist, strapped up bodice-tight in the black dress. Makepeace's return saw her come round. After a few sips of the tea, much diluted with milk and heavily laced with sugar, the lady had regained at least some of her composure.

'You knew him, too, I believe, Inspector.'

'I did, Miss Burchill. He was a most singular man. I recall my first rehearsal with the Hartley Choral Society. Your father's hold over the singers was truly wonderful to see. The discipline was extraordinary. Once a piece had been learned, there was no need for him to conduct. Two hundred people singing as if they were one voice. Every man and woman in that choir feared and loved him in equal measure!'

Watson worried his reminiscence of the good doctor would start Martha Burchill off again, but apart from a single tear running down her cheek, there was no further display of emotion. He imagined the woman sitting next to him to be about twenty years old. It was obvious, despite her diminutive frame, that she was Thomas Burchill's daughter. His jaw was her jaw; her eyes were his eyes; her curly black hair was his.

'Do you have any other family that you can turn to at this time, Miss Burchill?'

Martha shook her head. 'I am an only child. My mother died some years ago. She had been ill for a long time before then. She was always sickly.'

Watson cleared his throat. 'I am sorry to have to ask you this, Miss Burchill, but did your father have any enemies? Can you think of anybody who might have wanted to do him harm, to murder him, even?'

Martha sighed. 'My father was not an easy man to deal with. My mother found it hard, for one.'

'What makes you say that?'

'His rages. He was such a perfectionist, in everything that he did. My mother feared him, as I did, as we all did. I also loved him, very much.'

'What about others, though, Miss Burchill? As you say, your father was not an easy man to deal with. I saw that first hand at Choral Society practices!'

Martha Burchill clasped her hands tightly. Watson looked over at Makepeace. The two men waited.

'I can think of several people who did not like him, but I cannot believe any of them would want him dead.'

'I can understand that Miss. But successful people like your father are not always universally admired.'

'No, they are not. I accept that.'

'Who are the men who did not like Dr Burchill?'

'Men *and* women, Inspector.'

'Women as well?'

'Well, one woman.'

Detective Sergeant Makepeace sat ready with pencil and notebook.

'Some years ago, when Dr Banks came to Hartley, my father and the Vicar decided that the choir should lose its female singers with almost immediate effect. Sergeant Makepeace mentioned that fact, you will recall. Dr Banks wanted "the cathedral service", which meant there was no place

15

for women in the musical part of the worship, especially after all the changes to the building, with the chancel choirstalls and everything else that made the Parish Church what it is today.'

'I see. Do continue, Miss Burchill.' Watson tapped a finger against his lips.

'By then, my father had increased the size of the choir from seventeen to 70, most of the additional singers being men and particularly boys. The women were made to feel less than welcome; and their numbers dwindled, just as the number of male choristers increased. One or two ladies held out until the bitter end, when they were persuaded to resign, though one had to be sacked.'

'And Dr Burchill made an enemy of this last one?'

Martha Burchill nodded decisively.

'Her name, Miss Martha?'

'Smith was her name. Sarah Anne Smith. It was all made so much worse because of her husband's position.'

'Why was that?' Watson noticed Makepeace writing furiously as Martha Burchill spoke.

'It was a curious situation, Inspector. My father's predecessor as Organist and Choirmaster at Hartley Parish Church was a man called Edward Smith. He came with a good reputation and excellent testimonials but he was a poor leader. He kept *The Bargeman* public house in Holme Hill at one stage as a way of supplementing his income from the Sunday job. He appointed Sarah Anne Jessop, later to become his wife, to one of the paid choristerships soon after starting as Organist and she ruled the roost from then on. Edward was eventually sacked for some terrible misdemeanour and went off to be the Organist and Choirmaster at St David's.'

'The church Sir Templeton Taylor had built, "with no expense spared" as I recall?'

Martha Burchill nodded.

'My Fred is a chorister there, sir,' said Makepeace, more than a little concerned about what was to be revealed about his son's choir master.

'What was the misdemeanour?'

'I do not know, Detective Chief Inspector. What I do know, though, is that, because Sir Templeton wanted the best of everything, he insisted on a male-only choir from day one, so there was no opportunity for Sarah Anne to move churches along with her husband.'

'So, she stayed behind at the Parish Church?' Watson pursed his lips.

'Yes. She was a terrible thorn in my father's side ever thereafter. Sarah Anne never forgave my father for taking her husband's seat at the organ console. Even though she was paid a good salary – as much as eight guineas a year - she either missed practices or turned up late and was unprepared for performances. If you look in the choir records, you will see evidence of her being fined because of this. Later, my father discovered she was performing elsewhere without his permission. But it was her attitude to him that was the hardest thing to bear. I remember his coming home some evenings and carrying on over "that woman's impertinence, defiance, indolence, everything about her!" I can see him standing there in the hallway on a Sunday evening, raging about the latest crime that Sarah Anne Smith had committed. Once, he smashed a vase in anger, he was in such a temper.'

'Do you think that Mrs Smith would be capable of murder, Miss Burchill?'

'I am not sure. I suspect her husband could kill if Sarah Anne told him to get rid of my father'.

The Vicar of Hartley began the extraordinary meeting of the Organ Trustees with a minute's silence and then a prayer in memory of Hartley Parish Church's beloved Organist and Choirmaster. All members of the group were present, except Whiteley George and Arnold Entwistle, who was in Hull on business, seeing to his imports from Saxony. The Reverend Percy Banks then led discussion of the one item on the agenda: the appointment of a new Organist and Choirmaster.

'This is a bit previous, isn't it, Vicar?'

'We have no time to waste, Sir Arthur, if we are to maintain the high standards set by Dr Burchill and continue our push towards cathedral status. My meeting in London did not go well; there are many against us and Dr Burchill's death is just the opportunity our opponents will seize upon to say we are not the best place for the new bishopric.'

'Well, I am not convinced of the need for haste, Banks. Nor to be honest, am I certain that we should be chasing after this new diocese business.' Sir Arthur Hastings leaned back in his chair and drew on his large cigar. 'There's much better things to concern ourselves with here in Hartley. The rise of Methodism, for starters. We barely hold our own in the Church of England in these parts, thanks to all those non-conformist places springing up. They're like mushrooms. One minute, there's a row of old shops or something; the next, ABC - another bloody chapel!'

'I disagree with Sir Arthur, Vicar. It may seem a little hasty, given that TAB is not yet buried, but we have to move on. Things could so easily slip away from us, and Burchill will be a difficult person to replace – very difficult. We also need to put that episode about the organ finances behind us. That did our reputation no good at all, even though Whiteley George was exonerated – in the end.'

'Thank you, Dr Morse. I don't think we need to be reminded of Whiteley's mishandling of the pipe organ procurement. "Least said, soonest mended, as they say".'

There was a pause while Banks blushed and the other Organ Trustees looked down at their well-polished shoes.

'Gentlemen, you have heard from our two churchwardens. Arnold Entwistle sent me a note saying he was fully in favour of what I am proposing, so I intend to place adverts in the local and national newspapers at the earliest possible opportunity and to hire Dr Charleton Mann as our expert adviser at the organ trials.'

'Not so fast, Vicar! You haven't heard everybody's opinion yet. And we need to vote on your proposal, whether in its original form or as amended by any of us. Do I need to remind you that you only have one vote on this Committee, and that any motion has to be carried by a clear majority in favour?'

Banks banged his fist on the dining table. 'I am well aware of the constitution of the damn Organ Trustees, Mr. Sidebottom. Would that it were otherwise, for I am the Vicar, and I alone should rule in these matters!'

'Just saying, Dr Banks. I take your point, but we have never done things like that round here, not since we first had an organ installed in 1742.'

'God give me strength to work with these people. There are times when I could cheerfully kill every one of my bloody Organ Trustees. I will have my way in the end; I am the Vicar!' Banks thought to himself.

The motion to proceed to advertise for, and appoint a successor to, Dr Thomas Burchill, late Organist and Choirmaster of Hartley Parish Church, was carried by 5-2.

***

If he hadn't needed the money, Ernest Snelgrove would have closed the sweet shop for the day (if not the whole week) as a token of respect for Dr Burchill. A number of the larger shops in Hartley had done so, and the Town Hall flag was flying at half-mast. Much to many choir members' annoyance, the same could not be said of the banner flying from the Parish Church. Charles Verney, Assistant Organist, had petitioned the Vicar and Churchwardens to do the honourable and decent thing, but as yet there had been no response.

Snelgrove thought back to all the wonderful services and concerts TAB had conducted over the years. How the choir had improved, especially the move to the east end of the church and the change to all-choral services. The men and boys looked so splendid in their cassocks and surplices, washed, and ironed at great expense every three months.

It was the way the good doctor took practices that made him so different, and so successful. Every little detail had been considered, every note thought about, every singer made to feel part of the whole, whether they were the youngest boy treble, or the oldest adult singer. Not that TAB would let a chorister stay on beyond his best years. At the first sign of vocal decrepitude, a man was asked to undergo a rigorous vocal test every six months; failure meant immediate expulsion. Not that this mattered to Burchill; there were always plenty of altos, tenors and basses queuing up to fill any vacancy. For most applicants it was the prospect of performing under the greatest choirmaster in the land as much as the generous wage per quarter that made being a chorister at Hartley Parish Church so attractive.

Snelgrove had bored his wife to distraction over the previous year or so with his telling and re-telling of the day when the eminent American organists came to visit Hartley just so that they could hear Thomas Burchill's famed choir. He remembered word-for-word what Hiram H

Morton III had said of TAB's singers. 'I came expecting a good choir – an excellent choir. But I found paradise today in your singing. I have never heard anything like it; and I believe I shall never hear anything as divine ever again.'

There were tears in Snelgrove's eyes as he looked up to see who had entered the sweet shop. It had only been two days since TAB had called in on his way home from church after another great performance. In front of Snelgrove this time was no towering figure filling the whole space with his presence. In walked an old woman, bent almost double, dressed all in black. She came up to the counter and tapped it with her walking stick.

'I want to place an advertisement in the next issue of the *Hartley Almanac*, please. You can do that for me, I think?'

Snelgrove cleared his throat and wiped his eyes. 'Yes, I can. I am an agent for the publication, along with a number of others. What do you want to put in?'

'This!' The mystery shopper handed the shop keeper a torn piece of paper with the words 'RIP Thomas Augustus Burchill, Mus Doc, FCO. This is a memorial to all thwarted organists through the ages"

'Are you sure you want these words, Mrs...?'

'Miss! Yes, those exact words. The good doctor deserves it!'

Snelgrove thought the word 'thwarted' more than a little odd but had neither the heart nor the energy to persuade the old crone to change the wording.

'That will be 6d. It will appear in next week's issue.'

The money handed over, the woman hobbled out of the shop and into the cold autumn evening.

CHAPTER 5

A PRIME SUSPECT IS QUESTIONED

Royd Lane was not one of Wright Watson's favourite places. There was too much petty crime down that long row of terraced houses. He had urged Hartley Town Council to have the whole area cleared. All had been to no avail. The good burghers of Hartley could find money for a Town Hall designed by the finest architects in the land, but there was never the funding to take people out of squalor. Watson could still remember the murder of one of his uniformed colleagues during a brawl in *The King's Head*, the place where he and Makepeace were now headed. The Detective Sergeant's enquiries had revealed that Edward Smith, along with his wife Sarah Anne, had long left *The Bargeman* in Holme Hill and were back in Hartley itself. *The King's Head* had the great advantage of being within walking distance of St David's Church where Smith was Organist and Choirmaster. Watson had read Dr Banks's articles in the *Gazette and Argus* about the need for more churches (though not non-conformist ones) to act as 'citadels of faith': 'shining beacons of heavenly light' for the masses. The amount that Templeton Taylor had spent on St David's would have paid for proper accommodation and sanitation for everyone living in Royd Lane and more. But that was another story.

'Martha Burchill was correct about Mrs. Smith, sir. I asked Charles Verney and then Snelgrove, the lead tenor. There had never been anything but bad blood between her and TAB. It's amazing she stayed in the choir as long as she did. Verney said that every time Burchill wanted to sack her, the then Vicar, Archdeacon Hargreaves, would persuade TAB to reinstate her on account of her having such a beautiful voice. Snelgrove thought there was more to it than that. Sarah Anne had quite a reputation in her youth; still does, by all accounts.'

'Reputation, Sergeant?'

'You know what I mean, sir. Some say she is "an unfortunate woman".'

'Really?'

'Yes, sir. The gossip was that Hargreaves had – shall we say – a "soft spot" for Sarah Anne. Which is why Burchill was never allowed to get rid of her, despite everything that Miss Martha said about Mrs. Smith. When sacked by Burchill, supported by Dr Banks, she stopped being asked to perform in churches and gravitated towards the music hall and such like. That would have been something of a come down, especially when her husband was supposed to be an upright church organist in Sir Templeton's employ. But it might have given her an opportunity to ply her other trade, if what Snelgrove said to me is true.'

'I think you are getting ahead of yourself, Makepeace. There is no evidence for any of this being more than tittle-tattle, by the sound of it. The Church of England is rife with that sort of thing!'

'Given what we know about Sarah Anne and Dr Burchill, she has to be a possible suspect, do you not think? At least as part of a team with her husband.'

'I agree, Makepeace. It would surely have to be the two of them, given Dr Burchill's size and strength, though he was ageing quite rapidly, the last few times that I saw him. He was fifty-odd, after all. I used to see him huffing-and-puffing up the hill on occasion. Martha – Miss Burchill – did say he had a bad chest and suffered with his joints. "Too many hours practising in a cold church", especially when he was going for his degrees.'

'His degrees, sir?'

'Getting those degrees from Yorbridge was his pride and joy, apparently. First of all, it was a Bachelor of Music degree – Mus Bac; then his Doctor of Music degree – Mus Doc. TAB was a very hard worker. He came up from nothing; his father was a lowly mill hand over near Bradford. He was born in a place called Oakenshaw; turned out to be musically gifted; went to teacher training college; top of his class. Then set his heart and soul on being in charge at Hartley.'

'Why Hartley, sir? And how do you know all this about him?'

'Miss Burchill couldn't stop talking about him in the mortuary.'

'What about Mrs Burchill, sir?'

'I don't know, Makepeace. Miss Burchill said little about her mother. I doubt it is relevant to the case in hand.' Watson cleared his throat before continuing. 'Tell me more about Edward Smith as Choirmaster at St David's, Makepeace.'

'There's nothing much to tell, sir. Fred sings in the choir, though not for much longer.'

'How so, Sergeant?'

'He's fourteen sir. He is being promoted in the mill. He's going to be a fettler after Christmas.'

'Good for him, Makepeace. Nothing more you can tell me about Smith, then? Does he have a Mus Bac?'

'Not that I am aware of, sir. He's certainly not a Mus Doc like TAB is – or rather was.'

'Well, Harry, the walk from the station has done me good, even if we had to walk past all this terrible housing. This must be the place.'

Watson and Makepeace looked up at the sign swinging gently on its hinges. From inside came the sound of raucous laughter. The detectives peered through the dirty windows and saw two men engaged in drunken fisticuffs. Chairs were knocked over, beer spilt, and glass smashed. A man wearing a waistcoat and a long apron over his trousers rushed out from the bar and separated the inebriated fighters.

'Out, both of you!' he shouted, grabbing the men by the scruff of the neck, and single-handedly dragging them to the entrance and throwing them out of the pub.

'And don't you come back! Ever! You hear me?'

The man stood with arms on hips while he watched the drunkards stumble further down Royd Lane to the next hostelry.

'Excuse me, we are looking for Edward Smith,' said Makepeace.

'Well, you've found him! Who are you?'

'I am Detective Sergeant Harry Makepeace, of Hartley CID, and this is my superior officer, Detective Chief Inspector Watson. We would like a word with you, sir, and also your wife.'

Watson looked Smith up and down as Makepeace was making the introductions. There was something a little odd about a church organist keeping an inn, especially at the rough end of town. But then, how did a musician make an honest living if he did not teach, whether in school or privately? Martha Burchill had said how hard her father – despite his pre-eminence – had to work when he first arrived in Hartley as a 'Professor of Music', teaching piano, organ, singing, theory, and much more, for long hours, six days a week, on top of his church job. Then the financial situation had improved considerably, and TAB had reduced his teaching significantly. Martha Burchill had presumed this was on account of the royalties from his published compositions; she had no other explanation for his much-increased wealth in recent years, notably since Dr Banks had been appointed Vicar. If Smith had sullied his reputation at the Parish Church, then it was less likely he would be able to attract private students or find a position in a National Board School, especially if his wife really was 'an unfortunate woman'.

'You'd better come in. Sarah Anne is out t'back, though I can't think what you want with us!'

The two policemen followed Smith through the bar and down a little passageway to a small kitchen at the rear of the building. There sat a woman in a rocking chair humming to herself. A cat sat on her lap purring; a kettle was coming to the boil on the range; over the top of the mantelpiece tea towels had been hung to dry. The woman looked up.

'What's all this, Ed?'

'It's the police.'

'What you done?'

'Nothing. It's both of us they want to see.'

'Are you Sarah Anne Smith?' Makepeace looked at the woman, who stood up, took off her apron, and nodded to the two detectives as the cat howled in protest at the abrupt loss of its sleeping place.

'May we sit down?'

'If you must. Ed, you'd better make sure the bar's being properly looked after. We don't want any stealing.'

Sarah Anne Smith was an attractive woman. There was no doubting that. Despite her age – Watson took her took her to be about forty years old – she possessed a singular beauty, with the smoothest, whitest skin that the Detective Chief Inspector had ever seen. Her hair came down almost to her slim waistline. The long sleeves of her dress were narrow, emphasizing her petiteness. She carried a handkerchief inside the white frills of both arms. Above the dress's high neck, she wore a choker from which hung a small silhouette pendant. At the back of the skirt was a large bow. Watson was no follower of fashion, but from what his wife regularly told him, here was someone who knew how to look good, and could either afford – or had someone buying her – expensive clothes, with their thick, rich fabrics and trims.

Edward Smith reappeared in the kitchen, poured tea for all four of them, then put the kettle back on the range. 'I've left Gladys in charge. Nobody will get past yon! She's with us for an hour or so before she goes off to clean and wash at St Martin's.'

Watson could not help but notice the contrast between Sarah Anne Smith and her husband. Whereas she was immaculately dressed and coiffured, he was unkempt and untidy. His collar was undone and his waistcoat spattered with food and stained with oil and grease. The curly black hair was unkempt and over long; the face could not have seen a razor for at least three days. Was this someone who had turned up to church the previous day? Watson could see that Makepeace was uncomfortable at the sight of his son's choirmaster close up.

'I suppose you're here about Burchill!'

'What makes you say that Mrs. Smith?'

'Well, it's obvious, isn't it? Everybody knows what that man did to Ed and me. You think we had a grudge against the high-and-mighty Doctor, especially now the church is going to be a cathedral. What better way to put a stop to that than get rid of Burchill and blacken Hartley Parish's reputation? Just like Tartar Tommy blackened my reputation and got rid of my Edward here!'

'We've been nowhere near that infernal place in ages. I'm either here or at St David's most of the time. And Sarah Anne helps out as well, when she's not on other engagements'.

'We will have to talk to people who can vouch for your whereabouts over the last few days', Makepeace interjected.

'Easy; just ask anyone in Royd Lane. They'll tell you what we've been up to. Not that it will be true!' Edward Smith laughed raucously.

Sarah Anne Smith nodded in agreement. 'We have had our fair share of accusations over the years, Detective Chief Inspector Watson.

But – tempted though we might have been – we had nothing to do with Burchill's death. We will both swear that on the Holy Bible.'

'Well, thank you for your time. We may come back to you later during the course of our enquiries.'

'Please do so, Inspector. We have nothing to hide. Now my husband will show you out. I must get ready for my next engagement.'

The two detectives arose and followed Edward Smith out of the kitchen. Sarah Anne smiled at Watson as he glanced back towards her. The policemen could hardly hear themselves think, given the noise of singing and laughter in the public bar. Makepeace caught sight of a face that seemed familiar. The woman looked up as she pulled a pint, but quickly averted her gaze as the Detective Sergeant observed her at work.

Despite the acrid air, thick with the smoke from mill chimneys around the valley, Watson and Makepeace were glad to get outside. They were about to walk away from *The King's Head* when Edward Smith called the two policemen back.

'Honest to God, we had nothing – absolutely nothing - to do with Burchill's death. But I've a good idea who might.'

CHAPTER 6

SPECULATION MOUNTS

Choir practice at Hartley Parish Church on the evening of Thursday, 2nd October 1879 was a sombre affair. All 70 singers, 35 men and 35 boys, turned up, partly because they always had done, and partly because they wanted to find out what had happened, and what might be happening next. After discussion with the Vicar and his churchwardens, Charles Verney was asked to assume the post of Organist and Choirmaster until a worthy successor to Dr Burchill could be found. A date had yet to be fixed for TAB's funeral, but the adult choir members (including the older boys) agreed that it would have to be a grand affair, with the Hartley Choral Society and the Deanery Festival Singers also invited. Some of the boys burst into tears when Verney announced what had happened, though there can have been few choristers who were not already aware of the good doctor's death. As a memorial to their recently deceased director, the choir sang Burchill's well-known anthem *Ye choirs of new Jerusalem*, with Verney accompanying on the harmonium that TAB had procured for practices not long before. Some of the longer-serving men still muttered about the use of such an instrument when the choir was of such an advanced standard, but TAB had been forced to acquire it in order to save money, as the cost of water for the hydraulic blower was proving prohibitive. Snelgrove was the soloist in the anthem. At the end of the performance, there was a two-minute silence before the Grace and The Lord's Prayer were intoned to an accompaniment by Burchill. Banks had given instructions that the music for the following week's services, and thereafter, should not be changed but be performed as already selected. A vote was taken at the end of the rehearsal and Snelgrove was charged with the task of lobbying the Vicar and Churchwardens to have the flag flown at half mast, as was the case with that on Hartley Town Hall.

Many of the choir men were teetotal and would normally eschew the invitation to meet at one of the hostelries in the vicinity of the Parish Church, especially when some of the places were of ill repute. On this occasion, however, only those adult choristers who were under instruction from their wives to return home immediately after the practice declined the opportunity to mix socially with their fellow singers. Snelgrove and Verney led the party towards the *Cross Keys*. The publican, Arthur Bottomley, sang alto in the choir, kept a good house, and served a first-class pint. There was always lemonade or some other non-alcoholic beverage for those who did not imbibe. Much to Verney's amusement, the twenty-or-so choirmen who went for a drink divided into groups according to their voice: alto, tenor, bass. Some evenings, the drinking would have been interspersed with music: glees, part-songs, solos (including ones composed by Thomas Burchill); but not on this occasion.

The mood was far too sombre for song. Instead, the conversations revolved around the good doctor's murder and who could possibly have done it. There had been the occasion when TAB had raged against a member of the congregation for joining in the choral part of the service and ruining the performance as a result. There was much laughter as the men remembered how Burchill had got off the organ stool, gone over to the criminal in question and forcibly ejected them from the church. Would someone bear a grudge against the good doctor for doing that? The miscreant had never darkened the door of the Parish Church again, for certain.

Other potential suspects were evaluated during the course of the evening. Burchill had a reputation as a stiff examiner for the College of Organists, often failing candidates where other members of assessment panels would have given the player the benefit of the doubt. Charles Verney himself had struggled to pass his Fellowship examinations, thanks to TAB. The fact that Verney was Burchill's long-serving and trusty Assistant Organist at the Parish Church made no difference; in fact, if anything, Verney had been given a harder time in the practical tests than anyone else, not even scraping a pass, despite giving what he thought was his best ever performance.

'You should apply for the job, Charlie! You'll be a worthy successor to old Burchill. You knew his ways better than anybody. You'll be sure to get the job.'

Verney put down his pint and looked across at Snelgrove.

'I very much doubt it, Ernie.'

'Shame! Shame!' came the cry.

'Shhh. I am very flattered by your support, and I would love to succeed old Tommy at Hartley. But Banks will never give me the job.'

'Why on earth not, Charlie?'

'Because, Ernie, I don't have a degree – or not yet anyway.'

'Is that so important? Why should it matter if you don't have letters after your name?'

Verney laughed. 'It does to the Vicar of Hartley. He believes in degrees. Old Tommy advised me that I needed at least a Mus Bac if I was to get on. And I have started, I can assure you. I matriculated two years ago. But it is not easy when you have to earn a living; and I have a family to look after.'

'Burchill did it. He got his Mus Bac and then his Mus Doc, and in the minimum time you can do them as an external candidate. If he can do it, you can do it, Charlie.'

'I am not TAB, Ernie. I don't know how he kept going the way he did. That man must never have slept. No, Banks will never go for an ordinary man like me. He'll want a London organist; someone more in keeping with his own airs and graces. I bet the Vicar is already being measured for his bishop's mitre.'

Most choristers supped up after a short while and bade Verney and Snelgrove goodnight. The remaining few determined to have one last drink and a smoke before going home with work the following morning. Having had their glasses refilled, they gathered round the Assistant Organist and the Principal Tenor.

'Could it be somebody who wanted to scupper our chances of becoming a cathedral? The music at Hartley is far superior to that at either Halifax or Wakefield. With Tommy out of the way, Banks's chances of being in charge of a cathedral would be much diminished.'

It was Tomlinson, Principal Bass, as wide as he was tall, befitting someone with such a deep, rich voice. It seemed the larger he became, the better the sound that came out of his mouth.

'Surely, they wouldn't stoop so low, would they, Tombo? Who would think should a thing?'

'Well, I would, for one! There's a lot to be gained and lost from this new diocese business, and whichever place wins out will become a city, with all that entails. Think of the prestige and the status!'

The others laughed, if somewhat half-heartedly, for the singers could see Tomlinson's point of view.

'If I were the police, I would be looking nearer to home for a suspect.'

Gatenby, the Choir Librarian, slammed down his empty glass on the table, as if to emphasise his point.

'Funny goings on in the organ loft, eh, Jimmy?'

Everyone laughed as Gatenby shook his head.

'You may think it funny, but our Dr Burchill was no saint, I can tell you. He was in business on the side, you know, buying up land on the outskirts of town, though goodness knows where he got the money! Some say he had inside information from the council through his Freemason friends and knew where to place his bids and for how much; then when it came to expanding housing and factories, our good doctor would be able to make a killing by selling the land on at a much higher price than he got it for. Perhaps he got on the wrong side of someone else in the market, or he sold out his partners in crime and they got their own back.'

'A good try, Jimmy, but I think you are way off there. "Where's the woman? Seek her!" That's my two penneth!'

All eyes were turned on Warburton Sutcliffe.

'Believe me, gentlemen. Rumour has it that Dr Banks and his wife have not been on the best of terms for many a long year now. TAB gave Mrs Banks piano, singing and theory lessons, did he not? And what about the songs that he composed and dedicated to her?'

'That's ridiculous! I have never heard anything so funny in all my life!' Verney drew on his pipe and puffed out the smoke contemptuously in Warburton Sutcliffe's direction. The Assistant Organist had never had much time for the Choir Administrator's fantastical imagination. The suggestion that the Organist and Choirmaster was having a secret and illicit liaison with the Vicar's wife was sheer bunkum; proof, if proof were needed, of Sutcliffe's other-worldly flights of fancy. Snelgrove leaned back in his cratch, resting his case, looking at his fellow colleagues to confirm his judgement on Sutcliffe's idiocy.

'Well, I'm off, then', Sutcliffe snorted. 'I have a long shift tomorrow. I shouldn't have stayed so long, anyway.'

Once the Choir Administrator had departed, the remaining men looked at each other, wondering if there was any truth in the rumour. The Vicar's wife had certainly been fond of TAB. She always stayed behind to listen to his organ voluntaries and was an assiduous attender at the recitals he organised, at least when he was the performer, though not when other organists were invited, however prestigious they might be. She sang in the Choral Society, positioning herself prominently on the front row of the sopranos, only a few feet away from the conductor's baton. Could such a refined woman have been attracted to the Organist and Choirmaster of Hartley Parish Church? Thomas Burchill had many qualities, but refinement was not one of them. TAB made a virtue of being gruff and, if he took a dislike to something or someone, could be downright rude, and proud of it. Despite him pulling himself up by his bootstraps from poor beginnings, his obvious intelligence, and his significant academic and musical accomplishments, there was never any attempt to smooth out the broad Yorkshire accent. But perhaps that was what Rose Banks found especially attractive about Thomas Augustus Burchill.

'I just can't believe it, Ernie. And even if there were something between them, Banks would never do anything about it. He's too fixated on his own career and getting that bishopric for Hartley to be bothered about what his wife got up to.'

'So not the jealous husband, then?' Verney queried. The two men burst out laughing.

They downed their last drinks quickly. Both men had stayed far too long and would live to regret their drinking the following morning. Snelgrove wiped his lips with his hand. 'I think it's more likely to be somebody who covets the job, especially if we are to be a cathedral. You sure it's not you Charlie?'

Verney smiled and said nothing. He tapped the Principal Tenor on the shoulder and nodded in the direction of the door. Over in the far corner of the public bar, another late drinker watched the two men as they left the hostelry. The observer laughed as they thought of the conversations that had been overheard that evening.

'Little do they know what really happened!' The observer drank up, buttoned up and left the pub.

CHAPTER 7

BREAKFAST CORRESPONDENCE

'Let us pray. "Almighty God, the eyes of all look to you, and you give them their food at the proper time. Bless the earthly bounty you have provided now before us. Let these nourish and strengthen our frail bodies, that we may better serve you; through Jesus Christ. *Amen.*" You may now eat.'

Rose Banks looked across to the other end of the dining table. She watched as the maid served her husband breakfast, then motioned to the children to stay quiet as there were signs of disturbance. No talking was allowed at meals unless initiated by father and, as was his custom and practice, the Reverend Dr Percy Banks would not break the silence until he had finished eating.

He is putting on weight. I am sure of it. His cheeks are growing chubby, and his waistcoat is too tight for comfort. My beloved husband has always been a good eater, but he takes delight in his food more than anything else these days; more than his children and his wife.

'Thank you, Eliza. You may now serve my wife and then the children.' Banks took his napkin out of its embossed silver ring, tucked it inside his collar and spread it out neatly over his shirt front. Then he picked up his knife and fork and began to eat breakfast while Rose Banks watched him. Eliza moved down the table to serve the rest of the family.

Percy was such a handsome man when we first met; that determined face, those lively green eyes, the auburn hair, the Roman nose! I did love him then; I am sure of it. But what is left of my marriage now? My husband seems so preoccupied with the work of the church. There is no time for anything else in Percy's life. I so wish we were back in the south; even London would be better than this awful place. I have no friends, no help, no support. Nobody knows how miserable I feel.

Rose Banks waited and watched as Eliza served her with sausage and omelette. The breakfast smelt good.

'I will have one slice of bread only, Eliza'.

The maid nodded and curtsied, almost dropping the tray of food in the process. Rose Banks made sure that the children behaved themselves as they received their food. Anna was served first, as the eldest; then Grace; then Charlotte and Alice; finally little Augusta. Once all five youngsters had something on their plates, their mother bowed her head gently to indicate that they could begin their breakfasts.

Pray God that there will be no more children! Percy so wants a son, but I could not bear another confinement. I really could not go through that, ever again! It was bad enough with dear sweet Augusta. My husband was so angry when she was born!

By now the Reverend Dr Banks was reading the morning edition of the *Gazette and Argus*. Even from the far end of the dining table, Rose could see the headlines: everything was about Thomas Augustus Burchill; about *her* TAB. She smiled as she remembered when he gave her the score of *It was a dream*. Burchill had sat down at the piano and played it through for her. Rose Banks had joined in the chorus each time. She remembered how she felt when TAB read out the dedication; Rose Banks would always treasure that moment.

'Eat up, children! There is work to be done! I must get on, and you must attend to your schooling. Rose, you have a ladies' tea to organise, I believe.'

'Yes, Percy, dear. I do. Come children. We must leave papa to his day.'

'Let us pray. "What shall we return to you, O God, for all your benefits? Every day of our lives we are receiving fresh tokens of your favour. Oh, let your goodness lead us to repentance. And if we can do no more than express our gratitude, help us to do that in the sincerity of our souls, and yours shall be the glory, forever; through Jesus Christ. *Amen.*" You may leave now. Be good, my flock!'

Percy Banks permitted himself a smile as each of his children came up to him in order of seniority and kissed him on the cheek. Having bade good morning to his five daughters, Banks received his wife, who took him by the hand.

'Will I see you later, dear?'

'I fear not, dear. I have to meet Dr Charleton Mann to talk about the auditions for Burchill's replacement. It is a terrible business, but we must press on. You understand that my dear, don't you?'

'Yes dear, I do. I will wait up for you.'

'No need, my dear, no need.'

Rose Banks walked towards the door. She turned to look at her husband. He was already studying his correspondence, delivered by Eliza.

Percy Banks did not hear the door close. The first letter opened was from Entwistle. The Treasurer was not a happy man. The Parish Church's finances were in a woeful state. Far more had been spent on the church restoration than originally estimated; most of the budgets had been exceeded by at least 50%, some by much more. The worst culprit was the organ builder. Monkhill had charged twice the price for half the work and was still to supply the east case for the instrument.

'You know, and I know, Reverend Banks, what was really going on with Whiteley George and the organ procurement. That hearing you held was a complete travesty. There is no way that man should have been exonerated. He was guilty, I tell you: guilty! And Burchill was no innocent either. Why did you protect him and his blessed music? Is it so important? We have to resolve these matters otherwise we will go bankrupt!'

Banks stopped reading the letter aloud, put it down, took off his glasses and covered his face with his hands. Money will surely be found. The Lord will provide! I know it! The funds will flow in, as manna from Heaven!

The Vicar of Hartley put Entwistle's letter back in its envelope and opened the only other piece of correspondence that was on the tray. The address was curiously formed by some kind of machine, with a strange mixture of capital and lower-case. Inside, on a single sheet of paper, printed letters had been cut out and glued in to form the words:

IF YOU VALUE YOUR LIFE AND YOUR FLOCK YOU
WILL NOT APPOINT ANOTHER OF BURCHILL'S KIND
TO BE ORGANIST AT HARTLEY PARISH CHURCH.

'You really should eat something, Miss.'

'I am not hungry, Annie.'

'But you have hardly eaten for days now.'

'I have no need of food. I have lost my appetite and my sense of taste to go with it.'

'We can't have you like this, miss! What would your fether say? He would not want you to be grieving so! I have brought you cake and tea. Please just have a little something.'

Martha Burchill smiled. 'You are good to me, Annie. You have been a loyal servant over so many years. What will become of me – of us – now?'

'I am sure your fether will have provided well for you, Miss Martha. He loved you very much.' Annie laughed.

'What is so funny, Annie?'

'I was just remembering the time when he raced after that young man who wanted to court you. What was his name?'

'Wyn. He was called Wyn.'

'Dr Burchill followed Mr. Wyn all the way down into Hartley town centre just to tell him that he was not good enough for you, and never would be.'

'I remember that. Fether was so out of breath when he got back. He was in such a sweat. He was not a great one for exercise, except his daily walk to and from the Parish Church.'

Martha Burchill paused.

'I have never said this to anyone else, Annie. It will be our secret. Will you promise me that?'

Annie nodded, unsure of whether or not that was the correct answer.

'I loved Wyn, and he loved me; very much. My father took against him from the start. But that did not stop me seeing him. We used to meet when father was away, at church, at the Choral Society, giving his recitals and concerts all over the country, examining at music festivals and so much more.'

'How did you meet your young man, this Wyn?'

'Fether had gone to Blackpool for the annual music festival as the Senior Adjudicator. He wanted me to go with him, but I would have been even lonelier there than I was at home. He would have been busy all day and out at dinner in the evenings. No, I preferred to stay at home. It was a Friday morning about twelve months ago. There was a knock at the door. You were out shopping for food, so I answered the door. This young man was standing there. I remember it as if it were yesterday. He was wearing a bowler hat and an overcoat that was too big for him. He was clean shaven. He said he had an appointment to see Dr Burchill to do with becoming an articled organ pupil. I told him there must have been some mistake. I felt sorry for him because he had come all the way from Hull. I invited him in. We got on so well. It was – well – it was love at first sight. I never felt like that about anybody else.

'Fether eventually met Wyn, but he failed the audition and was told to go back home and work at his playing. Except he did not go back to Hull but got a job at Templeton's mill and started to see me. When fether found out he was furious, saying that Wyn was only after me for the money. Hence your seeing him chase my young man all the way into Hartley. Wyn got very angry. What worries me, Annie – what really worries me – is that Wyn threatened to kill my father.'

'Oh my! That's awful! Where is Wyn then, Miss?'

'I have no idea, Annie. I wish I did. I could certainly do with some company now,' she sighed.

'Would you like me to stay with you a while, Miss Martha?'

Martha Burchill shook her head. 'No thank you, Annie. But it is very good of you. No, I should look through all this post that has come. I imagine they are letters of sympathy. Look at them all!'

Annie decided that her mistress needed to be alone, at least for a little while. Coals glowed in the hearth. The grandfather clock chimed ten. Martha looked up at the huge portrait of Thomas Augustus Burchill hanging above the fireplace. He was the wrath of God personified, sitting there in his Doctor of Music robes, holding the mortar board in his right hand, his left loosely touching the fob of his pocket watch. Martha decided that her father would be pleased and more than a little amused at the encomia, including from organists who had been TAB's arch-rivals in the cut-throat world of church music. She resolved that the correspondence would need to be organised so that, after the funeral, replies and acknowledgements could be sent. She had arranged the letters in alphabetical order – there must have been more than a hundred – and made a note of the address. At the bottom of the pile, Martha noticed a larger brown envelope that remained. She assumed, given its size, that it must have contained the proofs of her father's latest composition. As she opened the parcel, a series of photographs fell out. The images made her feel sick. 'Not fether; surely not!' she exclaimed.

CHAPTER 8

WATSON'S MORNING REFLECTION

W right Watson prided himself on his appearance. Every morning he would get his wife and children to inspect him up and down, front and back, to make sure that he was in a fit state to go to work.

'That'll do, Wright.' Nancy Watson brushed some specks off her husband's shoulders, patted him on the buttocks and kissed his cheek. 'Off you go, my handsome police detective. Do what you have to do.'

The Detective Chief Inspector made sure the children were otherwise occupied, then hurriedly kissed his wife full on the mouth. Not content with his family's assurances, he looked in the mirror that hung over the fireplace. In order to get the fullest image of himself, he walked as far away as possible to check whether he really was fit for duty. It was not far from the hearth to the kitchen table, but he ended up being able to see everything but his shoes, which he knew were well polished, thanks to Albert. 'You're a good lad, Bert.' Watson's eldest son smiled. The Detective Chief Inspector smoothed his recently trimmed hair, twirled his moustache, buttoned up his waistcoat, checked his pocket watch against the kitchen clock, took his bowler from the hat stand, did his usual trick with it, much to the children's amusement, blew Nancy a final kiss and set off for work.

As Watson left his house, gas lamps were still being extinguished and knocker-uppers were rousing the last of their customers. It took a mere ten minutes for him to walk to the police station; just enough time for a cigarette. Nancy had told her husband not to smoke in the house. While she would have preferred him not to have the habit at all, Watson needed something to calm his nerves and help him think. And just at the moment, every part of his brain had to be diverted and devoted to the case in hand. It was Watson's most important murder to date. Though not the first case since he set up Hartley CID, this latest victim was by far the most prestigious. It was not only Burchill's musical standing that singled out the killing from previous cases, but also TAB's many connections in the town and across the region. It was one thing to determine who had killed a fellow drinker in the centre of Hartley on a Saturday night; quite another to find out who had done away with one of the most famed musicians in the land, and at a time when his reputation was more important than ever.

Watson looked down towards the town centre. The flag flew proudly from St Martin's central tower. Despite many pleas, it had not been lowered to half-mast as a token of respect. *What's all that about? Especially when the flag at St David's has been taken down? Is that some curious one-upmanship?* He shook his head, doubting that he would ever understand the machinations of the Church of England. Banks was a 'rum'un', that was for sure. He had not responded well, neither to the news of the death of his Organist and Choirmaster, nor the interview at the Vicarage the day after TAB's murder. The Vicar of Hartley had taken some persuading that Burchill had even been murdered. Banks argued that the good doctor was not in the best of health: he ate too much; he drank too much; he smoked too much.

'That is all very well, Dr Banks, but how do you explain the bruising to the victim's head and the marks around his neck? And why was he wearing his robes in the crypt?'

Watson replayed the rest of the conversation in his head as he continued his walk to work. There was no answer. In the end, the Vicar had reluctantly agreed that foul play must have taken place.

'I would be grateful, though, if discretion could be exercised at all times, Inspector. The negotiations concerning the new diocese do not go well. The standard of the music at Hartley Parish Church is one of the main factors being considered in our favour. To lose Burchill is a disaster.'

Banks had then announced that the advertisement for Burchill's replacement would be sent to the agent the following morning, to be placed in both local and national newspapers and the musical press. Even before TAB had been buried! *No respect for ordinary people, these Church* of England sorts! Watson threw his cigarette stub onto the cobblestones as he reached the police station.

'Give me Methodism anytime!'

'What's that, sir?

'Oh, it's you, Sergeant. I didn't see you behind me there. We often do that, do we not?'

'What's that, sir?'

'Arrive at work at the same time.'

'I was just speculating on the goings-on in the Church of England. It is all too complicated for me: bishops, priests, deacons, archdeacons, curates, and the like. Why not just have a minister and his people? Simple Sunday worship, with hymns and psalms, sung by all and not just by a choir in fancy robes, with no women allowed?'

'Beats me, sir! The missus says that it is good that Fred goes to St David's. It will help.'

'Help, Sergeant?'

'Give us a leg up.'

Watson burst out laughing.

'How do you mean, Harry?'

'Well, you know; help us to improve ourselves.'

Wright Watson sighed. 'I fear you will have a long wait. This town is in the control of a favoured few. We are meant to know our place. However hard we work, there will always be the toffs above us. And if it's not the old money; then it'll be the new money. Anyway, we have no time for politics, Detective Sergeant. "Ours is not to reason why; ours but to do and die". Isn't that how it should be?'

Makepeace nodded. 'I suppose so, sir.'

'Make us some tea, Harry. Then I can think.'

Watson entered his office while Makepeace put the kettle on. The Chief Inspector was tempted to light up another cigarette, but the wife had made him promise and he was a man of his word; always had been and always would be. He sat down and waited for his drink.

Makepeace arrived with two cups.

'Thanks. Harry, you make the best cuppa in the station. It calms my stomach something wonderful.'

'You got problems again sir? You ought to try Beecham's. I swear by them. And it does wonders for the old lady's movements.'

'Thank you, Detective Sergeant. The less said about your wife's movements, the better. I already know more about your wife's insides than I care to, thanks to your tales over the last couple of years!'

The two policemen laughed.

'So, what have you found out so far, Harry?'

Makepeace put down his tea, took out his notepad, flicked through the pages and began to read. 'Well, sir, I didn't know this until I questioned my Fred and then investigated further. But Smith only plays the organ at St David's now. He was told not to rehearse the choir any more a few months back.'

'Why is that?'

'Because Thomas Burchill complained about his treatment of the choirboys. My Fred had said nothing to me, but when I told him to tell me straight, he said that there had been some funny goings on with one of the head choristers. Smith got the lad very drunk, it was said. Sir Templeton then got another choirmaster in and – wait for it – the new man was one of Burchill's students.'

'There is certainly no love lost there, is there, Sergeant? What with Smith getting the sack and then his wife having the same treatment from the Parish Church and its Choirmaster. Both of them have a motive. Where were they when Burchill was murdered?'

'As far as I can make out, given his movements – if you will pardon the expression, sir – on the day of Dr Burchill's death, then both Smiths are in the clear. The whole of the afternoon and evening, they were at their pub or, in the case of Mr Smith, practising at the church.'

'Can that be verified?'

Makepeace nodded.

'Yes, sir. Plenty of witnesses saw them both at the *King's Head*, serving or otherwise going about their business. And there were people coming and going at St David's all the while that Mr Smith was practising on the organ.'

'I know nothing about these matters, Sergeant. How is the organ blown at St David's?'

'The same way as at the Parish Church, sir. I checked. The hydraulic engines were even installed by the same company.'

Is that Monkhill?'

'No sir. He was the organ builder at the Parish Church. He doesn't supply organ blowing equipment, except where the wind is raised by hand pump. No, if you want water or gas blowing, you have to go to a specialist.'

'And in the case of St David's and St Martin's, who was that?'

'Someone called Grindrod, sir. Based in Leeds, apparently.'

Watson laughed. 'That's a good name for someone who builds machines!'

'It is! I thought that.' Makepeace cleared his throat. 'There's a scandal attached to the procurement of the hydraulic blowing equipment at the Parish Church, sir.'

'Really? Tell me more, Harry.'

'It concerns a man called Whiteley George. He is a member of this body called the Organ Trustees that looks after – well, it's obvious, isn't it?'

'The organ, perhaps?'

Makepeace smiled. 'Yes, sir, and the choir; anything to do with the music, in fact.'

'I thought that the Anglican churches had something called a Vestry Committee. Shouldn't they be looking after musical matters?'

'Not at Hartley, sir. The Organ Trust dates back to the 18th century. It has complete power over music and the organ at the Parish Church. It was something to do with how the original instrument was purchased.'

'And is Dr Banks a member of this group?'

'He is, but he only has one vote. Even when it comes to appointing – or sacking – the Organist and Choirmaster.'

'I doubt the Vicar of Hartley is happy with that situation, Harry. Banks strikes me as someone who wants, and even needs, to get his own way, and all the time!'

'That's what a lot of people say of him, sir.'

'We digress, Sergeant. You were telling me about Whiteley George.'

'George is a senior partner in a firm of solicitors in Leeds. He became a member of the Trustees two years ago and had a lot to do with the fund-raising for the rebuild of the organ Burchill so desperately wanted. The problem was – Grindrod's business was largely owned by Whiteley

43

George. Even worse, it came out that Burchill also had a pecuniary interest in Monkhill's organ business.'

'And when Monkhill and Grindrod got the contracts to supply a new instrument and hydraulic engines to blow it, George and Burchill both stood to gain.'

'How much?'

'No idea, sir.'

'How did all this come to light?'

'There was an anonymous letter sent to the *Gazette and Argus*. A keen reporter followed up and it came out. George published a rejoinder (I think that was the word used in the newspaper article) protesting his innocence. Banks held an internal inquiry and exonerated both George and Burchill of all wrongdoing, but I don't think anybody really thought either of them was innocent, especially when the two of them were busy buying up land in north Hartley and charging tenants of any cottages on that land exorbitant rents and getting them out when they couldn't manage. They then got the hovels pulled down ready for the land to be bought by the council.'

'Is that behaviour enough for murder, Harry?'

'It could be sir. If a tenant was disgruntled enough by their treatment at the hands of George and Burchill.'

'We need to pursue this idea. Make a list of people who live – or lived – in homes owned by those two and see if any names stand out.'

'Will do sir.'

'Any other leads that we need to be pursuing, Harry? What about disgruntled students or choir members?'

'Not apart from our Sarah Anne, sir. The choir seems to be utterly devoted to TAB, man and boy. I don't know about students.'

'I seem to remember something in a newspaper article a while back about Burchill being a tartar, especially when it came to failing exam candidates. Draw up a list of his students and organise interviews. I think we should also question Miss Burchill again to see if she can shed any light on that particular line of enquiry. She may be more able to talk coherently the next time we see her.'

'Right away sir! Anything else?'

Watson mused for a moment. 'Yes Sergeant. One more thing.'

'Sir?'

'Another cup of tea, please!'

The two policemen laughed. Makepeace nodded and left Watson's office. The Chief Inspector turned to the pile of post on his desk. He carefully opened the letters one by one, reading their contents assiduously and making a note of any important points. All the correspondence related to Burchill's death: some of it was from crackpots with theories as diverse as direct intervention from God as a punishment for the iniquitous evils of music in church and Hartley's premier organist being a warlock; the rest of the pile contained references to sightings of the good doctor and suggestions as to who might have held a grudge against him and why. Watson determined that these last leads needed to be followed up, however tiresome and unproductive a task that might turn out to be.

One letter remained to be opened. Unlike the others, it had no stamp and the address had been printed by some kind of machine. Watson held the envelope to his nose. It had a strange odour that he had smelt somewhere before. He could not place it. It was not unpleasant, neither was it a tantalising perfume. He resolved to ask other members of his squad if they recognised the smell.

Some base instinct made Watson open the letter with the greatest of care. His knife sliced through the envelope thinly and cleanly. As he took the piece of paper out, he could see that a series of words had been cut from a book, a newspaper, or some other publication and pasted onto the page to spell the following sentence:

MAN THAT IS BORN OF A WOMAN HATH
BUT A SHORT TIME TO LIVE. THAT GOES FOR
BURCHILL AND ANY WHO FOLLOW HIM.

CHAPTER 9

A SUSPICIOUS DESTRUCTION OF EVIDENCE

Watson took out his pocket watch, looked at Makepeace, shook his head then put the timepiece away. Through the corridor window, the Inspector could see clerks silently studious in the next room. Occasionally, one of their number would get up and walk over to a colleague and ask a question or go to the bookshelves that lined three walls of the communal office to check a reference in one of the large, leather-bound tomes. Otherwise, the scene could have been from a chapel prayer meeting. At the far end of the room sat the chief clerk, writing, reading, or casting a roving eye over the subordinates.

'I doubt I could do this kind of work for long, sir.' Makepeace whispered. There was no-one else in the small waiting room, but the deathly silence made normal conversation levels seem inappropriate.

Watson smirked. 'I know, Harry. You can't sit still for five minutes, can you?'

Makepeace nodded. As he was about to say something more, the door opened and a junior clerk appeared.

'Mr. George will see you now, gentlemen. Please come through.'

Watson and Makepeace followed the young man down a long, oak-panelled corridor, whose walls were hung with portraits of partners, past if not present, of the legal firm of George, George, and Harrison. The door at the very end of the corridor bore the nameplate 'Mr. Whiteley S. George'. The clerk knocked and waited for a reply, but none came. He tapped a second time and called out. 'Mr. George, there are two gentlemen from the police here to see you. They tell me it is very important. They have been waiting for rather a long time.'

Watson looked at Makepeace, then motioned to the office junior to open Whiteley George's door. The boy went pale and shook his head. Watson turned to Makepeace, who had no hesitation in grabbing the handle. The boy ran off, not wishing to be party to the heinous crime of disturbing Mr. George when he had not given permission to enter the inner sanctum.

The two officers were met by the sight of a man throwing papers onto the fire, then pushing the documents to the back with a large poker.

'May we ask what you are doing, sir?'

'No, you may not! None of your business. I am just tidying my office and throwing away some papers that are no longer of use: old, unnecessary files. I needed more space in my office.'

Watson looked over to the roaring fire. Whatever evidence – if evidence it was – of any wrongdoing involving Whiteley George had now gone up in smoke. A few small pieces of half burnt paper flew off the fire along with showers of spitting sparks. There was a smell of burning as a half sheet landed on the rug in front of George's desk. Makepeace stamped on the fire that was starting and grabbed the remains of the document, handing it to Watson.

'I will have that! Give it to me at once!'

'Why is that Mr. George?'

'None of your bloody business!'

'Everything is our business, sir, especially when a man has died. I take it you know of Dr Thomas Burchill's passing?'

'I do. But what has it got to do with me? Who are you, anyway?'

'I am Detective Chief Inspector Wright Watson, of Hartley CID, and this is Detective Sergeant Harry Makepeace. He is assisting me with the investigation into Dr Burchill's murder.'

'Murder? Are you sure?'

'We are sir. And we wondered if you could help us with some matters pertaining to Dr Burchill's business interests and activities.'

'Why should I be able to do that, Inspector?'

Watson was conscious of the fact that the document retrieved so expeditiously by Makepeace was warm in his hand. He looked down at the browned, curled, crinkled paper. On it was neat copperplate writing that, as far as the Inspector could make out, referred to the purchase of land in north Hartley. The date at the bottom of the page was 29ᵗʰ September 1879.

'May we sit down, sir? I think we need to have a frank discussion with you about Dr Burchill.'

George nodded slowly. 'Very well, Inspector, Sergeant. Take a seat.'

Wright Watson watched the solicitor closely as he walked back to his large mahogany desk and sat down. The ornate long case clock in the far corner of the room struck four-thirty in the afternoon. Immediately behind Whiteley George's desk was a large painting. The Inspector could not take his eyes off it.

'Impressive, is it not, Mr. Watson?'

'It is sir. But what is it meant to be?'

'New Hartley, an artist's detailed impression of it, at least. My dream – our dream for the town of the future. It could be the capital of the north.'

George pointed out the many features of New Hartley: the neat rows of houses; the libraries; the schools; the institutes and colleges; the chapels and the churches. And at the centre, Hartley Cathedral.

'Is that the Parish Church?'

'What was the Parish Church, Sergeant. But it will be much improved when Dr Banks's plans are all completed.'

'But there is no certainty that it will become a cathedral, is there?'

George exhaled deeply. 'No, Detective Chief Inspector, there is not, especially now that Dr Burchill is no more.'

'That is why we are here, sir. To talk about your relationship with the Organist and Choirmaster of Hartley Parish Church.'

'Relationship? There was no relationship. Who said there was?'

'We understand that there were some "issues" to do with your involvement in the procurement of the new organ. Can you tell us more, sir?'

'There is nothing to tell, Inspector. I was completely exonerated of all wrongdoing. I am innocent of every charge laid against me.'

'What were the charges, exactly, sir?' Makepeace took out his notebook and began to write.

'That I was in charge of the selection process for both the organ builder and the hydraulic engine manufacturer. It was alleged that I stood to gain financially from the appointment of Ishmael Monkhill and Grindrod and Sons.'

'Really, sir?'

'The well-known organ building firm, Sergeant. They are based here in Leeds. You can see their manufactory just round the corner.' George pointed out of the window and across the square to a large factory, whose Doric portico was topped by a row of organ pipes.

'Thank you, sir', Makepeace replied. 'And Grindrod?'

'Most church organs are blown by hand, Sergeant, but the invention of the hydraulic engine has revolutionised all that. By the mere flicking of a switch the instrument's wind is raised without human intervention of any kind.'

'And this mechanism was applied to the new organ at Hartley Parish Church?'

'It was, Detective Chief Inspector. The first of its kind in Yorkshire, the realm and, indeed, the empire and the world. It was a very special day for the West Riding. And Hartley stole a march on everywhere else.'

'You sound very proud of the place, Mr. George.'

'I was born in Holme Hill, a little village to the west of the town.'

'I know it well, sir. And who made the allegations against you, Mr. George?'

'I do not know.'

'You were never told?'

'No, Inspector, nobody knows. The allegations were made anonymously.'

'And yet Dr Banks felt he had to investigate them?'

'He did. I wanted him to, and I expected him to carry out a full investigation.'

'And you were exonerated?'

'I was, Sergeant. Completely. I received not one penny from either contract.'

'Though it could be said, could it not, Mr. George, that you would benefit as a result of your shareholding in both companies?'

'The decisions to use Monkhill and Grindrod were both taken by the Organ Trustees as a whole. I was merely one vote on the committee.'

'Did the Trustees know you had a pecuniary interest in the two companies?'

'They did not, Inspector. But that was not relevant. The resolutions to proceed were taken on the grounds of merit alone, I can assure you.'

Watson looked at Makepeace, making sure that the Detective Sergeant was taking notes on George's statements.

'What about you and Dr Thomas Burchill?'

'What about me and Dr Burchill, Inspector?'

'You knew each other?'

'We were fellow members of the Organ Trustees. No, I tell a lie: I was a member of the committee; Dr Burchill attended meetings but was not, strictly speaking, a trustee.'

'What about your personal relationship with the Doctor?'

'There was none, Inspector. I hardly knew the man. I am sorry about his death and the circumstances in which it happened, but the work at Hartley must go on if we are to achieve our vision.' George turned away from the policemen and pointed to the picture on the wall.

'What about business activities, sir? Were you not in partnership with Dr Burchill in the acquisition of land, as in this document, Mr. George?' Wright Watson held up the charred piece of paper.

'I may have had some land purchases that also involved Dr Burchill, but he was one of a number of men who made up our consortium.'

'A consortium, sir. And the members of this group?'

'That is confidential information, gentlemen. It has no bearing on your case whatsoever.'

'I will be the judge of that.'

'Judge away, Mr. Watson, but you will not get any further information today, or any other day. Now I bid you good day.' Whiteley George rang a little bell on his desk and within a short while the office junior arrived.

'Bob, Detective Chief Inspector Watson and Sergeant Makepeace are just leaving. Will you please show them out?'

Makepeace closed up his notepad and got up.

'Inspector, could I please have my document back?'

'In due course, sir. I wish to keep it for now.'

'It is just a piece of paper, man! And it is mine!'

'It will be returned to you in all good time, Mr. George. I think it may have a bearing on the case, and I therefore cannot return it to you for the moment.'

'Then you will be hearing from the Chief Constable shortly, Inspector. He is a good friend of mine and will not allow this nonsense; I can assure you. Bob, show the gentlemen out, now!'

Watson stood up, ready to join his colleague at the office door.

'As you wish, Mr. George, as you wish. But before we go, sir, where were you on the afternoon and early evening of September 29th?'

'I was here in my office all day until I caught the 6.30 pm train home. Isn't that right, Bob?'

The office junior nodded.

'And can you think of anyone who would want to harm Dr Burchill?'

'As you must already know, Inspector, Tommy – Dr Burchill – was a singular man. He made many enemies – at least in the musical world – during his time at Hartley. But I cannot think of anyone who would hate him so much they would murder him. Except…'

'Go on, Mr. George.'

'In recent years, relationships between TAB and his assistant, Charles Verney, have been less than cordial. Perhaps you should talk to him at some point soon.'

'Thank you, Mr. George, that's very helpful. And we will have your document back to you as soon as possible.'

'You will indeed, Detective Chief Inspector.'

Once Watson and Makepeace had been ushered out and were well down the corridor, George rang the bell and the office junior came scuttling back.

'Have they gone?'

Bob nodded.

'Here, young man. For your trouble. And it is our little secret, remember?'

Bob looked down at the coin now in his hand. 'Thank you, sir! Of course, sir!'

'Now be off with you! I have work to do!'

George locked his office door and took a letter out of his coat pocket.

He read the brief correspondence over and over again. As the clock struck the hour, he looked over the note one last time then threw it on the fire and watched until it was no more.

'Pray God that this scandal never comes out. Let this be the end of it all!'

Whiteley George slumped down into his leather armchair and felt for the secret tray-drawer at the side. It sprang open sharply once he had found the button. He pulled out a large brown paper envelope. Opening it, he gazed at the photographs one by one and smiled.

CHAPTER 10

AN INTERVIEW TURNS SOUR

In all the years that Charles Verney had helped Thomas Burchill, there had never been an invitation to the Vicar's house. Now, the Assistant Organist had been summoned by Dr Banks twice in as many days, firstly to be told that he was to take charge of the choir and the organ playing until a more permanent arrangement could be put in place; secondly, to help with the funeral service for TAB.

Verney had been given permission by the Office Manager at Templeton Mills to take Saturday morning off work so he could attend on the Vicar. Banks's note insisted that the Assistant Organist be at the Vicarage at ten o'clock, sharp. Because he had been taken unawares at the suddenness of the first invitation, Verney was determined to be better prepared for this second encounter with Dr Percy Banks. The best way of doing that, thought Verney, was to go to the barber's shop and have a good haircut. In the meantime, Mrs V would make sure that his best suit was clean and his shirt properly starched.

If he were to make a successful claim for the Organistship at Hartley, encouraged by Sutcliffe and Snelgrove, Verney would need to be bold, starting with his appearance. Dr Banks was clean shaven, his one concession to facial hair being sideburns, not of the mutton-chop variety, but neatly clipped, stopping at the jawline. His hair was parted in the centre and fell to his neckline; the ears could be seen. That was how Charles Verney would now have his hair cut and styled.

The barber was more than a little surprised at Verney's instructions. But the Assistant Organist insisted on having his beard and moustache shaved off. It felt strange not to have facial hair any more, but when he looked in the mirror, Verney was pleased with the result, and hoped that the Vicar of Hartley would be impressed. He tipped the barber generously, put his jacket and bowler hat back on, left the shop and headed towards the Vicarage. He could hear the Parish Church clock strike nine forty-five. Verney decided to enter, knowing that the large gardens held much of interest (the first meeting with Banks was in an arboretum close to the house rather than inside it) and there would surely be no objection to the interim organist of the Parish Church admiring the horticulture, a particular hobby of the Vicar's, hence the many unusual varieties of tree, bush, and plant. The neat pathways led in numerous directions, towards and around the large building at the centre of the grounds. Beyond could be seen the tower of the Parish Church, its mediaeval intricacy contrasting sharply with the classical simplicity of its neighbour.

Verney looked at his pocket watch: another five minutes before it was time to meet the Vicar. Banks was in what looked like his study, talking to someone whom the Assistant Organist did not recognise. Verney thought the man to be about fifty years old; well dressed, with a full beard and head of hair. From a distance, it could almost have been Thomas Augustus Burchill himself, except that the good doctor would have won the argument every time! The conversation seemed heated. More than once the Vicar pointed fiercely at his guest, who raised his fists in reply. The man then left the room hurriedly. Verney assumed that whoever this person was, he must have used a back door, for there was no-one leaving by the main entrance, where the Assistant Organist now found himself. He took out his pocket watch once more: ten precisely, as confirmed by the chime of the Parish Church clock. The door was soon opened; it was Arthur Bottomley, one of the six curates who served the Parish and supported Dr Banks in God's work in Hartley.

'Ah, Charles. Good to see you, Come this way.'

Verney took off his bowler hat, put it on the stand along with his overcoat and walking stick, then followed the young priest along the broad, elegant hallway. The two men halted at the Vicar's study. Bottomley put his ear to the door. As he wondered what would happen next, Verney looked at the large painting on the wall immediately to his right. Eight pairs of eyes stared down at him. Percy and Rose Banks were seated, surrounded by their children. Verney tried to guess which was which, given that the portrait must have been painted some years previously. As he went through the names, it became clear that there was one offspring too many: a sixth child! Just as Verney had worked out which was the image of the missing offspring, the study door opened.

'Verney! Goodness, you look different. What have you done to yourself? Never mind. Good to see you! Welcome. Do come in. Bottomley, arrange for some tea to be brought. We have much to talk about.'

The Assistant Organist followed Banks into the study. All four walls were lined from floor to ceiling with bookcases. Opposite the entrance was a large fireplace, above which was an ornate gold mirror, and on either side were two armchairs. The Vicar of Hartley gesticulated to Verney to sit in one of these, while he went to the other.

'I am grateful to you for taking the choir and playing for the services, Verney. It is very good of you. You have been a loyal servant to Hartley Parish Church. It must have been a great shock to you when you found Dr Burchill down there in the crypt, his head submerged in the water tank.'

Verney nodded, wondering what the Vicar was about to say next. Surely it must be to confirm the trusted and loyal Assistant as the substantive Organist and Choirmaster of Hartley Parish Church. He had worked hard for it, studied for it, wanted it, needed it.

'Who do you think did it, Verney?'

'Sir?'

'Who murdered TAB?'

'I have no idea, Vicar. How should I know? Why do…'

At that moment a maid arrived with tea and seed cake. She served the two men, then left.

'You are sure you know nothing of what happened; of why Dr Burchill was killed, why he had to be murdered?'

'Nothing, sir! Absolutely nothing! Why would I know anything?'

'You have not heard any rumours about Dr Burchill?'

'No, Vicar. Nothing! Nothing at all! Why do you ask me?'

'I just wanted to be sure, that's all. I needed to know if you – if you knew anything that might assist the police with their enquiries.'

'I can assure you, Reverend, I have only ever sought to serve Dr

Burchill and the Parish Church. I would be honoured to serve you as Organist and Choirmaster.'

'As Organist and Choirmaster?'

'Yes, sir. I feel that I am ideally suited to the post. There would be no hi – hi...'

'I think you mean hiatus, Charles. It comes from the Latin verb "hiare", meaning "to gape" or "to yawn".'

'Thank you, sir. Of course, sir.'

'I understand that Charles, and you will do very nicely to keep things going until we have a proper replacement for TAB.'

'A proper replacement, sir?'

'Yes. Someone with at least a Mus Bac if not a Mus Doc. And a Fellowship of the College of Organists, of course. Don't you agree, Charles? We have to keep up standards, now, do we not?'

'Yes, of course, sir. Do I take it, then, that there will be no opportunity for me to be considered for the post?'

'The post of what, Charles?'

'Of Organist and Choirmaster at Hartley Parish Church. I have long harboured the ambition to succeed Dr Burchill.'

'I am sorry, Verney. But that would never do, unless you have gained your degree recently?'

'No sir, I have not. Dr Burchill wanted to teach me, but I have not had the time, with my job at the factory and all.'

'I am sorry. You are a worthy assistant, I am sure. Indeed, Tommy spoke highly of you, and you "know the service", but unless you have at least a Mus Bac, you cannot be considered. Do you, Charles?'

'No sir, I do not.'

'I have also heard that you play in a dance band sometimes.'

'I do, sir. The money is very good.'

'I cannot have that either. It sullies the reputation of the Parish Church to have people doing that; it would sully the reputation of Hartley Cathedral even more.'

'But...'

There was a knock at the front door. Banks and Verney could hear Bottomley answer it and then usher another visitor into the hallway. A moment later, the study door opened and the curate walked in.

'Dr Mann is here to see you, sir.'

'Thank you, Bottomley. That will be all.'

In walked a short, balding man with wisps of white hair round his temples and neck and down his sideburns. Verney thought the visitor had the most penetrating gaze he had ever seen.

'Charles, meet Dr Charleton Mann, Organist and Master of the Choristers at Yorbridge Cathedral. He is here to assist with the appointment of a worthy successor to Dr Burchill. The advertisement has already been placed in the local and national newspapers and I expect that a shortlist will be drawn up within a week at most, once the applications come in. You will arrange for the church choir to be present for the auditions and show the candidates the organ before they are asked, in turn, to play and accompany the singers.'

Mann smiled weakly at the Assistant Organist; Verney returned the compliment.

'I am pleased to meet you, Charles. Tommy spoke very highly of you.'

The Yorbridge Organist gripped Verney's hand in the special way, but the Assistant Organist was in no position to reciprocate.

'Now we must plan the funeral. Come, Charleton, there is much to talk about.'

'I assume you wish me to stay for that, sir.'

'No, I do not believe that will be necessary. We have it all well planned. Dr Mann will be in charge.'

'Very well, sir. I will leave you now. I had better be getting back to work. I only have the morning off.'

'I will show Verney out, sir.'

'Thank you, Bottomley.'

The curate motioned the Assistant Organist out of the study and closed the door so that Banks and Mann could talk in confidence.

'I am sorry, Charles.'

'Sorry for what, Bottomley?'

'Sorry that you have no chance of succeeding Burchill as Organist and Choirmaster. I know you would kill for that post.'

CHAPTER 11

BANKS ENTHRALLS; THE DETECTIVES MEET THREE SONGSTERS

Wright Watson was nervous, Harry Makepeace even more so. Neither policeman was comfortable attending the Sunday morning service at St Martin's. Nevertheless, both decided it would be worth seeing if anything could be gleaned from either the service or the worshippers.

'Was this a good idea, sir?'

'It seemed like it on Friday evening, Harry, but I am not sure now. Still, we are here, and it would be difficult to turn round and walk away at this stage.'

The two detectives observed the activity from their vantage point by the baptismal font near the main entrance, allowing them to observe members of the congregation enter the building. Hymn books were handed out together with a sheet giving details of Mattins and Communion. Makepeace read out the instruction at the bottom of the paper: the service would be sung by the choir alone, the congregation 'worshipping silently'. Dr Banks was listed as the preacher.

Carriages drew up at the main gates, from whence the gentry (old and new) of Hartley were escorted through the west door down the long nave and into their private pews nearest the chancel and the focus of the worship. The south door was for the ordinary folk of the town, who were ushered to the middling seats in the nave and the two aisles. The poor were directed to enter via the north door and allowed to stand or, in the case of the weak and infirm, sit on benches at the very back of the church.

Moments before the service began, the two detectives walked briskly up the north aisle and into the organ loft, where Charles Verney had said they could sit and watch the service.

The organ music grew in volume and timbre, reaching a climax as the choir began to process into the church, down the north aisle to the west end, then back up the middle of the nave and into the choir stalls. Watson and Makepeace counted over 70 singers and at least 800 in the congregation. At the end of the procession came the servers, the curates, and finally Dr Percy George Banks, Vicar of Hartley.

'Is this the way to worship God, Harry?' Watson looked at his Detective Sergeant.

Makepeace shrugged. 'I wonder, sometimes. Fred seems to like it and being in the choir at St David's helps with his education – you know, reading and writing and that.'

'Give me good Methodist singing any day. I can't be doing with all this ceremony.'

With this comment, the two detectives fell silent and turned to the task in hand. Over the next two hours, Watson and Makepeace did their best to follow the order of service. The choral singing was heavenly: Burchill had trained the singers well; no conductor was needed; the notes were absolutely in tune and the ensemble was perfection itself. On the few occasions when the congregation was allowed to join in the musical part of the worship, they too sang in a disciplined unison. Watson had never experienced anything like it in all his life.

'Now I understand why Burchill was so special, Harry.'

'So do I, sir. St David's choir is nowhere near as good as this.'

The time came for the sermon. Dr Banks ascended the enormous pulpit that loomed over the nave of the church. He clasped his hands as he led the worshippers.

'Let the words of my mouth, and the meditation of my heart, be acceptable in thy sight, O LORD, my strength, and my redeemer.'

Nearly 900 people answered 'Amen' in unison. Then silence. Banks bowed his head, looked up to the ceiling then scanned the people sitting in front of him, as they eagerly anticipated what the Vicar of Hartley was going to say to them. The sermon began quietly; the raising of Lazarus was the subject. The Bible passage was read out and repeated, the phrases dissected and reassembled, the words explained and expanded into new meanings: the theme of the day and the message for the week ahead.

Watson found himself being attracted to Banks and what he had to say. The Vicar of Hartley was very persuasive in his argument. The pace quickened; the volume grew. After an hour that seemed like minutes, the sermon ended.

'I am the resurrection and the life. He who believes in me will live, even though he dies; and whoever lives and believes in me will never die.' Banks shouted, raising his arms in the air. 'Let us pray', he then whispered.

Watson looked at Makepeace. There were tears in the Detective Sergeant's eyes. The two men nodded at each other and turned away to observe the congregation singing the last hymn and then leaving the church, row by row. Some parishioners were already known to the detectives, members of either the town's ruling class, its middling sort, or even its underclass. Workers made up the bulk of the congregation: the foremen and the mill hands; the shopkeepers and the stallholders; the council employees and the transport workers; the doctors and the nurses. People such as these not only worshipped at Hartley Parish Church, but sang in the choir or had sons who were choristers.

'We are going to have to do a lot more interviewing next week, Harry.'

'Sir?'

'We need to interview the choirmen and the senior boys. Then the Organ Trustees and Churchwardens, then Dr Burchill's students.'

'All of them, sir?'

Watson nodded. I see no alternative. We can ask for assistance, Harry, do not worry. I also propose to offer a reward for information leading to the apprehension of Dr Burchill's murderer. The *Gazette and Argus* have said they will put up some money, and I gather Dr Banks is willing to augment the amount from his own pocket.'

'Very generous. Guilt money, sir? The flag on the tower is not yet at half mast, despite a petition from the choristers. An article in the newspaper also comments unfavourably on the fact that the Parish Church is not prepared to mourn its great Organist and Choirmaster.'

Makepeace stopped talking and motioned Watson to turn around. Sarah Anne Smith walked down the central aisle as if she were royalty, turning from side to side and acknowledging, or rather pretending to acknowledge, the accolades of the members of the congregation still seated in their pews and listening to the final organ voluntary, fittingly a piece by Thomas Burchill himself, the well-known *Heroic March*, written to celebrate the complete reconstruction of the Parish Church and the finishing of the gargantuan organ now pealing out around the vast space of the nave.

'Good morning, Inspector, Sergeant. I did not know you were churchgoers. He is very good, is he not?'

'The sermon was very stimulating, Mrs Smith, I have to agree.'

The woman laughed. 'No, silly! I mean Mr Verney. He is such a talented player. I care not one jot for the religious bit. I did not listen to the sermon. Give me the music every time. Though I do find Dr Banks attractive.'

'I would have thought you would be at St David's, supporting your husband in his work.'

'I told you, Mr Watson, there is no place for women there.'

'And here, Mrs Smith? You said you had not been here for a long time.'

'I thought I would come and pay my respects, Inspector; and observe, of course. Just to see how things are going.'

'How do you mean?' Makepeace was tempted to take out his notepad, but decided against it, given they were still in church.

'Oh. I still love church music, Sergeant, even though I hated Thomas Burchill for what he did to me and my fellow singers.' Sarah Anne Smith pointed towards two other women who were following behind and had stopped and waited for the conversation with the detectives to end before continuing out of the building.

'Ladies, come and meet these two gentlemen.'

Makepeace recognized the first of Smith's companions immediately.

'You work at the *King's Head*. I remember seeing you there the other day.'

'What of it? I have to learn a living somehow!'

'Detective Chief Inspector, Detective Sergeant, meet Gladys Grimshaw. You are correct. She works for me, and the church.'

'The church?'

'Tell them, Gladys.'

'I clean the church – top to bottom – every week. And I wash all the choir robes. And I take pride in my work. They looked like angels, this morning, all of them, thanks to me!'

'And who is your other companion?' Watson nodded over to the short, slight woman standing behind Mesdames Smith and Grimshaw. The two men could not remain unaffected by her sheer beauty. Smith was attractive; Grimshaw plain; this lady beauty personified. The tight-fitting dress emphasised the curve of her bosom and the slimness of her waist. Everything about this woman exuded an inner peace.

'Come join us, Ottavina.'

Gladys Grimshaw held out a hand to her friend, who grasped it and walked towards the police officers.

'Let me introduce Ottavina Badland to you, gentlemen. Ottavina is a fine musician. You should hear her play the organ. Her music comes straight from God, I am certain. I have always been moved to tears by it.'

'I did not know that women could play the organ, Mrs Smith.'

Gladys Grimshaw snorted. 'They would be as good as the men, and better, given half a chance.'

Ottavina Badland held out her hand to the detectives. Watson and Makepeace later remarked to each other on the elegance of her fingers and the softness of her touch as she made their acquaintance. That was as nothing to the look in her eyes.

'Yes, gentlemen, our Ottavina is completely blind. She lost her sight years ago in an accident. But that has not stopped her becoming a very fine musician, has it, my dear?' Gladys Grimshaw stroked her friend's arm as she spoke.

'It was all so very unfortunate. And it could have been so easily avoided.'

'What happened, ma'am?' Again, Makepeace wondered if he should have his notepad to hand; force of habit could be strong, especially after all the Detective Sergeant's years in the force.

Ottavina Badland shook her head. 'I would rather not talk about it, sir. It is in the past, and I bear no ill will to anyone. Life is too short for that,' she smiled.

'We must be going, gentlemen. This is a special day for us, and we have a luncheon appointment that must be kept.'

'A celebration of some kind, ladies?'

'Yes, Detective Chief Inspector. It is just three years since we left the

Parish Church Choir. We meet every year on this Sunday to commemorate our departure. We think back to happier days. The choir was up there in the west gallery. Banks got rid of all that. There is nothing left of what was once there. William Grimshaw, my father, sang in that gallery choir all his life. He would have been appalled by what the Vicar did.'

'And what did you think of Dr Burchill and his role in your demise?'

'He was a singular man, Inspector. As many people hated the good doctor as loved him. There was no middle ground.'

'And what about you three ladies? How did you feel about TAB? Which camp were you in?'

'Despite everything, Ottavina and I loved him.' Grimshaw smiled.

'And you know how I feel, Chief Inspector. Given what he did to me and my husband. But that is all in the past, except for our annual get-together. For which we are now late, thanks to you! I could certainly kill for something to eat!' Sarah Anne Smith laughed aloud, then curtsied and led her two fellow singers out of the church into the cold October air.

CHAPTER 12

WATSON AND MAKEPEACE
REVIEW THE CASE

Wright Watson hated Monday mornings. There would be a pile of reports on his desk. Once he had read them, he would need to determine how to proceed. Watson checked to see if Makepeace had arrived, but there was no sign. Once his Sergeant was available, it would be possible – and, indeed, necessary – to divert all attention and energy to the murder of Dr Thomas Burchill and the swift apprehension of his killer or killers.

In the meantime, Watson determined to make swift work of the crimes logged over the weekend. Two reports caught his eye. The first related to a man charged with neglecting to maintain his wife and family. What struck him forcefully, as he read the report, was the fact that the man in custody was accused of bigamy; the woman he was refusing to care for was already married. Wright Watson looked at the second report, concerning the theft of a pig. Selina Brook, of Ainley Fold, Hartley, was locked in the cells. Watson read PC Hargreaves's report of her arrest the previous evening.

I attended the property in question at about 6 o'clock in the evening. Selina Brook had barricaded herself in the house as a Mr. Wally Scott was attempting to enter the premises to retrieve a pig. Scott had previously been given the pig by Brook in lieu of monies owing. I was called because of the commotion. Scott had broken a window and was shouting at Brook, who was hurling abuses back at him. I took the situation in hand and questioned both parties in the street. When asked why she had taken the pig, Brook (who was much the worse for wear) said that it had only been for "a lark". I arrested her and brought her back to the station.

Watson sighed. 'If pigs could fly...'

'Sir?'

The Detective Chief Inspector looked up suddenly. 'You surprised me, Harry. I was deeply engrossed in a report about a stolen pig.'

Makepeace laughed. I heard, sir. She is in the cells sobering up still. Along with the pig!'

'What?'

'The officers on duty last night did not know what to do with the animal, sir, especially since it is evidence. Mr. Scott wants to come and collect it, but I said not to let him have the pig until further notice. What would you like me to do, Inspector?'

'Don't tempt me, Harry. And no jokes about "bacon", either!'

'No, sir.'

'We have far more important matters to deal with, Sergeant. Pull up a chair. We need to review the Burchill case.'

'Very good, sir.'

'Thomas Burchill followed his normal routine on the morning of 29th September. According to his daughter he had been in high spirits the previous evening on account of his successful performance.'

'What was the music, sir?'

'I do not know. Too serious for me, I fear. Hymns and glees are more to my taste! There are far too few opportunities for lusty singing at the Parish Church. Yesterday morning was more like a concert performance by the choir than an act of worship, in my opinion. Anyway, let's get on! Burchill taught his students as he did every Monday morning and then, after lunch, went off to the church to practise on the organ, like he always did. Then there is a gap until Burchill was discovered, face down, in the water tank.'

'Held under until there was no breath left. Which suggests one or more people sufficiently strong to restrain a six-foot, sixteen-stone man for long enough for him to drown.'

'Yes, Sergeant. We are looking for a powerful, younger, man, I would say.'

'Perhaps we should visit Hartley Football Club.'

Wright Watson laughed. 'That is not a bad idea. I noticed at the service

65

yesterday some of the choirmen seemed very sturdy. Get a constable or two to ask around at the club and see if any of those song men have links there.'

'And Hartley AFC?'

'It would do no harm, Sergeant.'

'Having killed him, the murderer – or murderers – dressed Dr Burchill in his finery.'

'That seems a definite possibility, Makepeace. Unless TAB was already wearing his doctoral robes when he went down to the crypt. Martha Burchill said that he would not have done that. They were only for weekends, when he wanted to show off at the important services. Perhaps we need to find out if he had been wearing them at the concert the night before, and where he had put them at the end of the evening.'

'I wonder, sir, if he was murdered elsewhere and then his body moved down to the water tank.'

'You mean he was strangled rather than drowned? I suppose he could have been, but the doctor who examined him said that his lungs were full of water. No, he must have been attacked from behind once he was downstairs. That would fit with the fact there were no witnesses to his being accosted in the organ loft or anywhere else in the main body of the church.'

'Except perhaps the cleaners, sir.'

'What did they say when you interviewed them, Makepeace?'

'Nothing, sir. They were aware of the organ being played, and then Dr Burchill wandered off somewhere. He was apparently updating the music catalogue.'

'Updating what?'

'There is a complete list of all the music the choir sings. Verney showed it to me when I looked round the church. It is a real work of art. Wonderful, neat writing, and every detail included in this ledger book: number of copies, when performed, and more information that I could not understand.'

'I would not have expected a character like Burchill to have neat handwriting. Are you sure he compiled the catalogue?'

'According to Verney, sir. Burchill had a real eye for detail. It is what made him such a great choirmaster, apparently. There was somebody who was the "choir librarian", but TAB insisted on organising the scores himself.'

'Our librarian at the glee club would be incensed if the conductor were to interfere with the music!' Wright Watson snorted. 'And was Dr Burchill wearing his robes at any point when the cleaners observed him?'

'Not according to Gladys Grimshaw and her ladies.'

'Thank you.' Wright Watson clasped his hands and looked down at his own notes. 'I suggest we look at the list of possible suspects that we have identified so far.'

Makepeace nodded and cleared his throat, ready to read out his notes from the meetings and interviews of the past few days.

'Wednesday, October 1st, 1879: we interviewed Edward and Sarah Anne Smith. While both have a grudge against Burchill and Banks, there is no evidence to suggest that they were involved in the Doctor's murder. There are plenty of witnesses to show they were nowhere near the Parish Church when Burchill was murdered. Even if Mr. Smith had slipped out from his practice at St David's that afternoon, it would have been difficult for him to get to St Martin's and back in under forty minutes.'

'Difficult, but not impossible. And Mr. and Mrs. Smith both have cause to dislike if not hate Burchill. Not to mention Banks! Not a man I take to, Harry!'

'Me neither, sir, in spite of his sermon!'

'What was the "misdemeanour" that got Smith the sack all those years ago?'

'Drink, sir. He was found very inebriated in the organ loft one morning, just before an important service – for all the deanery, which was obviously something important. He was so far gone he urinated on the organ pedals. That was in the old days when the organ was in the west gallery and the choir was just a small group of men and women, of which Mrs. Smith was one.'

'And where did you find all this information out, Makepeace?'

'Interviews with the choir men, sir.'

'And if Smith was incapacitated, who played the organ?'

'Verney, sir.'

'You mean Charles Verney was assistant to Smith before Burchill replaced him?'

'Yes, Inspector. He had to cover up for Smith and then, to add insult to injury, was passed over for the job when Burchill applied. Some of the choir men said Verney thought he would get the job automatically and was very sloughened when he was only asked to stay on as TAB's deputy'.

'What do you make of Edward Smith's comment as we were leaving the pub, Sergeant?'

'What, that Charles Verney hated Burchill for stifling his career?'

'Yes. Everybody I have spoken to says what a "singular man" TAB was, and this included the Assistant Organist. According to Snelgrove, Burchill did most of the organ playing himself because the choir was so good and didn't need a conductor, so there was not much for Verney to do. Would I resent someone who got a job that I wanted? Not if he was better than me, but Verney may think more of himself, and I might get frustrated, I suppose, if there was so little for me to do. But then I would probably leave and find my own patch. Find out more about him, Sergeant, and then I think we should interview him.'

'Yes, sir.'

'Remember what those three ladies said after the service about Dr Burchill, Harry?'

'You either loved him or hated him! You could say that of Banks as well, of course. Let's hope that the Vicar of Hartley is not next on the list!'

'Pray to God that there are no more murders! This one is bad enough!'

'Yes, sir. Moving on, sir. Friday October 3rd, 1879: interview with Mr. Whiteley George, in Leeds.'

'Now that was interesting, was it not? I have yet to hear from my commanding officer, but I expect that I will. People like George have friends in high places, and the Chief Constable is no doubt one of them.'

'Do they shake hands in the same way, sir?'

'I suspect they do, Harry. I wonder if we can find out more about the Freemasons in Hartley and District.'

'I will see what I can do, sir.'

Wright Watson opened his desk drawer and took out the browned piece of paper rescued from the fire in Whiteley George's office. As he did so, more of the document disintegrated.

'Damn, our evidence is falling apart before our very eyes!'

'Is it evidence, sir?'

'Is it coincidence or not that this burnt document relates to the transfer of ownership of a large plot of land in north Hartley; more to the point, it is dated 29ᵗʰ September, the day that Thomas Burchill was killed? 'We need to find out more about George's business interests, I think.'

'Yes, sir. And those of Burchill as well, since they were both buying up land in the area, I assume?'

'We will interview Miss Martha again tomorrow, assuming she is well enough. I imagine she is heavily involved in the preparations for her father's funeral.'

'Of course, sir. I will send word that we wish to see her. Here or at her home?'

'At home, I think, if that is acceptable to her.'

'Very good, sir.' Makepeace closed his notebook and put it in his jacket pocket. He rubbed his chin, scratched his nose, and started to get up.

'You look as though there is something more you wish to say, Harry. Come on, man, get it off your chest!'

'Well, sir, you know we just agreed that Banks is loved and hated as much as Burchill was: what if the Organist and Choirmaster's murder was to get at the Vicar and his plans for the Parish Church?'

'You mean that with Burchill dead the choral tradition and the reputation for good – great, even – music would fade and Banks's dream of being in charge of Hartley Cathedral would go up in smoke, just like George's documents?'

'Something like that, sir. Even if they could appoint a worthy successor to TAB, the fact that a murder had taken place in the church would not go down well with those charged with making the decision about the new bishopric.'

'You make a very good point: another line of enquiry we must pursue! I need to find out where the power lies and who will take the decision about the new cathedral.'

Wright Watson looked down at his open desk drawer. After a moment's reflection, he pulled out an envelope and gave it to Makepeace.

'What do you make of this, Sergeant? It came the other day.'

Makepeace took out the piece of paper and read the letters pasted on the page.

'" Man that is born of a woman hath but a short time to live. That goes for Burchill and any who follow him". My goodness, sir. This puts another slant on this case!'

'It does indeed, Harry. Smell the envelope.'

'Perfume!'

Wright Watson nodded. 'Is it a case of:" Where's the woman. Seek her?" What do you think, Harry?'

The two men reflected on the enormity of the task ahead of them. They were both excited and fearful in equal measure. A knock at the door broke the silence.

'What is it, Constable Penfold?'

'It's the woman in the cells downstairs, sir. Selina Brook.'

'Don't tell me, the pig wishes to confess.'

Makepeace burst out laughing; Watson smirked; Penfold grimaced.

'No, she says she has information about Dr Burchill's death and needs to speak with you urgently.'

CHAPTER 13

AN INTERVIEW AND A SHORTLIST

The walk from the police station to Thomas Burchill's house took no more than twenty minutes. Number 84, New Station Street, was the last in the row of neat, four-storey terrace houses that had sprung up alongside the railway lines into Hartley Central. The Lancashire and Yorkshire Railway had been late coming to the town, despite the pleas and protestations of the local industrialists and because of the difficult terrain leading into the valley. There had been similar difficulties with the construction of Hartley Canal in the early 1800s. In consequence, water and rail followed the same route through the narrow gap in the hills surrounding the town. Now there were two stations, Hartley Central and Hartley North, the first mainly for passengers, the second primarily for goods.

As Watson and Makepeace arrived at 84's gate, the noise and smoke of the engines was overwhelming, for next to the terrace end was the point where the two sets of lines – one to Central and the other to North - were conjoined as they bridged Hartley Canal.

'I would hate to live here. It is bad living next to Templeton Mills, but the trains coming in and out day and night must be a nightmare.'

Wright Watson nodded at his Detective Sergeant and shrugged. 'I can think of far worse places to live, Makepeace.' He lifted the doorknocker on its hinge and let it fall back, once, twice, thrice. The two policemen looked to the right of the doorway to see if there was movement inside. The curtains were drawn tightly across the bay window. The same was true of the upper floors.

Watson took out his pocket watch and checked the time against the Town Hall clock chiming in the distance.

'What do you make of our pig-owning songstress's evidence, Makepeace?'

'Selina Brook, sir? Yet another lady in the choir before Burchill and Banks ruined her musical livelihood because they wanted an all-male choir like a proper cathedral. Or so she said. I think it was more the demon drink that was her downfall, assuming she ever was in the choir. I will check the records.'

'Records?'

'Yes, sir. Burchill kept meticulous records of all the singers. How much they were paid; what they sang; when they were absent (and fined for non-attendance!). We would be able to find out whether or not Mrs. Brook is telling the truth.'

'The rest of her story seemed to be pure fiction, though, Sergeant.' Wright Watson lifted the door knocker a final time. There was no response. The Detective Chief Inspector looked at his watch, sighed and turned away from the door.

'No doubt Miss Martha is in mourning, Sergeant. Perhaps we had better come back another day.'

Makepeace nodded and walked down the two steps from the doorway. As Watson followed behind, he noticed someone emerging from the basement window. The Detective Chief Inspector tapped his Sergeant on the shoulder and pointed. They watched as a young man emerged with a parcel, looked back into the house, then tiptoed up the steps and out into the street.

'Stop! Police! Now!'

The man looked back, then sprinted towards the canal. Watson nodded to Makepeace to chase after the thief while he himself went to the nearest bridge. There, he saw the escapee running down the tow path and towards him, with the Detective Sergeant in hot pursuit. A barge was steaming past. Wright Watson leapt onto the vessel's roof, ran towards its stern and, much to the surprise of the navigator, jumped down onto the deck and threw himself at the thief on the tow path. The stranger was strong and used his fists to fight. It was only when Makepeace arrived that the man could be subdued.

72

'I didn't do it! I didn't do it!'

'What didn't you do?'

'I didn't kill him, I swear.'

'Kill who?'

'Burchill! I hated him, but I didn't kill him, honest to God!'

'And what were you doing, stealing from Dr Burchill's house?'

'I wasn't stealing!'

'Wyn! Wyn! Leave him be, Inspector. Leave him be!'

Martha Burchill appeared. The thief took advantage of the distraction to give the two detectives the slip.

'Wyn! Come back!' Martha Burchill cried out.

'Who is this man?'

'He was only trying to protect me, Inspector. He meant no harm.'

Makepeace chased the thief as Martha Burchill burst into tears. Watson stayed behind to keep an eye on the Organist's daughter. Some of the bargees jumped onto the towpath in order to block the man's escape route. They were much aided by the horse towing a barge. The animal refused to budge once the vessel was stopped and the escapee had no way of getting past. Seeing he was now heavily outnumbered, with all routes closed off, the man stopped, bowed his head, turned round and, as Makepeace approached him, held up his arms so that he could be handcuffed and led back to where Watson and Miss Burchill were standing.

'I am sorry, Martha. There is no point in pretending any more. I am responsible and no-one else.'

'Who are you? Identify yourself!' Watson barked.

'He is my fiancé, Inspector.' Martha Burchill smiled, went over to the man, put her arm in his and kissed him on the cheek.

'My name is Wyn Williams.'

'And how long have you and Miss Martha been engaged to each other?' Watson put his hands on his hips indignantly.

'Since this morning, officer. We are very much in love.'

Watson looked at the bargees as they listened intently to the conversation. 'Thank you for your help. It is appreciated.' The navigators nodded and went back to their barge, looking over their shoulders as they did so.

'Have a quiet word with them, Makepeace, and then join us back at number 84, if that is acceptable to you, Miss Burchill.'

Martha nodded. 'It is, Detective Chief Inspector.'

'Thank you, Annie. That will be all for now.'

Martha Burchill waited until the servant had closed the door.

'Would you mind taking the handcuffs off my fiancé?'

Makepeace looked at Watson, who nodded. Williams held out his hands while the Detective Sergeant did the honours.

'Thank you. Do help yourselves, gentlemen.' Martha Burchill pointed to the teapot.

Watson and Makepeace shook their heads, despite the many temptations of Annie's tea-tray.

'Who are you, Mr. Williams? And what were you doing in the basement of this house earlier?'

Williams looked at Martha Burchill, who nodded to him.

'I was retrieving some papers.'

'What papers were these, sir? And why were you leaving through the basement window?'

'That was my doing, Inspector. I did not want Wyn to be seen by anyone, especially now. It was force of habit, really.'

'Force of habit, Miss?'

Martha Burchill bowed her head and sighed.

'Miss Burchill and I are in love, gentlemen, and we have been for quite some time.'

'How long, Mr. Williams?'

'Since I came visiting Dr Burchill about an opening with him last year. I wished to become an organist and what better apprenticeship than to work at Hartley Parish Church?'

'Wyn is very good, Mr. Watson, except that my father did not think so. He said my fiancé was not good enough for me; he forbade me from seeing Wyn and decreed that he would never let us get married.'

'But that did not stop us, Inspector. We have been seeing each other surreptitiously for the last twelve months. It was not too difficult, given the amount of time that Martha's father was out of the house.'

'Did he ever find out about you two?'

'No, Mr. Watson. Or at least we do not believe so. If he knew we were "carrying on", he never did anything about it. But I cannot think my father would do that, given that he was so vehemently opposed to my seeing Wyn.'

'And how did you feel about Dr Burchill's views on your relationship with Miss Martha? Did you feel strongly enough to kill him, Mr. Williams?'

'No, I did not, Inspector.'

'Are you sure?'

Williams looked at his fiancée. 'I thought about it, gentlemen, more than once, I'll admit that. The way he treated Martha; giving her so little freedom; forbidding my love from having any say in her own life. Yes, I was tempted. Thomas Burchill's death means we can be together; we can marry and be man and wife as we have wanted to be since we first saw each other. But for all that, Detective Chief Inspector, I swear on the Holy Bible I did not kill Martha's father.'

'Where were you on the afternoon and evening of Monday September 29th, Mr. Williams?'

'I was doing a shift in the mill. I am a stuff presser at Templeton's. Ask anyone there; ask the foreman. They will all vouch for me.'

Watson nodded at Makepeace, who took due note.

'What is it that you were taking from the house earlier this afternoon, Mr. Williams, when we saw you leaving through the basement window? That envelope there; what is inside it?'

Williams looked at his paramour. Martha Burchill nodded.

'Are you sure?'

'Yes, Wyn, I am sure. Give Mr. Watson the envelope. He needs to know what my father was really like. Hand over the photographs, now!'

<hr />

The Reverend Canon Percy George Banks was pleased with himself. He looked at the pile of applications for the post of Organist and Choirmaster at Hartley Parish Church. He counted no fewer than forty letters and the closing date was not till Friday, so there was plenty of time for more people to write in. Charleton Mann's letters to his colleagues in other cathedrals had done the trick, and a number of good people currently in assistant posts had thrown their hats into the ring with a little prompting from their superiors. Perhaps Burchill's murder would not mean the end of Banks's vision after all. The Vicar of Hartley went over to the fireplace, poked the coals back into life and looked into the mirror. He smiled at the reflection.

'The Right Reverend Percy George Banks, MA, DD, Bishop of Hartley. That sounds so good! It is what I deserve! It is what I have worked for. It is what I want and it is what I need! Nothing, and no-one, will stop me!'

The Vicar of Hartley returned to his desk and looked through the applications. Using the criteria that he and Dr Charleton Mann had agreed, Banks sorted the letters into three piles: definitely not; possibly; definitely. Charles Verney's papers went on the first pile, along with those of Marshall and Hainsworth, two of TAB's pupils, and several organists at local non-conformist churches.

'Hum! None of that lot will know the service. I cannot have them ruining my plans. And Verney is worthy but dull. He will do until a successor is appointed but no longer.'

Two more went into this group: Kathleen Holmes and Joan Whittaker.

'Pray God that a woman never becomes Organist of Hartley! How could a female be capable of such a post?'

The second pile was the largest, containing organists from Anglican churches across Great Britain.

'None of these people will be auditioned. None has a degree. We must have men who have already attained at least a Mus Bac.'

This meant that the final pile only had six letters on it. Banks smiled.

'We have our list. Just one more name to add.'

Banks took out a key from his waistcoat pocket, unlocked the bottom drawer, took out a letter and opened it.'

'My best candidate.' The Vicar of Hartley laughed. As he put the document on the last pile, he noticed the large brown envelope that had recently arrived in the post.

'I will look at those "papers" later,' he smiled.

CHAPTER 14

THE END OF ONE CHAPTER AND THE BEGINNING OF ANOTHER

The church was full to overflowing. Even with the additional seats left in the building after Burchill's final performance, there was insufficient space for all who wished to attend the funeral. When the church opened at 10 o'clock, there was a long queue waiting, ready to jostle for the seats set out for ordinary people. The middling sort appeared over the next hour as their carriages deposited them at the main gates. Reporters from the *Gazette and Argus* asked for comment; sometimes it was given, sometimes not. As the time of the service approached, the leading men of Hartley arrived to take their places at the head of the nave: the Lord Mayor, the Lord Lieutenant, the Members of Parliament for Hartley North and Hartley Central, the Duke and Duchess of Hartleydale. Burchill would have been stoutly proud at the sight of the high-and-mighty attending his funeral. At the last came Martha, dressed all in black, a black crepe veil covering her face and a black cap on her head. She walked slowly, with head bowed. Wyn Williams walked alongside her, watching closely as she put one foot in front of the other, never looking at the coffin that was being carried up the nave by six of Burchill's organ students.

The procession was met at the chancel screen by the Reverend Canon Dr Percy Banks, resplendent in his robes, and accompanied by his six curates. Behind the Vicar of Hartley, the 90-strong choir stood in silence, heads bowed, while Charles Verney played the *Dead March* from Handel's oratorio *Saul.* Once the coffin was in the chancel, Banks began the service. The hymns were Burchill's favourites, while the responses, setting and anthem were the late Organist and Choirmaster's own. Wright Watson and Harry Makepeace, who had been allowed by Charles Verney to observe the service from the organ loft once more, were moved both by the dignity of the ceremony and the excellence of the singing. The two detectives sat in an alcove near to Verney's bench so they could look out for possible suspects, other than those already identified. The series of mirrors that allowed the organist to see the choir, the vicar and the nave proved to be just as useful in giving the policemen the best view of both singers and congregation.

Nothing seemed out of the ordinary. Makepeace took the south side, Watson the north. They worked their way along every row, starting with the berobed, bewigged, bechained, uniformed authorities in the front pews, safe in the knowledge that every one of the attendees had signed the book of condolences on arrival. A group of police constables were ready to check all the names listed, as and when required. Immediately behind the great and the good of Hartley sat the churchwardens and the Organ Trustees, including a somewhat dishevelled looking Whiteley George, who looked around the congregation nervously, not talking to his fellow worshippers. Next in order of precedence were the many organists, choirmasters, and other musicians, a number of whom had at some time been students and even articled pupils of Burchill. Verney whispered to Watson and Makepeace that they were the group most likely to be at the service to pay their genuine respects to the Organist and Choirmaster, despite – or perhaps even because of -- the fact that he had dominated the town's music making to the point where he had a stranglehold on it. Verney drew the detectives' particular attention to the arrival of Dr Charleton Mann, of Yorbridge Cathedral, one of the finest players in the country, a contemporary of Burchill's and a close friend of Banks.

By the time Watson and Makepeace had surveyed the whole congregation, the service was coming to a climax. Percy Banks was walking up the steps to the imposing pulpit where he, and only he, held sway. As the Vicar of Hartley read from the Bible passage that was to be the basis of his eulogy, Watson noticed a group sitting near the back, all together in a row, without any men accompanying them. They included Sarah Anne Smith, by far the most elegant of the ladies in question, along with Ottavina Badland (the most beautiful), Gladys Grimshaw (the glummest) and a newly released Selina Brook (the dirtiest), minus her pig, which, thanks to Wright Watson, was back in the hands of its rightful owner.

The Detective Chief Inspector thought back to the meeting with the pig thief. She had been less than coherent in interview, but what Brook was asserting needed to be investigated, now that Miss Martha and her fiancé had shared the contents of that brown envelope with them. Not that it would be easy, given the high rank of those implicated in the woman's testimony. Watson and Makepeace had talked about how they might best go about their business when it concerned such a sensitive issue. Watson had heard of these circles from his former colleagues in the Metropolitan Police, and they were becoming more prevalent as the techniques and technology of the photographic arts continued to improve. Burchill had certainly appreciated the finer points of the female form, if the pictures in the envelope were anything to go by, and Watson and Makepeace had some sympathy with Miss Martha wanting nothing more to do with her father's illicit hobby. It would have come as a shock to TAB's daughter if she had discovered more material. Wright Watson did not have the heart to tell her it was unlikely to be the first parcel requested and received. In the same way, he and Makepeace determined that, for now, they would not share the identity of the models depicted in the prints with anyone else at Hartley Police Station. Would Burchill's penchant for naked men and women in graphic poses get him murdered? Was he the ringleader of a group that exchanged these expensive and hard-to-acquire works? Was he blackmailing others? Did he know too much? Was another 'leading light' in Hartley set to lose all if it became known they shared the Organist and Choirmaster's secret pastime? Could it be several members of the town's upper echelons; a whole conspiracy of them?

Watson turned his attention back to the service as Verney began playing the final hymn. The instrument was so loud that the two detectives were physically intimidated by its noise. The Assistant Organist had warned him and Makepeace that with so many people in the building, it would be necessary to use all the stops when it came to the congregational singing; a full building needed an even fuller organ. Makepeace watched in admiration as Verney demonstrated his mastery of the instrument and the music. The Detective Sergeant nudged his Inspector and pointed at Verney's feet as they danced across the organ pedals. Makepeace could understand why the Assistant Organist was bitter: at Burchill, at Banks, at the churchwardens and the Organ Trustees, at the Vestry Committee for not backing his claim to be Burchill's successor. Not that it would have done Verney any good, given the Vicar of Hartley's implacable opposition to someone of such lowly rank being appointed. Yet Burchill himself had been an ordinary sort, born and bred of working people. But the great Organist and Choirmaster was already well established by the time that the Reverend Canon Dr Percy George Banks was installed in the Vicarage at Hartley. Whatever Banks had thought of Burchill, and vice versa, the two men had agreed (according to the Vicar) that Verney just would not do; neither would a charge that the Assistant Organist had murdered his superior, for he was at work, as he had protested, on the afternoon and evening of TAB's murder.

The hymn came to a rousing conclusion. Banks then gave the final blessing from the high altar, his voice clear and resonant, his right hand held high above the congregation. Watson watched the singers bow their heads in unison. The boys in their crisp, newly starched surplices, looked like angels. Watson realised what perfection had been achieved at St Martin's. Every last detail had been considered. Perhaps Banks and Burchill were right; Verney might be a good, worthy Assistant, but there was no way in which he could take up the mantle of Organist and Choirmaster at Hartley Parish Church. It would need to be someone very special indeed to fill TAB's organ shoes. The coffin was led out of the church by the choir and followed by Martha Burchill and Wyn Williams (there was no other family present). Both policemen thought they could detect a thin smile on Williams's face, though it was difficult to be certain from such a distance. Then came Dr Banks and his six curates. Other local clergy were present, together with representatives of every denomination; Burchill had been especially popular amongst the local Methodist churches, where he often played recitals and conducted concerts with the Parish Church Choir, despite Banks's protestations. The Vicar beckoned the dignitaries in the front rows of the nave to join in behind as he passed. Wright Watson noticed that Banks shook his head at Whiteley George as the ever-growing procession passed the solicitor's pew.

It was more than half an hour before the Parish Church was empty of people, notwithstanding the precision and thoroughness of the arrangements and the efficiency with which the twenty or more sidesmen shepherded the multitudes out through the many exits. Watson and Makepeace decided they had seen enough and would decline the invitation to refreshments. They looked over to where the National School pupils were lined up in rows, ready to pay their respects to Dr Burchill; row upon row of ragamuffin children standing there behind the iron railings. The Detective Chief Inspector wondered whether or not to go over to talk to the group of women surrounding Sarah Anne Smith as she held court. Watson and Makepeace counted at least ten of them, including Grimshaw, Brook, and Badland. After a few moments, Mrs. Smith noticed that Watson was observing her and her friends. She smiled and pointedly gave a little curtsey before turning away and leading her group towards the nearest hostelry.

Banks was tired. Leading Burchill's funeral service and hosting the reception afterwards had been both physically and emotionally draining. The Vicar of Hartley hated social occasions, but it was a necessary evil if he were to realise his ambition. Now, he was one step closer, despite the setbacks of the past few weeks. He gathered the meeting to order, looked round the table to make sure that all the attendees were paying attention, then began.

'Gentlemen, I have made my decision. Dr Charleton Mann is in complete agreement.' Banks nodded to the Organist of Yorbridge Cathedral, who bowed his head slowly in response. 'Here is a list of the seven candidates shortlisted. They will be interviewed and auditioned this Friday. Dr Mann and I will lead the process; Mr. Verney will be in attendance with members of the choir; you are very welcome to join us, though we must all make sure not to be seen by the candidates – that would never do!'

'This is a bit steep, Banks!'

'Why the hurry?'

'We should have been consulted!'

'The Trustees are in charge here, Vicar!'

The Vicar of Hartley stood up. 'Not any longer, gentlemen. I have here a ruling from the House of Lords that clearly states I am in charge, not the churchwardens, not the Organ Trustees, not the Vestry Committee; nobody but me, and I will have my way!'

CHAPTER 15

PREPARING FOR THE AUDITIONS

Banks and Mann retired to the study. Having served the two men with port and cigars, the butler added a final scuttle of coal to the fire then nodded goodnight.

'You have an impressive family, Banks.'

The Vicar of Halifax smiled.

'Thank you, Charleton!'

'Of course. I was just thinking: "Happy is the man that hath his quiver full of them: They shall not be put to shame, when they speak with their enemies in the gate".'

'Psalm 128, verse 5! You know your Bible well! I would not have expected an organist, even of your standing, to be so well versed in the scriptures.'

'Nonsense! I have known it from my youth up; and the psalms are my daily meat. You of all people should appreciate that!'

'My apologies. Indeed, I do very much appreciate that, and I am also grateful that you are assisting me in the auditions tomorrow. The Organ Trustees asked me to tell you how keen they were to have the great Dr Charleton Mann to advise on the selection process.'

Mann smiled. 'It was the least I could do to help you find a worthy successor to dear old Tommy. I felt very sad as TAB's coffin was lowered into the grave yesterday and you said the words of the committal. The manner of Burchill's departing this life does not bear thinking about. Who would do such a thing?'

Banks thought for a moment then replied. 'I can think of a number of people. Everybody said what a "singular man" TAB was. It is impossible to be successful in this country without making enemies. I should know. I have worked every hour that God has sent me for the Church, and for such little reward and recognition. I should be a bishop by now, but I have been told I am not yet eligible. I have been thwarted at every turn over my plans for Hartley Parish Church, and whatever I do and however I approach matters, the people of this dale do not like me one jot.'

'Where were you born, Percy?'

'Not in Yorkshire! That is the problem. And that is where Thomas Burchill had the advantage over me and my kind. He was born but a few miles from here, in a little village called Oakenshaw, I think.'

'I know it well. Several celebrated singers have come from those parts. Sarah Anne Jessop, for one.'

'I do not care for music of the secular and social order, Charleton. I look for someone who will get on with the authorities and be conciliatory. Too often, I found that Burchill would not bend to my will when he needed to. I felt absolutely at his mercy during the service. Up in that organ loft, anything could be going on, and often did, believe me!'

'I find that hard to accept, Percy. I have heard Burchill render the service in such a devout and sensitive fashion over many years, both here in Hartley and when he took his choir to other places of worship. Why, I recall the time that the Parish Church singers came to Yorbridge. I was more than a little ashamed of my own choir's rendition of the service in contrast ever thereafter.'

'I give you that, Charleton. There is no doubting TAB's qualities as both organist and choir director. But he could be impatient and insolent towards me and others. He was constantly composing and forcing his compositions on the choir and the congregation. There was no need for that at all.'

'So, you are not sorry that Tommy is dead?'

'Goodness, no! I would not say that at all, and I never meant to imply such a thing! Shall we say that…well, that I wish I had known him longer and sooner; before he became so set in his ways.'

'Perhaps we should turn to the shortlist, Percy.'

'Indeed we should, Charleton. More port?'

'No thank you. I need a clear head. I believe that we both do.'

'You are right. Let me fetch the applications.'

The Vicar of Hartley rose from his armchair and walked over to the bureau. He unlocked the drawer where he kept his confidential papers and took out the file marked 'Organ'.

As he returned to the fireside and his musical advisor, he poured himself another glass of port.

'Here you are, I have written out a list of the candidates. You will not know the order in which they will play, nor will you be able to see them.'

'And what about the other way round? Will they be able to see me?'

'No, they will not, though they know you will be listening and judging their performance. I have asked Verney to have the choir in attendance – or at least those who can get off work or school – and they are ready to sing the music that you requested. What else do the candidates need to do?'

'Everything that I said in my letter to you. I will use the pro forma to note down my comments on every test.' Mann took the handwritten shortlist from Banks, put on his reading glasses, and proceeded to inspect the names of those he was going to assess the following day. 'These all seem excellent choices. I congratulate you and the Organ Trustees on your selection. I know some of these men. They will all do nicely, though we shall have to see who wins on the day. May I see their letters of application?'

Banks handed Mann the remaining papers in the file.

'I can see we will have a difficult choice tomorrow if truth be told. Burford is a good man; so too is Macintosh. I know them both personally; at one time they were my students. I have heard good things of Bennett, Turner, and Warley. I know nothing of Casement, though he comes with a good *curriculum vitae*.'

Mann paused. He took out the final letter and read it carefully.

'Who is Stanford George? He seems an oddity. Far too young, I would have said!'

'I added him to the list at the last minute. There was something about his application that struck me as worthy of consideration.'

'He is but 22 years old, Percy. That is no age for someone who is to become Organist and Choirmaster of Hartley Parish Church. Is it wise to consider a man with so little experience of an important and demanding role?'

'TAB was the same age when he was appointed!'

Mann laughed. 'That was a long time ago. The world was very different and the music here in a terrible state. There was nothing to lose by appointing an ambitious young man. Now there is everything to lose! You need someone like Burford or Macintosh. They have both served their apprenticeships in cathedral organ lofts. They will command the respect of the choir, the congregation, the town and, most importantly of all, you. The same, I imagine, will be true of the others. But not George. I do not think we should audition him tomorrow. It will be a waste of his – and our – time.'

'I disagree, Charleton. A younger man like George can be moulded. He will be ambitious like TAB was once ambitious. He will want to prove himself; to make Hartley Parish Church choir even greater than it already is. The other men have less to prove. They will see the post as a sinecure.'

'You are wrong there, Banks! Trust me. I know these people. Burford or Macintosh for preference!'

'Well, we shall see. But George stays on the list. See what you think when you hear him, along with all the others, of course. And you will be the final arbiter. I promise you.'

'Very well, Vicar. If that is how you wish it to be, then that is how we will conduct the audition and these seven men are the ones whom I will assess.'

'Capital! I so wish to move on with filling the post. Then we can return to the work in hand.'

'And what is "the work in hand," Percy?'

'Can I speak to you in confidence? There is a major development planned for this town. You might be interested in becoming a shareholder in our venture. You would do well to join us. Significant financial gains are to be had for men of vision who are prepared to take risks.'

'Tell me more. I might well be interested in such a proposition.'

'Banks has spoken, then! And we obey.'

'Like we always do! TAB would never have let the Vicar get away with what he wants to do now!'

Verney, Snelgrove and Sutcliffe sipped on their beer. It was a long time since they had patronised *The King's Head*. And they would not have been there now if they had not been invited by the landlord, and his wife.

'Here he comes: our former Organist. He has not worn well, has Edward, unlike his wife. I wonder what they want with us, the evening before the auditions at Hartley Parish Church.'

CHAPTER 16

NOTHING GOES AS PLANNED

'Is everything ready, Verney?'

'It is, Vicar. I have managed to assemble twenty choir members: ten men and ten boys, with a goodly number in all four parts. They have been given the music, as instructed by Dr Mann, and they are ready to be rehearsed whenever you require them for the auditions.'

'And a table for Dr Mann to sit at while he listens?'

'All arranged, sir. If you look over there you will see everything is set up for him behind the chapel screen. There is pen, paper and ink, and a jug of water and a glass to go with it.'

'Thank you, Verney. I am much obliged.'

'Very good, sir. I will station myself at the vestry door so that I can show the candidates to the organ loft.'

'Thank you. And remember, Dr Mann has given strict instructions that no assistance is to be given to any of them; no help with stop changes, page turns, relaying the beat, nothing!'

'Of course, Dr Banks. That is all very clearly understood.'

'And what about Snelgrove?'

'What about him, sir?'

'He knows how to conduct the choir and where to put the mistakes into the music, as Dr Mann has ordered?'

'Of course, Vicar. You have no need to worry. Everything has been taken care of, down to the last detail. Monkhill came yesterday and fettled up the organ until she sang like a bird. The ladies are just doing the final cleaning of the organ loft as we speak, and then everything will be ready.'

'Cleaners, Verney? That should have been done hours ago. Quick man! Get rid of those infernal women. They are not to be in the church when the auditions start! Do it! Do it now!'

Hartley Parish Church's Assistant Organist sloped off sheepishly. Verney was uncertain as to which he was more afraid of: the Vicar or the cleaning ladies. He determined that in the end, he had to tell Gladys and her army of women their work would have to be completed later.

'I am sorry, Gladys - Mrs Grimshaw, Dr Banks has spoken, and his word is law, as you and the others well know – we all do!'

'It's Miss. How many times have I told you? Doesn't his lordship want the loft neat and tidy? Burchill left it in a right state!'

'I know. But the first candidate will arrive any moment now, and you know how the Vicar is a stickler for punctuality in all things.'

'Don't I know it!'

Grimshaw fell silent, nodding to her fellow cleaners to stop work, gather together their dusters, cloths, mops, and buckets and leave the building via the choir vestry, where they would deposit the tools of their trade before leaving the building and locking the door behind them. Verney made sure they had left the Parish Church and all was secure before returning to the chancel. The choir had robed and assembled. It seemed strange to see Snelgrove in Burchill's old seat, but it made sense for the stand-in conductor to be there at the far end of the front row of the choirstalls; it was the ideal place for the organist to see the beat. Verney smiled at the lead tenor and then walked to the south chapel, where Mann and Banks sat in silence, ready to judge who should be Burchill's successor.

The Vicar looked at Mann and then signalled to Verney. 'We are ready for candidate number one, thank you.'

The Assistant Organist walked back to the north aisle entrance to the Parish Church. The candidates had been told to report there at the appointed hour for their audition. It was a convenient location, not least because from there, the applicants could be guided to the organ loft on the left of the chancel without being seen by either adjudicators or choir members. Verney went to the porch and opened both doors. There was a strong autumn breeze as he went outside to call Dr Harcourt Bennett, Mus Doc, FCO, to his audition. Verney thought he might recognise Bennett, for he had given a recital at the Parish Church when the new organ had been opened in a series of concerts. It had not gone well, and the more discerning members of the audience had determined that he was past his best. Nevertheless, the choir members had not been surprised when they found out Bennett was on the list. Having a doctorate counted for a lot with Banks.

Verney looked around the churchyard. The National School children were singing some trifle or other and performing it well. The occasional passer-by nodded to the Assistant Organist as he searched for candidate number one, but of Harcourt Bennett there was no sign. Verney took out his pocket watch and checked the time. It was now more than five minutes past the hour at which Bennett should have been there. There was nothing for it but to let Banks know.

'What? Where is he?'

'I do not know, sir. There is no sign of him.'

Banks looked at Mann. 'What shall we do?'

'There is nothing for it but to go onto the next candidate.'

'Very well. Send word to the landlord at *The Station Hotel* to ask candidate number two to attend now.'

Verney ordered one of the choirboys to take a message. Within fifteen minutes, the lad had returned with Robert Casement. Once settled in the organ loft, Banks rang a bell to signal the start of the audition. The playing was less than impressive, and every one of the tests was botched. Banks was all for curtailing the audition, but Mann persuaded the Vicar to let the assessment continue until its timetabled conclusion, despite the fact that the performance got worse rather than better.

'I simply do not understand it, Percy. Casement comes with good references and a Mus Bac – admittedly not from Yorbridge, but good enough – and Wilpshire Parish Church is of excellent standing for its music. It beggars belief that he should have played so badly. It cannot be nerves or having been called before time. It was almost as if he was deliberately playing badly.' Mann shook his head. 'I will write to Mr. Casement. Such a performance will not do if he is to advance within the profession. But enough; we had better continue with candidate number three.'

Banks nodded to Verney, who went to the north door. John James Turner was waiting in the porch, but only to hand the Assistant Organist a letter. 'Take this to Dr Banks and Dr Mann, please, would you? I have come all this way only to find that the post is not for me. I need to earn an honest living and there is no way I could do that as Organist here.'

Verney was shocked at the way in which Turner shoved the envelope into his hands, touched the brim of his hat and then ran away from the church door and towards the railway station. It was several moments before the Assistant Organist had regained his composure to the point where he could deliver the message. Banks had his head in his hands, while Mann wrote up his report of Casement's audition.

'A message for you both, from Mr. Turner.'

Banks snatched the note and opened it roughly to the point where the letter inside was torn in two. As the Vicar pieced it together, he swore. 'Goddammit! What is going on here? Turner says that he will not be able to make an honest living if he comes to Hartley and withdraws from the auditions with immediate effect. What is going on here, Verney?'

'I have no idea, sir. It is most perplexing.'

'What do you make of it, Mann? Is there some kind of plot afoot here?'

'I have never encountered anything like it. It is a bad dream!' Perhaps we should abandon proceedings. Someone does not want these auditions to be concluded.'

'No. We shall continue. I will not be thwarted! Go get candidate number four. Perhaps he will make more of a showing, that is assuming he turns up at all!'

Verney found himself running out of the Parish Church and across Market Street to *The Station Hotel,* where all the candidates had been accommodated. Burford was known to him and he had made Macintosh's acquaintance at a Deanery Choir Festival many years earlier. He would not recognise Warley or George but assumed that the hotelier would tell him where they could be located, if and when required. Macintosh was meant to be the fourth player to be heard, but such had been the Vicar's agitation on hearing of Turner's withdrawal that Verney determined that he would invite the first organist that he found. Warley and George were nowhere to be seen, no doubt because they were not due to perform until the afternoon. The man on duty at the hotel reception desk explained that the two residents had chosen to take the air together and would not be back for at least an hour. No matter, for Burford and Macintosh would still be available.

'Not Mr. Macintosh, sir. He left the hotel and took the mid-morning train back to London.'

Verney went pale.

'Are you alright sir?'

Verney shook his head.

'Not really. I am rapidly running out of organists to send to the Vicar.'

'I am still here and ready to play.'

The Assistant Organist of Hartley Parish Church turned round. 'Who are you?'

'Algernon Burford, at your service. And you are?'

'Charles Verney, Assistant Organist at Hartley Parish Church. I have been deputed to bring the candidates from the hotel to their auditions. But we seem to be falling victim to a spate of non-attendances.'

'Really. Why is that?'

'I do not know, Mr. Burford.'

'Dr Burford. I obtained my Mus Doc from the University of Yorbridge last year.'

'My apologies Dr Burford.'

Burford acknowledged Verney. 'I am ready to be heard, even if somewhat earlier than I had expected.'

'Macintosh was due to play before you so I am not sure how Dr Mann and Dr Banks will react.'

'Macintosh and I agreed that only one of us should remain for the auditions. I called heads and won.'

'You mean you tossed a coin? Why should you both not stay?'

Burford laughed. 'You are obviously not aware of the ways of the cathedral organ fraternity, Verney!'

'What fraternity is that sir?'

'We take it in turns to be auditioned for the top posts so that we each stand a better chance of being successful. Macintosh has withdrawn from Hartley while I will not attend at Ribchester so that he and I can both have a clear run.'

'Isn't that dishonest, Dr Burford?'

Candidate number five burst out laughing. 'It is what has to be done to get on! And you would do well to heed that advice if you want to leave Hartley and be successful in obtaining a better position. Now take me to the organ loft, post-haste. I have an audition to win.'

Burford put on his hat and coat, picked up his music case and followed Verney out of the hotel and towards the Parish Church. There was no conversation. Burford whistled the theme of one great Bach organ fugue after another until the north door was reached.

'The organ loft is this way, Dr Burford. I will let Dr Mann and Dr Banks know that you have arrived. Please start your pieces and then the tests once you hear the bell each time. Then Mr. Snelgrove will position himself so that you can see him conduct the anthem. Please be patient with the singers – especially the boys – they have had a long and frustrating morning.'

Burford took his place on the organ bench. Within five minutes the first bell had rung. Full organ sounded from the first chord in a performance of Mendelssohn's *First Organ Sonata*. The rendition was so brilliant that the choirmen burst into spontaneous applause at the end of the final movement. The candidate made short – and excellent – work of the various tests Mann had set. Burford even spotted the deliberate mistake that the Organist of Yorbridge Cathedral had inserted into the sight reading. As he directed the choir in the chosen anthem, Snelgrove could not help but feel that here was a worthy successor to Thomas Burchill. The stand-in conductor looked across at the Assistant Organist and smiled. Verney nodded.

There remained but one test. A choirboy ran up to the organ loft to give Burford the theme that was to be used as the basis of the final improvisation. The music began softly, almost imperceptibly, growing in intensity and dynamic as Mann's few notes were turned into an organ symphony of epic proportions. When the listeners thought that all was concluded, the composition began again, and again, relentless crescendo after relentless crescendo. There came a final pedal point that signalled the triumphant coda. Every stop was in play, each ounce of wind was being pumped through the bellows. Then the last chord. As Burford pressed down the keys and pedals of a great C major chord, a terrifying rumble came from high up in the organ. The choir watched in horror as the largest central pipe in the chancel case came away from its mounting and fell down onto the organ console. The improvisation died away to a chronic, painful moan. Snelgrove and Verney rushed up to the console, but to no avail. Candidate number five lay sprawled across the bloodied keys, his head smashed completely open.

CHAPTER 17

WATSON AND MAKEPEACE INSPECT THE CRIME SCENE; THE ORGAN TRUSTEES PLOT AND PLAN

'Has anything been moved or touched?'

'No, Inspector. We left everything as it was when poor Burford met his end. The choir men and boys have been sent away, of course. Some of the trebles were very distressed, I can tell you. This is such a terrible blow.' The Vicar of Hartley wrung his hands, shook his head, and looked at his fellow assessor. 'Let me introduce you to Dr Charleton Mann, Organist and Master of the Choristers at Yorbridge Cathedral.'

'This has been an awful shock, gentlemen. Things have gone horribly wrong, have they not?' Mann extended a hand to Watson.

The Detective Chief Inspector was surprised at the strength of the Doctor's grip. 'Pleased to make your acquaintance, sir. These are trying circumstances, I give you that, and so soon after Dr Burchill's demise. We would like to take statements from you both, but first, I need to examine the body in the organ loft, if I may.'

Banks looked at Mann and then nodded to Watson, who beckoned Makepeace to follow him up the steps to the console. The Vicar and his expert assessor followed. Music and other papers were strewn about the loft. Access to the organ was blocked by the enormous metal pipe that had fallen from its mounting. The performer's head had been broken open.

'This is Dr Algernon Burford, sir. According to Charles Verney, the

Assistant Organist, Burford was meant to be the fifth candidate to play today, but because of the non-attendance of other applicants he ended up playing sooner than he expected.'

'Non-attendance?'

'Some of the organists did not turn up for their auditions, Inspector. I cannot understand why. I have never come across anything like it.' Mann shook his head.

'What about the ones who did turn up? Were they all auditioned?'

'No. There were two more candidates to go, though we were very impressed with Burford, were we not, Percy?'

Banks nodded. 'Yes, though we might have been just as impressed if not more so with the others.'

Watson turned to Makepeace. 'We will need to investigate that later, Sergeant, and we must take statements from the choir members.'

'Yes, sir.'

'Can we have names and addresses for all the applicants and the shortlisted candidates please, Dr Banks?'

'Of course. I have the paperwork back at the Vicarage if you would care to collect it later.'

'I will. And what of the people who were yet to play, Vicar?'

'I do not know, Watson. They may still be at the hotel. I doubt they will know what has happened, though the time for their auditions is long past.'

The Detective Chief Inspector turned to Mann. 'Tell me, Doctor, you say that nothing has been moved or touched, but why is the organ not sounding? Burford's hands and head are depressing all those keys. Surely the instrument should be making a noise?'

'Verney pushed the stops in and switched the engines off once we realised what had happened to Burford. As you imply, Inspector, it was a terrible row. It was sending some of the boys off, and they were badly sparked enough already with the collapse of the organ pipe. I told Charles to silence the beast.' Mann smiled thinly as he spoke.

'So, the Assistant Organist was in here after Burford was killed?'

'He was, Inspector, but only to stop the noise.'

Watson sighed. 'Is Verney still present, Dr Banks?'

'No, Inspector, I told him to sort the boys out. Then he asked to be excused so he could get back to work.'

Makepeace continued to write in his notepad as Watson approached the corpse. The pipe was leaning precariously over the edge of the balustrade at the front of the loft. The Detective Chief Inspector looked up to the hole in the casework where the pipe had been.

'It must have been dislodged by the vibrations. Burford was playing on full organ when it happened. It is a very powerful instrument. One of the biggest in the kingdom, and almost certainly the loudest!' Mann snorted.

'Could this have been an accident, the result of poor workmanship?'

'I think not, Inspector. Ishmael Monkhill is one of the best builders in the country. I wish he would attend to the organ at Yorbridge Cathedral. He could do wonders with it, just as he has done here at Hartley!'

'And when was the work done?' Makepeace stood ready with his pencil and notepad.

'It was initially completed some two years ago, though there is always more to do. TAB wanted yet more stops, and the casing to the east of the main organ is yet to be completed. We are still fund-raising to pay off the debt and to finish the woodwork there.' Banks pointed to the scaffolding that had been erected to the right of the organ console.

Watson went to the edge of the organ loft and looked up. 'Would it have been possible for someone to gain access to the front of the case and tamper with the big pipes?'

Mann looked at Banks before replying. 'I believe that it would Inspector, but you would need to confirm that with Monkhill.'

'I shall do, that, sir.'

'You will not have long to wait, Watson. Our organ builder is here now. He was due to continue work on the instrument when the auditions were over – which they should have been half an hour ago. The successful candidate, Dr Mann and I were meant to be having a celebratory meal. Who would do such a thing? It is all aimed at me and my ambitions, I know it!'

Mann squeezed the Vicar's arm. Watson nodded to Makepeace. 'I do not believe we have any further need of you two gentlemen at this stage. Sergeant Makepeace and I will call upon you at the Vicarage tomorrow, if we may. I assume you will be staying in Hartley overnight, Dr Mann?'

'I will, Inspector, though I must get back to Yorbridge for evensong tomorrow.'

'Very good, sir. I will make sure that we have spoken with you before 10 o'clock tomorrow morning.'

Banks and Mann descended the organ loft steps. As they did so a rotund, red-faced man clambered past them. Makepeace could not help but notice the largest mutton-chop whiskers he had ever seen. The man was bald in the middle of his head, with two hedges of white hair on either side, as if to make up for the lack of follicles in the middle.

'O my God! What has happened here? This is awful! Simply awful! It is a disaster.'

'Disaster, sir?'

'Yes, a disaster. My beautiful instrument, so damaged!'

'Not to mention the dead organist, of course, sir.' Makepeace looked askance.

'What? O yes, of course, the poor man. That big CCC pipe was heavy: some several hundredweight, in fact. He would have been killed in an instant, no doubt of that, no doubt whatsoever.'

'I take it that you are Mr Monkhill?'

'I am indeed. Ishmael Monkhill, and this instrument is my *magnum opus*. My pride and joy'. By now the organ builder had become fascinated with his organ pipe's effect on Burford's head.

'I wouldn't touch that, if I were you, Mr Monkhill, at least not until the doctor has been – the medical doctor that is. Too many people with doctorates round here!' Watson snorted, Makepeace smirked and Monkhill grimaced.

'They are a fine sort, these Mus Docs. Think they know it all. They might be able to play the organ, but only I can build one! Where would they be without me? Nowhere!'

'Indeed, Mr Monkhill.'

'Call me Ishmael. Everyone else does!'

'Very well, Ishmael. Why were you meant to be here today?'

'To finish off the work on the east side of the organ'.

'Where exactly?'

'Yon. It's for the new case. Not that I should be doing it. None of it!'

'Why is that?'

'Because the buggers haven't paid me for the last lot o' work! £700 yon owe me! Big ideas and small pockets, that Banks has! Him and his cronies!'

'That is a lot of money, Ishmael. Is that how much the organ cost?'

Monkhill burst into laughter. 'What? It were £2,000! The blowers were on top!'

'So, the church owes you a lot of money?'

'You could say that!'

'And are they likely to pay?'

Monkhill shook his head. 'Deep in debt, this place, an' not just to me! Stonemasons, builders, stained glass makers, the lot. Then there is the business with Grindrod's hydraulic engines. They've never worked properly. Give me hand blowing any day.' The organ builder stopped and looked up. 'What happened here?'

'How do you mean, sir?' Makepeace put his notebook down and came over to where the pipe had fallen through the casework and onto Burford's head.

'Look for thissen. All these stays and supports sawn away. No wonder t' pipe fell down!'

The two policemen followed the organ builder's finger as he pointed to where blocks of wood supporting the organ front pipes were situated. One of these 'stays' (as Monkhill described then) had been neatly sawn almost all the way through.

'I see what you mean. Presumably the vibrations of the last chord Burford played would have been the final straw.'

Monkhill nodded. 'Aye. No doubt.'

'This is murder, Makepeace, that is clear.'

'Someone in Hartley does not want this organ loft occupied, for certain, sir.'

The Detective Sergeant closed his notebook and followed the Detective Chief Inspector down the steps and into the body of the chancel, where the mortuary staff were ready to remove Burford's body from the church. Monkhill waited to begin removing and repairing the murderous pipe. The cleaning ladies stood in the south chapel where Charleton Mann and Percy Banks had sat earlier. Once instructed, they would do their best to clean away the blood and sanitise the organ keys.

'It will not do. We cannot be treated like this!'

Sir Arthur Hastings warmed his posterior by the drawing room fire, then looked round at the Organ Trustees. All but two were present: the Vicar and Whiteley George had not been invited. When asked why, the self-appointed chairman of the breakaway organ group argued that George was not to be trusted with confidential matters; because the single agendum item was Dr Banks's behaviour towards the Trustees, it was only right and proper he should not be present, at least until the present group had formulated a plan for regaining their authority over all matters musical at Hartley Parish Church.

'We have the law on our side', said Sidebottom, 'I am sure of it. This paper that Banks quotes is a nonsense. Our constitution cannot be overturned in the way that the Vicar asserts. I propose that we just go to him and say so.'

'What good will that do, Arnold? Banks will take no notice. He has friends in high places, that one.' Worsdell puffed at his pipe.

'I agree, William. There is no arguing with that man. He will not be told. He has got his sights set on being the Bishop of Hartley; nothing will distract him from that course. If we do not fall in behind him, we will be cast aside like all the others who have crossed him. He has been wanting to rob us of our power since he first set foot in that Vicarage.' Hastings looked round at the rest of the Trustees. 'Are we agreed on a course of action before it is too late? I ask you for a show of hands to confirm your commitment to my proposal. All in favour?'

Hands went up slowly at first, then more rapidly as the waverers saw how the meeting was going.

Hastings counted the votes. 'Thank you, gentlemen. All are in favour. We have agreed, *nem con,* that the Vicar must be dealt with.'

CHAPTER 18

THE AFTERMATH OF AUDITIONS

Rose Banks knew something was wrong as soon as the Vicarage door slammed shut. She had heard that sound so many times. Percy would be in one of his rages. As always, it was best to keep out of his way until the morning. At least the children were in bed. She looked at the picture of herself beside him on their wedding day. It was a different world and another Rose Steward who had married the dashing young curate; she had fallen in love with him so rapidly, so fully, and so earnestly. She remembered that first Sunday at the family church in London. It had begun like any other morning worship. Then Percy George Banks had got up to preach the sermon.

For an instant, Rose felt the tingle of desire as she remembered their first encounter. She took the silver-framed photograph from the sideboard. How happy I was! What we had to look forward to! And now, what is there? She looked round the drawing room. There was comfort, respectability, security, safety. There were the children: all but one, that is; the one Percy had most wanted; the one that he cherished more than all the girls put together; the one who had so bitterly been removed from their earthly lives. 'The Lord giveth and the Lord taketh away'. He took away not just my – our – son, but my husband as well. Percy has never been the same since Archibald passed away. The man I loved and married died too. We were happy and could still be happy if my husband would give up his rampant, greedy ambition, would throw away his stupid plans for Hartley to be a cathedral and him to be its bishop. None of it will make him happy;

nothing ever makes him happy. We would need another Archie to make us happy, well, and whole again. And that will never happen.

Rose Banks could hear voices in her husband's study as she walked over to the piano and sat down. She rifled through the scores on the music stand until the piece most dear to her was located. Then, she found her glasses, put them on, and began to play and sing. It was not the same without the composer present. Rose stopped after only a few bars, closed the manuscript, shut the piano lid, and returned to her reading by the fire. The tears made it difficult for her to see the words; the volume was returned to the side table after only a few paragraphs. She thought to ring the servant's bell for more coal, but decided there was no point, given the hour and her tiredness.

The voices could still be heard. Her husband's rage seemed to have subsided, judging by the volume and timbre of his utterances. It was also noticeable that the second person – presumably Charleton Mann – was speaking more as the conversation wore on. What is it all about? This should have been a good day for Percy: a successor to TAB was being chosen. Something must be wrong. Not that anyone could ever replace Tommy Burchill.

<hr />

'I do not understand it, Charleton. Everybody is against me!'

'I doubt that, Percy. You are imagining things!'

'Imagining? Imagining? Were we imagining the killing of Dr Burford today? Inspector Watson has already said that there has been foul play in that organ loft – **my** organ loft. That pipe did not tumble of its own accord. They are out to get me and they know that if the music tradition and reputation falters, there is no cathedral and no bishop in Hartley!'

'Who is the "they", Percy?'

Banks picked up the decanter and poured himself and his organ adviser a large whisky. 'I have never been welcomed in these parts, Charleton. The good burghers of Hartley do not want change – at least not my kind of change – especially when it is effected by an outsider. They have been against me from the start, I swear. Then there were those damn Organ Trustees, interfering and asserting their rights to be in charge of all the music. Though I scored a victory with them recently; the law is on my side there!'

'Do not be so hard on them, Banks. They only want what is best for the music and the organ.'

'Do not be so sure, Mann. There was far more to the Whiteley George scandal than meets the eye. I was not party to all the shady goings on involving him and Grindrod. And I expect other Trustees were just as culpable.'

'Put it behind you! The matter is over and done with!'

Banks shook his head in reply. 'That was just the beginning. There have been letters – anonymous ones of course – smearing my good reputation and my wife's honour. I know who wrote them, I can tell you! I would not put it past those Trustees to be behind today's shambles!'

'You are getting beside yourself again, Percy. You are imagining conspiracies where no conspiracies exist. Every church community has its factions and antagonisms – Yorbridge Cathedral is a good case in point – but I am sure that your ambitions for this place are shared and supported by the vast majority of people in the town and, even more so, in the Parish Church.'

Banks grunted as Mann continued.

'Now what do you say we determine what to do next? I take it that Verney is willing to continue for the time being?'

'Ha! Good old Charles. Yes, he will continue for as long as I wish and require him to do so. There is no issue there. Where I lead, he will follow.'

'And what does that mean, Percy?'

'He is a man of little imagination and even less ambition. Tommy used to say of him that the "vital spark" was missing when it came to Verney and he would always be an assistant and never a master. Did you not think so at TAB's funeral service? His playing lacked that "snap" for which other players – including yourself, of course, Charleton – are so famed.'

Mann blushed a little as he nodded in agreement. 'But do not take Verney for granted, Vicar. He has the support of the choir men, and the boys like him. You need to keep him sweet, especially given our inability to appoint an Organist and Choirmaster today.'

'Could we not just invite one or other of the remaining candidates to take the post? You seemed to think that they were both good men.'

103

'Well, we could, but surely, you would only want to select one of them after a proper examination.'

'Hmmm. You mean like today's "proper examination"?'

'You know what I mean, Percy. I also believe that we should determine why Dr Harcourt Bennett was not in attendance. He is probably the best of the men on the list after Burford.'

'So, you think it was our best candidate who was slain?'

Mann nodded. 'Burford is – or rather was – one of the most talented younger players in the land, and a Mus Doc at only 27, to boot! He will be sorely missed, and he would have been a worthy successor to Tommy Burchill.'

Banks sighed. 'Is there any point in continuing with this charade?'

'Of course! The other men are all very good – except I do not know George, the last candidate. As well as Bennett, we must ascertain why Macintosh withdrew and see if we can persuade him to reinstate his application. He is older than the others, and perhaps not so talented a player, but he is good with choristers and achieves his results through sheer hard work – something that I admire in a man.'

'Do I take it you do not believe Turner should be recalled?'

'Well, Percy, his letter made it plain that unless the salary were to be increased to £150 from £100 per annum, then he could not entertain the post. Are you prepared to offer more?'

'No, I am not. At least not to start with. I was prepared to pay TAB extra out of my own pocket, but that was different, especially when I needed to retain Burchill's services to help our case.'

'So was Tommy thinking of moving on?'

'There was some talk of it.'

'Really? After all these years? Why would he want to leave Hartley when he had built the musical reputation of the church choir to such an apex? It would be a backward step for him. And why bother at his age?'

'I believe there had been some – some personal difficulties of late. Between him and a lady.'

Mann laughed. 'I would have thought Tommy would have been too old for that. But then he always did have a twinkle in his eye. Except that he was not much liked by the ladies of the choir when he got rid of them!

Not that they could do anything about it. Once TAB had made up his mind, there was no stopping him, was there?'

'That is very true, Charleton, very true indeed!'

'We shall cross Turner off our list, then.' Mann sighed.

Shall we consider the other candidates?' Banks looked at his pocket watch.

Mann scratched his head. 'If you believe it is worth it, Vicar. Howell Warley comes with good references, and you are obviously keen on Stanford George, despite his seeming lack of experience. And neither man has had a chance to prove himself before us. It would seem unfair to penalise them because of the events of today. On the other hand, I do not know what to say about Casement. He would have failed his Fellowship examination if he had turned in such a performance, and yet he won the top prizes. I know, I was the examiner and gave him good marks! If you are looking for a conspiracy, Percy, ask Robert Casement if he had been warned off the job and played badly to get out of being appointed!'

⸻ ◆ ⸻

That evening, October 10th, 1879, three men each read a letter they had just received. The addressees were unaware that the words, cut out from newspaper articles, formed the same warning in each case:

ATTEND THE NEXT AUDITIONS AT YOUR PERIL. IF YOU PLAY FOR BANKS AND MANN AND GET THE JOB YOU WILL DIE, JUST LIKE BURCHILL AND BURFORD DID. YOU HAVE BEEN WARNED. YOU ARE BEING WATCHED. TAKE THIS ADVICE IF YOU WANT TO LIVE!

Two of the organists threw the letter away and determined to have nothing more to do with Hartley Parish Church, its organ, and its choir. A third, being of sterner mettle, resolved not to heed the warning.

CHAPTER 19

SUSPECTS PAST AND PRESENT

Wright Watson walked slowly up the steps to the police station. He remembered the day eighteen months earlier when the Prince and Princess of Wales had visited Hartley to open the building. The factories had stopped work while the royal parade made its stately way through the town; all the school children had been given the day off. The streets were lined with flag-waving, cheering, happy folk, determined to make the most of Hartley's moment of fame. A brass band played, the Mayor gave a stirring speech, and the Vicar, Dr Banks, said a prayer. Members of the Parish Church Choir were in attendance. Dr Burchill conducted them in one of his own compositions, written especially for the occasion. It was not the only time when the good doctor was to the fore in civic celebrations. There had been the opening of the Town Hall in 1875 and, going back to when Watson had first joined the police, the completion of the first railway line into Hartley. All these events paled into insignificance compared with the re-opening of the Parish Church in 1877, when Queen Victoria, the Duke and Duchess of Hartleydale, the Lord Lieutenant, the gentry and middling sort of the area, all and sundry had been present as the Archbishops of Canterbury and York rededicated St Martin's Parish Church after its complete refurbishment.

Watson, then a Detective Sergeant, had been on duty, along with every other officer. By then, the Hartley and District Women's Social and Political Union had been in existence for two years, a period of time during which its leader, Gertrude Rankin, had done her utmost to further the cause of women's suffrage within the town, whether by peaceable, legal means or through other, more nefarious methods. Her inner circle of suffragists determined that Hartley women would do things differently from the circles springing up in other parts of the kingdom. Wright Watson had been charged with the task of keeping a close watch on the Rankinists (as the *Gazette and Argus* had christened them) when the monarch was in Hartley to celebrate the refurbishment of the Parish Church.

Police constables were deployed at key points along the route of the procession and at the entrances to St Martin's. Hartley Central Station was similarly well protected, with the added reassurance of a guard of honour supplied by the Queen's Own Hartleydale Light Infantry. There appeared to be no opportunity for mischief, even by Rankin's army of hotheaded suffragists.

As it turned out, the police did well to contain the Rankinists and make sure all was in order by the time the Queen arrived, but for a few moments, the Parish Church was a scene of utter mayhem as women shouted and screamed from every corner of the building. One or two tried to throw paint and ink over the newly whitewashed walls; others distributed leaflets. Gertrude Rankin herself ascended the pulpit and began to preach on the subject of 'Women's Right to Ballot'. She had uttered no more than two sentences when Dr Thomas Burchill had the presence of mind to play a triumphal march on full organ. Mrs Rankin was carried out of the church, along with the rest of her followers. The fracas was over within ten minutes of it starting, but not before much disquiet had been engendered. The monarch, the aristocracy, the gentry, and the archbishops never knew any different, for, by the time that they arrived, the Rankinists were well on their way to the police station to be charged and imprisoned.

Detective Chief Inspector Wright Watson hoped never to have to deal with an event like the 'Rankin Revolt', as it became known, ever again. Gertrude's imprisonment had seen a falling away in support for radical action. Most of her followers had either gone back to their day-to-day domestic lives or, for those who still harboured sympathy for the universal suffrage movement, less aggressive branches of the sisterhood were available. Could there still be a Rankinist league in Hartley? Might such a group have been involved in the deaths of Burchill and now Burford? Both were men. Burchill had certainly not wanted women in his choir and it had turned out that the second victim had come from the 'Anglo-Catholic' tradition, which relegated women to subsidiary roles within all aspects of the ecclesiastical set-up in parts of the Church of England. Watson had read of Burford's recommended alterations to the lofts in churches where the organist was a woman. It was not so much a case of seen and not heard as the other way round: a female could play the instrument provided that she could not be observed from the church. Screens had been erected round the keyboards to that effect. Burford – far more extreme than Burchill in such matters – had even proposed changes to the College of Organists' examinations that would have precluded females entering, in the way that women could not study for, and gain, music degrees.

'A penny for them, sir.'

'A penny for what, Makepeace?'

'A penny for your thoughts, Detective Chief Inspector.'

'Oh yes, of course, Sergeant. Except I do not think you want to hear my thoughts. I have just had an outlandish idea about who might be behind the murders. Except that it is so far-fetched you would laugh if I told you.'

'Are you sure, sir?'

'I am sure, absolutely. Now let us get on with the investigation into who really killed these two men, and who may kill again, given the letters I and Dr Banks have received.'

'Banks has received the same note as you did, sir?'

'A similar one, Detective Sergeant. Come into my office and I will show you.'

The two policemen walked down the corridor. As they reached the stairs that led to Wright Watson's office, the Detective Chief Inspector stopped and turned to Makepeace. 'You remember all that to-do with Gertrude Rankin, do you?'

'Breach of the peace at the Parish Church when the Queen came?'

'That's the one. Find out what happened to her, will you. I suspect that she has just about finished her prison term. Could she be back in Hartley, by any chance?'

⋯⋯⋯⋯◈⋯◈⋯◈⋯⋯⋯⋯

'When can we get married, Martha? I do so love you, and I want to be with you all the time.'

'Not so fast, Wyn. Father is only just buried. We have to observe a decent mourning period.'

'I know, Martha. But how long is a "decent period"?'

'A year, Wyn. At least a year.'

'A year! But that is – but that is an eternity!'

'Oh Wyn, you are a one! That's what I like about you. You are so straight and honest. You wear your feelings on your sleeve!'

Martha Burchill leaned over to kiss her fiancé but as their lips were about to touch, in walked the maid.

'I wish you had knocked, Annie.'

'Sorry, Miss. I got so used to coming straight in when Dr Burchill was in charge.'

'Well, I am in charge, now, and there are going to be some changes round here, I can tell you!'

'Wyn! You are not in charge at all. You are not my husband – yet – and I will not have you speaking to Annie like that. She has been a loyal and devoted servant to me and my father for many years now. Annie has become like a sister to me, haven't you?'

'Is there anything more I can get you Miss, Sir?' Annie bobbed.

'No thank you. Mr. Williams will be leaving shortly.'

'But Martha…'

'In fact, could you show Mr. Williams out? I have a headache. I am sure an early night will sort it.'

'Very good, Miss. This way, Mr. Williams.'

Annie Meredith walked ahead of her mistress's fiancé. She tried to keep a safe distance from him as they headed towards the front exit, but he managed to catch her up and grabbed her bottom.

'You'll be fondling much more than that door knob when I move in, young lady, when I am the master of this house,' Williams whispered.

Annie looked beyond Williams at her mistress. She could see the tears and the anger in Martha Burchill's eyes. That woman has been a slave to her father all these years; now he is dead and she has a chance of happiness she meets a chancer and a philanderer. She ought to get rid of him, if she knows what is best for her. But she won't. She is too old to attract a good husband.

Realising his fiancée was watching him, Wyn Williams turned round, touched the rim of his bowler, blew Martha a kiss and tripped down the front stairs. Annie looked at her mistress and shook her head.

'It won't do, will it, Miss?'

Martha Burchill shook her head. 'No, Annie, I don't suppose it will.'

<hr>

'How long would it have taken someone to weaken the pipe supports, Mr. Monkhill?'

'Not long, Sergeant. Not if you knew what you were doing and where to unhook and unscrew them. Then it would just be sawing through wood, where I showed yon t'other day.'

Makepeace put his pencil down and gazed at the organ builder. Monkhill looked exhausted.

'Can I get you a cup of tea, sir?'

'No ta, Sergeant. When I've finished 'ere, I 'ave to get back to t' Parish Church.'

'To finish the extra stops and the casework on the eastern side?'

'Well remembered, Sergeant Makepeace! Thee's an organ expert!'

Makepeace laughed. 'Hardly, sir. I just take good notes and can read them back when I need to.' The Detective Sergeant waved his pad in the air as he spoke. 'Tell me, sir, why is it that you do all this work when the church is in so much debt to you? £700 is a lot of money! It is what I will earn in a lifetime!'

'It's a prestigious contract; I gets lots of other work that gives me profit.'

'That is no reason to let them get away with not paying you!'

Monkhill smirked. 'Isn't it? There are other people involved in Monkhill and Sons apart from me.'

'Shareholders?'

The organ builder nodded.

'Who are they?'

'Too many to mention. And their names are nay matter, I can assure you.'

'Let me be the judge of that, Mr. Monkhill. Now who are these shareholders? And what are their links with Hartley Parish Church?'

Monkhill paused for a moment before he spoke. 'Talk to Grindrod. He knows about business side of things and yon Dr Banks.'

Edwin Snelgrove was tired. He thought back to the death of his beloved Choirmaster. All the men missed TAB. Things would never be the same again. Even if Burford had lived, he would not have been the good doctor. Snelgrove took out his pocket watch. The Parish Church and Town Hall clocks chimed in duet as he pulled down the window blinds, turned the sign from 'Open' to 'Closed' and took out the key from his waistcoat pocket ready to lock up the shop and go for his late supper. As he was about to go upstairs, there was a loud tapping on the door.

'Let me in!'

'I have shut up!'

'You are early. The clocks have not struck the final hour. Let me in!'

Snelgrove sighed. 'God give me strength! Is there no rest for me?'

The tapping became more insistent.

'Very well. Hang on!' Snelgrove took the key out of the lock, opened the door, and watched while the customer shuffled inside and up to the counter.

'You!'

'What does that mean?' The old woman looked at the shopkeeper.

'It means that I remember you from last week. What do you want, and at this time of night? I have had a long day and it is time for my food!' Snelgrove walked wearily to the back of the shop and waited to see what his customer wished to purchase.

'I want this placed in the next edition of the *Hartley Almanac*, just like the last one.' The woman slid a note across the wooden worktop.

Snelgrove put on his reading glasses, picked up the piece of paper, read it, looked at the woman, then spoke the words out loud.

'" RIP Algernon James Burford, Mus Doc, FCO. This is a memorial to all thwarted organists through the ages." This is what you paid for last time, except the name was different then.'

'What of it? Just do your business and take my money. Here it is: the exact amount. Don't forget! The next issue!'

By the time Edwin Snelgrove had counted out the pennies and made sure the correct money had been proffered, the woman was gone.

112

CHAPTER 20

TWO PEOPLE TAKE STOCK OF EVENTS

'I have to leave that house! There is something wrong with that man. He is not what he seems!'

Annie Meredith burst into tears and crumpled into her friend's arms. 'Who do you mean?'

'Wyn Williams, of course; Miss Martha's fiancé; he wants to marry her for the money and the house. I saw Dr Burchill's papers one time. What with his playing and his conducting and his compositions and everything else – all that land he was buying up, and big money transfers – he was a rich man. I don't earn in a year what he got paid for one of his songs! TAB even owns – well, owned -- the house! The master saw through him straight away. "Williams is no good as an organist and he will be no good as a husband to my daughter". That's what the master said. Williams knew he had been caught out. Dr Burchill had written to people in Hull and found out the man was a ne'er-do-well. Williams never did any of the things he said he did – certificates and that were all made up! I heard the master rowing with Miss Martha many a time about it all. But she would have none of it. The mistress said the letters proving Williams was a fraud were all made up to dissuade her from marrying. She said her father was a selfish, lonely man who wanted company in his old age. Miss Martha even threatened to kill TAB if he got in the way of her and her "true love", her "Winny", as she called him. And he called – calls her – Matty.'

'That's awful. Now dry your tears, dear. Have another cup of tea. It will do you good. There is nothing better than a good brew in these circumstances. Do you really think that Martha Burchill would kill her father?'

'I do. I swear to God, I really do. She is a lonely woman – always has been – at least as long as I have known her and worked for her parents. It got a lot worse after Mrs Burchill died. Things were never the same after that. TAB used to taunt Miss Martha you know. He would call her "the spinster of this parish". It hurt her – it hurt her a lot. She so wanted to be married and have children. He had a real tongue in his head did the master. He was very tart in some of the things he said. He didn't mean it though. It was his way of telling a joke, or so he made out. Dr Burchill could be the kindest man on earth. He never saw me wanting, I'll tell you that an' all. He gave me extra every Christmas to look after my old fether. I loved him, in my own way. That's why I never wanted to leave, until now, that is.'

'It must have been a real shock to you when you found he was dead.'

'It was horrible. I will never forget it. Running up and down the street, here there and everywhere, trying to see where he had got to. It was odd, though.'

'What was?'

'When she received the news.'

'That he was dead?'

'Yes, when the police constable came. She was so calm. There were no tears, no sadness or anger or shouting or carrying on. Miss Martha just thanked the man for the news and offered him a cup of tea, which he said "no" to. Later, she told me how her and Williams met. I knew it were a put-up job as soon as she told me. But I didn't have the heart to tell her otherwise. I agreed with the master. I still agree with him, now I see what "Winny" is up to.' Annie Meredith snorted.

'Is that why you are so upset? More milk, dear?'

'Thank you, just a touch please. Well, you could say that. It's funny, isn't it, that Williams reappears just after Dr Burchill's murder. He was supposed to have gone back to Hull when the master chased him away, but Miss Martha said he stayed local and worked in a mill. Well, if he did, I never saw him. It must have been when I was having my time off, or when I was asleep or out shopping. That was when they must have been doing their courting. I suppose they had to keep quiet when you think Dr Burchill said he would kill Williams if he ever darkened the door of number 84 again. What worries me is that if Williams – and Miss Martha - could be so deceitful about their carrying on, then what else might they get up to? He wanted her money and she wanted a wedding ring and a bairn. She will need to get a move on; some might say she's already past it. Williams is a lot younger than her you know.'

'Really? That's a bit scandalous!'

'Tongues are wagging already I can tell you!'

'What is it that Williams has done to upset you so?'

'He came to me the other night.'

'What! Where? How?'

'He said things and…'

'Go on.'

'And he – he tried to – touch me.'

'No!'

Annie Meredith took out her handkerchief and blew into it loudly.

'Dear me, Annie, that sounded like the last trump!'

'I am sorry. I do not know what to do about him. I used to have a lot of time for Miss Martha. I thought she deserved better, especially at her time of life. But now I am not so sure. And I know what will happen if Mr. Wyn moves in. He will be after me – and other women, I'll warrant – before you know it.'

'You will have to make sure your door is locked at night, my dear.'

'I will have to do far more than that! I have already begun looking for other positions. Somebody with my experience will have no difficulty, I am sure.'

Annie Meredith finished her drink and stood up, ready to make her exit.

'O my! He's here!'

'Who is?'

'Williams! What shall I do?'

'But surely he cannot have followed you here!'

'I can see him walking down the street, as bold as brass.'

'He could not possibly be coming here! He would be shown the door if he did!'

Annie Meredith sat back down in the chair. 'He has walked past. It must have been coincidence. I am just so completely wrung out with all this.'

'There, there, dear. It will be all right. I doubt Mr. Wyn Williams will be staying in Hartley for very long'

'I know. I thought you had seen Williams walking towards your house. I have to keep reminding myself that you cannot see.'

'I hope never to be in such a position again. It was horrible.'

Charleton Mann gave his hat and coat to the maid and entered the drawing room of 'Cathedral Hatch', the grace-and-favour home of the Organist and Master of the Choristers of Yorbridge Cathedral.

'Really dear, what happened? Winifred Mann looked up from her embroidery, over her *pince-nez* spectacles and at her husband. 'Pour yourself a brandy and tell me all about it. I presume Banks was at his best, as usual?'

'Far worse than that, I can assure you, Winnie. One of the candidates was murdered.'

'Ow. I just stabbed myself! What did you say?'

'I said that one of the candidates for the post of Organist and Choirmaster at Hartley Parish Church was killed, and it was no accident, I am sure. The police are investigating and they are certain that it was foul play.'

'Foul play? On top of old Tommy's death! What is going on in Hartley?'

'I wish I knew, Winnie. I have never seen anything like it. The people we selected for the auditions either failed to appear or did arrive and then played badly – so badly that it must have been deliberate so that they would be failed. Then the strangest misadventure I have ever come across in all my many long years in the organ loft befell the one who outshone the others.'

'And what was that dear?'

'I am not sure you would believe it if I told you.'

'Sit down by the fire, drink your drink, and tell me. I will believe you; I promise.'

'He was called Burford. He played exceptionally well. Every test passed with flying colours. Right down to the last chord of the last improvisation – every stop pulled out – a triumphant sound – then, would you believe it, the biggest front pipe came loose, crashed down into the organ loft, onto the player's head, killing him instantly.'

Winifred Mann burst out laughing. 'O surely not! That is just a bad joke, Charleton. Please tell me it is not true.'

Mann shook his head.

'O Charleton! I am sorry. I am so sorry! You mean it don't you? It really happened, didn't it?'

Charleton Mann sank back in his chair. Winifred put down her embroidery and came over to kneel in front of her husband. She took his hands in hers.

'It was bad enough when Tommy was murdered. Some twisted individual who should be hung if they are ever caught. Not that I have much confidence in Hartley CID's "finest". Now this. Banks is not the easiest man to deal with, as you already know, but he deserves better than this. He is seeing his dreams destroyed almost at a stroke. In a few short weeks Hartley Parish Church has gone from a serious candidate for the new See to being a complete laughing stock and worse. It is as if these organists have been murdered to make the place look bad and seal the fate of Percy's bid for the bishopric. I can't see Cantuar and Eboracum backing Hartley now, if ever they entertained the idea.'

'Hartley has always been a difficult place for the Church of England. All those Liberals and Methodists and worse. I read in the paper that the awful Gertrude Rankin has recently been released from prison. The one who would have disrupted the grand reopening of the Parish Church when you and TAB shared the honours on the organ bench.'

'Goodness. I had forgotten about that fracas and that awful woman behind it. I wonder what she will get up to now she has been unshackled.'

The couple laughed.

'Come, my great Doctor Mann, Mus Doc, FCO and a thousand and one other things. It is time to retire. You have been away far too long.'

'I know, Winnie. My train from Hartley was late back into Yorbridge, so I had to go straight to the Cathedral for evensong.'

'Well, you are home now, and I am here.'

'Thank you!'

Mann stood and linked arms with his wife. As they walked out of the room, he noticed a letter on the sideboard. The address had been reproduced by mechanical means; there was no stamp.

'When did this arrive. Winnie?'

'What?'

'This letter.'

'I have no idea. It is late and you have a busy day tomorrow. The Dean wishes to see you, remember?'

'I know. But there is something about that letter.'

'It is just a letter.'

'I saw one like that when I was with Banks. With the same duplicated writing on the envelope.'

'Very well, Charleton. You had better read it.' Winifred handed her husband the letter opener that he always kept on the writing desk. The blade sliced neatly through the top of the envelope. Mann carefully took the single folded sheet out. The scent was almost overpowering. Having unfolded the letter, he read its contents then handed the correspondence to his wife in silence. She took it and read the message out loud.

'Man that is born of a woman hath but a short time to live. That goes for you Dr Mann, if you appoint another like Burchill to Hartley's organ loft.'

CHAPTER 21

AN ORGANIST DECIDES; TRUSTEES SCHEME

Stanford George and Howell Warley were the last candidates to leave *The Station Hotel*. Both had waited to be called for the auditions, but no message ever arrived. Then the landlord told them what had happened at the Parish Church. Warley had scuttled back to Cardiff on the first train available. George had no need to rush away, being the only one of the shortlisted applicants to live locally.

Unlike the others being considered for the post at Hartley Parish Church, Stanford George had yet to complete his degree. For this reason alone, he was surprised to be shortlisted. He had not even applied for the post. He had seen the advertisement in the *Gazette and Argus* and wished more than anything for such a majestic role. Think of it! Successor to the great Thomas Augustus Burchill, Mus Doc, FCO. In another twenty – no, ten – years, perhaps, but not in 1879. Not when there were far more qualified people queueing up to fill the vacant organ seat. There had even been rumours that jealous rivals had done away with Burchill so they could claim the throne. That was understandable, if unthinkable. 'Thou shalt not kill'. Surely no organist would murder a fellow practitioner, however prestigious a post!

Stanford George thought about his rivals for the Hartley position. If one of them was a killer, then not only had they killed Burchill, but Burford as well. Judging by the anonymous threatening letter he had been sent, this was a possibility. George took the note out of its envelope and read it once more. Was he the only one to receive the letter or had the others been sent a similar missive? What would Uncle say? There had been some strange goings on over the organ at Hartley and Whiteley George had been in the newspapers more than once over fraudulent financial dealings. Uncle's statement in the Parish Papers had gone some way to retrieving his reputation, but the general view (even within the family) was that there was 'no smoke without fire'.

Stanford George took out a second piece of correspondence from its envelope. It had taken him long enough to decipher the untidy scrawl the first time. Even now, after several readings, he was not entirely confident that he fully understood the Reverend Canon Dr Banks's message. Why would the Vicar of Hartley, one of the most eminent clerics in Yorkshire, want a young man like Stanford Aloysius George as his Organist and Choirmaster? Banks's argument was plausible: better to 'blood' an up-and-coming young player, rather than appoint a well-established man, as Burchill's successor. TAB had been an unknown when he arrived at Hartley, so why not the next occupant of the organ loft there? Given the grand reputation of the choir, a more eminent applicant might see the post as a mere stepping stone to a cathedral situation, even though the Parish Church singers were as good as any group of lay clerks in the country and better than most, if not all. Not unreasonably, then, Banks wanted someone to 'stay the course', as the Vicar put it, who, like Tommy Burchill before him, would be there for the next twenty years or more.

George put the letter down on his little writing desk and smiled to himself. Think of it! Organist and Master of the Choristers, Hartley Cathedral, and at a salary of £200 per annum, for Sunday services only! That meant extra monies for mid-week work, and plenty of time to build up a sturdy teaching practice. No more teaching at that dreadful National School next to the Parish Church! The number of times he had heard the organ and longed to be playing it, especially since Monkhill had turned it into the most ravishing instrument imaginable. George decided that even he might be persuaded to kill for such a prize.

It was not going to be necessary to commit murder, now that Dr Banks had more than implied that the post was his. Uncle Whiteley had helped enormously; having a Freemason as a close relative had its advantages! Perhaps one day he would be invited to join Absalom Lodge. Whiteley George and

Percy Banks were certainly members, and there were men of even greater rank who embraced the local branch of that fraternal organisation. Had Burchill been a member? No doubt, once he was 'in his pomp', he would have been deemed sufficiently worthy of an invitation. Stanford remembered the day when he told his father he wanted to become a musician and to earn his living from performance. 'That will not do', Pater had said. 'It will not do at all! How could you contemplate being a journeyman of the lower order? This family has worked hard to gain its present standing and you will destroy it in one action by becoming a musician?' Uncle Whiteley had been more sympathetic, no doubt because of his own passion for music as a gifted amateur, though even he had reservations until Dr Banks stepped in and guaranteed a secure future and a steady income, with the possibility of additional sources of funding if all went to plan.

What would the choir think of the appointment? There had already been words with Snelgrove, lead tenor, and Sutcliffe, the Choir Administrator, had made his antipathy to younger players well known. The two men had already threatened to leave the Parish Church and take the best singers with them to somewhere like Halifax, Leeds, or even Wakefield, towns that all aspired to cathedral status, every one of which would welcome singers who had been 'Burchill-trained'. Was that such a bad thing? Stanford George looked at the rough copy of the letter he had hastily written and submitted (after the closing date) to Canon Banks. 'A new beginning is required, and I am humbled and eternally grateful for the confidence that you are set to place in me to fulfil your wishes. I will do your bidding at every turn. I am the very churchman that you require.'

Stanford George read the threatening letter once more. Will this job be the death of me? The enmity of Snelgrove and Sutcliffe is bad enough; but what about Verney? He must surely be the one behind this awful jest – if it is a jest when two people have already been murdered! How many times has that man raged against his lot and cursed Burchill and Banks, and anyone else whom he has cause to blame for his lack of advancement? George took off his glasses and rubbed his eyes. The hour was too late to be concerned. Surely, no more murders were planned or likely. Was Burford's death a murder? Burchill had complained to his fellow organists at the way Monkhill had rushed the work on the Parish Church organ, cutting corners in order to save money. Then there had been the vile disagreement between TAB and

Banks about the use of Grindrod and the choice of water rather than the more efficient gas engines. But the Vicar, against the advice of his organist, his trustees, and the selected organ builder, placed the order for hydraulic apparatus. The machinery had never worked properly since its installation, according to Burchill, who complained bitterly at every turn. It might have been a deliberate act of damage to the organ front or, if TAB's own words were to be taken seriously, an example of Monkhill's shoddy workmanship.

'I may live to regret what I am to do now.' Stanford George looked up at the print of Our Lord and Saviour above his minuscule desk as he took out his pen, dipped it in the ink well and began to write.

'Dear Dr Banks, I am more than happy to accept the post of Organist and Choirmaster at Hartley Parish Church on the terms offered...'

Sir Arthur Hastings stared into the fire and wondered what was keeping his fellow Organ Trustee. The long-case clock in the smoking room struck eight. He took out his pocket watch, which confirmed the hour. It was not like Worsdell to be late. Quite the contrary; the Lord Mayor of Hartley was one of the most punctual men Hastings had ever had occasion to meet. Perhaps there had been a problem with the railway system. Sir Arthur himself had previously fallen victim to delays getting to and from Hartley, especially when the connections at Wakefield were missed. Oh, for a direct service to London! That would be one of the benefits of becoming a cathedral city. Hastings decided to order a second brandy and motioned to the servant on duty to fetch him a glass of his favourite drink. There was no need to enquire what the required alcoholic beverage was; Sir Arthur's long membership of the Athenaeum meant that his predilections and quirks were well known.

William Worsdell arrived along with the brandy. 'I am sorry to be so late, Arthur. The trains were badly disrupted by an incident at Hartley junction. The police have been called.'

'Good lord. The police? What is happening in Hartleydale? The place is going to the dogs. Why, I was only talking to fellow masons at the Lodge the other day. The stories about lawlessness among the working classes made me shudder. Have you heard about the Rankinists? Those blessed women will be the death of us, mark my words.'

'I sincerely hope not, Arthur. We need you for our grand plan.'

'Sit down, Worsdell. Never mind the grand plan. There won't be one if we don't sort Banks out. That man is becoming a liability. He acts more like a *pontifex maximus* than Vicar of Hartley!', Hastings snorted, then downed the remains of his glass in one go. He signalled for two more brandies; one for himself and another for his recently arrived colleague.

'I agree with you, but it would seem our Vicar has the law on his side, now he has somehow managed to have it changed to his advantage. Banks obviously has friends in very high places.'

'Are you sure he can sack the Organ Trustees and take sole charge?'

Worsdell nodded. 'I fear so, Arthur, though when I consulted Whiteley George he implied we would have a good case in court. For all the man's failings George knows the law.'

The two brandies arrived. Hastings and Worsdell toasted each other quietly.

'For health and food, for love and friends, for everything Thy goodness sends, Great Architect, we thank thee.'

'What do the other Trustees think, Arthur?'

'The same as you and I do, William. Banks has to go. But hold fast, Worsdell, our Vicar has just arrived!'

The two Trustees watched with more than a little surprise when Dr Percy George Banks walked in. The Vicar of Hartley did not seem to notice his erstwhile colleagues on the organ committee, perhaps because he was intent on steering Sir Templeton Taylor to a place by the roaring fire at the other end of the smoking room.

'Well, I never, Worsdell. What are those two doing together?'

'Strange bedfellows, indeed, Arthur. I thought there was no love lost between Banks and Sir Templeton, ever since Taylor said he would not support a cathedral in Hartley unless it were based on his own church and not that of St Martin's.'

'That was my understanding also, William. Given the enemies that Banks has made of late – including you, me, and the rest of the Trustees, if not the whole of the Vestry Committee – he has probably decided he needs all the friends he can get. Look at them. I would not be surprised if they are planning something underhand. Let us hope it is not another murder!'

CHAPTER 22

AN UNSATISFACTORY INTERROGATION

It took four turns on the bell pull and several sharp knocks at the front door before anyone answered. Wright Watson tut-tutted and paced up and down the entrance steps while waiting for a reply. Makepeace knew his commanding officer well enough to recognise when he was in a bad mood; not that it would have been difficult on this occasion. The train journey from Hartley to Leeds Central (changing at Halifax) was the telltale sign. Few words had been exchanged once the two men had left the police station. By the time they arrived at Grindrod's factory in the north of the town, the trickle of phrases had dried up completely.

Makepeace comforted himself with the fact that Watson had black moods from time to time. Because of the years they had worked together, the Detective Sergeant knew only too well that the best response was to do nothing; the darkness would pass, and the Detective Chief Inspector would be his old self again, in as far as someone with the weight of responsibility for Hartley's CID and the biggest murder investigation ever could remain calm. Makepeace remembered how PC Watson would patrol the back-to-back terrace houses in Holme Hill. The village was a rum place in those days, but Watson had gained people's respect; he was *their* local bobby and the residents welcomed his strong presence and firm but fair attitude to local disputes. Watson had become Makepeace's hero, and the reason he had joined the force. The boy would look out for the bobby, who would keep an eye on 'my little lad', making sure that his charge kept away from Makepeace senior on pay day.

Harry Makepeace had never wanted to work with anyone apart

from Wright Watson. The Detective Sergeant could not believe his luck when the Criminal Investigation Department was formed and the newly promoted Detective Chief Inspector specifically asked that Makepeace join the team. What a lot had happened since then, and now the biggest case of them all! It must be anxiety that had made the Detective Chief Inspector fall silent. Makepeace guessed that a stern word from the Chief Constable was to blame, though it was unlikely that Watson would ever confide in his Sergeant if such a difficult meeting had taken place.

'Yes, what is it? What do you want?'

'I am Detective Chief Inspector Wright Watson of Hartley Criminal Investigation Department, and this is Detective Sergeant Makepeace. We wish to talk to Mr. Ignatius Grindrod.'

'What about?' The man at the factory door was so bent over that the detectives could see the back of his head, while he must have had an excellent view of the policemen's shiny shoes.

'That is for us to discuss with Mr. Grindrod. May we come in?'

'No. Not until you tell me what you want him for. Mr. G is very particular about whom he sees. You might be stealing his business secrets.'

Wright Watson sighed. 'And what would those be, pray?'

'His inventions. Lots of people are after his designs, you know. You could just be pretending to be policemen so you can steal Grindrod's ideas.'

Makepeace could see that Watson was becoming impatient. 'Here is my badge, sir. You will see that I am a Detective Sergeant with Hartley CID. And I can assure you that Mr. Watson is a Detective Chief Inspector with the same force.'

Spurred by Makepeace's intervention, Wright Watson showed his badge also, making sure that it was placed right under the old man's nose.

'May we come in then?' It had started to rain heavily. 'We wish to see Mr. Grindrod. It is in connection with the deaths of Dr Burchill and Dr Burford.' Makepeace began to hope and pray that they would be allowed on the premises before his commanding officer lost his temper.

'Burford? Who's Burford? Never heard of him.' The old man tried to look up.

'If we can come inside, sir, and see Mr. Grindrod, we can explain as much as we are able.'

'As much as you are able, eh? What's your name again?'

'Makepeace, sir. Detective Sergeant Makepeace. And this is my colleague, Detective Chief Inspector Wright Watson.'

'Wright Watson. Wright Watson. I will remember that. Well, you had better both come in.'

The old man swivelled round slowly as if practising some arcane dance move then shuffled along the corridor. Watson and Makepeace followed, noticing the poor state of the place: cracked plaster, a damp patch on the ceiling, dust everywhere. The three men came to a set of steps. The old man gripped the rails on either side and inched his way up. Makepeace wondered if he should support their host but decided this would reduce the chances of significant co-operation further. There was nothing for it but to wait until the Matterhorn had been scaled. As the peak was reached, the two detectives noticed that the inner sanctum lay immediately opposite; the office door glass bore the inscription 'Ignatius G. Grindrod' in flowery gold leaf letters.

The old man walked in without knocking. The office was empty. Grindrod must be elsewhere, probably on the factory floor, thought Watson. It was therefore a great surprise to him and Makepeace when their guide walked round to the far side of the enormous desk, sat down, and stared at the two detectives.

'What is all this about, gentlemen? I doubt I can help you.'

'You are Ignatius Grindrod?' Wright Watson grunted.

'I am. Who did you think I was? Now, be quick. I have an important order to see to.'

Watson looked at Makepeace, who realised he would be doing the questioning.

'We are here in connection with the deaths of Dr Burchill and Dr Burford.'

'Yes, yes, yes. You have said that already. Never heard of Burford, but I knew Tommy. A very singular man. Everybody said so!'

'Yes, Mr. Grindrod, we have become well aware of that.' Watson rubbed his eyes as he agreed with the factory owner. 'What is it you make here?'

'Hydraulic equipment. That's what we make.'

'For church organs?'

'For all manner of things, Inspector Wilson.'

'Watson.'

'Watson?'

'My name is Watson, Mr. Grindrod.'

'Wilson, Watson, whatever your name is. Church organs are but a small part of our business. We have some very, very important clients, I can tell you. If it weren't for Burchill and George, I would not be bothering with blowing machinery. There is no money in it. The equipment is expensive and most churches would rather have hand blowing – far cheaper and easily more reliable!'

'Do you mean Whiteley George, Mr. Grindrod?' Makepeace asked tentatively, afraid that Grindrod's willingness to talk was only temporary.

'Yes, do you know him?'

'We have met Mr. George in connection with our enquiries.' Wright Watson nodded wearily as he replied to Grindrod.

'Well, I can't tell you anything that George won't already have mentioned, I can assure you.'

'Who invented the organ blower system, sir? Was it you?'

Grindrod snorted. 'No, it was Burchill and George between them. They designed it for George's house organ. The trouble was – and always will be – that what worked for a small instrument with but a few stops is not the same as that vast beast that Tommy wanted at Hartley Parish Church.'

'The invention was imperfect?' Makepeace thought of his son as he asked the question. Fred would love to know how a hydraulic blower worked.

'You could say that. But George persisted despite Burchill's objections.'

'Really? Tell us more, Mr. Grindrod.'

'It was all to do with yon Vicar.'

'Which one? Do you mean Dr Banks?'

'Aye, that's him, the Vicar of Hartley. He's a strange one! Always wanting the latest and the best. Banks had found out that Halifax and Wakefield Parish Churches were to have their organs replaced and rebuilt and Dr Percy wanted the Hartley organ to be the biggest and the best. The problem was, there was no way that the hydraulic blowing would cope with everything he wanted. Burchill knew it and wanted to go over to a gas engine, but George insisted that the Organ Trustees stay with the original plan. There were some real arguments, I can tell you.'

'And what was your involvement in all this, Mr. Grindrod?'

The factory owner burst out laughing. 'I kept out of it, good and proper. Burchill and Banks came to blows over it. Nothing to do with me; none of it. I have lost money on every one of those damn blowers. I think Tommy Burchill was right. They would have been better off with gas.'

'But the blower worked, didn't it? Inspector Watson and I heard the organ only the other Sunday and it sounded fine to us.'

'Oh, it works alright, after a fashion. But give it full organ for more than a chord or two and you have had it. Then there's the cost of it all. There's the rub!'

'How do you mean, Mr. Grindrod?'

'It uses so much water as to be unaffordable for all but occasional use, that's what I mean!'

'And gas?'

'Far cheaper, Sergeant! A quarter of the price!'

'So why keep making them, sir?'

Grindrod stopped grinning. 'That is a very good question, Inspector. Because George and Banks wanted me to.'

'For what purpose?'

Grindrod shook his head. 'I have no idea, gentlemen; no idea whatsoever.'

'Do Mr. George and Dr Banks have a pecuniary interest in the making of these engines?'

Grindrod waged his finger. 'That is not for you to ask, nor for me to tell you. Now it is time to meet a customer, so I will bid you good day. Please see yourselves out.'

Neither policeman thought to continue the conversation. Grindrod was already busy scribbling in his notebook as Watson and Makepeace got up, then opened the office door and left. Once the detectives' footsteps could no longer be heard, Grindrod shouted: 'You can come out now.' Slowly the oak panelling behind the old man's desk moved and out came a younger version of the factory owner.

'Thank you, father. I am grateful to you. There is much at stake with this invention. The government will pay handsomely for it, but the plans must on no account fall into the wrong hands.'

'I know, I know, Ignatius'. The old man laughed.

'What is so funny, father?'

'Those two policemen; that is what is so funny. They asked for, and got, Ignatius Grindrod, but senior not junior. They were too stupid to realise that. Little did they know this is your office and not mine any more. Though I do wish you would let me into your confidence about the hydraulic equipment and why the War Secretary is so keen to acquire it.'

'I fear for your safety if I tell you, father. Look at what happened to Burchill.'

'Is that why he was murdered?'

Ignatius Grindrod the younger shrugged his shoulders. 'Who can say, father? The Germans would certainly kill for the design, I'll be bound'.

Meanwhile, the two detectives were walking out of the factory, unsure as to whether the story just told was credible or relevant to the case in hand. As they came to the main entrance, Makepeace noticed a small office to the right through which, because the door had been left ajar, it was possible to see the occupant, a pretty woman, smartly dressed for office work, typing furiously. Watson was striding ahead impatiently, so Makepeace determined he could not delay for more than a moment, before his Detective Chief Inspector's rage boiled over. The young lady was more than a little familiar to him, but try as he might, he could not recall where he had encountered her before, or whether or not he had ever spoken to her. It was only that night, when he was unable to sleep, that the Detective Sergeant realised what was unusual about Grindrod's typewriter; she was blind.

'Ottavina Badland', he cried out, much to his wife's consternation.

CHAPTER 23

AN ARRIVAL FROM ABROAD; SUSPICION TURNS IN A NEW DIRECTION

Olivier Laverne stepped off the train. His eyes stung like never before. It took him several minutes to acclimatise to the heavy air. Acrid smells accosted the Frenchman on every side. He searched for a porter; none was available. Fellow organists had warned him about Hartley; now he believed them. Had there been a direct train back to London he would have used his return ticket then and there. But the furthest he could travel that evening would be Wakefield, which might be just as unwelcoming. In any case, Laverne had made a commitment, and he was a man of his word. There was no way he was going to break his promise, much as he already knew he would hate every minute of his time in Hartley.

'May I help you, sir?' The porter's politeness came as a contrast to the bustling crowds getting on and off the trains; passengers were only too willing to push and jostle each other for places, knocking Laverne off balance several times in the process.

'Yes, you may. I have a reservation at *The Station Hotel* for two nights.'

'Very good, sir. Let me take your cases. Follow me. It is only a short walk from here.'

Laverne decided that Hartley was not such a bad place after all, given not only the porter's attentiveness but also his willingness to carry the luggage all the way to the hotel.

'A heavy load, sir. What have you in here – a dead body by any chance?'

Laverne laughed. 'No, only my organ music.'

'You play the organ then, sir?'

'Yes.'

'I wish I played. It is such a fine instrument. I used to sing in the Parish Church Choir, but I have no time for it now.'

'I am sorry to hear that, especially since it does not sound as if your voice has broken yet.'

'No sir. I can still get them top notes!' The porter laughed.

'Are we there yet, boy?'

'Not quite, sir. I am sorry the hill up from the station is so steep, sir. It's a very narrow valley and the canal and the railway line only just fit down next to the river.'

'I see.'

'You see, sir?'

'Metaphorically speaking.'

'Meta what, sir?'

'Never mind. I have been almost blind since birth. I can see shapes out of the corners of my eyes but nothing more. I cannot see you, for instance, but I can hear you very well. And I can smell you!'

'Sorry about that, sir. We don't get much chance to wash at work, and there's only one bath a week for the whole household. Fourteen of us, there are, sir.'

'Is that the Parish Church clock I hear striking?'

'It is sir. It keeps good time. Almost as good as the station clock!'

'Surely, we must be near the hotel by now, boy. I am growing very tired after such a long journey. I have come all the way from Paris!'

'Goodness, sir! That is a long way! That's foreign, that is!'

'It is. Now where is this damn hotel?'

'Nearly there, sir, Nearly there, I promise you, sir. You speak English very well for a Frenchie, sir.'

'My mother was English, and my father was French.'

'Well, well, sir. You speak them both, then, sir?'

Laverne sighed. 'I speak them both. May we just stop a while, please? I am growing very tired.'

'Of course, sir. Sorry, sir.'

Laverne took out a Sobranie from his cigarette case, fumbled for a match in his waistcoat pocket, lit up and inhaled deeply. 'I was invited here by Dr Thomas Burchill to give a celebrity recital on the Parish Church organ.'

'Goodness sir! That's quite something, you being blind, and all. How can you play the organ if you are unable to see? And Dr Burchill; well, he is the most famous man in this town. He has made such a reputation for Hartley, he has.'

'I have been playing since I was five and I have a musical ear and an excellent memory. It is a gift that I have.'

'Well, well. That's incredible, sir. I often can't find my own fingers when they are right in front of me. Especially when it comes to sorting out the tickets at the station.'

'I thought you said you were a porter.'

'That's right, sir, but I also get to clip the tickets sometimes, when we are busy. It's all hands on deck then, sir. And I hope to be promoted soon.'

Laverne's cigarette smoking was beginning to calm him down. He thought how strange it was that there had been nobody to give him a welcome at the train station. Thomas Burchill was renowned for his generosity to fellow players, especially of the recital class, and for the warmth of his welcome to musical visitors. And yet here he was, Olivier Aristide Laverne, one of the foremost players of his generation, and blind to boot, left to fend for himself in a strange town! Just as he was preparing to gird himself to complete his walk to his accommodation, Laverne felt his scarf tighten. He found it difficult to breathe. He was aware of shadowy movement out of the corner of his left eye. The cigarette was pulled from his fingers, his arms dragged behind his back and his wrists tightly tied. The last thing Laverne heard was the Parish Church clock strike the quarter.

Wright Watson adjusted the minute hand on his pocket watch so the time accorded with that on the face of the Town Hall clock. Makepeace was busy reading through the notes of the interviews carried out since the deaths of Burchill and Burford.

'Harry – in here, now!'

Sergeant Makepeace jumped up from his seat and strode into the Detective Chief Inspector's office.

'When will you have finished tabulating the statements?'

'Very nearly done now, sir.'

'And what does the table tell us?'

Makepeace inspected his boots. 'It tells us … very little sir.'

Watson sighed. 'This cannot be! It should not be! It must not be!'

'I agree sir. But we are doing our best. All the men have put their hearts and souls into this case.'

Watson sank back into his chair. Makepeace observed how tired his commanding officer looked.

'Let us consider the facts, Detective Sergeant.'

'Of course, sir.'

'Burchill and Burford were both eminent organists. The musical reputation of Hartley Parish Church is of paramount importance if it is to become a cathedral. Many people stand to gain from that move, including, of course, Dr Percy Banks, who will be thrust into the limelight when the new Diocese is formed and the town becomes a city. So could the murders have been carried out in order to put paid to Banks's ambitions and those of the other people pressing for city status, including the businessmen who are investing in land to the north of Hartley, where expansion is most likely to take place over the next few years?'

'That all sounds very plausible, sir. I get the impression that Banks is not much liked by many in the town. He is very much against the non-Conformists, for one thing, and is often at odds with his Organ Trustees.'

'The Trustees are a strange group, are they not, Sergeant? I wrote to a colleague in another force who has knowledge of ecclesiastical matters and he tells me that the arrangement at Hartley is most unusual. The Vicar would normally expect to have sole authority in all matters relating to the music and the organ. In our Parish Church, he only has one vote alongside the others. A man like Banks is never going to accept a situation like that, while the Trustees will not want to have their power withdrawn. Could they have arranged the murders to ruin the Vicar's plan?'

'It seems an extreme way to carry on! Would those men's hatred of their incumbent be so great as to lead them to murder – or at least to arrange for the murder – of those two men? Surely not!'

'I agree, Makepeace. But just as there is much to gain from Hartley becoming a cathedral city, there is much to lose if it does not. Think of all the investment: in the church, the music, the land to the north.'

'What about Sir Templeton, sir?'

'What about him, Harry?' Watson smiled appreciatively at his Sergeant.

'He is an ambitious man. Look at St David's Church up there on the hill. Templeton Taylor spent nearly £100,000 on that building. It is a cathedral in all but name, with its spire taller than anything else in Hartleydale. Would it not be to his advantage if Banks's bid failed?'

'And St David's became the cathedral instead?' Watson warmed to Makepeace's line of thinking.

'That seems a more likely possibility. My son would then be singing in a cathedral choir – and me a humble policeman!'

The two detectives laughed.

'Perhaps we should interview Sir Templeton. That is if the Chief Constable will allow it. They are good friends, I am told, and they shake hands in the same way.'

Olivier Laverne shivered. He was cold and fearful. He could not tell how long he had been asleep. Now he was conscious once again. There was no light in the corner of his eyes. He heard the sound of footsteps, of people talking, of children laughing. The periodic trit-trot of horses' hooves suggested he was near a street, down which passers-by walked and talked. An organ grinder played in the distance. The drone-tune irritated him. Most of Laverne's clothes had been removed: coat, hat, suit, socks. His modesty only remained thanks to a pair of shorts. There was a cold moistness in between his legs.

Laverne tried to move, but quickly found he was restrained to a chair of some kind. He pulled and tugged to no avail. 'What do you want? Who are you? Where are you? Why are you doing this to me?' He called out, but there was no reply. A clock struck the hour; he could tell that it was the same one that had chimed earlier when he had been led from the station to his accommodation. But this was no hotel room.

A door opened. Two sets of feet walked towards Laverne. He could feel breath on his face and hands on his neck. Then the pressure began to be applied.

'Dieu me garde! Dieu me garde!'

<hr />

That evening, a traveller checked into *The Station Hotel*. The receptionist thought that the new arrival looked tired.

'Good evening, sir. Welcome to Hartley, and my establishment. Joseph Tomlinson at your service. I am the proprietor and have been for the last twenty years.'

The visitor smiled and nodded.

'If you could just sign the register for me, please.'

Tomlinson held out a pen. The new guest took it and scribbled a name and address on the next available line in the book.

'Very good, sir. The lad will take your luggage upstairs to your room – number 19, sir.'

A bell was rung and a small boy appeared.

'James, could you take these cases upstairs for the gentleman?'

'Yes, father.'

Tomlinson junior struggled with the luggage and had to call his sister to help him.

'What's in here? A dead body?'

'Don't be daft, you dozy little bugger. Sorry for that sir. He means well. Will you need any assistance yourself, sir? I observe that you cannot see very well.'

The guest shook his head and continued walking towards the staircase.

'Well, be careful on those steps, Mr... Sorry, sir, I can't read your signature here in the register.'

The guest stopped and half turned to Joseph Tomlinson.

'My name is Laverne. Olivier Laverne, from Paris, France. And I am here to give a performance on the organ of Hartley Parish Church.'

CHAPTER 24

SIR TEMPLETON REVEALS ALL

It was possible to see the whole of the western end of the Hartley Valley from Templeton Towers. Sir Templeton Taylor had made sure of that fact by a combination of deforestation and demolition between 1868 and 1875, when the gargantuan castellated construction was completed. The edifice symbolised the rise of the Taylor family from humble home workers, toiling at their cottage looms, to the pre-eminent dynasty in Hartleydale. Only Ernest Riddles, of Holme Hill, could rival Templeton and his empire was a pale imitation of Taylor's conglomeration.

The building's design was loosely based on the fortresses built by the Knights Templar in the Holy Land and elsewhere. Sir Templeton had even sent his architect (who had also designed St David's) to study the architecture of his supposed ancestors. At some point in time, the occupant of the Towers had decided he was descended from the Knights Templar. What better symbol of his lineage or greater tribute to his noble ancestors than to build a replica castle atop Hartley Crag? Lighting, plumbing, décor, and the like were all of the latest design, style, or fashion, as appropriate. Once occupied, the Towers was home not only to Sir Templeton, Lady Maude and their remaining four boys, but also more than twenty servants of various descriptions. Ernest Riddles only had five staff to look after a house a quarter of the size.

Sir Templeton was not expecting visitors so early on a Monday morning. Indeed, Mondays were typically given over to administrative work, reading the newspapers and then a stroll in the grounds with his dog Saladin. Templeton thought nothing of it when the bell rang and his butler's shoes squeaked across the hall floor. Three voices could be heard: his servant and two men with Hartley accents.

How pleased I am that the boys are off to public school. I could not have them speaking like the locals do! Templeton smiled as he looked up at the portrait of grandfather, stern and grave, the epitome of thrift and guile; the foundation on which the Taylor empire had been built. And there was more to come if only he could dominate the town – no, the city – of Hartley. If only David were still alive!

'Come!'

The study door opened slowly. Albert Eccleston should have been stood down as butler long ago, but Templeton Taylor did have a heart of sorts, especially when it came to the man who had been with the family for nearly fifty years and who had taught every Taylor for three generations how to fish in the River Hart.

'What is it?'

'Two gentlemen to see you, sir, from the Police. I told them to go away, but they insist on seeing you, my lord.'

'Eccleston! I am not a lord yet! Desist from calling me that!'

'Very good, Sir Templeton. But it is only a matter of time before the news is made public. Your father and grandfather would have been so pleased to see you in ermine! What shall I tell the policemen?'

'Tell them – tell them…I will meet the officers. I must not be seen to be withholding my co-operation from the police, even though I cannot fathom what business they would have with me.'

'Very good, sir. Very good.'

Eccleston trudged out of the study, closing the door behind him. Sir Templeton wondered what the police knew. Surely nothing could have been traced back to him about the goings on in Hartley!

On his second visit to the study, the butler opened the door without knocking and beckoned the two policemen into the room. Templeton Taylor stood up from his seat, put both hands firmly in the pockets of his smoking jacket and turned to greet the officers.

'Come in, gentlemen. I trust that this will be brief. I have important work to do – today and every day - and I cannot spare any time for trivial matters.'

'Good morning, sir. Thank you for seeing us. I am Detective Chief Inspector Wright Watson, and this is Detective Sergeant Makepeace.'

'I am more than a little surprised to see you here. I do not think officers of the law have ever visited the Towers before.'

'We are very sorry to disturb you, Sir Templeton. But it is a matter of some importance.'

'Very well. Say what your business is, Detective Chief Inspector. As I have already made very clear, there is much to be done.' Taylor pointed to his desk, littered with plans and papers.

'Thank you, sir; of course, sir.' Watson noticed a large street plan spread out, with red crayon markings over almost every grid square.

Sir Templeton Taylor sat back in his armchair while Wright Watson explained the purpose of his visit to the Towers. The two detectives remained standing.

'You mean to impugn that I have had a hand in those murders? Of organists? How could you possibly think I would have any interest whatsoever in the goings-on at the Parish Church? I have my own choral establishment. It will one day be the best in the land!'

'Do you have any connection with Dr Banks, Sir Templeton?'

'No, I do not, Sergeant. I have not set foot in his church since the destruction of my family vault.'

'Destruction, sir?' Makepeace took out his notepad, pencil poised to note down the reply.

'And you will put that thing away before I say another word!' Sir Templeton rose from his armchair and pointed at Makepeace, who complied immediately, bowing his head as he did so. 'There are some of us who have a long association with this town; we *are* Hartley, Sergeant! I will have you know that I am descended from ancient Templar stock. Why, on the ridge above this house can be seen the remains of the noble knights' chapel; *my* chapel!'

'I am sure Makepeace meant no offence, Sir Templeton. The Detective Sergeant and I – we merely wish to ascertain the facts; nothing more and nothing less.'

'Well, Watson, the facts are this: the Reverend Canon Doctor Percy Banks willfully arranged for all the tombstones in the Parish Church to be removed and broken up so that he could turn our beloved place of worship into a damn cathedral! The ancestral church gutted, the family vault desecrated, the old music books thrown away, and all for that man's vanity.'

'Vanity, sir?'

'Yes, Chief Inspector, Bishop Banks will have his way, and no-one shall thwart him!'

'I see, Sir Templeton. And what about your own church?' Wright Watson shifted the weight from left to right foot as a way of easing the pain in his back from standing all the while.

'What about it, Watson? What are you impugning?'

'I am not sure as I know, sir. I do not know the meaning of the word.' Wright Watson scratched his head as if to distract from his own ignorance.

'Then I suggest that you look it up in the dictionary, man!'

'Very good, sir.' Watson nodded to Makepeace, who dutifully made a note of the instruction.

Templeton Taylor sighed. 'St David's Church is a monument to my beloved son, Inspector, taken from us far too young.'

'How old was he, then, sir?'

'He was but five years old. A mysterious sickness took him from us. It is not right that the child dies before the parents.'

The conversation paused. Sir Templeton pointed to the picture hanging over the wall immediately to the side of the large study desk. It portrayed a small boy with black curly hair wearing a green satin suit. A dog sat on the child's lap. In the background was a large church surrounded by oak trees. Around the spire were large black storm clouds.

'No, sir. It should not be so, not at all, sir '. Wright Watson wiped a tear from his eye. 'One of my children died a few years ago. He was barely one when the Lord took him home.'

Seeing that the Inspector had been moved by the story of his David, Sir Templeton relented and beckoned the men to sit down.

'I am sorry to have been harsh on you, gentlemen. Forgive me. I have much to think about at the present time.'

'Understandable, Sir Templeton.'

'What did you need to know?'

'Just some more information about your own St David's Church, and any rivalries with St Martin's.'

'You have already heard most of the story, Inspector. I withdrew my support for the Parish Church when Banks did his detestable worst to that wonderful old building. I had decided many years ago to immortalise my son in stone, hence the construction of St David's. There is no rivalry, though; none at all. I merely want the best that money can buy. I always have done, and I always will.'

'Does that include the musical parts of the service, Sir Templeton?'

'It does, Sergeant. The organ, the choir, the pieces performed; everything.'

'What about your organist, Sir Templeton?'

'Edward Smith? He is a good performer but lacks the skills to train the singers. I made him stand down from the role of Choirmaster recently. It has been the one area where I could not better the Parish Church. It was never possible from the day Smith left and Thomas Burchill was appointed.'

'My son sings in the choir at St David's, sir.'

'I did not know that Detective Sergeant. I will see that the lad gets an extra shilling now and again for his trouble.'

'That's very good of you, Sir Templeton. Fred will appreciate that very much, though he will not be able to attend for much longer.'

'Has his voice broken, then, Sergeant?'

'No, sir. When he goes full time at the mill it will be difficult for him to spare the hours. Pardon me for saying, sir, but on the few occasions when I have heard the choristers, they have all sounded good to me.'

'Good, perhaps, Makepeace, but not excellent; not divine; not heaven on earth. That was the sound of Hartley Parish Church choir; they gave you paradise every single Sunday.'

Watson nodded slowly. 'And who is going to replace Mr. Smith as Choirmaster, Sir Templeton?'

'Why, only one person could have fulfilled the role and given me what I so wanted.'

''Really, sir? And who might that be?'

Templeton Taylor laughed out loud. 'Why, who else? Dr Thomas Augustus Burchill.'

'Surely not, Sir Templeton! I thought that TAB was wedded to the Parish Church, especially after all he has done to secure the choir's reputation.'

'Not in the least, Watson. Burchill was looking for a new challenge after all this time. I have the letter here from the good doctor confirming his acceptance of my offer. In fact, he was the one who approached me. He said he wanted nothing more to do with the "goings on" at St Martin's, as he put it. He was due to start in the New Year.'

'What goings on were those, Sir Templeton?'

'Something to do with the Vicar and the Organ Trustees and the income to the Organist, I believe. But you had better ask the Vicar about all that.'

Watson smiled at Sir Templeton. 'And Smith would have remained as Organist, with Burchill as Choirmaster?'

'Good Lord, no, Watson. I had just given Smith notice. Him and that interfering wife of his. I had employed her as a cleaner to help Edward financially, but the woman was neither use nor ornament. Good riddance to both of them! Burchill had already accepted my offer of four times the salary, *for Sunday services only*, as he was getting at the Parish Church. Though he said – much to my surprise – that the money did not matter to him. Burchill seemed to be a wealthy man to say that he was only a musician, good though he was. He would also have had free use of the instrument for practice, recitals, performances and much more; a bone of contention at the Parish Church, I understand.'

'What bone of contention was that sir? Makepeace queried.

'The Organist at St Martin's had to pay to practise because of the cost of water for the hydraulic engines. There would have been none of that at my church. And I was going to pay each and every bass, tenor and alto more than they would ever get from the Reverend Canon Doctor Percy George Banks! But do not come to me for answers to your questions about Burchill's murder, gentlemen: as I have already said, go see the Vicar of Hartley Parish Church!'

CHAPTER 25

VERNEY CONSIDERS HIS POSITION; A DISTINGUISHED ORGANIST PRACTISES

Charles Verney could hardly keep his eyes open. Night shifts at the mill were bad enough but doing the work of Organist and Choirmaster at the Parish Church as well would be the end of him. He sat alone in the choir vestry and looked across at the harmonium where TAB would play the notes for the singers. First there would be the vocal exercises, then the hymns and chants and finally the fully choral music that would be sung the following week. Burchill was always writing some new piece or other, and he would expect the Choir to be able to sight read the notes and perform them to the required level of perfection within days of the new composition being penned. After the 'initial outings' (as Burchill would call them), during which the composer would make final amendments to the score as necessary in the light of practical experience, the material would be sent off to the publisher. TAB had occasionally shared some of the 'profit' from this activity as a thank you to his Assistant Organist for helping with the proof reading. Sometimes, TAB had given Verney a free organ lesson as well, though the two men always had to be mindful of the cost of the water for the hydraulic engines, given the regular admonitions from Banks and the Organ Trustees about saving money. How would it ever be possible to succeed in the necessary music examinations if it were not possible to practise for the requisite number of hours?

What was the point, anyway? Why work so hard for nothing? Verney could practise for fifty hours a week, 52 weeks a year, and the Reverend

Canon Dr Percy George Banks would still not appoint him as Organist and Choirmaster! Never! And yet, the Vicar of Hartley was always ready to call for him when he needed something doing, like the order in which the candidates for the post at the Parish Church were to be heard. Why was it so important that Stanford George went last? Was it because the Vicar had decided that Whiteley George's nephew was going to be the new Organist and Choirmaster all along? That business over the hydraulic engines and all those backhanders from George. Verney had even seen old Tommy taking something from one of Whiteley's clerks before the order with Grindrod was placed. And Banks was hardly blameless if the mutterings of some of the Organ Trustees were anything to go by.

Verney got down the choir attendance book from the shelf above TAB's old desk. He opened the heavy leather-bound volume at the latest page and started to update the lists of attendees. Burchill had always insisted on completing the records himself: who was present; who arrived late or left early; who had misbehaved and deserved to be fined; who should be rewarded for 'extra diligence'. For no particular reason, Verney found himself going back through the previous weeks' logs. Burchill's handwriting was as meticulous as ever. Did the man ever sleep? Except that TAB now slumbered forever in his newly dug grave by the north vestry door, as near to the organ as possible. No doubt the good doctor was busy preparing a composition for the 'dreadful day of judgement, when the secrets of all hearts shall be disclosed'. Verney looked up at Burchill's portrait. It sent a shiver down his spine; it always had done, and it always would do. Most people believed in the wrath of God; Hartley Parish Church choir were much more afraid of the wrath of Tommy Burchill. And that rage, once unleashed, had been a fearful thing to behold. Even now, the choir members could not believe that the great choirmaster would not storm through the vestry door to admonish them for their indiscipline, their appearance, or some other misdemeanour. In the light of this terrifying reminiscence, Verney resolved that he must complete the records forthwith. As he turned the pages back to the current entries, he could not help but notice a strange pattern of attendance – or rather absence – in the weeks leading up to TAB's murder. It was as if there was a rota of choir men taking their turns at being absent. Was this of significance? Verney resolved to look more closely at the records when he had the chance and, if the pattern repeated itself during earlier months, he would report it to Messrs. Watson and Makepeace.

Verney heard footsteps. He put away the choir attendance book and tried to look lively.

'Come in!' The Interim Organist and Choirmaster croaked. Taking the choir practices was taking its toll on his vocal cords. There was no answer to his call.

'Please, come in!' Verney coughed. There was a shadow below the door; two shadows, in fact. No answer and no movement.

'Very well. I am coming!'

Verney got up from TAB's old chair and walked wearily to the door.

'Who is it? I am very busy.' Verney cleared his throat, placed his hand firmly on the knob, paused for a moment, then opened the door firmly.

'Gladys! What are you doing here? You know you are not supposed to come anywhere near the Choir Vestry! And who is this?'

Verney looked at the two people standing perfectly still in front of him. One was the workaday cleaner who did the most menial tasks the Parish Church had to offer and had done so ever since women had been expelled from the choir apart from a short period away from Hartley immediately after the sackings. The other was a stranger.

'Sorry Charlie. I know I'm not supposed to be down here. Not even after the good doctor has passed away, not even to clean the place. But I had to show Mr. Laverne here how to find you.'

Verney looked at the man. The eyes were darkly clouded; there was not even a blink, just a passive, peaceful stare. The face was pale, the complexion sallow. He had a slight, almost unmanly physique. The hands were slim and long fingered; the feet like a ballet dancer's; the shoes the shiniest that Verney had ever seen. Laverne's suit must have cost at least a year's wages.

Laverne held out his hand. 'Enchanted to meet you, Mr. Verney. I am so sorry to hear of Dr Burchill's death. He was a brilliant man I can tell you. Shocking! Absolutely shocking!'

Verney reciprocated. 'Pleased to meet you too, sir. And how can I help you?'

'Your master invited me to give a recital on the Parish Church organ. Here I am. I have travelled all the way from Paris via London. I am due to give my recital in two days' time. I need to practise. My programme is a very demanding one!'

'I am sorry about the lack of a welcome, Mr. Laverne. And I must apologise for the lack of arrangements for your recital. I knew nothing about it! Dr Burchill took care of all the details himself, and, what with his death and all, I am not sure if anything has been done.'

'*Mon Dieu*! Is nothing done properly in this place?' Laverne stamped his feet and moved his head from side to side.

'I am afraid we are not ourselves in Hartley and have not been so since Dr Burchill's murder.'

'Murder? *Sacré bleu*! What is happening here?'

'We do not know, sir.' Verney looked at Gladys Grimshaw. The old cleaner shook her head. The Interim Organist and Choirmaster agreed that it would be unwise to tell the distinguished visitor of Harcourt Burford's untimely accident.

'I – we – do not know, sir, but I will personally ensure all goes to plan and your performance takes place. I am sure we can muster a good audience. The Thursday evening recital series has been a feature of the musical life of Hartley Parish Church since the new organ was installed. It will be good to restart the programmes again, and what better way to do so than by having you play for us?' Verney looked at Gladys Grimshaw, who nodded and turned to go back to her duties.

'Come, Mr. Laverne, I will show you the organ.'

Verney and Laverne linked arms as the Interim Organist and Choirmaster guided the guest recitalist out of the Choir Vestry and towards the Loft. Despite the lack of sight, Laverne proved to be remarkably adept at negotiating the chancel steps and then the access route to the console. Verney looked up at the main case, hoping that the repairs effected by the organ builder would be robust enough for another accident to be avoided. The Interim Organist and Choirmaster helped the distinguished visitor onto the bench, then explained the layout of the keyboards and the stops. Laverne asked a few questions and then felt every stop head on both sides of the console before asking that the blowing engines be switched on.

'Why not do it yourself, sir? You will need to know how to get wind into her lungs sooner or later!'

Laverne laughed. 'So, you treat her like a lady, this wonderful machine of yours? I approve of that, being from France!'

The visiting organist's hands were guided to the large iron crank handle to the right-hand side of the organ keyboards. Once the mechanism was engaged, the hydraulic feeders underneath the instrument flowed into action with a loud 'whoosh'. Verney and Laverne could hear and feel the bellows fill with wind.

'A very satisfying sound, is it not? It is time for the bird to sing.' With that comment, Olivier Laverne pulled out all the loud stops, coupled the four manuals together and began a rich improvisation, the like of which Verney had never heard before. The performances of Tommy Burchill, Charleton Mann, Harcourt Burford and a hundred other organists who had graced the keys of Monkhill's *magnum opus* could not hold a candle to this man and his music. It started with a pompous, majestic prelude, full of rich chords and novel harmonies. Then Laverne used the composition pedals to reduce the sound as he began a fugue, using the same melodies as had opened the work. The softer stops of the organ were displayed to great effect in what Verney now realised was the middle, contemplative section of a three-movement sonata, all drawn from the performer's head. The sound and the intensity built up as the pace quickened. The opening theme returned, cleverly and cunningly intertwined with the counterpoint that had followed it. There was more to come, for as the improvisation seemed to be nearing its end, the contemplative mood returned before a final crashing coda, in which all the themes were brought together in a single, unifying whole. As the final chord died away, it was as if the soul of the organ was smiling down on Laverne and his single listener. Neither man spoke for several minutes.

'I do not know what to say, Mr. Laverne. Your playing is not of this world; it is from God, just as Dr Burchill's choir brought heaven to earth. It is a pity that you and he will not be able to perform together.'

'Why, thank you. You need not say anything. My reward is the performance itself. Nothing more.'

'I wish I could play like you. Will you teach me while you are here, if I can get the time off work for an hour or two?'

'I would be delighted to do so. But I hear footsteps. We are not alone.'

'No, we are not, Olivier. It is the new Organist and Choirmaster of Hartley Parish Church, and he does not look best pleased.'

CHAPTER 26

AN ARREST IS MADE AS THREE WOMEN CELEBRATE

'Another one, for old time's sake?'

'Why not?'

'Yes please!'

The three women laughed as Edward Smith served them stout, then poured himself a whisky, downing it in one gulp.

'Steady on, Ed, you know what you are like! Take it easy with the drink. It has already cost you your job at St David's!'

Sarah Anne Smith looked her husband up and down as he stumbled back to the bar. He had been handsome once; a real catch when she first met him. She had been Sarah Anne Jessop then, just beginning to make her mark on the Hartleydale music scene. The *Gazette and Argus* had found her performance of the soprano solos in *Messiah* 'immense' when she had first sung with Hartley Choral Society. Everything was set fair. 'I will be the Jenny Lind of Hartley', she used to say to herself, 'and Edward Smith my accompanist!'

She thought back to Sundays in the old organ gallery. There were just nine singers, the town's élite: three sopranos, two altos, two tenors and two basses, sitting either side of the organ. Sarah Anne always made sure she was the one next to the organist. That was easy to do if you arrived early enough. The only other person in the loft would be Verney. Dear faithful, loyal, diligent, dull, boring, Charlie. He had professed his love for Sarah Anne Jessop so often it had become monotonous. The Assistant Organist would never interest a woman like her. Or so she thought back then. Now, Sarah Anne Smith was not so sure. At least Verney was dependable. He had argued against the sacking of the female singers when Banks decided in favour of the 'cathedral service'. It was bad enough when Burchill replaced Ed as Organist and Choirmaster, but Banks's changes were the final straw.

'Don't you think you've had enough?' Edward Smith poured himself another whisky, despite his wife's mouthing admonishments at him. She looked at her two companions and shook her head. 'It broke my husband, you know. Losing the job at Hartley Parish Church.'

The other women looked at her. 'But Sir Templeton pays well enough, doesn't he?' Gladys Grimshaw was the one to speak; Ottavina Badland merely nodded in agreement.

'Well, he did, Gladys. It worked well enough to start with: no expense spared; a grand organ; a choir of eager men and boys; no discipline problems. Not like Burchill had from me!'

The three women laughed so raucously that the other patrons of *The King's Head* stopped their drinking, smoking, talking, and their games and looked across to see what the cause of such hilarity might be. Two men raised their glasses and pointed at Sarah Anne. She smiled back. Gladys Grimshaw looked at Ottavina and wondered if she had realised what Sarah Anne really did for a living nowadays. Edward Smith was such a wastrel. All the money from St David's or his private practice as a Professor of Music went on drink. It had been that way for a very long time now. Certainly, since his latter days as Organist at St Martin's. He had been a good man and a good musician and a good many women had been attracted to Edward Smith. Just as Sarah Anne Jessop sat at one side of the organ console up in the old west gallery, so Gladys Grimshaw located herself at the other. She had seen the way in which Jessop had looked at Smith, whether during rehearsal or service, and wondered if there was any point in pursuing the organist herself, for Edward only ever had eyes for Sarah Anne.

Gladys had always known the relationship between the Organist and his Principal Soprano would not end well. She was surprised it had lasted so long. It had obviously been to do with their continued amorous congress, at least in the early years of their marriage. This was especially the case when being the Principal Soprano at Hartley Parish Church meant something, and Sarah Anne could command a substantial fee both for services and concert performances in Greater Hartleydale and beyond. She had even performed in Yorbridge Cathedral for Charleton Mann, both in performances of Handel's great oratorios and more modern works, including by Mann himself. Then came the day of reckoning for Edward Smith. It was one thing for her husband to be 'merry' while playing the organ and conducting or rehearsing the choir; being found 'bread and butter fashion' in the loft was more than anybody could ever tolerate. Sarah Anne pleaded both ignorance and innocence and, as the man, Edward admitted his guilt and resigned without demur.

Gladys herself had never had such fame (or notoriety), even 'in her pomp' and, once Edward Smith had plumped for Sarah, the Principal Alto had determined not to bother herself with men. Burchill hated female altos and was only too glad to get rid of her when the opportunity arose. By the time that 'Miss Grimshaw' (as TAB always addressed her) sang for the last time in the west gallery choir, Sarah Anne had been sacked for disobedience on a grand scale, according to Burchill. Mrs. Smith was more than willful; she was manipulative and self-seeking. Everyone knew that. But however good she was at her deviousness, she was never going to beat Burchill. He was a real master. Gladys Grimshaw had to smile in admiration as she remembered the way in which TAB always won over the years. Even the new Vicar of Hartley had succumbed to the great Organist and Choirmaster's guile. Percy Banks might have thought he was in charge, getting his own way on everything from the colour of the new stained glass to the source of the communion wine, on the size of the new Vicar's Vestry to the number of times a year the choirboys' surplices would be laundered. That could not have been further from the truth: Thomas Augustus Burchill, Mus Doc, FCO, ruled the roost at Hartley Parish Church. It was said that he even governed when it came to the Vicar's wife.

'A penny for your thoughts, Gladys!' Sarah Anne Smith raised her near-empty glass as she spoke.

'Nothing, Sarah. Well, nothing really. I was just remembering happier days when we three were the prime movers in the choir.'

'And what about you, Ottavina? Has the cat got your tongue this evening?'

Ottavina Badland smiled. 'I do not feel like talking much tonight.'

Sarah Anne Smith grabbed Ottavina's hand. 'Cheer up, Ottie. It may never happen, whatever it is.'

'It already has, Sarah. It already has.' At which point, Ottavina Badland burst into tears.

'Oh no, what is the matter?' Gladys and Sarah spoke in unison.

Ottavina shook her head. 'I am not sure I can do this anymore.'

Gladys Grimshaw squeezed Badlands's hands. 'Yes, you can, Ottie. Yes, you can! You do so wonderfully well! You always have and you always will do!'

'Do you think so Glad?'

'I do, Ottie. We both do, don't we, Sarah?'

'I'll say! It's for the best. Think of the money it gives you – gives us! And what can't you do with all that brass?'

'Not to mention what those men won't do for us, eh?'

'I suppose you're right, Sarah. But it still feels wrong. What if – you know – something happens?'

Gladys Grimshaw and Sarah Anne Smith moved closer to their companion. 'We'll see you alright, Ottie. We know about these things, don't we, Glad?' Sarah Anne smiled across at Grimshaw, who nodded and grinned back.

'Anyway, you have other business just at the moment, and we know it is to your liking, isn't it Ottie?' Gladys squeezed Badland's arm tightly.

'Ow! Glad, you're hurting me!'

'Sorry! I meant no harm, honest! Another glass of stout. That will do wonders!'

'No, Glad. I have to be going back. I need to try and make an honest living, at least some of the time!' Ottavina Badland laughed at her own remark. They all laughed.

Sarah Anne Smith motioned to her husband to refill her glass. He dutifully complied. As he carried the empty jug back to the bar, two new customers appeared at the entrance to the public house. They surveyed the scene then walked purposefully over to the landlord.

'Good evening, gentlemen. This is a surprise, if not a pleasant one. What can I get you to drink? On the house, of course!'

'Nothing to drink, sir. Makepeace, over to you.'

'Of course, Mr. Watson.' The Detective Sergeant cleared his throat before continuing. 'Edward Smith, I am arresting you on suspicion of the murders of Thomas Augustus Burchill and Harcourt Burford, both in the organ loft of Hartley Parish Church, on the 29ᵗʰ of September and the 10ᵗʰ of October 1879 respectively. Please come with me, preferably as quietly as possible, if you would, sir.'

'But this is ludicrous! I was nowhere near the Parish Church when those murders took place. Ask my wife, ask Gladys, ask anyone!'

Wright Watson shook his head. 'I am afraid that we have a witness – witnesses, in fact – who are prepared to swear that you were in the vicinity of the crime scene on both occasions.'

Edward Smith looked at the two policemen and then across at his wife and her two companions. Sarah Anne shook her head almost imperceptibly.

'But I did not do it – I had nothing to do with either of those killings.'

'We'll see about that, Mr. Smith. Now will you please come with us? We don't want a scene, do we?' Makepeace got out his handcuffs and showed them to the landlord. 'We can either do this now, or when we get outside. Which is it to be, Edward?'

Smith bowed his head, as if in contemplation of his fate. As the two police officers waited, the landlord took hold of two full jars of beer that were stored below the counter. When he was ready, he pulled them out and threw the contents over Watson and Makepeace. 'You'll never take me! I am innocent, I swear!'

The element of surprise gave Smith an advantage. Without waiting to see how the policemen reacted, the landlord of *The King's Head* ran from the bar, down into the back rooms and out through the rear exit. He was surprised how cold it was, in contrast to the convivial warmth of the inn. By the time Watson and Makepeace had regained enough composure to pursue their suspect, Edward Smith was nowhere to be seen. Makepeace twirled his rattle, in the hope that a bobby or two might hear and join in the chase, but nobody appeared.

Watson took in his surroundings before determining what to do next. Along the rear wall of *The King's Head* there was a narrow lane running parallel to a waterway. The Detective Chief Inspector decided that this must be a spur from the Hartley Canal, for it led to Templeton Taylor's factory and no doubt was used to carry goods and materials to and from the works.

'Smith must have gone down the towpath, Harry. I can see no other means of escape. You go the factory way and I will head into the town.'

'Very good, sir! I will keep twirling my rattle, in amongst!'

The two policemen parted. As they did so, Edward Smith watched them from the safety of his hiding place on the barge he and his wife had bought in happier times. It had been a way of using Sarah Anne's earnings to good effect, and the money from hiring out the vessel to carry goods back and forth to Hartley and beyond represented a tidy sum, at least until the pub work started to go downhill and the landlord began to drink the profits. That was what Smith needed now: a good drink. As he sat there under the tarpaulin, he felt his mouth go dry. He heard Makepeace's rattle in the distance. Once the repetitions had faded away into silence, Smith relaxed a little.

'Who saw me? Why would they tell against me? I believe I know, and I will have them!'

CHAPTER 27

THE SMITHS BEGIN TO REVEAL THEIR SECRETS

'Have there been any sightings, Harry?' Watson cleared his throat, then drew on his pipe.

'No, sir. Nothing. Something of a "wild goose chase".'

Makepeace closed the office door so no-one would overhear the conversation. Bobbies on the beat were grumbling about the boot leather they had worn out searching for Edward Smith. Makepeace looked at his commanding officer. Watson had been under pressure from the Chief Constable to make an arrest. The detectives had tried to do that, based on a second piece of anonymous correspondence. This letter – using words cut out from the *Gazette and Argus,* like the first Watson had received-- suggested two things. Firstly, despite being witnessed at the St David's organ, Smith had absented himself from practice and gone to the Parish Church during the afternoon of Monday, 29th September (when Burchill had been murdered) before returning to complete his rehearsal. Secondly, that he had been seen in the organ loft at St Martin's early on the morning of Friday 10th October, the day of the ill-fated organ trials, when poor Dr Harcourt Burford had met his unusual and untimely end.

It made sense to pursue Edward Smith, especially now Watson had discovered the St David's instrument could be played automatically, without human intervention, as with a fairground organ. Smith could have set the thing going and then left to murder Burchill murder, the St David's instrument sounding all the while. Smith was a strong man and would not only know where the hydraulic engines' water tanks were located but also, in the case of Burford's murder, had a knowledge of the innards of an organ, as confirmed by Monkhill. Burford would have known little or nothing as the metal came crashing down; no doubt it was a fitting way for an organist to die – playing a triumphant chord on what Verney had explained would have been *organo pleno* - the full power of the organ. The anonymous letter had even suggested that Smith had been in the loft waiting for the moment when Burford completed his performance.

It had also come to light that Robert Casement had been 'got at'. An anonymous letter sent to the hotel the night before the auditions had told him that if he were to excel in performance the following morning, he 'would be a gonner'. Casement had taken the message to heart and decided to play badly to prevent his being offered the post. Was this also the case with Dr Harcourt Bennett? It would never be known, for it turned out he had passed away on the morning of 9th October, just before leaving home to catch the train to Hartley. Verney had explained Rowntree Macintosh's early departure, adding that 'divvying up the posts' between the top candidates was apparently a common occurrence.

All this information had made Watson and Makepeace ponder, especially when Sir Templeton Taylor had revealed that Burchill was to leave St Martin's and take his reputation and much of his loyal choir with him. Edward Smith had already lost his choirmastership, and it was clear that Taylor wanted rid of his organist completely, especially if Burchill were to take the reins and raise St David's to cathedral status.

It all made sense. Banks would be so desperate to fill the vacancy and squash any further scandal that Smith would be an obvious candidate to return as Organist and Choirmaster at Hartley Parish Church. What a triumph that would have been for him! But the anonymous letter had prompted action. The witnesses to Smith's practising at St David's at the time Burchill was murdered, when re-interviewed, could not be sure their organist had not 'popped out' or for how long, leaving the instrument playing as an automaton. While the cleaners at St Martin's had thought there was someone in the organ loft tuning up the evening before the auditions for TAB's successor. Monkhill denied it was him since the organ had been thoroughly 'gone over' before the performance on the evening of 28th September at Burchill's insistence.

Wright Watson had decided it was imperative to arrest Edward Smith before there were any more misdemeanours, especially since Stanford George was now the occupant of the Hartley Parish Church organ loft, despite his youth and inexperience. Surely the murderer would not be able to tolerate a 'pimply youth' (as Verney described him) as Organist and Choirmaster when Smith would think himself to have the greater claim to Burchill's crown.

Watson was still cursing himself for not deploying bobbies at the back entrance to *The King's Head* before arresting Edward Smith. Just as the Chief Constable was pleased the likely murderer was known, so was he angry the prime suspect had been 'allowed' to escape. Another 'bungle' like that, and Wright Watson was in danger of being demoted. How could Smith disappear so quickly and completely? If he had not used the towpath, either to run towards the town or up towards Taylor's factory, then where was he?

'Sergeant, did we search the pub after Edward Smith ran out of the bar?'

'We did, sir. Nothing was found – or rather – nothing to do with Smith and his possible role in the murders.'

'What did the men find, then?'

'Love letters.'

'Love letters?' Wright Watson looked up. 'Who from, and who to?'

'Well, sir, you remember we thought that Sarah Anne was an unfortunate woman.'

'Yes, we suspected it. Mrs Smith is an attractive woman, especially for her age.'

'The bobbies found sponges in her room.'

'Sponges? Her room?'

'It looks as though Mr and Mrs Smith lived separate lives. He had his own space at the other end of the house. Sarah Anne said that they had not been man and wife for some time.'

'And what about the sponges?' Watson rubbed his chin vigorously.

'I assume that they are to be used when she has her gentlemen friends round for tea.'

'Do we know who they are?'

'No sir, except for the one who wrote her letters.'

'Really, Sergeant. And who was that?'

'You will never believe it sir. Inside her dressing table drawer, we found a whole bundle of letters. Here they are.' Makepeace handed over the tightly-bound correspondence and watched while Watson untied the red ribbon and laid the envelopes on his desk. There were ten of them in all. Watson took the first piece of paper out and read it. Makepeace smirked as he saw the Inspector blush. The face reddened further as Wright Watson took out the second and third letters. By the time of the fourth, he had read enough.

'This is quite a turn up for the books, is it not, Harry?'

'It is. I would never have expected Burchill of all people to be sweet on Sarah Anne Smith. Perhaps we are dealing with a crime of passion.'

Edward Smith was cold; and hungry. He had lost all sense of time, even though he could hear the clocks of St David's and St Martin's chime in competition with each other. He knew which was which; the Parish Church peal was lower and more resonant, and further away from his hidey-hole than his own church. Smith heard the comings and goings of other boats as they fed Templeton Taylor's factory with materials and took away the finished goods for sale all over the country and then beyond to every corner of the empire. This gave him some idea of day and night, though the traffic never stopped; only slowed. Sleep came from time to time, but there was no way to get comfortable lying in the bottom of a boat built for coal and coke rather than people. The hull leaked and his feet were permanently damp. The rats did not seem to mind either the environment or the new occupant of their watery home. Smith wondered periodically if he should peek out from under the tarpaulins but determined each time that it would be unwise to show his face, even for an instant. He heard bobbies talking to each other as they walked up and down the towpath. Smith knew they were searching for him. The conversations had now ceased, but that was no guarantee that police were no longer in the area. A constable could be guarding *The Kings Head* in the event of the landlord's return.

Smith wished he were at the inn; the organ loft even more so. How had it come to this? Life had been so full of promise all those years ago at

Hartley Parish Church. Think of it! The world was going to be his oyster; a whole plateful of oysters. Then Sarah Anne Jessop had come along. O the glory of it all! They would be the golden musical couple of Hartley; the West Riding; the whole of Yorkshire! The Kingdom! Sarah had the most divine voice that Smith had ever heard, with a face and a body to match. It had been love at first sight. Nothing else mattered thereafter; not his music, his career, his reputation; nothing. As long as he had her, Edward Smith did not care when he had to leave Hartley Parish Church. It came as a total surprise when he was offered the post at St David's, on twice the salary, without competition or references. Someone with considerable influence must have spoken on his behalf. But soon, the drinking was no longer a pastime; it first became a necessity; then a total addiction. The business as a Professor of Music had dried up almost entirely, while the profits from *The Kings Head* were frittered away on ever more booze, interspersed with bouts of gambling that left Smith even shorter of cash. The fines levied by St David's for non-attendance and poor performance meant the church income no longer covered even the couple's basic outgoings. It was only Sarah Anne's continuing popularity on and off the platform that kept them out of the debtors' courts.

'Enough!' Smith said out loud. 'If ever I get out of this mess alive and free, I will repent and reform.'

He heard a rustling as the tarpaulin at the far end of the barge was untied and a figure stepped down into the hull. As the aperture closed over, it was too dark to see who the visitor was. The steps suggested a man; or was it a woman in boots?

CHAPTER 28

STANFORD GEORGE FAILS; THE CHOIR REVOLTS; A PRISONER'S FATE IS SEALED

As a little boy, Stanford George was taken by his Uncle Whiteley to Halifax Central Station one Sunday morning to see the trains. This was no ordinary event, for there had been a terrible accident the previous evening as two trains had collided and a third, diverted into a siding, had run off the track and over the edge of the viaduct, killing the occupants of the houses below and severely injuring the driver and fireman of the locomotive, aptly named *The Death's Head*. By the time that uncle and nephew had arrived at the scene, the bodies had been removed. The scene was still horrific; a mangle of twisted metal, splintered wood, and shattered glass. Workmen were lifting what materials they could by hand and throwing them into the wagons that were there to take the spoil away. Two steam cranes were *in situ* on the main lines through the station lifting the engines back into place so they could be towed away for scrap.

Stanford George never forgot the image of a badly damaged engine, still snorting steam from its cracked open boiler, being lifted off the end of Platform 1 and back onto the metals. The move was too much for the bruised machine, and the frame disintegrated with a loud sigh and a clanking of broken parts. That memory was in his head as he stood there mid-way through his choir first practice at Hartley Parish Church. The rehearsal had gone badly from the start. The Vicar had insisted on accompanying George and making a short speech in front of all the choristers. Percy Banks had never been liked by the choir and the way in which he addressed them on the evening confirmed their opinion of the cleric. Snelgrove, lead tenor, and Warburton Sutcliffe choir administrator, mouthed at each other from their places on either side of the chancel. Some of the boys worked out what the two men were saying and began to snigger loudly. Banks continued unabashed. George wished that he would just be allowed to get on with the business in hand. Though inexperienced in the ways of choral direction, Hartley Parish Church's new Organist and Choirmaster had seen enough of rehearsal technique to know when a choir was bored stiff.

Eventually, Banks concluded. 'Mark my words, gentlemen, boys, this choir will become greater than ever. I have every confidence in Stanford here. He will be – no, he already is – a worthy successor to Dr Burchill. Let us pray.'

Choir members snorted and grunted as they bowed their heads. The Vicar lifted his hand and blessed them before departing back to the Vicarage and the writing of his next sermon. Stanford George smiled at the choristers, who stared back at him blankly. Unusually, the rehearsal was to take place in the choir stalls rather than the choir vestry. This was the first of many changes and innovations that the new choirmaster intended to make, partly because he thought they were for the better, but mainly to signal that he was his own man and would not be swayed, especially when the choristers kept muttering 'this was how TAB always wanted it.'

Because they were singing in the chancel, it was necessary for the big pipe organ to be used (the harmonium was too heavy to move from the vestry) as George had determined that the piano was not a good instrument on which to accompany the choir. Verney was asked to go to the organ loft, but he did so reluctantly, given the earlier altercation with George, when Olivier Laverne had been told to leave the organ loft after his brilliant improvisation. Verney was still seething when he switched on the hydraulic engines and began to pull out the stops. Unlike Burchill's clear movements, Verney found George's conducting almost impossible to follow. He could not easily be seen over the choir stalls and the heads of the taller tenors and basses, while his soft voice resulted in some of the instructions not being heard properly. George managed to maintain a semblance of order for the two hours that allotted to full practice. All the music for the following week was rehearsed after a fashion, though the performances were less than convincing.

The ordeal finally over, the singing men repaired to their usual hostelry. The choristers sat in silence, stunned by the awfulness of what had just happened. Eventually, Sutcliffe stood up, tapped his spectacles against his tankard and drew the meeting to order.

'Well, gentlemen. What did we think of this evening?'

The choristers roared and grumbled in about equal measure.

'What an effing shambles Warburton!'

'Tommy would be turning in his grave.'

'It was a load of shite, that's what!'

'What have we come to? A great choir like ours, reduced to this?'

All eyes turned to Sutcliffe, who beckoned to Snelgrove and Verney to join him at the head of the throng.

'It won't do, will it?' declared the choir administrator. 'Stanford, has been appointed because our Vicar owes the lad's uncle a favour or more. Percy Banks wants a weakling who will do his bidding. Not like old Tommy! He wouldn't have been told what to do! Not even by God Almighty.'

The choirmen laughed and cheered at the thought.

'We don't want to be Banks's lackeys, do we, eh?' Snelgrove added.

'I know what we will do! We will go on strike until Banks withdraws the offer of employment to Stanford George! It's about time people like us had a voice, and this is our ideal opportunity to make our mark!' Sutcliffe slammed his drink down on the table; everybody cheered.

Finally, Verney spoke. 'We must get the Organ Trustees on our side. They have fallen out with Banks and can be persuaded to support our cause. It is not enough just to get rid of Stanford George. We must provide the Organ Trustees with another way forward, and one that Banks will not be able to counter.' There was nodding and grunting and clapping as the choirmen agreed. 'And I have the ideal proposal. Recently, I heard the most brilliant organist, a Frenchman by the name of Olivier Laverne. He was invited to give a recital at Hartley Parish Church. Laverne arrived, not knowing that our beloved Organist and Choirmaster was dead. What if we forced Banks to replace George with Laverne? We would then have an even greater player than the good doctor ever was!'

'An excellent idea!'

'Capital!'

'Bravo, Charlie!'

'Laverne will be Organist before the month is out!'

It was cold and damp in the basement where the visitor was captive. Every so often, someone brought bread and water, and at least twice a day he was untied and guided over to a bucket where he was encouraged to go to the toilet. There was little or no conversation at these times, despite the prisoner's attempts to engage his jailers. Why had they done this to him? What was his crime? Who were they? What did they hope to achieve?

There was never any response. The jailers had a more pressing question to answer - what to do with their prisoner? There could only be one way forward on that front. It was not long before the deed was done.

CHAPTER 29

SARAH ANNE COMES CLEAN, OR SO IT SEEMS

'Where is he? You must tell us, now!'

'I have no idea, Inspector. No idea at all. How should I know? Why should I know?'

'I do not believe you, Mrs Smith.'

Sarah Anne Smith giggled unexpectedly. 'Do you like my perfume?'

Watson's idea of scent was a good scrub with carbolic soap.

'It is my favourite. Here, smell this.' Sarah Anne held out her handkerchief and invited him to inhale the perfume. Watson shook his head, walked back to his desk, and sat down. He slammed shut the open drawers, clasped his hands tightly and turned to look back at Mrs Smith.

'It is called "Otto of Roses". Have you ever heard of it, Inspector? It is made from the petals of *rosa centifolia* – the hundred-leaved rose.'

'I have not.' Watson shook his head. 'Is it very expensive?'

'It is the costliest of all the perfumes and the most powerful, Wright. May I call you Wright?'

Watson laughed. 'No, you may not. I am in charge of this interview, not you!'

Watson walked to the office door, opened it, and called Makepeace to join them.

'Shall I bring my notepad, sir?'

'Yes please, Harry. I think that would be wise.'

Makepeace saw how pale his commanding officer had become. He wondered about saying something but then thought better of it. Instead, he walked into the office in silence, nodded at Sarah Anne Smith, then sat in the far corner of the room, behind Watson, but able to look over his shoulder and observe the suspect from a distance.

'May I go now, please? I have nothing further to say to you.'

'You know where Edward is, don't you?'

'No, I swear to you, on the Holy Bible, I have no idea where my husband has gone.'

'Do you believe him guilty of murder?'

'Murder?' Smith laughed. 'My husband is too weak to do anything like that. He has no stomach for blood of any kind. If you pricked his finger he would faint at the sight! He is a sad man. He could have been a great organist; he could have been "Mr. Music" in this town. If only he had been a real man!'

'Are you sure, Mrs Smith? Appearances can be deceptive, can they not?'

'What do you mean?'

'How can you afford expensive perfume? I know how much your husband earns; and running *The King's Head* is not going to bring you in a fortune, is it?'

'My husband earns enough!'

'Not enough to afford expensive dresses and fine hats and coats!'

'How dare you insult me like that! You have no right!'

'Then tell me where your husband is!'

'I do not know. The last time I saw Edward was in the pub when you tried to arrest him!'

Watson paused the interrogation while he whispered to Makepeace, who then left the room.

'Do we have to have your Detective Sergeant present? I would far rather talk to you on your own. You might get more out of me that way.'

Watson refused to turn round until he heard the office door open and shut. When he returned to his seat, however, there were three other people in the room, not two.

'What are you doing here?'

'Sorry, sir, she insisted on joining the meeting; said it was wrong for the suspect to be on her own with you and me.'

'Very well, Mrs – Miss Grimshaw. How can we be of assistance?'

'Detective Chief Inspector, I would be glad if you would explain to me why Sarah Anne is here.'

'We seek Edward Smith. We believe he is responsible for the murders of Thomas Burchill and Harcourt Burford. Miss Grimshaw, do you have information as to the whereabouts of Edward Smith? I have seen you at *The King's Head* and the Parish Church. Have you not seen Smith of late? You do work at the public house, do you not? And you clean for Dr Banks.'

'No, I do not have any information. Neither does Mrs Smith. But I – we – swear to you, we have no knowledge of his whereabouts, so I would be glad if you would let us go.'

Watson nodded to Makepeace, who opened up the small case he had brought into the office. 'If you would be so good as to open it, Detective Sergeant.'

The two women sat there as Makepeace spread a group of letters out on Watson's desk.

'This correspondence was found in your bedroom, Mrs Smith.'

'What! You had no right to search my room.'

Watson laughed. 'We had every right, Mrs Smith. We were – and still are – looking for a murderer. We found your love letters from Thomas Burchill.'

Sarah Anne Smith looked at Gladys Grimshaw then turned to the two detectives.

'Those letters were not written to me, Detective Chief Inspector.'

'Oh really? I find that hard to believe, Sarah Anne.'

'What do you mean by that?' Gladys Grimshaw growled.

'Sarah Anne knows what I mean.'

Smith shook her head; tears started to drip down her cheeks.

'You have no idea, Watson. No idea at all. I know what you are thinking of me, but none of it is true. I am a singer, and a good one, and I am well paid for my engagements.'

'Leave her alone! Mrs Smith is distraught! Her husband is missing, and you are saying that he is a murderer! Then these unfounded allegations about her behaviour and her morals! We are going!' Gladys Grimshaw stood up and took Sarah Anne by the arm to pull her out of the other chair.

'If you try and leave this office, I will have you both placed under arrest!'

'You are bluffing, and you know it!' Gladys Grimshaw linked arms ever more forcefully with her companion.

'Don't, Glad. I ought to tell them!'

'But you said it was a secret you had sworn to keep!'

'I know Glad, but it is going to come out sometime. Better now than later.'

Gladys Grimshaw let go of Sarah Anne and sat down. 'Very well. It is your choice.'

Smith clasped her hands and then began to speak. 'Inspector, have you read those letters?'

'I have, and so has Makepeace.'

'All of them?'

Watson and Makepeace nodded.

'Tell me, Inspector, am I mentioned by name in any of the correspondence from Dr Burchill?'

'He called you "My Dearest Flower".'

'And never "Sarah, or "Sarah Anne"?'

'No, but...'

'But nothing, Inspector. I never had a relationship with Thomas Burchill. He sacked me from the choir, remember? And I was never his flower; a nettle, more like!'

'That is no defence. These letters were in your possession! That is all the evidence that we need in this matter.'

Sarah Anne Smith bowed her head and whispered. 'They were in my safe keeping for a friend. It would not have been possible for her to store the correspondence, so I agreed to look after the letters. I was going to give them back only the other week, then Dr Burchill's murder made that impossible.'

'Impossible? Why?'

'Because the owner's husband might have grown suspicious with all the fuss about the dead Organist and Choirmaster. Questions might be asked about TAB's past and his liaisons with women; or at least one woman. They say Burchill was a gal-sneaker, even before his wife died.'

'There was more than one woman, then?'

'I believe so, Inspector, but only one he really cared for.' Sarah Anne Smith clasped and unclasped her hands in a rhythmical motion.

'You had better tell the detectives, Sarah.' Gladys Grimshaw put an arm round her companion. 'Best that it all comes out. You cannot keep a secret like this for ever. It's not your responsibility, and it's not fair to burden you with it all.'

'Very well.' Sarah Anne Smith looked at the correspondence, neatly arranged in chronological order. She picked one of them up at random. 'These letters are from Thomas Burchill; but they were not written to me – not one of them. They were meant for – they were meant for –' Smith looked at Grimshaw, Makepeace and Watson in turn.

'Go on. You need to tell us. This could be important.'

'Very well. I will tell you. They were meant for Rose Banks. She is the "dearest flower", not me. I could never mean anything to that man; nor vice versa! '

There was silence. Gladys Grimshaw patted Sarah Anne's hands and tried to smile at her. Makepeace and Watson looked at each other.

'Are you sure?'

'I am sure, Inspector. No doubt of it. Gladys even found them one time in the organ loft, "bread and butter fashion".'

'That I find difficult to believe! I met Thomas Burchill. He was not the kind of man to indulge in such goings-on.'

Sarah Anne Smith laughed. 'You know nothing when it comes to men and women, Inspector!'

CHAPTER 30

MARTHA AND WYN ARGUE, WITH ANNIE AS A WITNESS

'Go on, Matty, you know you want to.'

'Winny, please. Not till we are married.' Martha Burchill pushed her fiancé away and stood up. He followed her over to the fireplace, putting his arms around her as she looked up at the portrait of her father.

'Matty, we love each other. It is the most natural thing in the world to – to – well, you know.'

'No Winny. Not until we have been married!'

Williams broke off his embrace and went back to the sofa.

'Do you really love me, Matty?'

She remained silent.

'What's the matter? Surely you love me! Don't you?'

'I do. Well, I did. Now I am not so sure.'

'What makes you say that? What have I done wrong?'

'I do not want to say.'

'Tell me!' Williams stamped his feet.

'Very well, I shall!'

Martha rang the servant's bell and sat down opposite her fiancé. It was not long before Annie Meredith knocked at the drawing room door.

'Come in, please.'

The maid appeared and looked nervously at both Wyn Williams and Martha Burchill.

'Yes, Ma'am. What is it, Ma'am?'

'Come over here Annie and sit down.' Martha Burchill pointed to the sofa on which Wyn Williams was sitting.

'What? Next to Mr Williams?'

'Yes Annie, that's right. Next to Mr Williams.'

'Why have you brought the maid in here, Martha? She has nothing to do with our conversation.'

'Are you sure, Wyn? I think the facts may point to Annie being very relevant to our conversation.'

'Nonsense. Annie, please leave us at once. I am sorry you have been brought into our argument. Go back to your duties.'

Annie Meredith rose. 'Yes, sir. At once, sir.'

'You will do no such thing. You are to stay here, sitting on that sofa, until I give you leave to go.'

'Yes, Miss Burchill.' Annie Meredith curtsied and went back to her seat.

'Annie. I want you to tell Mr Williams what you told me earlier today.'

'What? But I could not possibly do that!'

'You must, Annie. Please tell Mr Wyn what you told me.'

Wyn Williams ran his finger round his collar and looked at the maid. A bead of sweat ran down his forehead and onto his lips. It caused him to sneeze. He got out a handkerchief from his jacket pocket, wiped his brow, then blew his nose loudly.

'Must I?'

Martha Burchill nodded at her maid.

Annie cleared her throat and began. 'Mr Williams has been taking liberties.'

'What? I have done no such thing. This is preposterous!' Williams stood up and turned to Annie, sitting meekly on the sofa. 'You are lying!'

The maid sat in silence, curling in on herself.

'Sit down, Wyn, and keep away from Annie. Let her finish her story, please.'

Williams ran his hand through his long locks, paced up and down for a few moments then, realising his fiancée was not joking, he sat down, adjusted his jacket and trousers (to avoid any creases appearing) and folded his arms. He looked up to the ceiling and waited for the remainder of Annie Meredith's testimony.

'What are these liberties that Mr Williams has been taking, Annie? Speak clearly, will you?'

Annie Meredith stole a glance at Williams. 'Well, he said he was an artist.'

'An artist? What kind of artist?'

'Well, at first he said he wanted to sketch me. He showed me some drawings that he had done of me without me knowing. They were very good. He has a talent for it.'

'Nothing happened, Martha! What is wrong with a few sketches?' Williams buttoned his jacket, then unbuttoned it and adjusted himself on the sofa. 'Drawing is my hobby. I swear to you. If I had not been an organist, I would have trained at the art school, but there was no way that I could have afforded to go to the college.'

'I might have believed you, Wyn, if it were not for what else Annie told me – and worse than that – what she showed me.'

Williams blushed and sighed.

'You might well do that, Wyn Williams!' Martha Burchill walked up to her maid and looked her straight in the eye. 'What did my beloved fiancé do next, Annie?'

'He asked me to pose for him, without any clothes on, while he took photographs of me.' Annie Meredith burst into tears. 'It was awful; I didn't know what to do.'

Williams shook his head and bit his nails.

'But what did you do, Annie?'

'He kept coming to me at night, after you had gone to bed. I would not let him in. I swear I did not let him in!'

'I believe you, Annie, I really do.' Martha Burchill turned to look at the grand portrait of TAB, growling down on the *contretemps* taking place. 'Perhaps my father was right about you all along, Wyn. He told me you were a ne'er-do-well. And I believed you – I so wanted to believe you – and not him.'

'Miss Martha, he showed me some photographs of his art work, or so he called it. It made me feel sick. It wasn't just pictures of ladies with little on. Some of the photographs had men in them. I have never seen anything like it. I did not know that a man – well, a man looked like that!'

'I understand, Annie. It must have been very upsetting for you.' Martha Burchill put her hand on Annie Meredith's shoulder and squeezed it gently.

'Thank you, Miss. Can I go now?' The maid looked up. Her eyes were swollen, her cheeks reddened.

'Yes, please go. I need to talk to Mr Williams on my own.'

Martha Burchill watched every step of Annie Meredith's journey from sofa to drawing room door and beyond. Once the maid had left, Martha went over and locked the door, took the key out and put it on the sideboard.

'It was you who took those photographs that I found in that envelope, wasn't it? Why my father wanted such "art work" I will never know. Did he know it was you, sending them through the post?'

Williams buried his head in his hands. 'I needed the money, Martha. I so wanted to prove myself to you and your father. I would never get on in the musical world without my degrees.'

'You need not have bothered on my account, Wyn. I would have loved you with or without a Mus Bac. That is not the point. You have not answered my questions: did my father know it was you supplying him with these pictures?'

'No. He did not. At least I do not think so.'

'Are you sure?'

Williams thought for a moment. 'Yes, I am sure. It was all meant to be secret, so there was never any direct contact between me and the people who wanted the – the "art". I swear it.'

'Were you blackmailing my father?'

Williams laughed loudly.

'Of course not! I would never do that. I promise you, Martha, that is the truth, I swear it. The money I was paid for my art work was more than enough for my needs!' Williams stood up quickly and went over to the fireplace. Pointing at Thomas Burchill's portrait, Williams spoke again. 'I will swear on your father's grave if it helps!'

'You will do no such thing! Sit down. I have not finished with you yet!'

Williams went back to the sofa. He clasped his hands and waited for the next question.

'Was my father your only "customer"?'

Williams shook his head. 'No, he was not.'

'How many more do you have?'

'I am not at liberty to say, Martha.'

'You will tell me! I need to know so that I can help to root out this obscene evil!'

'Martha – Matty – I cannot tell you because I do not know. I take the pictures and make sure they are suitable for – well, for the customers' needs. I swear I did not know your father liked "art work" until you asked me to remove the envelope that was delivered the other week.'

'Was it the first delivery?'

Williams blushed. 'I – I believe not. He was a regular from before my time.'

'And there are other men in Hartleydale who appreciate this "art work"?'

Williams nodded.

'And you do not know who they are?'

'No. I do not. But I know what they prefer. And they all have nicknames. I know those. The man who organises the service created them. It is funny really. He must be an organist or know about the organ.'

'What a stupid thing to say!'

'Not stupid at all, Matty.'

'Don't ever call me that again!'

'Sorry, Martha. I meant no harm, I swear it. The pictures aren't so bad. Men like me just appreciate the female form and, in some cases, the male version too. Nothing more!'

'What are these names then?'

'They are names of organ stops like Clarabella; Tromba; Vox Angelica. I have a list of them all and their particular preferences.'

Martha Burchill had heard those names often enough, especially when her father would talk over breakfast about the rebuilding of the Parish Church organ and all the extra stops he wanted. Had he been thinking of something else all this time?

'And you have no idea who this person is, the man in charge of your little "studio" services?'

Williams shook his head. 'No. I simply drop the envelopes and pick up the money from an agreed spot in Hartley town centre.'

'And where is that?'

'It varies, but I always know because it is wherever the organ grinder and his monkey are.'

'And you have never met the man behind this obscene and perverted practice?'

'No, Matty – I mean Martha.'

'I believe you, Wyn. I really do believe you. Now go. I never want to see you again!' Martha Burchill went to the door, unlocked and opened it, then waited for her former fiancé to leave.

Wyn Williams did not demur. He got up and walked to the exit, then paused and looked Martha in the eyes. 'I really did love you, Matty, I swear. That bit is true – it always was true!' He tried to kiss her on the mouth, but she quickly turned her face away from him; his lips touched her cheek.

'Go! Get out of my sight! Now! Please!'

'Very well. But I will be back! I haven't given up yet. I promise you!'

Martha Burchill watched Wyn Williams walk down the corridor, put on his hat and coat, open the front door, and leave the house.

Downstairs, in the basement kitchen, Annie looked out as Williams sloped down the steps and out onto the street. She saw him look both ways, as if wondering where to turn next. After a few moments, her erstwhile seducer and *artiste extraordinaire* had determined to go towards the town centre. Once the footsteps had subsided to nothingness, Meredith went over to the dresser and took out an envelope from the bottom drawer. She hesitated for several moments before emptying the contents onto the wooden worktop. The basement lamp was dim, but it was light enough for the maid to see the detail in the photographs. Annie looked at them one by one. Some of the men's faces seemed so familiar. She had seen them before, of that there was no doubt. Where, though?

She decided to make herself a cup of tea. That would calm her nerves. Once her drink had brewed, Annie sat down at the work table and considered her next move. She felt tired. If she did not go up to bed soon, she would end up falling asleep where she sat. As she rubbed her eyes, Annie Meredith noticed a strange shape in the opposite corner of the kitchen.

'I must be dreaming. I should go to bed.'

The shadow moved, grew taller and larger as it came towards her.

'Not yet, Annie. We need to talk first.'

CHAPTER 31

LAVERNE SAVES THE DAY

Hartley folk would never forget the evening of Sunday, 19th October 1879. The annual archdeaconry service always attracted a full congregation and this one was no exception. Quite the contrary; it was the best turn out ever, according to the vergers and sidesmen on duty. Chairs were brought to seat the many additional singers (the choir stalls were full to overflowing) and the massive congregation, many of whom had turned up to see what the Parish Church's new Organist and Choirmaster was like.

Optimism was in the air. Stanford George had recovered from the disaster of 16th October (or so he thought) and the morning service had been negotiated without incident. The choir members were in full attendance: 70 in all, resplendent in cassocks and surplices; not a hair out of place; not a murmur during the silences or the sermon; the service was sung to perfection. Thomas Augustus Burchill was still in control at Hartley Parish Church. The Vicar referred in his sermon to the glory of music in worship and urged the choir, the congregation, the parish, the town, and the dale to put the horrors of the past few weeks behind them. No-one disagreed. All was well. Evening worship was eagerly anticipated, not least by Dr Percy Banks, who decided that he had weathered the controversial storm of young George's appointment as Organist and Choirmaster. Uncle Whiteley certainly thought so, for he handed the Vicar a cheque for £100 towards the organ fund immediately before his nephew ascended the organ loft to herald the start of the evening service.

Whereas the morning's organ preludes had been well received, there was a collective shudder as George began playing the preludes to evensong. Even at his drunken worst, Edward Smith had never played as badly as this. Whatever the new Organist and Choirmaster did, the cacophony continued. Switching the organ off and on again did no good; the wind was just as weak as before. The squeaks and groans got worse as the player tried different stop combinations; nothing resembling a musical sound could be achieved.

'What are you doing, man? This is ridiculous!' It was Dr Banks, in all his religious finery, his Doctor of Divinity hood flapping behind him as he stormed up to the organ loft.

'I have no idea, sir. Everything was well this morning, and when I practised this afternoon.'

'Well, George, it is not good enough; not good enough at all. You will have to play the piano instead.'

The Vicar of Hartley stomped down the loft stairs; the Organist and Choirmaster half ran, half fell after him, rushing to the piano located at the head of the chancel steps. It was now almost past the hour at which the service was to start. Banks ordered the choir to process, which they did, immaculately in step and order, as always; not a sound as they walked into their places in the stalls and the extra seats beyond. Once there, they waited as one until the opening prayer had been said.

Banks announced the first hymn. Stanford George attempted to play it. However hard the keys were pressed, no sound emerged. The Organist turned to look at the Vicar, who merely shook his head in disgust. George turned round to the assembled congregation, then back at the choir. A thousand pairs of eyes seemed to stare at the young organist. In the absolute silence of the moment, Stanford George lost his nerve. He got up from the piano, closed the lid, and walked briskly out of the church. Uncle Whiteley wondered about persuading him to return but thought better of it.

The dignitaries in the front rows of the nave looked at each other. The Duke and Duchess of Hartleydale had never witnessed anything like it. The Lord Mayor, the Lord Lieutenant, the Members of Parliament for Hartley North, Hartley Central and Hartley South were shocked and appalled by the scene. Behind the great and the good, bedecked in their aristocratic and official finery, sat the former Organ Trustees, who looked at each other and smiled.

Dr Percy Banks could not move. What could he do? Nothing! Never had he felt more powerless than he did now. All his dreams lay in tatters. There was nothing for it but to pray. As he began to mouth some words to his Lord and Saviour, Charles Verney walked towards the Vicar.

'Sir!' Verney whispered, trying to attract Banks's attention. The Vicar's eyes remained firmly closed.

'Sir!'

'What is it? Can you not see that this is a disaster? I am praying for a miracle. That is the only thing that can save me now.'

'Your miracle has already happened, sir. The most brilliant organist that I have ever heard is here this evening. I am sure he will be able to play for the service, if you give him the chance to do so.'

'Who is this organist? What is he doing here?'

'He is called Laverne, Dr Banks. He was meant to be playing here at Dr Burchill's invitation. No-one told him the recital had been cancelled. He should have been playing yesterday evening. I have been entertaining him ever since he arrived.'

The Vicar of Hartley looked around the vast church that had been his domain. Could it still be if what Verney said was true? Why had he let himself be blackmailed by Whiteley George? It was never going to work with Stanford. Charleton Mann had warned him, and he had taken no notice.

'Very well. Where is Laverne now?'

'Already at the console, sir. Announce the first hymn again and we can begin.'

Banks did as he was told, apologising for the false start in the process and asking everyone to remain calm and to prepare for an evening of musical worship.

Having announced the hymn number, for a moment, nothing happened. Banks felt sick unto death; then the most glorious sounds pealed forth from the organ. The choir joined in; the congregation followed. Hartley Parish Church was filled with rapturous praise. 'Onward Christian Soldiers' was just the beginning. The accompaniment to the responses was ingenious; that for the canticles and the anthem restrained and daring all at the same time. The singers felt led and supported, without any domineering by the accompanist. There was no need of a conductor; Laverne's playing gave the singers direction when necessary; no more, no less. All was in place to perfection.

The guest preacher was the retiring Bishop of Ayton-on-Hebble, who spoke movingly about the role of music in worship. The man had been so inspired by the rendition of the sung parts of the service that he kept returning to the way in which performances like that just experienced brought heaven to earth in a unique way. 'I will never hear anything finer than this choir until I reach paradise; even then, I am not sure I will ever be treated to anything better than Hartley can produce!' Upon hearing these words, the congregation burst into such hearty applause that Banks had to gesticulate wildly in an attempt to calm the listeners down.

The final hymn was the pinnacle of the congregational singing, matched and exceeded by the choral amen (a setting by Burchill). Laverne's final improvised voluntary stole the show. The four hymns were used as the basis of a triumphant off-the-cuff composition, first separately, then in masterly combination in a double fugue. The music critic of the *Gazette and Argus* was later to report that the improvisation itself was 'from God; surely no earthly hands were capable of such divine polyphony?'

Once the postlude was over, the choir processed out in silence and the congregation began to disperse. Dr Banks and his six curates stood at the back to bid goodbye to the parishioners, who filed past in order of rank. Except that many did not join the queue for the Vicar of Hartley's individual blessing and farewell. Rather, they waited in the north aisle by the door to the organ loft. Prominent among the expectant crowd were the Organ Trustees. All but one, that is; Whiteley George was notable by his absence.

It was many minutes before the organ loft door opened. None of those waiting thought to depart without meeting and greeting the mysterious substitute organist. Was there really someone who could play like God himself? Eventually, the door opened. Out came Charles Verney, full of smiles.

Sir Arthur Hastings strode forward. 'Verney. That was brilliant playing! I never knew you had it in you! Why have we never heard music like that before?'

Verney shook his head vigorously. 'Please, Sir Arthur, it was not me, I swear. I wish it were. It was Monsieur Laverne.'

'Who?' The other Trustees joined in the interrogation.

'Olivier Laverne. The French organist. He was meant to be giving a recital here.'

'Ah, yes, I remember. Burchill organised these jamborees. They made a lot of money, did they not?' William Worsdell moved his hands, as if counting coins.

'So where is this musical genius and saviour of Hartley's musical reputation? What a disaster Stanford George was going to be! Thank God that appointment ended before it had begun!' Hastings laughed sheepishly, then looked round, making sure that Uncle Whiteley was nowhere to be seen.

The door remained tantalisingly half open, just as Verney had left it when he came down the organ loft stairs. Beyond was only darkness. Had the mysterious maestro escaped while attention was diverted elsewhere?

Movement could be heard inside the loft. Someone was slowly descending, gently, cautiously, step by step. Verney looked around the assembled crowd, twiddling his thumbs to some rhythm or other. Then he looked back to the organ loft entrance.

'Olivier, bravo! You have an audience of admirers who wish to greet you. Let me introduce you to them.'

Laverne stepped forward to rapturous applause. As Verney guided the virtuoso towards the central chandelier so that his admirers could obtain a better view of their new hero, there was a collective gasp: how could someone as slight and slim as this produce such glorious sounds from the Parish Church organ, especially when they did not have the gift of sight?

The Assistant Organist looked at Olivier Laverne, standing there, surrounded by a crowd of at least 100, who clapped and cheered the Frenchman. The maestro gave a simple bow, raised his walking stick slightly and then asked that Verney take him back to his hotel. All attempts to engage the organist in conversation (with an invitation to dine with the Organ Trustees at their expense in addition) were met with polite shakes of the head and the words '*Non, merci!* I am very tired now. Perhaps another time. I thank you.'

In order to ensure that Laverne did not trip or collide with the pews,

Verney took the maestro by the arm, as a loving couple would do when out courting on a sunny afternoon. 'I will guide you, sir.'

'It is very good of you, Charles. But there is no need, I promise you. I have no eyes, but I have ears and touch and smell. I do not require sight. We are at the west door now, and if I am not much mistaken, here is the Reverend Canon Dr Percy Banks. I will need to converse with him at some point, but not yet.'

The Vicar of Hartley stood ready to greet his saviour, at least for the evening of Sunday, 19th October 1879. Banks proffered a hand; Laverne walked straight past and up to *The Station Hotel*.

CHAPTER 32

BANKS AND GEORGE, WATSON AND MAKEPEACE; MEN IN DEEP CONTEMPLATION

'What am I supposed to do, Whiteley? Your nephew was an abject failure last night and, as I now know, at the previous Thursday's choir practice. He lost the respect of the choir men before he had even tried to gain it! You sold me a dog and a half!'

'He was never allowed the opportunity to succeed, Vicar!'

'Stanford George needed to succeed from the very first. I believed you when you said he could do the job! What a fool I looked at the archdeaconry service! And in front of the great and the good of Hartleydale! If it hadn't been for that Frenchie everything would have gone awry! Absolutely everything!'

'It was not Stanford's fault! He is a good player, and you know it. Those men in the choir took against him from the start.'

'Which men? Tell me!' Percy Banks grabbed onto the edge of his study desk with both hands as he leaned over.

'I will tell you. Look no further than Warburton Sutcliffe and Edwin Snelgrove. They put cheats in the organ bellows and removed the hammer mechanism from the piano yesterday afternoon, I am sure of it! And was it mere coincidence that Olivier Laverne was in the church and ready at a moment's notice to take over, at which point, suddenly and miraculously, the organ was functioning perfectly again? Verney must have had a hand in the plot as well. I have never trusted those three, and especially not the Assistant Organist. Why did Burchill never give him any real responsibility; just like Snelgrove and Sutcliffe?'

'You are just making excuses for your nephew, Whiteley! I am sure there was nothing amiss with either instrument! I know we have had problems with the hydraulics, from time to time, but Tommy always knew how to sort it and Stanford should have been able to do the same!' Banks walked round to where his visitor was seated.

George stood up, not wishing to be overshadowed by the Vicar of Hartley. 'Do not be so sure, Percy. How long have we known each other? Remember the good old days when we were students together. Have I ever let you down? What about all those business deals I struck for you; all very much to your advantage if I may say so! Why would I ruin our relationship – whether professional or personal – when there is so much still to be gained?'

Banks sighed as George put a comforting hand on the Vicar's shoulder. 'I know, Whiteley, I know.'

The former Organ Trustee smiled. 'We need to think rationally and clearly about what is going on and how we not only counter it but also use it to our advantage.'

'Whatever the cause of yesterday evening's problems, the appearance of Laverne saved your bacon. Indeed, by the end of the service, Hartley Parish Church's reputation was just as high as it had always been, if not more so.'

Banks nodded at George's assessment of the archdeaconry service. 'You are right. The number of people who greeted me as they were leaving and said how wonderful it had all been. There were many promises of money in amongst; in fact, more in ten minutes than the whole of the last six months put together!'

George laughed and beckoned Banks to sit down, but this time by the fire. The Vicar did so.

'There are times when I want all this to be over, George. I grow very tired!'

'Have faith, man! There are great riches to be had in Hartley, both temporal and spiritual! I promise you. Just trust me for a little longer.'

'What must I – we - do then?'

'I do not believe for one moment that Verney, Snelgrove and Sutcliffe are capable of the sort of deceit and deviousness necessary to pull off last night's plan.'

'Really?'

'Yes, really, Percy. They are mere mill workers; used to the hard toil of the loom and the lathe, content with their beer and their babes, their women and their singing.'

'That seems rather harsh, Whiteley!' Banks shook his head.

'Others are behind this dastardly work. Look no further than my fellow Organ Trustees, I'll warrant!'

'My enemies from the start, I will give you that! All except you, that is, and that is only because I appointed you!' Banks laughed and clapped his hands triumphantly.

'That's more like it, Percy! I haven't seen you laugh in ages!'

'What do we do with those menaces?' Banks offered his friend a large glass of port.

'Thank you. I don't mind if I do. Did you notice how Hastings and Worsdell were at the head of the queue to greet Laverne at the end of the service last night?'

'No, I did not. I could not see the organ loft door from the west end of the church.'

'Well, they were there, I can assure you, only too ready to heap praise on the Frenchman. I believe it was all their doing. I am sure if we got in touch with Monkhill or Grindrod, one or the other will confess to tampering with the organ and the piano. Once my nephew had left the organ and moved to the piano, it would have been a simple enough job for someone – Verney probably – to remove the cheats from the wind supply or whatever other parts of the mechanism had been temporarily shut off and reconnect it all. You will recall that Verney was near the organ loft door when Stanford went to the piano.'

'I do. But what about the piano?'

'Anyone could have made the instrument unplayable. It is a simple matter. I have studied these things and could think of several ways in which it could be done.'

'And is there no evidence the piano was made unusable?'

George shook his head. 'I am afraid not. By the time I was able to inspect it, all was well. Someone had reassembled the instrument and it was working perfectly.'

The two men sat in silence for several moments, sipping their port and contemplating their next moves.

'Hastings and Worsdell are the leaders, are they not?' Banks put down his empty glass.

'Indeed, they are, Percy. The rest are just like sheep, who could no doubt be led astray if suitably tempted.'

'Should I not have sacked them in the way I did, Whiteley?' The Vicar tapped his fingers on the side table as he spoke.

'You did what you had to do, but perhaps you could have done it with more subtlety. That temper of yours always did lead you to do bad things, did it not?'

'I know. I know only too well. "For I acknowledge my transgressions: and my sin is ever before me".' Banks bowed his head.

'Look at me, Vicar. Look at me!'

'What?' Banks raised his head.

'That was all a long, long time ago. And you were a very different person then. So was I. We all were.'

'I accept that, but it can be very difficult sometimes, when I remember what happened.'

Whiteley George stood up. 'Percy: "Sufficient unto the day is the evil thereof!"'

Banks rose in answer to his friend. 'Yes! "Deliver me from mine enemies, O my God: defend me from them that rise up against me. Deliver me from the workers of iniquity and save me from bloody men!" The Organ Trustees really have had their day!'

'Burchill was in love with the Vicar's wife after all. The rumours were true!' Harry Makepeace laughed. 'And I always thought it was spiteful gossip put about by TAB's enemies.'

'I think most sensible people thought that. What do they say? "There's no smoke without fire".'

'My missus would say you *can* have smoke without fire, especially in our kitchen. That stove has never drawn properly in all the time we have lived there!'

Watson smiled. 'Thanks for cheering me up, Harry. We seem to be getting nowhere with this case, and no sign of Edward Smith even now. The man has to be somewhere. The thing is, I believe Sarah Anne when she knows not where he is.'

'I do too, sir. Though I believe she knows what he has done. That woman is no innocent.'

Watson snorted. 'I agree with you there! I had one of the constables check how much Mrs Smith is paid for musical engagements and unless that bobby has missed some, there is no way she could afford all her finery from singing fees.'

'And the earnings from *The King's Head*?'

'What do you think, Harry? I doubt they make any kind of living from that, not with Edward Smith drinking most of the profits, by all accounts.'

'I agree, sir. And Mr. Smith's organ work has collapsed.'

'So, Smith is still our main suspect?'

'Who else might be responsible for those deaths?' Makepeace shrugged. 'We have to redouble our efforts to find him, and soon!'

'Indeed, sir. What do we do about the letters in the meantime?'

'That is a very good question, to which I have no obvious answer.' Watson scratched his head.

'We are sure the letters are from Burchill to Mrs Banks, are we?'

Watson nodded. 'I checked the handwriting against other documents written by Burchill. Remember those choir records, for one thing; and his musical scores and letters to singers – all the things that Verney showed us when we investigated the church. It is Burchill's writing; there is no doubt.'

'And those letters are for Rose Banks?'

Watson nodded. 'I have now read them all carefully – very carefully. I am almost certain this is a correspondence between Burchill and the Vicar's wife: the references to the services and the singing and the lessons. Then he talks about the music he has written and dedicated to her. I asked about those songs at the music shop – you know, the one by the Town Hall, that sells harmoniums and pianos and other things – and they let me borrow the scores. Here they are.' The Inspector took out a batch of compositions from the bottom drawer of his desk and gave them to

Makepeace. 'If you look at the words of the songs, you will find many of the phrases in the letters. It looks as those two had a strong affection for each other.'

'Do you believe what Sarah Anne Smith told us about the letters, sir?'

'That Rose Banks gave them to her for safe keeping? I do not, Sergeant. I think that those letters were stolen from the Vicar's wife by one of Mrs Smith's "gentlemen", or, just possibly, one of the cleaners at the Parish Church. They also clean the Vicarage, or at least some of them do. Once in Sarah Anne's possession, she was intending to use them to her advantage, either with the Vicar, or his wife, or both.'

'Or Burchill himself? It would not be good for TAB if it came out that he had been having a liaison with the Vicar's wife, would it?'

'I agree, Harry.'

'What are we going to do about Mrs Smith and her men friends, sir?'

'For now, nothing. There is enough scandal coming to light in Hartley without letting the world know of that woman's alleged dalliances with the great and the good men of the dale.'

'Very good, sir. You know best in these matters. Do you think Sarah Anne was already blackmailing the Bankses, or was it as yet only her possible intention to do so?'

'No. She had not got round to blackmailing them. I believe her when she said there had been no contact between her and Percy or Rose Banks. You will note that the most recent letter was only written a few days before Thomas Burchill's death. That correspondence is interesting in itself. I think you should read that last letter, Harry.'

'How so, sir?'

'Because it is as if TAB knew he was about to be murdered.'

CHAPTER 33

A BLIND MUSICIAN LOOKS BACK; WHITELEY GEORGE IS WORRIED

Being blind, or nearly blind, had its advantages. Without the gift of sight, the other senses became much enhanced. That was the prisoner's experience and had been for over forty years. Smell, hearing, touch, memory, were all sharpened in ways that those who had eyes to see would never experience. Olivier Laverne determined he was being held in a basement because of the level at which the many street noises were reaching him. Given that there was rarely any time of absolute quiet, day or night, he surmised his prison must be somewhere in the industrial and commercial part of Hartley. Or was it even that town? Could he have been tricked into getting off at some other station? Halifax? Leeds? Wakefield? Anywhere?

Laverne thought back to his journey. There had been the train from Paris to the coast; then the abominable voyage across the channel. Another train to London; a hackney carriage across the metropolis and then the journey north to Hartley, via Wakefield and Halifax. Burchill had warned Laverne there was no direct train service to the town, and to alight at the correct places for the requisite onward connections. Unusually, the traveller had not stayed overnight in London. Burchill had been keen to entertain Laverne in Hartley and the renowned French organist was only too happy to accept his good friend's invitation to play at the Parish Church on one of the best organs in Britain.

'Monsieur Tommy' was not his usual self. That was obvious from the tone of the letter to Laverne. The Organist and Choirmaster of Hartley

Parish Church was renowned the world over for his organisational abilities: everything was planned months if not years in advance in TAB's world. The invitation to play on the evening of 19th October 1879 was therefore more than a little uncharacteristic. Laverne's amanuensis had remarked on the haste with which the letter was written and the sharp tones in which the request to travel to West Yorkshire had been made. 'Come at once; your presence urgently needed to play at Hartley Parish Church, 18th inst. As ever, TAB.' Laverne had even asked if the correspondence was in Burchill's hand; the assistant thought it was, though the scribbled handwriting could not be attributed with full confidence.

Laverne had thought it would be an opportunity for the two men to rekindle their friendship and reminisce about their time together at the School for the Blind. He laughed to himself as he remembered the tricks Burchill would play. TAB's favourite was re-arranging some of the organ pipes in the small instrument in the music room and seeing how the pupils reacted when the sounds came out wrong. Not everybody had appreciated the bluff Yorkshireman's sense of humour; one female student regularly ended up in tears at the end of a lesson with the good doctor.

Laverne had taken a softer approach with women like her – of whom there were a number at the School for the Blind. He never knew her name (the students were all known to their individual tutors by number), but he would never forget her playing. 'Nineteen' was the best organist that Olivier Laverne had ever heard. He often wondered what happened to her. Unlike in France, there were so few opportunities for blind players, and even fewer for women. There was a time when he tried to find out, but she left no forwarding address and the School for the Blind seemed reluctant to help him pursue his enquiries.

Laverne imagined what the staff common room at the School for the Blind must have looked like. He could still remember the smell of the fire and Burchill's pipe tobacco. You always knew when TAB was on his way; first the aroma, then the humming of a tune (usually his latest composition), the squeak of his shoes as he walked through the door, the sag of the leather as he landed his posterior in an armchair and finally the rustle of newspaper. The sequence of events had become a ritual, observed if not welcomed by Burchill's fellow tutors. There would be guffaws and snorts depending on how favourable the reviews of his latest performances were. Then he would engage the rest of the staff with tales of Hartley and the antics of the Parish Church authorities. Tommy knew how to handle them all! He would regale his colleagues with stories of how he was playing them off against each other: Vicar and Organ Trustees; Sir Arthur Hastings and Sir Templeton Taylor and a hundred other protagonists that Laverne could not be bothered to remember. He could recall TAB's trying to persuade him to 'buy into' a speculative land purchase in north Hartley. 'It mun mak a 'ole lot o' brass fo' thi, Oliver!' Laverne had constantly declined the offer, despite the spectacular returns on any investment made, according to Burchill. Tommy was certainly a wealthy man; too wealthy for an organist.

Laverne recalled their last meeting. There had been a sadness about the encounter. Both men realised that their careers were taking them in different directions: Olivier to work in Paris and Thomas to ever greater glory 'oop north'. TAB had placed his great big hands on Laverne's shoulders and promised him he would be one of the first to play the grand new organ at Hartley Parish Church once the restoration of the building was finished and the instrument could be completed and installed.

'I will hold you to that, Thomas!'

Laverne giggled once more at the expression that would have been on Burchill's face as the Frenchman kissed the Yorkshireman on each cheek as they bade farewell to each other.

The fond memories faded as Laverne came back to the cold reality of his situation. Here he was, almost naked, tied to a chair, fed and watered, if he were lucky, twice a day, only allowed to perform his *toilette* when his captors deemed it appropriate. He never heard them speak. There were occasional snippets of conversation in an adjacent corridor, though it was difficult to tell what was being said; the whispered dialect phrases were all but unintelligible to Laverne, despite the time spent with Burchill. The prisoner sensed that there were three of them talking outside his cell, but only two of them ever came in, and never together. One of them might have been a woman, judging by the lightness of her step and the occasional whiff of what smelt like perfume (though nothing like the sort worn by French women, of any class), but the disorientation brought about by captivity had rendered Laverne's senses less acute than usual. They remained sharp enough for him to smell death; most likely his own.

'We are here to see Monsieur Laverne. Is he available?'

The landlord of *The Station Hotel* turned to the row of hooks behind his desk.

'I don't think so, gentlemen. His key is on its hook, so he must be taking the air. He has done so each day since he arrived in Hartley, though he leaves for London tomorrow morning.'

'Really?'

'That's what it says in the book here.' The landlord pointed at his ledger and then shrugged at the two visitors. 'It's Reverend Banks, isn't it? My son James sings in the choir at your church!'

'Does he now?'

'That he does, sir. He told me what happened at the service last night.'

'And what did he say?'

'You can ask him yourself, Vicar. Here he is!'

James Tomlinson appeared from behind the curtain that separated the back office from the counter.

'Jim – tell the gentlemen here what you told me last night about the service at the Parish Church.'

The boy blushed as he recognised the Vicar of Hartley. 'It were marvellous, sir. The way that blind man played. We all thought so. I wish I could play like yon. It made all the boys want to learn. It were even better than old TAB! And we though a lot of him! We didn't reckon much to the other one though!'

'What other man, Jim?'

'The one who were supposed to be playing last night. We all thought he were neither use nor ornament. He couldn't play for toffee. He …'

'Thank you, boy. We get the picture.' Dr Banks looked at Whiteley George then gave the lad a coin. 'Now be off with you. We need to find Monsieur Laverne before he takes leave of us in the morning.'

'I know where he is', the boy replied. 'And thanks, sir!'

'Where is he, then?' Banks leaned over to scrutinise James Tomlinson as he asked his question.

'He's at Parish Church, sir. Mr Verney called for him this morning and they went down there. Mr Verney said he wanted Laverne to teach him how to play proper.'

Banks growled. 'Did he now?' Turning to Whiteley George, he whispered angrily. 'These organists are all the same! What have I said? What has been agreed? No-one, but no-one, has permission to play that instrument unless I say so. I am the single authority in that Parish Church. And I will have my way!'

At which point, the Vicar of Hartley stormed out of *The Station Hotel* and down towards St Martin's. Whiteley George made his excuses to the Tomlinsons, father and son, and chased after Banks.

The rain was bucketing down, and George was getting wetter by the minute as he attempted to catch up with his colleague. Banks was a difficult man at the best of times, but these were now the worst of times as far as the plans for the Parish Church, the town, and the new developments to the north were concerned. All could so easily be lost if the Vicar's hot temper could not be assuaged. There was so much to gain and so much to lose.

He could see Banks striding away a few minutes ahead. He would need to run to catch up with him. He must do that before Percy encountered Laverne and Verney and said something so horrendous that both men would walk out of the church on the spot and never return. That could not happen, for if Stanford were ever to hold the premier position, there needed to be a period when the choirmen could be brought round during Laverne's temporary appointment as Organist, with Verney and George's nephew sharing the burden of choral direction (surely a blind organist would not be capable of leading the choir). In due course, it would become right and proper for a substantive appointment to be made.

So deep in thought was he that Whiteley George was unaware he was being followed. Only when he felt a hand on his shoulder did he realise Wright Watson and Harry Makepeace had been walking just behind him, step-for-step.

'Sorry to bother you, sir. But we would like a word with you about the organ loft murders, if we could ask you to come with us to the station.'

'Not now, Watson. I have an urgent appointment with Mr Laverne. I need to make sure that he and Dr Banks reach an amicable agreement about music at the Parish Church.'

'Do you now, Mr George. I wonder if that relates to what Mr Laverne told us earlier this morning. What do you think, Sergeant?'

Watson turned to Makepeace, who smiled and shrugged.

CHAPTER 34

WHITELEY GEORGE CONFESSES; ANOTHER BODY IS FOUND

Whiteley George need not have worried. Despite the former Organ Trustees' concerns about Percy Banks and his periodic outbursts, the Vicar's encounter with Laverne and Verney at the Parish Church went well: no remonstrating with Verney about unauthorised use of the organ and no hostility to the French visitor. Quite the opposite: Banks was charm itself, realising that he could not afford to offend either player if his ambitions were yet to be realised. By the evening of 20th October, it had been announced that Olivier Laverne would become Organist of Hartley Parish Church. Given that the appointee was from the French tradition, where the *titulaire* was not responsible for the choir, and because Laverne had insisted on maintaining his role as a concert organist, the Vicar also agreed to appoint Charles Verney and Stanford George jointly as Choirmaster and Assistant Organist.

'It is for the best. This way I get to "learn my trade" with Laverne and Verney and the choir might respect me more.' Stanford George looked across at his uncle. It was many months since the two of them had dined together.

'I only wanted the best for you, Stanford. You have the potential to be a great player, and a wonderful influence on music and more in this town, especially when Hartley becomes a city. And I want you to be at the heart of it all!'

'I am very grateful to you, Uncle. But I would have preferred – and still prefer – to be successful on my own terms, not yours.'

Whiteley George stopped eating and put down his knife and fork. He patted his lips with his napkin as he finished off the last mouthful of roast beef. 'Well, I applaud that, Stanford, but a little helping hand from time to time never did anybody any harm. I was given an occasional push up the ladder; and I have always been grateful for it.'

'Let us agree to differ, Uncle. Laverne is a brilliant organist and Verney is loyal and hard working. The three of us will do wonders for the Parish Church and its music!'

'I am sure you will. Let us only hope that there are no more murders in the organ loft before it becomes Hartley Cathedral!'

It was Stanford's turn to stop eating. 'If you don't mind me asking you, Uncle Whiteley, what did the police want with you this morning? The Vicar thought you were going to join us at the Parish Church. He said that you had been with him at *The Station Hotel* looking for Monsieur Laverne, but then you were stopped by the police and taken to the station. Why?'

Whiteley George blushed. 'It was nothing. A minor business matter that required resolution.'

'I am not sure I believe you. Your face does not tell me what your lips are saying.'

Whiteley George laughed nervously. 'You are just like your mother, Stanford. She could always tell what I was really thinking!'

'Then tell me, Uncle.'

The older man looked at his nephew. How Stanford looked like Gertrude! The same eyes, the same wicked smile, the same laugh, the same ability to look right inside you. If only she had accepted his offer of marriage all those years ago and he had been Stanford's father and not his uncle! Except since his brother Wilson's death, and Gertrude's disgrace, Whiteley had brought the boy up as his own.

'Very well. But not here. In my study. We will have some port.'

Stanford followed his uncle. He was rarely allowed into the 'holiest of holies' (as Whiteley George called his study) and surmised, therefore, that a serious conversation was about to ensue. Once the port glasses had been filled (to the brim), uncle began to confide in his nephew.

'What I am about to tell you, Stanford, remains within these four walls. Is that understood?'

'Yes, Uncle.'

Whiteley George downed his glass of port in one expansive gulp and began. 'This morning, Monsieur Laverne – our new Organist – told Detective Chief Inspector Wright Watson that Tommy - Thomas – Burchill feared for his life.'

'Really? How? Why? What?'

'I know. It is very worrying, given what happened to TAB not long afterwards!'

'After what?'

'After Laverne had been invited to come to Hartley to give a celebrity organ recital.'

'And how does Laverne know all this?'

'Because Burchill said so in the invite letter!'

'Where is this correspondence?'

'With Watson and Makepeace. They showed it to me and asked what I knew about it.'

'And what did it say, Uncle?'

'I cannot remember every word, Stanford, but the implication was that Tommy was being blackmailed and that if he did not comply with the blackmailer's wishes, then he would be killed.' Whiteley George poured himself another large glass of port and offered his nephew a refill.

'No thank you, Uncle. I am not a great devotee of port.'

'Really? I thought you enjoyed a glass or two.'

'Just the occasional one. But my time as an organist for the Methodists put me off alcohol, given some of the stories they told about "the demon drink" and what it can do to people; how it can ruin lives.'

Whiteley George looked into his port glass, already half empty, thought about topping it up, then slammed it down on his desk. 'You are right, of course. I really should stop drinking!'

'What else did this letter from Dr Burchill to Monsieur Laverne say?'

'Not very much, other than by implication. There was a reference to land acquisition.'

'Weren't you involved in buying to the north of Hartley along with TAB?'

Whiteley George nodded. 'Yes, I was. Tommy and I, along with a third party, have been buying up land there in anticipation of a big building project once Hartley is a city.'

'And who was – or is – the third party?'

Whiteley looked at his nephew and shook his head.

'Are you saying "no" because you are unaware of the identity of the third party or that you are unwilling to say who it is?'

'The latter, Stanford; I am sworn to secrecy.'

'But you can tell me in strict confidence, Uncle. I can be trusted.'

'Can I? Can I really? Can anybody be trusted?' Whiteley George refilled his glass after all and then offered the decanter to his nephew, who again refused to imbibe.

'Of course, Uncle. What would I have to gain from breaking any confidence that you shared with me?'

Whiteley George rose from his armchair, put his arms in his pockets and started to pace about the room. 'Once I have told you, you will be party to knowledge whose possession may threaten your life.'

'Surely not, Uncle!'

'I am. With two people dead already?' Whiteley George sat down firmly in his armchair. 'Very well. The third person involved in the land acquisitions was – is – Dr Banks.'

'The Vicar? That is ridiculous!'

Whiteley George shook his head. 'Do not be fooled, nephew, dear. Percy George Banks is a cunning and devious man. His ambition – and his greed -- know no bounds. I should know, I was at university with him!'

'Was it Banks who was blackmailing Dr Burchill, then?'

Whiteley George smiled. 'Not according to Laverne.'

'What did he say, then?'

'According to the detectives, Monsieur Laverne said correspondence between him and TAB had named the blackmailer.'

'Who was the blackmailer, then?'

'It was me, apparently.' Whiteley George smirked.

'And was it, Uncle?'

'Of course not, Stanford. What do you take me for?' Whiteley George smirked a second time.

Despite the dominance of railway transport across the valley since the 1850s, Hartley Canal remained a major route for trade across the Pennines. As Templeton Taylor (for one) regularly argued, there was more than enough demand for both train companies serving the town and, at least in the case of less urgent traffic, the moving of goods by water. Tuesday, 21st October 1879 was no exception, and the bargees at work that morning had their work cut out to load the finished goods from the wharves by Taylor's factory and begin the long journey through to Manchester and beyond. Ten barges in all were required – more than were available at the moorings – so extra vessels were hired from private owners to fill the need. The last of these additional boats was pulled by horse up to the factory basin ready to be loaded. Two lads were deployed to pull off the tarpaulin along the length of the 70-footer. They had nearly completed their task when one of them noticed a large sack in the bottom of the otherwise empty hold. It was too heavy for them to move, so the foreman was called. He could not lift it either; it took three to manhandle the sack off the barge and onto the quayside.

Because there was an urgency about completing the filling of the barges, the sack was left to one side and forgotten about. The barges moved off; workers came and went; it rained, then the sun shone. Only when the gas lamps were being lit did a passer-by notice rats gnawing away at the sack and, in the process, exposing a human hand. Workers were called from the nearby mill. As the cloth was torn away, a whole body was revealed: torso, arms, legs; only the head was missing.

Watson and Makepeace were off duty when the report of a corpse being found came into the police station. Bobbies were despatched to inform them of the discovery, however, and within an hour both detectives were on the scene, along with uniformed officers.

The body was naked. There was nothing obvious about the torso to suggest the man's identity other than the fact that the deceased had been bound and beaten before being killed, perhaps by decapitation.

'Is it Smith, sir?'

Wright Watson shrugged. 'I do not know, Sergeant. It could well be, given that the barge was moored near *The King's Head*, and we have not been able to locate him anywhere else, have we? Without a face, it might be difficult, though one assumes that Sarah Anne will be able to recognise any distinguishing features from what is left of this gentleman.'

Watson knelt to examine the lifeless body in more detail. There were no rings on any of the fingers and no sign there had ever been. The hands looked as they had been used to write rather than to labour; the nails were neatly clipped. One of the legs might have been broken at some point and then not healed properly, leaving a bend in what should have been straight. Watson was no expert, however, and determined the body should be taken to the mortuary for further, detailed examination.

'Makepeace, instigate a search of the area. We need to find that head; his clothes; and any other belongings.'

'What if it isn't Edward Smith, sir? Could it still be connected to the other murders?'

'Your guess is as good as mine, Harry. We don't have many murders in Hartley, so I am inclined to think the appearance of this corpse is more than mere coincidence.'

'But there are other killers out there, sir. You and I both know that. This could be part of a feud between the types that live in the terraces round here; a revenge crime, perhaps?'

'That would make sense. Or even something as simple as a drunken brawl gone wrong. Remember when we first went to *The King's Head* and Smith was breaking up a fight? The fight might have continued.'

'Or some of the customers might have come back later and murdered the landlord in a fit of pique.'

Makepeace motioned to a constable to cover up the body then looked around the canal basin as the moon came out.

'At least this one wasn't found in an organ loft, eh, Sergeant?'

The two detectives smiled at each other.

CHAPTER 35

CALLS TO ARMS ARE ISSUED

'It is good to see you, Gertrude. The sisterhood have waited for your return, and now you are among us, once and for all! The Hartley and District Women's Social and Political Union rejoices. Hallelujah! our day has come!'

'I am overwhelmed by your kindness and the warmth of your welcome. I am deeply moved.' Gertrude Wilson Rankin embraced every one of her followers as they lined the hallway of 82, New Station Street, Hartley. Once she had completed this task, the leader of 'the movement' walked into the large parlour at the rear of the house where a celebratory spread of sandwiches had been prepared.

Inundated with requests to speak to the assembled group of women, 'GWR' held up her hands. 'Sisters, please. Let us first eat together. I have had a long journey, and an even longer sojourn away from you all. When my hunger has been satisfied, I will address you, and gladly. My wishes are your wishes; your will, my will.'

With that, Gertrude Rankin sat down at the head of the table. Her followers jostled with each other to serve the woman who had been away from them for far too long. All were shocked at their leader's appearance. Even though her prison sentence had been shorter than many, it had aged the founder of the HDWSPU terribly. In place of the long, free-flowing auburn locks was a short, almost masculine mop of grey-white hair, parted to the left. Rankin's legendary smooth skin and beautiful face had been replaced by a leathery complexion and a careworn countenance. The graceful, elegant hands, once the instruments through which she played such glorious music, were rough and calloused, the nails broken, the skin bruised. Only when the members of the Union looked into Gertrude Rankin's eyes could they be reassured that the woman's spirit had not been broken; quite the opposite, for the reforming zeal was as strong as ever; stronger, even.

The meal over, the gathering gradually fell silent, the members readying themselves for the long-awaited speech from their leader. They were not disappointed. After a final cup of tea, Gertrude Rankin clapped her hands to bring the meeting to attention. Everyone looked at her. She rose to address them, looking round to make sure everyone was fully attentive.

'Sisters, I thought about you all when I was in prison. I could not have survived in there without your support.' Gertrude Rankin nodded at the members of the HDWSPU. 'Not a day went by when I did not say a prayer for the members of the Union; not a moment passed when I was not thanking God for the sisterhood. Not a second was spent other than preparing for this day! You are my life! All of you! And I will repay your trust in me a thousand times over! My time in the gaol was not wasted. I thought long and hard about what must now be done to achieve our aims, and I know now; I really do, my sisters! It is time for action; not the kind of protest that you saw at Hartley Parish Church, but *deadly* action. Until or unless we do something that will bring the disenfranchisement of women to the attention of the authorities, then our movement will never make progress. We will forever be oppressed second-class citizens. We deserve to be treated as equals in every respect!'

The members clapped, cheered, and stamped their feet.

'Shhh! Be careful. We do not wish to draw attention to ourselves; at least not yet. Over the next few days, I and the other officers of the Union will be working on a campaign that will succeed. All eyes are already on Hartley because of the recent murders, and we must capitalise on that opportunity for the good of the movement. I am in touch with other branches of the Union and the central office in London. All are agreed that the focus should be on Hartley: think of people like Templeton Taylor and Percy Banks and their pronouncements on the role of women in society. Until men like them are persuaded otherwise, there is no hope for us. If they become advocates for the movement, speaking for women's liberty and equality in national debates, everything would then be possible!'

'So how are we to do that, sister? How shall we win them over?'

'Yes. You are asking for the impossible! There is no chance that Taylor and Banks will advocate for universal suffrage and equality of opportunity!'

Gertrude Rankin held up her hands to calm the meeting.

'Enough, sisters! Only believe; have faith! All will be revealed, and everything will be granted to us! Our time has come! Believe me!'

Everyone cheered as the leader of the Hartley and District Women's Social and Political Union left the room, walked along the hallway and up the stairs to the bedroom that the sisters had prepared. Gertrude Rankin felt wearier than she had done since her arrest and trial. But it was a happy tiredness. All was going to plan. The murders of Burchill and Burford had done wonders for the movement; that was only the beginning. Hartley, the Riding, the country, would be different places by Christmas 1879.

The members filed slowly and silently out of the house, making sure they did so singly or in pairs, so as to avoid attracting attention. Annie Meredith was the last to leave. It was easy enough for her to sneak back into number 84, just like she always did after Union meetings.

'It was good of you to come and see me, Banks. Especially at this hour.'

'The least I could do, Sir Templeton, especially after our meeting at the Athenaeum.'

'Drop the "sir", please. First name terms here! Have another brandy!' Templeton Taylor rang the bell for more drinks. He waited until the butler had poured them and left the study before continuing the conversation. 'I have thought long and hard about your offer, Percy. It is a most attractive one; it appealed to me from the start. Is it still available?'

'It is – er, Templeton – it is.'

'So, as I recall from our discussions at the club, you will arrange for me to acquire all the land in north Hartley owned by the church and yourself in return for my abandoning my campaign to have St David's become the seat of the new bishopric. In addition to which, I will have control of the music at the Parish Church – sorry, Cathedral – and be enabled to name the choir school that will be formed in my son's memory.'

'That was what was offered to you.' Banks clasped his hands, as if in prayer.

'And with my name at the head of the list of proposers, the plan will succeed?'

'It will surely succeed, especially when you have been promoted to the House of Lords.' Banks bowed his head slightly.

Sir Templeton blushed. 'It has yet to be confirmed, Percy, but I am reasonably confident all will be well. Now tell me more about the land. You have the surveys for me, I think?'

Banks opened the case lying next to him on the sofa and passed over the required documents. 'I think you will find all in order. I have taken the liberty of having our solicitor draft a possible agreement between us. It is the last of the papers – there – the one at the bottom.'

Taylor fanned through the plans and the other material. 'You have certainly prepared all this very thoroughly.'

'Do not thank me, thank Whiteley George. I could not have made all these arrangements without him.' Banks closed the now-empty case.

'Is he not one of those infernal Organ Trustees? They were one of the reasons why I wanted my own establishment!'

'The Trustees are no more, Templeton. I found – or rather George found – a way of circumventing their power, whether over the organ or the land that was gifted to pay for the music and the Organist and Choirmaster; the land that I am now selling to you!'

'Are you sure, Percy? Hastings and Worsdell are powerful, cunning men. They will not take any of this lightly.' Templeton Taylor got up from his armchair, walked over to where Banks was seated and leaned over him. 'Are you really sure, Vicar? There is a good deal at stake here, and those two men are no friends of mine, nor me of them. Once this agreement is out in the open, they will fight it to the House of Lords!'

Banks laughed. 'Where you will be, sitting in splendour in your ermine!'

'That may be so, Percy, but do not dismiss them, nor their ability to cause trouble! Can they not be persuaded round to our way of thinking?'

Banks thought for a moment then shook his head. 'They have enjoyed wielding power as Organ Trustees. They sorely miss that dominance. Perhaps not so much the other men, but Hastings and Worsdell are a different kettle of fish, I can assure you, especially now that Burchill is no more. It is as if TAB bequeathed his awkwardness to them upon his death.

That is one of the reasons I was so keen for Whiteley George's nephew to become Organist and Choirmaster.'

Taylor gasped slightly. 'Not Burford? I would have had him at St David's any day in preference to that drunkard Smith.'

Banks snorted. 'Burford would have been as much of a thorn in my side as Tommy used to be.'

'If I didn't know you better, Vicar, I would almost think you are happy that those two men are dead.'

It was especially cold that night. It was after 11 o'clock when the Reverend Canon Dr Percy Banks left Templeton Towers. The Vicar and his host exchanged pleasantries for a few moments before the horse and carriage arrived. This gave them the opportunity to look over the town and point to the planned new developments, and what the further extensions to the Parish Church to make it into a cathedral with a choir school, cloisters and the like might resemble. Sir Templeton could be heard jesting that St David's would still be taller than St Martin's, however magnificent the alterations to make the Parish Church a suitable home for a bishop might be. Banks replied that the topic would be one for debate when they were both in the House of Lords. By this time, the Vicar's transport home was ready, and Taylor was getting cold. The two men shook hands heartily, the host slapping his guest on the back as the latter ascended the carriage.

The vehicle was observed as it drove off down towards Hartley. The same two pairs of eyes watched as Sir Templeton smoked his cigar a little more before throwing the remains onto the gravel immediately in front of the porch.

'We could have done it tonight!' the first observer said to the other. 'We could have killed two birds with one stone!'

'No. We have to be patient. We bide our time for now. Once everything is in place, then we strike. We have waited this long for our revenge -- we can wait a little longer.'

The first observer sighed as the second put out a comforting hand.

'We should be going. We have to keep up the pretence of being ordinary people living ordinary lives for a little while longer. Now be careful and quiet! We cannot afford to be discovered, especially by Sir Templeton's guard dogs!'

With that, the two observers crept back to the walls surrounding the mock-castle grounds, eventually managing to locate the hidden passageway out onto the road into Hartley. Once they were far enough away, they began to whistle cheerfully, confident in the knowledge that it would not be long before the Reverend Canon Percy George Banks and Sir Templeton Taylor would be singing a very different tune.

CHAPTER 36

THE BODIES MOUNT; A TRAIN TRIP GOES WRONG

'So, what do you make of the head being sawn off after death, Sergeant?'

'I don't know, sir. I suppose it could be to hide the victim's identity.'

Wright Watson lit a pipe and leaned back in his chair. As he puffed out the tobacco smoke, the Detective Chief Inspector tried to take in the facts surrounding the latest death.

'That makes sense, Makepeace: no head, no name, no clothes, no obvious identifying features.' Watson looked at his number two, ran his hand through his hair, cleared his throat, then continued. 'Do you think that this victim had anything to do with the organ loft murders, Harry?'

Makepeace shrugged. 'I have no idea, sir; there is no evidence either way, is there?'

Watson shook his head. 'No, there is none. What troubles me, though, is that there is no obvious sign the man was murdered.'

'I agree, sir. The doctor could only propose that our victim had starved to the point where his heart gave out. There was the bruising on his hands, of course, suggesting the man had been tied up at some point.'

'He might have refused food to assure his demise, I suppose, but he could not have sawn his own head off and then disposed of it.' Makepeace laughed. Watson snorted.

'I think we can assume that foul play was involved, Sergeant, even if *post mortem*. Has anyone been reported missing within the last few weeks?'

'No sir. No-one.' Makepeace shook his head vigorously. 'I checked thoroughly. Apart from Edward Smith, that is.'

'I know, Harry. I know.' Watson sucked his teeth. 'Had you heard that Gertrude Rankin was back in Hartley?'

Makepeace laughed. 'Her? God help us!'

'She was released from prison some three weeks ago.' Watson waited for Makepeace's reaction.

'You mean just before Burchill was killed?'

Wright Watson nodded.

'And you think there might be some connection?'

The Detective Chief Inspector nodded again. 'I do not believe in coincidences, Sergeant.'

'Why would Gertrude and her tribe want to murder Burchill and Burford, sir?'

'Remember why Miss Rankin was sent to prison, Harry. It all revolved around the Parish Church celebrations. Why not return to the scene of the original crime and continue where you left off?'

'Isn't that rather obvious?'

'Perhaps so, but if you believe in your cause passionately enough, and you have been incarcerated for the last three years, unable to fight your fight, why waste time when you have been given back your freedom? Would you not want to get on with it?'

Makepeace looked at Watson. 'Yes sir, I would; I would think that there was no time to lose and every reason to move forward while I still had the opportunity! Why kill two organists though? What purpose would that serve?'

'What better way to scupper the plan to make the Parish Church a cathedral and Hartley a city and all that would give this place?' Watson opened his arms as he turned to the office window and looked out over the smoking chimneys.

'A plan put together by the leading men of the town, all of whom have strong views about the role of women.'

'Yes, Harry. And those leaders all stand to lose, and lose significantly, if we are not looking out at Hartley Cathedral within the next two years.'

Makepeace joined Watson at the window. The business of the day was being conducted in the way it was done every morning, every afternoon, every evening, and had been conducted since water and coal and iron and wool had been forged together to create the industrial cauldron that was the town of Hartley. The two detectives watched the horses and carts and carriages and men and women and boys and girls; lives being lived, singly and collectively. Stall holders were selling their wares all around the central market place. An organ grinder wound the handle of his instrument while the monkey sat on his shoulder. From time to time, pennies were dropped into the animal's collecting tin.

Makepeace tapped on Watson's arm. 'Do you see what I see, sir?'

'Yes, I do, Sergeant. Quickly! We must give chase!'

The two men strode out of the office, down corridor and stairs and onto the street. The suspect was still there, in the distance, talking to the organ grinder.

'Gently, Sergeant. We do not want to arouse suspicion, do we?'

'No, sir.'

Watson and Makepeace walked steadily up Market Street. They were within twenty feet of their destination when the organ sounded again. The suspect had finished his conversation and begun to move off. The two detectives quickened their speed so as to remain within striking distance of their prey. Within a short while, the suspect had turned off Market Street down a narrow alley lined with yet more shops, the occasional ale house, an undertaker's establishment and, at the far end, a small Methodist chapel.

The distance between the policemen and their suspect lessened as the chase continued into Church Street.

'Where are they headed, sir?'

'Difficult to say, Makepeace. It could be Hartley Central. The boat train to Liverpool is due in fifteen minutes.'

'And then a boat to America, sir?'

'That's my fear, Sergeant. Let us close in!' Watson quickened his pace; Makepeace followed dutifully, amused to see they were marching in step.

The suspect looked around, as if to make sure they were not being followed. Watson pushed his number two into a shop doorway to avoid detection. Once it became clear they had not been noticed, the two policemen emerged back onto the street and continued the hunt. The distance had grown again, and there were times when the pursuers felt they were not on the right track. Then the suspect was sighted once more, and they quickened their pace.

'It **is** the station, and the boat train is the aim!' The Detective Chief Inspector nudged his Sergeant as the suspect's destination and intent became clear.

Watson began to run; Makepeace joined in the chase. The porticoed entrance to Hartley Central was in plain sight. The station rose like a great Greek temple out of the random array of untidy old buildings, soon to be demolished as part of the grand city plan. The two detectives bounded up the steps, anxious not to lose their suspect in the crowded entrance area. Watson motioned to Makepeace to split up and circle round the two sides of the massive hall. A hundred conversations echoed round each other underneath the dome, adding to the cacophony of whistles and snorts and puffs and growls from the locomotives beyond.

The suspect had bypassed the ticket office and made straight for platform number one, where passengers for the boat train waited in large numbers. Watson and Makepeace pushed past the inspectors at opposite ends of the platform and began to make their way towards each other. The suspect had to be somewhere amongst the expectant throng. The Detective Chief Inspector cursed himself for not having apprehended the fugitive sooner. He could see his Sergeant advancing towards him, checking out the waiting passengers as he did so. Watson saw the huge billows of steam heralding the arrival of the boat train, like a monster emerging angrily from its cave-home. The noise was deafening, even as the beast slowed its advance into the station. People pushed towards the edge of the platform, making it difficult for the two detectives to do their job. A warning whistle from the locomotive told them to keep back, but few took any notice.

Watson and Makepeace simultaneously caught sight of their prey once more. The suspect stood motionless, staring straight ahead, seemingly unaware of the recent pursuit and their imminent capture.

'Police! Stay where you are!' Watson shouted, but the cry fell on deafened ears. The beat of the locomotive's puffing and pounding grew ever louder as the train slowed to a near halt. Finally, the suspect turned and saw the Detective Chief Inspector. Looking the other way, the prey observed Makepeace advancing purposefully towards the middle of the platform. The Detective Sergeant paused briefly to move a blind man out of the way.

The two detectives were now but a few yards from the suspect, who looked both ways and then shouted 'I am innocent. Please believe me. They made me do it!'

Though the cry could not be heard above the sound of the iron monster close by, Wright Watson knew me-mo well enough to read the suspect's lips and respond. 'You are under arrest! Stay where you are!'

The suspect shook their head and advanced towards the edge of the platform.

'No! Don't do it!' The detectives shouted at the top of their voices.

As the locomotive drew near, the suspect looked both ways and then down at the track. Before Watson and Makepeace could make their next move, there was a jostle amongst the passengers nearby. The prey was pushed forward, losing their footing as a result. Now prostrate on the track, there was no time for a rescue, no chance of being saved. The engine driver put the brakes full on at once, but the impossibility of halting the train was clear to all. Apart from the final clanking of the locomotive, there was silence all along platform one.

'Reverse, man! Reverse at once!' Wright Watson gesticulated to the driver, who did his best to move the train back along the track.

'Move back everybody! Move back at once!' Makepeace did his best to calm the crowd and clear the area. He twirled his rattle in the hope of attracting nearby uniformed officers, but none arrived. The ticket officers formed a passable substitute once the Detective Sergeant had located them and given orders.

The locomotive finally began to reverse. Boat train passengers craned necks and heads out of the windows, trying to get a view. Two children were sick as they beheld the sight.

'Stand back! Stand back, I beg you!' Watson pushed the gawping crowd near him away from the platform edge. Once he felt it safe to do so, he jumped down and made for the body. The engine had now stopped. The driver walked along the side of his locomotive and joined the two policemen on the metals.

'Is he dead, sir?' The driver took off his cap, as if in answer to his own question.

Makepeace shook his head. 'I fear so!'

Watson bent down and put his ear to the suspect's mouth. 'He still breathes, Sergeant. He is alive! He is trying to say something.'

'What is it? What do you want to say?'

The suspect looked up and pointed to the crowd. 'They did it! They are the ones to blame! Not me!'

With that, Edward Smith's eyes glazed over. The former Organist and Choirmaster of Hartley Parish Church, and then of St David's, innkeeper at *The King's Head,* was no more.

The engine driver looked at Watson and Makepeace. 'Did he fall or was he pushed?'

CHAPTER 37

LAVERNE TRIUMPHS; BANKS BREAKS DOWN; SMITH DECEIVES; WATSON LOSES CONSCIOUSNESS

C hoir practice on Thursday evening, the 23rd of October, was a sight - and a sound – to behold. In the wake of the festal service the previous Sunday evening and the brilliance of the playing, the choristers (man and boy) were eager to find out more about the new organist, even if he had only been appointed on an interim basis.

Charles Verney was to take the rehearsal, with Stanford George assisting (though nobody was entirely clear what the Vicar had meant by 'assistance'). As agreed, Olivier Laverne would accompany the singing and play for the major services until further notice.

The evening did not go to plan. Stanford George's train back from Leeds to Hartley was delayed because of a derailment, and Verney was nowhere to be seen. This was most unusual for the trusty Assistant Organist, as he prided himself on being on time for everything, mainly because Burchill had made sure of it over the years. Nobody dared thwart TAB: never; ever.

The Parish Church clock struck seven thirty. The singers could not bear it. Choir practices always started on time. It could not be otherwise. Even from beyond the grave, TAB was looking at his pocket watch, tapping with his foot, looking around with his accusatory stare, making the choristers stand as one, and raising his baton ready to begin. Sutcliffe and

Snelgrove nodded to each other. The two men approached Laverne as he sat quietly and patiently at the harmonium. Sutcliffe was the first to speak.

'Mr. Laverne. I am Warburton Sutcliffe, the choir administrator, and this is my colleague, Ernest Snelgrove.'

'The lead tenor. Yes, you have a very fine voice, Mr. Snelgrove. I appreciated your solo last Sunday evening. It brought tears to my eyes. And you are also a good singer, Mr. Sutcliffe. Your bass range is exceptional if I may say so.'

'How do you know that?' Sutcliffe looked at Laverne's cloudy eyes.

'I have very sensitive hearing.' Laverne laughed. 'I heard you talking about me a moment ago. And the answer is, yes.'

'Yes, what?' Snelgrove looked at Sutcliffe.

'Yes, I will take your choir practice this evening. I have directed singers before. It will be a pleasure and a privilege, given the wonderful reputation of the Hartley Parish Church choir.'

'You heard me and Ernest whispering to each other a moment ago?'

Laverne nodded and laughed. 'I am afraid so, gentlemen. How do you say it in English? You will have "to mind your Ps and Qs," I think, from now on.'

Snelgrove and Sutcliffe returned to their places in the choirstalls. 70 pairs of eyes looked at Laverne; 70 sets of vocal chords hummed quietly.

Within minutes, the diminutive figure standing by the harmonium had captivated the choristers. Even Thomas Augustus Burchill could not have inspired such awe. How could a sightless person know so much about the singers; could pinpoint exactly which chorister was off-key; could treat the choir as a single unit and as 70 different individuals all at the same time? There was not a moment of mischief from the choirboys, nor any element of waywardness from the 'back row', as Burchill always called the adult singers. Laverne even mimicked TAB's mannerisms and sayings, to the point where some of the men wondered if the great doctor had been reincarnated inside the tiny Frenchman.

Laverne insisted the rehearsal be conducted entirely without accompaniment; nothing was to detract attention from developing the purest tone possible. Within an hour, ears had been sharpened and voices tuned in ways not previously experienced. The music was prepared to perfection within the time allotted: not a minute more; not a minute less. As the practice concluded, the choristers burst into a warm round of applause, intermixed with cheering from the younger singers.

Once the choirboys had been dismissed (Sutcliffe having completed the attendance records), Laverne was asked if he wished to join the men for a drink.

'Yes, I will. I would like that. On one condition: that you buy me a pint of your English beer.'

The laughter that ensued echoed round the choir vestry. Snelgrove and Sutcliffe took Laverne in hand and marched him towards the *Cross Keys*.

'I did not think someone from Paris would like beer, especially of the northern variety.' Sutcliffe queried.

'Ah, that is where you are wrong, Warburton. I am half English, and some of my training took place in London, so I am perfectly capable of appreciating the good points about this country of yours!' Laverne sensed the choristers looking at him and weighing him up.

How was it that someone so small and slight could command the respect and awe of a worldly-wise choir of experienced and accomplished singers who would never suffer fools gladly, as Stanford George had so bitterly found out?

'Is that what you think of me, gentlemen?'

'What do you mean, Mr Laverne?' Sutcliffe downed the last of his beer, studied his empty glass and motioned for a top-up.

'Please, call me Olivier, or even Oliver, as some of my fellow students used to call me in London. You know what I mean. I sense these things. Nothing escapes Laverne.'

'We realised that this evening, Oliver!' Snelgrove snorted. 'Tommy Burchill is alive and well – in you!'

'That is the greatest compliment anyone could ever bestow! A toast to the great man! To Tommy!' Laverne raised his glass.

They all raised their glasses. As they did so, two souls drinking quietly in the corner of the room looked at each other and smiled.

'Have you heard of him, Charleton?'

Mann nodded. 'Yes, of course. A great player. I met him in London more than once. But I never had any connection with the schools for the blind, so I cannot comment on Laverne's training, whether in England or abroad. More tea, Percy?'

Banks shook his head. 'Burchill knew Laverne well enough to issue an invitation to play at Hartley. He is a brilliant player, I give him that, but there is something very strange about this Frenchman. Where did he train? And why is his English so good? TAB never mentioned him to me, of course, though why should he? I have always left the musical part of the service to Tommy; and the concerts and recitals. Do you have any sherry, Charleton?'

The great bells of Yorbridge Cathedral struck the hour. Mann went over to the sideboard, took the top off the decanter (given to commemorate the 25th anniversary of his appointment as Organist and Master of the Choristers) and filled two large glasses almost to the brim.

'Here you are, Percy.' Mann handed the glass to Banks who took it and downed the sherry in one go.

'Banks! I have never seen you like this before! And you and I have known each other for more years than I care to remember! What is the matter?'

The Vicar of Hartley looked up at the Organist and Master of the Choristers of Yorbridge Cathedral, then buried his head in his hands.

'I have sinned, Charleton. I have sinned grievously. These murders are all my fault. I know it!'

'I am sorry, but I must ask: is this your husband?' Wright Watson looked at Sarah Anne Smith. Her face was the palest he had ever seen; her stance bent and worn. Before, she had been a bold, confident lady; now there was a shrivelled-up woman, dressed forlornly in black.

Makepeace held up the sheet covering the body, then waited while the formal identification was completed. How many times had he done this; how many more times would he do it before his career was complete? He was a happy Sergeant; proud to be a detective; content that Wright Watson commanded him. Ambition was no longer important to Harry Makepeace, if ever it had been.

Sarah Anne Smith looked at the dead man's face. 'It is as if he was asleep and will wake up any minute now.' She stroked his face, then bent over and kissed him on the forehead and the mouth. 'Yes. This is my husband, Detective Chief Inspector. This is Edward Smith.'

'Thank you, Mrs Smith'. Watson nodded to Makepeace, who laid the sheet down over Smith's upper body.

'Will that be everything, Mr Watson?'

'Yes, thank you, Mrs Smith. My condolences to you. We would like to ask more questions, but not now. That can wait till a later day. Would you like me to arrange for a constable to escort you home?'

Sarah Anne Smith shook her head. 'That is very kind of you, Mr. Watson, but there is no need, I can assure you. I will walk home. The fresh air will do me good.'

'Very well, Mrs Smith.' Watson nodded. 'Sergeant, see Mrs Smith out, will you?'

'Of course, sir.' Makepeace opened the mortuary door and waited until the newly-widowed woman left.

Watson went back to his office. He went over to the window and looked out. For a few moments, he saw nothing of interest. Then, he noticed Sarah Anne Smith walking on the opposite side of the road up towards the railway station. Watson reminded himself that her house was in the opposite direction. He ran out of his office, down the stairs and into the street. Once again, Watson was on the chase. Makepeace asked him where he was going. 'Not now Sergeant, not now!' he replied.

Sarah Anne Smith quickened her pace. Watson followed. Was she escaping Hartley, just as her husband had attempted to do? The woman looked around once, twice, thrice, to check that she was not being followed. On each occasion, Watson managed to evade detection. As before, the organ grinder was at his work, playing the same tunes as the previous day. At first, it looked as though Smith would walk past the man, his monkey, and his music, but then she stopped, put a coin in the collecting tin, then engaged him in conversation, just as her husband had done. After a few moments, the organ grinder handed her a small parcel, doffed his cap to her, then continued with his performance.

As Watson was attempting to catch up with Sarah Anne Smith, a fracas broke out on the street between two men much the worse for wear. The Inspector tried to walk round the impromptu fight, but as he did so, one of the combatants was punched so hard that he bumped into Watson, who took a tumble, hitting his head on the cobblestones. The last thing he remembered was a vision of Sarah Anne Smith, dressed all in white, singing like an angel while she thrust a dagger into his stomach.

CHAPTER 38

BANKS BEGINS TO REPENT

'Are you alright?'

'Yes, dear, I am quite well, thank you.' Percy Banks nodded, smiling weakly at his wife.

'You seem awfully pale. Was your train delayed?' Rose Banks watched as her husband gave his overcoat to the maid, brushed down his hair, straightened his waistcoat and jacket, then walked into his study, where the fire was burning brightly.

'I had a good deal of business to transact with Dr Mann and I missed the through train to Hartley as a result. Then the connection from Wakefield was late. All in all, it was a dreadful journey. Would that we had a better service!'

Rose Banks rang the bell for the maid to attend. Once the servant had arrived, she ordered tea and cake for her husband.

'I think I will have something stronger in the meantime! Fetch me the port, Rose.'

She did as she was told, walking over to the far side of the room to retrieve the decanter and a glass. Her favourite song – *her song* – by TAB lay open on the piano. Humming the tune to herself, she poured a large glass of her husband's favourite drink.

'Here you are Percy. Rest awhile now that you are home.' She put her hand on her husband's shoulder. 'You seem so troubled. You were once happy in your work; and you and I were such good companions. I wish with all my heart that it could be so again; for your sake, for my sake, for the children's sakes. Can we not try to change?'

Banks took Rose's hand and kissed it. 'I fear too many things have happened for you and me to be man and wife like we used to be. We have both sinned in our different ways. I have not been entirely truthful with you of late. This business with the cathedral proposal has taken its toll on my constitution and my mind. Then when I learned that you were so affectionate towards Burchill, I – well - I turned elsewhere for comfort.'

'But Percy – nothing ever happened between me and Tommy! Yes, he gave me piano and singing lessons, and wrote those pieces for me, nothing more! I have always maintained my innocence, and I always will. I married you, not him! Yes, I admired TAB very much, but as a musician, not a man, I swear to you!'

'So you say, Rose. And part of me so wants to believe you; I have always wanted to believe you. But I cannot get it out of my head that you had an *amitié amoureuse* with that man: with my Organist and Choirmaster!'

'It is simply not true! I would never do anything like that!'

Percy Banks shook his head. 'I really wish that were the case, Rose. I really do!'

Rose Banks sank back into her armchair and put a handkerchief to her face as she sobbed. After a few moments she stopped and looked up. 'What do you mean you "turned elsewhere for comfort", Percy?'

'I meant nothing. Forget what I said!' The Vicar of Hartley took a large swig of port.

'I do not believe you, Percy. It meant something. We may have been estranged in recent years, but I still know you too well to dismiss words like that.' Rose got up and came to kneel in front of her husband. 'Tell me! I can forgive you if you forgive me. Is Christianity not about forgiveness?'

The Vicar snorted. 'Would that it were about forgiveness! Not in Hartley it isn't!' He downed the rest of the port. 'Fetch me another, now!'

Rose Banks filled the glass then sat it down on a small table next to his chair. 'Look at me, Percy. Look at me!' She cupped his cheek in her hand. 'What has happened? What have you done? Where did you seek "comfort"? Was it with another woman?'

'How dare you ask me that, Rose! Who do you think I am? What do you take me to be?' Banks shouted.

Rose Banks paused for a moment, then stood up. 'If there is nothing more you want of me, Percy, then I intend to retire.' She looked at her husband in the hope that he would ask something of her, but there was no reply. She turned and left the room.

Banks heard the door close gently. He stared into the embers of the fire for many minutes, then glugged down his drink, spilling some of the liquid on his chest as he did so, then threw the glass into the shimmering coals.

'Damn!' he shouted. 'I should not have told Mann my secret! It was a moment of madness to tell him.'

Percy Banks got up and paced round the room. 'I could not bear it anymore! I had to tell someone else. Mann is right. I have to stop this madness! Now!'

Banks went over to his desk, sat down, and reached for the button underneath. Pressing it, a concealed compartment sprang open. He slipped his hand into the hidden drawer and took out a bulky envelope. Inside were four smaller envelopes. Banks emptied the contents of each one and spread them out on the desk. There were 100 photographs in all, now carefully placed in chronological order of receipt, up to and including 28th September 1879.

Banks removed everything from the desktop, including the inkwell presented by the adoring parishioners of his previous incumbency, then picked up the photographs in turn. The earlier ones were the most 'artistic'. He traced the lines of the bodies, smiling as he did so. 'I should not be doing this!' Despite this self-admonishment, he continued. The later depictions were stronger in style. The art was nevertheless appreciated and had been from the first. There was always a sense of wondrous anticipation when the envelopes arrived. Firstly, the thrill of secrecy: it was something that Percy George Banks knew about: nobody else in his household comprehended; no-one had the slightest inkling. Secondly, there was the anticipation: waiting all day until he was finally alone in his study, with the door locked. Thirdly, and finally, taking out the new envelope and inspecting its contents, the enjoyment heightened in the knowledge that the others around him – his wife, his children, his servants, his curates – thought that he was writing his sermon.

Banks had persuaded himself from the beginning that collecting and inspecting illustrations such as these was not in itself a sin. After all, one only had to read *The Song of Solomon* to know that. Banks and Burchill had even joked about a partnership to write words and music based on the

Old Testament text! Why not appreciate the human form? God created man in his own image – images such as these!

At least the earlier ones. They were beautiful, these women. There was no doubt about it. Number nineteen was the most beautiful of all: an angel above all angels: that beatific smile; the perfect form. God is love! And this was love in human form!

Banks traced his finger over the later photographs. Why had he agreed to accept this material? It had stopped being art, he knew that. He had known it from the very beginning; but it excited him. The illustrations were 'classically' posed, it was true, but the scenes were out of his mind, out of any man's mind.

Then came the later photographs. At that point, Banks began to wonder who was supplying this material. One face – a man's – had stood out from illustration number 73. Though the features were not clear, it was obvious enough who had been photographed. Then came picture 79, and another familiar face. It was not possible to stop, not only because the envelopes fulfilled the Vicar's artistic needs, but also because there was no way of knowing and then stopping the person who was sending them.

Banks thought back to the first encounter with 'Clarabella'. It had been innocent enough. He had stood there, listening to the organ grinder playing a silly tune that he remembered from his youth. He could not pass without reminiscing about his childhood. After all, poor though these people were, they were still his parishioners and he needed to engage with them. That had been twelve months ago, but Banks could smell the odours, hear the sounds, and see the sights of Hartley as clearly now as then.

The organ grinder had turned out to be remarkably erudite. As he continued to turn the wheel and keep an eye on the monkey, he had regaled the Vicar with stories of Hartley and its history from the year dot. On subsequent visits, the organ grinder had turned to politics, economics, music and, finally, art. By now, Percy Banks was mesmerised by this unusual man. It became part of his regular routine when walking the short distance from the Vicarage to Hartley Central. Given that the incumbent of Hartley had to make frequent visits to London, Leeds, Wakefield, Halifax, and every part of England (especially to preach) by train, the priest and the organ grinder became firm friends.

Banks looked over the illustrations once more. What a strange relationship it had been! For some reason – and he never determined what it was – it had been easy to talk to this man. To tell him things he never told anyone else. There they used to be, in the middle of Hartley, some silly tune playing, the monkey chattering away, with Banks talking to the organ grinder about contemporary art. That was when it started. Banks had been offered sight of a picture – pictures – of foreign artworks. How the man had come by them was never explained, but the initial illustration had been accepted and retained. For a good while, it was the only picture. Then, some weeks later, another had been proffered. It was only high art, after all; especially number nineteen.

Banks shook his head; he should have gone to the police. But what was the crime? Who was the perpetrator? Banks resolved that carrying out his own investigations had been a mistake. At the time, it had seemed the right thing to do: to make discreet enquiries without alerting either the people producing the artwork or Hartley CID. A scandal had to be avoided at all costs, especially when it involved his parishioners and – the ignominy of it – two of his choirmen!

That was not the worst of it. If Clarabella was supplying the artwork, and Percy George Banks was Hautboy, then Open Diapason was Thomas Augustus Burchill and Algernon Burford, it turned out, was Cornet. Clarabella had been threatened with exposure, but to no avail, for the organ grinder demonstrated clearly and easily how it would be possible to ruin all their reputations. The next thing Banks knew, Burchill and Burford were both dead. Someone – Clarabella perhaps, or the brains and the power behind the organ grinder, more likely – had made sure that Banks was the only one left who could reveal the dark secret to the world; the Vicar would have nobody to corroborate his evidence.

Banks gathered up all the illustrations and took them over to the fireplace, where he threw them on the flames; all except number nineteen, which he put back in the secret compartment. Having locked it, he had a last glass of port. Once that was drained, he walked out of the room and ascended the stairs. As he got to the top, he stopped and looked at the door to his wife's bedroom. He then turned the other way, walking along the landing to his own chamber.

CHAPTER 39

A NEW CHASE IS ON; TAYLOR AND VERNEY ARE BOTH IN TROUBLE

Harry Makepeace rarely visited Wright Watson's house. In all the time the two men had worked together, whether as bobbies on the beat or in the CID, the Detective Sergeant had hardly ever paid his commanding officer a visit at home. 'There's always a first time for everything', his mother used to say. It was her favourite phrase. Hilda Makepeace had used those words on her death bed.

Harry Makepeace wondered how Watson would be. The assault of the previous day had rendered the Detective Chief Inspector unconscious. Even when Watson had come round, he had talked little sense. Back at the station, the police doctor had pronounced him fit after a cursory examination but recommended he take the rest of the day, and the following one, off work. The day after that being Sunday, Watson would be ready to start the new week fully rested.

The knock on the door was soon answered. Makepeace thought Nancy Watson pretty in a plump sort of way. He detected the smell of baking and remembered the delicious pies that Mrs Watson baked for her husband to take to work for his lunch. The Inspector always shared the confection with his Sergeant.

'He is still in bed, Harry. I made him stay there, though he is the worst patient in the world! You can have him back as soon as you want!' Nancy Watson and Harry Makepeace both laughed. She pointed to the stairs.

Makepeace tiptoed up to the bedroom, keen not to disturb Watson if he were asleep.

'No need to be quiet, Sergeant. I am awake and in full possession of all my faculties.'

'I am pleased to hear it, sir. Good to see you!'

'Pull up a chair, Harry.' Watson waved impatiently.

There was only one seat in the room. Makepeace carried it over to the bed and sat down. 'How are you feeling, sir?'

'I told you, Sergeant. I am well. Don't believe anything that my wife tells you. The sooner I get back to work, the better.'

Makepeace laughed. 'I don't think you need worry, sir. She agrees with you, though she worries so. Just like my wife!'

'All women worry, Sergeant, except perhaps for the woman that we are dealing with.' Watson shook his head.

'You mean Sarah Anne?'

The Detective Chief Inspector nodded.

'Is she behind the murders? Including killing her husband?'

Watson laughed. 'I wish I knew, Harry. There is something going on. My brush with those men was no accident, I swear it. That fight was for my "benefit". It allowed Mrs Smith to escape. She must have known I was following her.'

'And Sarah Anne ordered those men to start a brawl which ended with you unconscious on the pavement?'

'Yes. I believe that was the case. Remember, Harry, that this woman has "acquaintances" among the men of Hartley. They would probably do anything for her. And if they did not, then there would be hell to pay when their wives found out, would there not?'

'I suppose there would, sir. By the way, we have been unable to find the organ grinder. He has disappeared off the face of the earth. What do you think was inside the envelope he gave Mrs Smith? And what was the connection between the man and Edward Smith?'

'If we knew that, we might have the key to these murders. Get the men to redouble their efforts at finding our organ grinder, Harry.'

'Of course, sir. And what about Mrs Smith? She has gone to ground also, as far as we can tell. There has been no sign of her at *The King's Head* since she left the police station yesterday. That Grimshaw woman was there when I went earlier today, and she swore blind that the landlady had not been back.' Makepeace took out his notepad to remind himself of the morning's interview.

'Grimshaw?'

'Yes, sir. The cleaner and general help at the public house. She also does the same at the Parish Church and the Vicarage.'

'Ah yes, I remember. We saw her with Sarah Anne and that blind girl. What was her name? It sounded strange if I remember rightly. We were at the Parish Church for that service. When was that, Sergeant?'

Makepeace flicked through his notepad. 'It was the 5th of October. And she was called Ottavina; Ottavina Badland.'

'And blind?'

Makepeace nodded as he closed his notepad. The two policemen remained silent as the footsteps on the stairs turned into hands holding cups of tea.

'I assume that you take milk and sugar, Harry. Wright likes it strong and sweet, so I thought you would too! And there is a piece of pie for each of you.' Nancy Watson smiled at her husband. 'How do you find him, Detective Sergeant?'

'I find him very well, Mrs Watson. His old self, believe me!'

Nancy Watson laughed. 'I will leave you two gentlemen to your detecting. I have the kids to look after. That will do me!'

Once they were alone again, the two policemen pondered.

'Do you think Sarah Anne is a Rankinist, Sergeant?'

'I thought they were against men, sir.'

'Not as such, Harry, but they believe they are equal to the male of the species. They want to be allowed to do everything that we can do – and more!'

'It will never happen, sir. Not in our lifetimes, thank God!'

'Be that as it may, Detective Sergeant, we have already noted the "coincidence" of Gertrude Rankin's release from prison and the commencement of the organ loft murders. And what did Edward Smith say as he lay dying on those train tracks?'

Makepeace took out his notepad once more. It took him several moments to find the relevant page. 'He said, "I am innocent, I swear it!

They did it! They are the ones to blame! Not me!" Those were his exact words; I remember them well.'

'You will notice, Sergeant, that he said *they*. More than one person. Who knows what these women will not do to further their cause? Go downstairs and wait for me. I will be shaved and dressed in ten minutes. I think we need to talk to Gertrude before any more happens in Hartley!'

'Is my carriage ready, Eccleston?'

'It is, Sir Templeton.'

Taylor looked at his elderly butler. He would have to go. Albert Eccleston made too many mistakes, and that could not be tolerated any longer. When the latest business in Hartley had been concluded, the butler would be pensioned off.

'Very well, Eccleston. I am on my way!' Taylor put down his copy of the *Gazette and Argus,* took a last drink of his morning coffee, stood up, brushed down his jacket and trousers, and walked out of the room. Eccleston followed meekly behind. At the front door, Taylor waited while the butler helped him into his coat, gave him his hat, gloves and cane and then led him out to the carriage. The driver was standing by his horse, so Eccleston opened the carriage door and helped his master up. As the door clicked shut, Sir Templeton called out: 'I will not be long. Just a few papers to sign, then the deed is done!'

'Very good, sir!' Eccleston noticed that the driver had already clambered back up onto his seat. The butler's back was bad that morning, so the lack of a greeting was the least of the old man's worries.

Taylor settled down to the glowing anticipation of a meeting where he would sign an agreement with Banks about St David's and the transference of ownership of land from Hartley Parish Church to his own organisation. He pulled out a cigar and tried to light it; not easy when the carriage was jolting him to and fro so violently. Taylor looked out of the window; what a strange route from Templeton Towers into Hartley! Rather than taking the macadamised road (the most direct way), the driver had chosen an old dirt track. It would still lead down into the town, but take twice as long, and be four times as uncomfortable.

'Stop! Stop at once! You are going the wrong way! Where are you taking me?'

Sir Templeton's orders went unheeded as the driver cracked his whip and the horse sped up.

'Stop! Stop! I will have you punished for this! Who are you? Don't you know who I am? You will obey me now!'

The ride was unbearable. Taylor fell onto the floor; he was unable to get up, wedged as he was between the two seats. Then he could sense the carriage slowing down. The wheels were turning on a smoother surface. The confused passenger tried to get up, but without his cane, it was impossible. Then the carriage stopped, and the door opened.

'Will you please get out?'

'Who are you? What are you doing? What is the meaning of this?'

'Will you please get out?'

Templeton Taylor looked up. A figure dressed all in black, with a veil over the face, stood waiting.

'Who the hell are you?'

'You will find out in due course, Sir Templeton. Now for the last time, will you please get out?'

Taylor managed to clamber up and stumble out of the carriage. As he turned to the driver, he felt a sharp pain on the back of his head, then collapsed to the ground, wondering what would happen to his plans for Hartley.

It was the best performance of his life. Burchill would have been proud of him. Not a wrong note; not an expression mark missed; not a nuance lost. The organ sang like never before. Having ended this triumphant performance, Charles Verney swung his legs over the side of the organ bench, jumped down onto the floor of the organ loft, then strode down the steps and into the north aisle. Hartley Parish Church was full to overflowing. The audience stood, cheered, clapped hands, stamped feet, shouted, 'more, more, more!' Verney bowed slowly and slightly to acknowledge the praise, then raised a hand to calm his frenzied admirers.

The Vicar came forward and shook Verney by the hand. 'I knew you had it in you, Charles. Will you please accept the post of Organist and

Choirmaster at Hartley Parish Church with immediate effect? And at a salary commensurate with your exceptional talents! £400 per annum for Sunday services only in the first instance. What do you say to that?'

Verney was speechless. 'Of course; I accept! It would be an honour to serve!'

The Assistant Organist of Hartley Parish Church opened his eyes and looked around. 'What? Where am I? Who are you?'

The next thing Verney knew, a glass of water was being thrown over his face; then another; and another.

"You are serving no-one, Verney. Nobody but us. Do you understand! Do you want to live? Then do everything we tell you!'

CHAPTER 40

A MARCH, A MISSING PERSON, A MAN TRANSFORMED, A MYSTERY

'Wake up. It is time.'

'I am sorry, sisters. My time in Woking prison has weakened my body. I have barely slept for any length of time over the last three years.' Gertrude looked at her carers; both were in tears.

'What brutes they were. How could they?'

The leader of the Rankinists laughed. 'Very easily. The solitary confinement was the worst thing. But I did not let the loneliness break me. Quite the contrary. It strengthened my spirit, for I had the time to formulate my plans.'

'We admire you so, Gertrude! You are an inspiration to us all.'

The leader of the Hartley and District Women's Social and Political Union sat up on the chaise longue where she had been napping. She tried to stand, but then thought better of it.

'So, all is ready?'

The members of the sisterhood looked at each other, then nodded at their leader. 'All is prepared!'

'Good. Let us proceed. Help me up!'

Two of the sisters held out helping hands, which Mother Gertrude was only too happy to take.

'It will all have been worth it! I have waited long for this day. The hour is upon us. Come; we must advance. Let battle commence!'

The sisterhood laughed and cheered as their leader walked to the front door of number 82 ready to begin the fight. The cold made Gertrude Rankin catch her breath. It felt strange to be out in the open air; spaces seemed so large; day-to-day noises crowded out rational thought. How different it had been in Millbank! One of the sisters squeezed Mother's arm, just as her son had done as a child.

'Stanford!' Gertrude whispered to herself, smiling as she remembered the newborn at her breast. 'How different life might have been if I had not married the wrong brother!' The house was still there, standing as proud as ever atop Hartley Moor.

'What is the matter, Mother Gertrude?'

'Nothing, sister. Absolutely nothing. I can assure you.'

'But you have tears in your eyes.'

Gertrude Rankin shook her head. 'Nonsense, sister. I am not used to fresh air. It makes my eyes sting! Quick – give me a handkerchief! Now let us begin.'

The sisterhood marched forward. Their numbers grew as the procession wended its way into the centre of Hartley. The singing began, quietly at first, then ever louder, as the members of the Union gained in confidence. Crowds began to form on the pavements as the women strode towards the Town Hall. Most stood in silence, some booed, and a few cheered.

'This will be a triumph! Our triumph! My wilderness years are over!' Gertrude Rankin could see the civic buildings ahead as she shouted out to her followers. The last time she had been here was to be tried and sentenced at the law courts. No more servitude! Liberation for women from now on!

The boos drowned out the cheers, but the sisterhood were unwavering in their determined marching towards the civic centre of Hartley. Eggs were thrown and obscenities shouted but the women took no notice. The Town Hall steps were soon reached; Gertrude Rankin ascended them. Reaching the top, she turned to address her followers, raising her hand to still the cheering sisterhood. As she was about to speak, she noticed a figure at the side of the street. Her eyesight was as sharp as ever, despite the years of prison.

'Whiteley!' She mouthed. The man in the bowler hat nodded.

'Dear, sweet, Whiteley! All these years!' Gertrude whispered.

'Speak to us, Mother. We wait for your order to begin the fight!'

Gertrude Rankin was rooted to the spot. 'But I was told Whiteley was dead. And Stanford had been sent to live with relatives in Australia. But my beloved is here! Here in Hartley! Is Stanford here too?'

'Speak to us, Mother, please! Just say the word!'

Gertrude Rankin looked across the street once more; the man had faded away, just as a dream dies at the dawn of day. Having regained her composure, the leader of the Hartley and District Women's Social and Political Union began to speak.

'Sisters! This is our day! We will not be swayed from the cause! We are here to fight the good fight! We will...'

Those were the last words that Gertrude Rankin spoke before two uniformed policemen grabbed her from their vantage point immediately inside the imposing doors of the Town Hall. Bobbies rushed out from the side streets to detain the members of the sisterhood before they could escape. The hostile elements of the crowd made sure any woman trying to make an exit was unable to do so.

'Gertrude Rankin. I am arresting you for breaking the terms of your licence from prison. I am now going to read you the relevant section of the Riot Act. If your followers do not disperse when I have done so, they will be held in custody and prosecuted! Do you understand?' Wright Watson demanded, breathlessly.

There was no reply, the only reaction a smile.

'Do you understand?' The Detective Chief Inspector pointed at Gertrude Rankin then turned to the assembled sisterhood. 'You are all under arrest!'

'Wait, Inspector. You would do well to make haste slowly.'

'Why should I?'

'Before you imprison me and my sisters, you should ask the officials inside this building if Sir Templeton Taylor arrived for his business meeting this morning.'

'What do you mean, woman?'

'Just do as I say, Inspector.'

Watson nodded at Makepeace, who ran into the building. After a short while, the Sergeant reappeared. 'Sir Templeton should have been at the Town Hall two hours ago.'

'What is the meaning of this, Mrs Rankin?' Watson barked.

'What do you think it means? You are the policeman, not me.' Gertrude Rankin laughed. 'And I am "Miss", not "Mrs", if you please.'

'What have you done with him, woman? What have you done with Sir Templeton Taylor?' Watson looked around as the sisterhood cheered. 'My God, this is all we need!'

⋯⋯⋯⋯◆◆◇◆◆⋯⋯⋯⋯

Charles Verney had been glad to finish his shift after a long day, and an even longer week: the worst of his life. He knew it would get worse before it got better, assuming it ever did. But there was a chance – just a chance – of a brighter future at Hartley Parish Church. He thought back to 28th September, not quite a month before. What a stunning performance! TAB had been at his best; the choir had been at its best; and he, Charles Verney, Assistant Organist at Hartley Parish Church, had been superb, though he said it himself. Then his world had been changed irreparably with Burchill's murder. How could he have been so stupid, so foolish, so naïve as to think the Vicar would make him Organist and Choirmaster in succession to the 'master'? His remembered all the slights and insults and degradations he had suffered over the years. At least Burchill 'knew his stuff' when it came to playing the organ and training the choir, but what about people like Banks? He and the Organ Trustees were a cut above ordinary working men. And Charles Verney was a working man; nothing more.

Verney had been hit on the head when checking the organ blowers at the Parish Church. He awoke in unknown surroundings. His captors had said he had a chance to redeem himself; and he took it! How strange that at the point where he thought he was to lose his liberty and perhaps his life, he had gained a kind of freedom: freedom from being the dutiful servant; freedom from others telling him what to do; freedom from his own subservience. Thanks to his new colleagues, Charles Verney had a golden opportunity; a chance to settle all the old scores he thought would never be settled. That would show them! All of them!

But what if he got caught? Then how would things turn out? He wrapped his scarf tightly round his neck and pulled his cap down hard as he walked through the factory gate. Verney whistled as he walked towards the Parish Church, determined to follow his instructions to the

229

letter. What if he were caught? Better to die infamous than live a mouse! He guffawed. Faint heart never won fair lady! 'Not that my mistress is especially fair', he muttered.

***

Ernest Snelgrove was glad the day was over. The shop had been busier than ever. All those people! Only later had he found out why there had been such a throng. Think of it! Those women marching through the streets and threatening to take the Town Hall over. Then the news about Sir Templeton Taylor being kidnapped. It had all been good for business; he was run off his feet. Still, they needed the money more than ever. 'It's an ill wind that blows nobody any good, eh, Mam? I'll be up in a minute'.

Snelgrove cashed up then locked the till. He walked to the door and put the key in the lock. Looking through the glass and out into the October evening, he saw a small figure clad all in black advancing toward the shop. Snelgrove deliberated whether or not to retreat and evade this strange customer. His initial action was to lock the door and turn around, but something made him change his mind. He waited for the figure to shuffle into his emporium.

'I suppose you want to place another advertisement in the *Gazette and Argus*. Do I assume the same words as last time?'

The customer nodded and handed Snelgrove a piece of paper. He took out his glasses, put them on the end of his nose and read out the sentence:'" RIP Edward Smith, former Organist and Choirmaster of Hartley Parish Church. This is a memorial to all thwarted organists through the ages". That will be ...'

Before he could complete his request for money, the correct change had been pressed into his hand and the customer was gone. Snelgrove traced his finger over the words. It seemed so strange that, as on the two previous occasions, the text had been cut out from the newspaper and pasted onto the sheet. Why not just use pen and ink? Snelgrove pondered for a moment then decided his mysterious visitor was unable to write but could perhaps read enough to find the right words in the newspaper. That had to be the explanation, he determined, and thought nothing further of the incident.

CHAPTER 41

FINAL PLANS ARE PUT IN PLACE; MANN MEETS HIS MAKER

The tree was coming into bloom. Soon it would bear the most luscious fruit imaginable. How long had it taken to grow? Too long! There had been so many slights and innumerable indignities suffered over the last ten years and more. But then, 'of human virtues, patience is most great; everything comes to he who waits.' The wait had been long, certainly. There were times when it had been tempting to act; to let battle commence. Caution had won the day on every previous occasion, and rightly so.

The momentous hour was now at hand. All was ready; nothing taken for granted; everything planned and executed. Burchill, Burford, Smith - dead; Stanford George, and his 'uncle' - discredited; Banks – compromised. Time to pick the fruit. Templeton Taylor's disappearance was unplanned and unforeseen, but it could be employed to great advantage. It was a godsend, in truth.

The scissors cut through the morning's edition of the *Gazette and Argus* as a scythe mows hay. Memories of youth on the farm came to mind! The work of harvesting had not ruined the hands; later work in the mill had done that. Where once there had been elegance and delicacy there were fingers and thumbs like gnarled bark. Bat-acute hearing was heading into muffled oblivion by the incessant sound of looms: hour after hour; day after day; night after night, with no respite, even at this age. The voice was still firm and bright, if across fewer notes than formerly. The keyboard technique was dulled and the ability to memorise complex music all but gone through lack of practice. The heart, mind, mission, and purpose were stronger than ever. Hartley would never be the same when the year was over!

The excisions finished, the author laid letters and words on the blank page in the required order. One by one, the cuttings were pasted in, then smoothed over with a tight fist. Excess glue was wiped away and the whole left to dry. While this happened, the author played the piano: music (waltzes for the most part) by Burchill, Burford, and Smith. Once the messages were ready, their creator checked them, in turn. The first, to be deposited at Hartley Police Station for the specific attention of Detective Chief Inspector Wright Watson, read:

'If you wish to solve these organ loft murders, look no further than Gertrude Rankin. That woman and her sort have much to answer for. Who else would want those poor men dead and buried like that? What was the sisterhood doing at the time of the killings?'

The second message, addressed to the Reverend Canon Dr Percy George Banks, was simpler:

'You know what you have to do, Vicar. It would be a pity if your wife and children became the victims of your stubbornness.'

It was cold outside, but the task of delivering the letters was soon accomplished, without detection. Then home, to plan the final murder.

'Do I have to appoint this man? He is not my sort; not my sort at all!'

Charleton Mann looked at Percy Banks. The Vicar of Hartley had aged visibly since Burchill's death: the hair was greyer, the face thinner, the stance less confident.

'What have you got against Laverne? He is a wonderful player. Is it that he is blind? Do not be afraid, Percy. He plays better than most sighted men can! I don't mind admitting it: he is a better organist than I am!'

Banks snorted. 'Surely not, Charleton. I have always admired your playing. I know TAB thought that you were the very best!'

'I know. And Burchill was a good player. But nothing like Olivier. Really, Percy. You would do well to make Laverne permanent.' Mann put a hand on the Vicar's shoulder. The eyes were bloodshot. 'I am worried about you. Make a decision, then let your new Organist get on with the job in hand!'

'But does he know the service? He is – well, he is a Frenchman!'

'Oh, Percy'. Charleton Mann laughed. 'Olivier is as English as he is French, I can assure you. He speaks the language as well as we do; I have heard him play for cathedral services. There is nothing to worry about.'

'And what about the choir? How can a blind person see to the choir?'

'Just like Tommy or I would do. Olivier Laverne may not be able to see, but he can hear, and smell, and touch, and feel and sense.'

Banks sat back in his armchair and sighed. 'I suppose you are right, Charleton. I have to admit that his playing at the service recently was of the first order; the very best, in fact. Tommy would have been proud. And, according to Verney, Sutcliffe and Snelgrove, the choir practice taken by Laverne the other evening was beyond compare. The singers are all in favour – to a man and boy.'

'Then what are you worrying about?'

'Would a man like Laverne be – well -- be good enough to be a cathedral organist? What will people think?'

'I will vouch for him at any and every meeting of the College of Organists! He will be welcomed with open arms. Men of his standard will do much for our profession: raising standards; improving our status.'

'Status, Charleton?'

'Status, Percy. We are not servants; we are professionals. And we deserve recognition as such!'

Banks clasped his hands to his mouth and tapped his feet. 'Very well, Charleton. On one condition.'

'Yes?'

'That you go and talk to him now, before you go back to Yorbridge. If you are satisfied that he can do the job, then I will appoint him permanently to the post.'

'And if – when -- Hartley Parish Church becomes a Cathedral?'

'Well, I am not sure that…'

'Trust me, Percy. Olivier Laverne will be well capable of being a Cathedral Organist and Master of the Choristers. Thanks to Tommy Burchill, you are already a cathedral in all but name, at least in terms of the music!'

'Very well. But please go and see Laverne. He will be at the Church, practising. I gave authority for an hour a day on the instrument. It uses so much water! We cannot afford more.'

'I will see him, as you suggest. Do not limit his time for playing, Percy. It is an insult to a great player to have to watch the clock, and the water!'

Banks smiled and held out his hand. Mann took it. Having exchanged final pleasantries and moved to the front hall, the Organist and Master of the Choristers at Yorbridge Cathedral donned his hat and coat, took the cane proffered by the Vicar's maid, waited for her to open the door, then began his walk to the Parish Church. He heard the clock strike. There would be time for a brief discussion with Laverne before his train left for Yorbridge (changing at Halifax and Wakefield).

Hartley was not Yorbridge, and Charleton Mann found himself coughing as he began to inhale the smoky air. Looking round the town centre, he counted no fewer than twenty mill chimneys belching away. Then there were the steam locomotives and their carriages, coming and going. By the time that Mann reached the Parish Church, his eyes were itching, and his coat covered with specks of soot.

Mann was surprised to be greeted by Charles Verney.

'I did not expect to meet you here!'

'It was the least I could do, Dr Mann. You have been so helpful to the Parish Church in finding an Organist and Choirmaster for us. Dr Banks asked me to be in attendance. He said you might call in on your way home.'

'In difficult circumstances, Verney. I have never encountered anything as curious as these killings. What are people calling them? I forget the phrase.'

'The organ loft murders, sir. Though Edward Smith met his death at Hartley Central railway station.'

'Smith? Of St David's? The one who was sacked all those years ago?' Verney nodded.

'Well, I never! Now I would like to meet Mr – or should I say "Monsieur" – Laverne. It is some years since we last met. It will be good to renew our acquaintance! I remember that wonderful recital he gave for me at Yorbridge. His Bach was immense!'

'Of course, Dr Mann. Mr Laverne is in the blowing room.'

'The blowing room! What on earth is he doing there?'

'He wanted to know more about how the instrument was winded. I took him down there and left him to inspect the machinery. Would you care to join us? I don't think you have water engines at the Cathedral, do you?'

'Gas, Verney. The organ is blown by gas engines at Yorbridge. More efficient – much more efficient!'

'I think you will find Grindrod's engines superior, Dr Mann.'

Mann laughed. 'We shall see, Verney. We shall see! Now lead on! I want to meet with Olivier!'

Verney led the way. Mann found the stairs steep and narrow.

'Mind your head, sir! Oh – sorry Dr Mann – too late!'

Mann rubbed his forehead where it had hit the hard, low, stone ceiling. Once underneath the church, the narrow corridor opened out into a series of large rooms. Flickering light beckoned Verney and his guest towards the far chamber.

Mann coughed and sneezed. 'It is very dusty down here. Is this place never cleaned? Look at my coat!'

'Sorry, sir. The lady cleaners could sort it for you if you like.'

'No matter, Verney. Now where is Laverne? I have a train to catch!'

'Just in here, Dr Mann.' Verney pointed towards the tanks that fed the hydraulic engines.

'Laverne! Olivier! How good to see you!'

The figure standing by the water supply turned round.

'Wait a minute. By Jove! You are not Laverne! Who on earth are you?'

There was no answer. Suddenly, Mann felt an extreme pressure on his throat. He tried to pull the hands away, but to no avail. The air became sparser as his neck became more and more constrained.

'No! Please! No! I beg you!'

Mann was pushed forward. His head was soon immersed in the water tank. He could no longer inhale without ingesting water. The Organist of Yorbridge Cathedral began to hear music; sweet harmonies; heavenly melodies. Then nothing.

CHAPTER 42

THREE INTERVIEWS: RANKIN; TAYLOR; LAVERNE; ALL WITH CONSEQUENCES

'Where is he? What have you done with Sir Templeton Taylor? Have you done away with him?'

'I am saying nothing, Inspector, until you release the members of the sisterhood.'

The woman stared straight ahead, resolutely avoiding Wright Watson's questioning gaze.

'This is a serious matter, Miss Rankin. If you do not reply, then you will go back to prison for a very long time.'

'And your women friends will go with you. That would never do, would it? Your delicate sisters banged up in a terrible prison!' Harry Makepeace laughed.

'How dare you! My sisters are brave warriors. I have known prison. The others are ready to join me. They will fight the good fight to the end; until we triumph, believe me. We deserve recognition; we need equality; we demand the vote!'

'Not in my lifetime! What do you think, sir? Do you think women are our equals?' The Detective Sergeant looked at his commanding officer and winked.

'That is a very interesting question, Makepeace. I think we may find the world turned upside down before long!' Watson stood up and went to sit on the edge of his desk, immediately next to Gertrude Rankin. 'If I release your "sisters", for the time being, at least, will you tell me where

Sir Templeton is? And who killed the other men? Which of your followers did the deed? Who are the murderers?'

'What other men, Inspector? Murder? We are peaceful protesters. We would never harm anyone, let alone kill them.'

'And yet you have detained Sir Templeton, have you not?' Watson leaned over and looked Gertrude Rankin in the eye.

'I will not answer that question until you release my sisters. I tell you this, though, Mr. Watson, I know of no Rankinist who would take a life, even that of a man! I have given strict orders that no one – and I mean no one – is to be harmed; ever!'

'Have you ever heard of Dr Thomas Burchill?'

'Of course! Everyone has heard of Burchill! Members of the sisterhood even sang in his choir before he got rid of women singers! Not that he should have done that! I never heard of anything so ridiculous!'

'Then you and your sisters would have a grudge against him!'

Gertrude Rankin laughed. 'We have more important things to fight for than women singing in church choirs! What does it matter? Females are in the Choral Society are they not? They perform next to the males there, do they not? They are welcome in the Methodist Chapels, are they not? Why should they be bothered about being excluded from the Parish Church Choir?'

'Have you ever heard of Algernon Burford?' Watson returned to his seat and waited for a reply.

'No, I have not, Inspector.'

'Are you sure?' Watson stroked his chin and looked at Makepeace. The Detective Sergeant shrugged in response.

'I am certain. The name means nothing to me.'

'What about Edward Smith?' Makepeace asked.

Gertrude Rankin laughed. 'A good many people are called "Smith", Sergeant!'

'But only one was a former Organist at the Parish Church.' Watson added.

'I am none the wiser. Now will you *please* release the sisters. You may do as you will with me, but free them. Do it now!'

Watson shook his head. 'Not until you tell me what you have done with Sir Templeton Taylor and why your blessed sisterhood killed those three organists?'

'I have told you, Watson, the sisterhood had nothing to do with those murders; nothing!'

'What about Stanford George?'

'Stanford? Stanford is dead? It cannot be! No! No! No! Please – tell me that he is alive!'

Watson stood up, leaned over the desk, and barked at his guest. 'Why is that so important to you, Miss Rankin?'

'No reason; no reason at all.' Gertrude Rankin looked down at her feet.

'I do not believe you, Gertrude Rankin. What is Stanford George to you? Why would it matter to you if he were dead?'

'If he were dead? Does he no longer live?'

'What does it matter, woman? Why is Stanford George important?'

Gertrude Rankin burst into tears. 'Because he is my son! That is why!'

'Will you agree to help us?'

'No, I will not! For the last time, release me! If you free me now, then I will not take any action.'

'You are in no position to dictate terms to us, Templeton Taylor!'

'Sir Templeton Taylor to you! And from next year it will be Lord Hartley!'

'And that is why we want you to help us!'

'Who are you anyway? Why the masks? Reveal yourselves to me, and I will listen to your demands!'

The two figures looked at each other, then back at Taylor. They shook their heads. 'We are not at liberty to divulge our identities.'

Sir Templeton observed his captors. They were tall, slim, slight; not old, judging by the lightness of their voices. The noble-lord-in-waiting tried to recall the appearance of the carriage driver who had brought him. The hat had been pulled down so far over the head that the face could not be seen; apart from ruddy cheeks and pale, soft skin; and delicate hands that had not seen rough work. And his prison must be somewhere near Hartley, given the route the anonymous cabbie had followed. Templeton

Taylor was a Hartleyian through and through. His family had been there for generations; always would be, until the day of judgement.

'I may not know who you are, but I know where I am.'

'What do you mean?'

'Tell me what you want, and I will tell you where we are. And then it will not be long before I have revealed your identity to the police! There will be all hell to pay!'

The two captors looked at each other and shook their heads.

'We do not believe you', said one.

'You could not possibly know where you are, Taylor.'

Sir Templeton laughed. 'Oh yes I do. I am at Hartley Vicarage.'

The final chords of Bach's great *Fantasia and Fugue in G minor* rolled around the empty building. The organ bellows refilled as the sound died away.

'What a wonderful instrument this is! One of the best I have ever played! Monkhill is a fine builder; and Burchill knew what he was doing when he designed the organ. A pity that TAB had to die in such a horrible fashion.' The player pushed in all the stops, turned the blower switch to the 'off' position and listened for the exhalation of air that signified the stopping of the hydraulic machinery. Footsteps could be heard at the back of the nave. They grew in volume; slow, deliberate steps. The visitor was now mounting the stairs into the organ loft.

'Are you ready for tomorrow, sir?'

'All ready, Verney. I am looking forward to it so very much, but please, why so formal? Call me Olivier, and I will call you Charles. At least in private. A certain amount of decorum must be observed when we are in public, not least in front of the choir – men as much as boys. In front of them, and everyone else for that matter – clergy, congregation, choral society, glee singers and so on – I propose that we call each other "'Mister". Are we agreed?'

Verney looked at the new Organist and Choirmaster of Hartley Parish Church. What a contrast he was with Burchill! TAB had been tall and broad and loud and gruff; Laverne was petite and slim and soft and gentle. Where Tommy was six feet tall, Laverne was less than five. One could see;

the other was blind. Past and present Organists had one thing in common: an incredible presence that dominated all around. Olivier would be a worthy successor; and there would be no more loyal assistant to the new man than Charles Verney.

'Charles?'

'Yes sir – I mean, yes, Olivier.'

'What do you make of the business with Dr Burchill and Dr Burford, and then Edward Smith?'

'I do not understand. What are you saying?'

'They were murdered, were they not?'

'I do not know, Olivier. Dr Burchill might have drowned; Dr Burford's death could have been an accident and, well, Edward Smith slipped and fell onto the railway track, did he not?'

'Is that what they are saying, Charles? Do people really believe that? Three unfortunate accidents, all to organists with links to Hartley Parish Church?'

'If you put it like that, Olivier, it does seem very strange; quite a coincidence.'

Laverne laughed. 'No coincidence, I fear, Charles.'

'Do call me Charlie, everyone else does. Even old Tommy called me Charlie!'

Laverne paused for a moment. Verney thought that his new colleague was looking at him as if sighted, but then the moment passed, and Laverne turned away to gaze emptily at a pillar instead. 'No, I would rather call you Charles. That is more – how do you say – more respectful. And you deserve respect. I will be counting on you in the future, Charles Verney; we all will.'

Laverne walked over to the organ loft stairs where Verney was standing and put his arms round the Assistant Organist.

'Now take me to my hotel. You can advise me on what I should do about more permanent accommodation.'

'That I will do, and gladly, Olivier.'

As the two men walked out of the Parish Church, others were busying themselves in the crypt preparing the late Dr Charleton Mann, Mus Doc, FCO, for transport to his final resting place.

CHAPTER 43

REAPPEARANCES AND RELATIONSHIPS

Albert Eccleston had not slept since his master left for his business meeting in Hartley the previous day. The joyous pealing of bells calling the faithful to worship at the Parish Church gave him no comfort. The loyal butler would not rest easy until Sir Templeton Taylor had been found, alive and well.

'I should have questioned that cab driver before I let Sir Templeton get in. I knew there was something suspicious about him!'

The maids smiled sympathetically at Eccleston as he lambasted himself out loud for his error. They then got on with their Sunday morning chores, ignoring the old man as he watched and waited at the front door of Templeton Towers. He remembered the day they had moved into the grand edifice. What an opening ceremony, complete with Burchill and the Parish Church Choir! The singing had been exquisite, as always. Edward Smith had played the organ, though not before his wife had got him sobered up well enough to play. What a spat that had been! Dr Burchill stamping and shouting at Smith; then Smith's wife threatening the good doctor: 'I will see you rot in hell, Thomas Augustus Burchill.' Eccleston could still hear the words echoing round the great hall.

The butler looked up at the ornately-cased instrument. He remembered how Sir Templeton had assembled all the house servants and lectured them on the symbols hidden in the carving, including the depictions of Taylor himself! The butler had taken to Monkhill as he put the innards of the organ together. It had been fascinating to watch the organ builder construct the instrument. The two of them even drank together after normal working hours, Monkhill answering Eccleston's questions about how an organ worked. Grindrod, on the other hand, had been an awkward so-and-so, constantly grumbling about the poor water supply and the difficulty of getting enough water pressure to make the hydraulic engines work properly; shouting at everybody; turning up at all hours; leaving a mess everywhere; never engaging in conversation with anyone. Even Sir Templeton was given the cold shoulder.

Eccleston snapped out of his reverie. A carriage was pulling up by the front door. The old butler prided himself on his excellent hearing; Monkhill had even offered him a job voicing organ pipes! It was the same carriage that had taken Sir Templeton away. And now here the master was, back at the Towers!

The butler opened the door as fast as his bones would allow him. The carriage had already turned round and moved away. Sir Templeton was just standing there, resting on his cane.

'What is the matter?'

Taylor beckoned to his butler. 'Help me up the steps, Eccleston. I have not had the use of my legs since I last saw you!'

'Oh, sir! What became of you? We were all terribly worried! Here! Lean on me as you walk. One step at a time!' The butler gasped as he took his master's weight; he bore his burden dutifully, nonetheless.

'Stop here, Eccleston! I will rest awhile on this sofa. Bring me a drink.'

'Tea, Sir Templeton?'

'Tea? No, you bloody fool! Whisky! And a large one! Now!'

Eccleston had never run so fast in his life. It was less than five minutes before he was back with a silver tray on which sat a large glass.

'What is the matter, sir?' The butler was shocked by his master's gaze.

'Who is that Ecclestone?' Taylor pointed at the organ, perched at the far end of the great hall atop its minstrels' gallery.

'I do not know, Sir Templeton.'

'Did I not say that no-one – but no-one – was to touch that instrument without my express permission?'

'No sir – I mean yes, sir!'

'Then who is that sitting up there at the organ? Tell him to come down, and now!'

Eccleston scuttled off to the far end of the hall and called to the unknown organist. There was no reply. He called louder; still no answer. The butler turned to Sir Templeton, who gesticulated for him to climb the stairs to the little loft below the ornate front casing. Eccleston wondered if his old heart would take it, but he managed to get there. Having surveyed the scene at the console, Eccleston turned round and shouted to his master: 'I think we had better summon the police, sir'. The butler then attempted to grip the rail at the front of the loft: in vain. Eccleston fainted before he could get a hold of the support.

'You may go.'

'What about the sisterhood?'

'They have already been released and sent on their way, Miss Rankin.'

'Why, Inspector Watson? I have not told you where Sir Templeton Taylor is being held!'

'No, you have not. But then, he is not being held.'

'What do you mean, "not being held"?'

'Sir Templeton sent word an hour ago to say he had gone away on business and not told his staff he would only return today. When he heard we were looking for him, he got one of his people to come and inform us of the misunderstanding. He has apologised for the inconvenience caused.'

'A man like Templeton Taylor apologising. My goodness! What a turn up for the books!'

'Watch your tongue, Miss Rankin. That man is well respected in Hartley; he has done much for the town!' Makepeace unlocked the woman's handcuffs as he spoke.

'He has, Sergeant, and made all that money in the process! On the backs of ordinary working people!

'And what of the other organists, sir? Do we not need to question her further?'

'Yes, Chief Inspector. Tell me about these other men. The ones that my sisters may have murdered.'

Watson laughed loudly. 'I doubt that Miss. They would not have the strength, even if they had the brains to carry out such crimes!'

'How dare you, Chief Inspector! Women can do anything that men can do, given half a chance!'

'But you and your Union have not had the chance, have they? We have found no connection between "Gertrude's ladies" and the organ loft murders.'

'And what about my son? What about Stanford?'

'What about him, Miss Rankin? Do you think he killed those other men, those organists?'

'No! Of course not, Inspector! Why would he do that?'

'So that he could become Organist himself. I gather that he was, briefly – very briefly.'

Gertrude Rankin smiled. 'What? My Stanford? Organist and Choirmaster at Hartley Parish Church?'

Watson nodded. 'Dr Banks was keen to appoint him but, well, shall we say there were difficulties.'

'Difficulties, with my Stanford? What happened?'

Makepeace looked at Watson, who determined, nevertheless, to answer Gertrude Rankin's question.

'I think – I think – I think it was felt that he did not have the experience nor the maturity to undertake such an important post.'

'What happened, Inspector?'

'He is to be Assistant Choirmaster.'

'Only an Assistant, Inspector? Assistant to whom?'

'A man called Laverne.'

Gertrude Rankin laughed. 'You mean Olivier Laverne?'

'Yes, I do. Do you know him?'

'I do. He was one of the few who showed me any kindness in prison. In the last months before my release, inmates like me were allowed to have some lessons, as a way of preparing us for release back into the world. He taught me to play the organ in the prison chapel. He was – is – a lovely man. I must meet him again to thank him for everything he did for me. Unlike some of the others in that horrible place.'

'I am sure you will be able to hear him regularly at Hartley Parish Church. He will be there now playing for the Sunday morning services.'

'I will. It will be good to renew my acquaintance with that wonderful man.'

'Have you touched anything?'

'No, Mr Watson. The body is just as it was when I – when I fainted.'

The Detective Chief Inspector looked around the loft and over the edge of the balustrade.

'You could have had a nasty accident if you had fallen the wrong way. I trust you are sufficiently well to answer our questions now, Eccleston.'

'Mr Eccleston to you! You are nothing special, so no airs and graces!'

'Now, now, Albert. Give the officers their due!'

A fourth person entered the tiny organ loft.

'Sorry, Sir Templeton. Of course. Gentlemen. May I leave you now?'

'You may, Mr Eccleston. The Detective Sergeant will take your statement once you are both downstairs. Makepeace, go with Ecc – Mr Eccleston.'

Watson and Taylor waited until they were alone and could talk freely.

'Are you well, Sir Templeton?'

'I am perfectly well, Chief Inspector. Why do you ask?'

'There was considerable concern about your whereabouts yesterday and earlier today, sir.'

'There was no cause for concern or alarm, I can assure you. It was a simple misunderstanding. I had a good deal to think about this weekend. It had slipped my mind that I would not be returning home until today.'

'And the threatening letter?'

'What letter, Watson? I know of no correspondence. Some ruse by the Rankinists. A mere prank. You know what those women are like!'

Watson sighed. 'Very well. I will ask no further. Do you know this person, Sir Templeton?'

'Sadly, I do, Inspector. It is Dr Charleton Mann, late Organist and Master of the Choristers at Yorbridge Cathedral. Along with Tommy Burchill, he designed this organ.'

CHAPTER 44

THE RANKINISTS ARE IN THE CLEAR; WATSON DRAWS CONCLUSIONS; SIR TEMPLETON TURNS

'What happened? Why did you let him go?'

'What were we meant to do? There was nothing more to say. He agreed to our demands. I could not believe it! Sir Templeton is one of us! He has long supported universal suffrage, at least in private. He will be a real asset to us in the House of Lords! He is not pressing charges. The great man even made excuses to the Police as to why he had "disappeared".'

Gertrude Rankin stroked her chin as she looked at the two bright-eyed sisters. 'I know, my fellow soldiers. Inspector Watson had no option but to let me and the other warriors go.' The leader of the Hartley and District Women's Social and Political Union rubbed her wrists where the handcuffs had chafed her skin. 'Our great initiative is somewhat thwarted.'

'How so, Mother?'

'I had expected much more resistance from Sir Templeton. Much more. I simply do not understand how or why he acceded to our demands so quickly and so easily.'

The two sisters looked at each other and blushed. Gertrude Rankin faltered as she stood up. 'Forgive me. I am still weak from my ordeals. I need to know what happened with Sir Templeton. You are not telling me everything. I can sense that. Now look me in the eye and describe what happened when you – when you "invited" him to join you.'

The older sister spoke. 'It was hard, Mother Gertrude. He is a dominant and stubborn man.'

'What? Balderdash! We women are strong! Stronger than men! Always remember that! You must never be cowed by the male sex! Never!'

'We know, Mother. But we still got our way.' The younger sister smiled.

'Yes, Mother Gertrude. It really is true that Sir Templeton – Lord Hartley – will support our movement from now on. He is a Rankinist through and through!' The older sister burst out laughing.

'Cease! Now tell me what happened to persuade Taylor – that's assuming you really have persuaded him – to espouse our cause!' Gertrude Rankin walked over to the sofa, aided by an assistant, then crumpled up and fell over.

'Mother! What is wrong?'

'Nothing. I am perfectly well. The cause is more important than the individual. Proceed! Tell me what happened!' Mother Gertrude adjusted herself and sat waiting expectantly.

'He will propose a vote from the House of Lords. He will campaign for the vote for women, and he will gather support not just from the Tory Party but across all political groups. He said that it will not be easy, but he already knows of men who will join him in the task.' The older sister then presented a letter to Gertrude Rankin. 'Read this. If you need proof of Lord Hartley's intent, here you have it.'

Rankin looked at the almost indecipherable scrawl on the envelope, opened it and took out the single sheet of paper. She drew a finger over the embossed coat of arms on the page, put on her spectacles, then read the missive. The writing was difficult to fathom, and it was several minutes before the contents could be digested in full. Once this work was complete, Mother Gertrude looked up at the sisters and smiled.

'This truly is an auspicious day. My congratulations to you both. I never thought you would achieve it. At least not without a good deal of "encouragement". I am so glad that was not necessary.' Gertrude Rankin sighed and smiled. She relaxed onto the sofa, then picked up the letter once more. 'Now tell me the truth – the whole truth. What hold did you have over him; what made Taylor write this?'

The elder sister walked over to Mother Gertrude. 'May I sit?'

'Of course, sister. We are all equal in this Union.'

'Thank you, Mother. You are correct. There was more to our acts of persuasion than meets the eye.'

'Go on, sister. Tell me everything. I will not be angry with you, I promise.'

'There are certain facts about Sir Templeton – Lord Hartley – that are not well known.' The sister blushed as she spoke. 'For all his faults, he has been a staunch member of the social purity movement, has he not, Mother?'

Gertrude Rankin nodded vigorously. 'He has indeed, sister. He is not all bad!'

'Well, what he says in public is not what he does in private.'

'What do you mean?'

The sister blushed even more. 'Well – well, he – he prefers the company of men to women.'

'And so?'

'I do not mean social company, Mother Gertrude. I am referring to far worse than that.' The sister burst into tears as she blurted out the news of Sir Templeton.

'I understand what you are saying, sister. You mean this "guardian of the righteous", as he calls himself, is far from what he seems! Calm yourself! Be strong! Tell me all!'

The sister looked at her colleague, still standing on the other side of the room, then back at Gertrude Rankin.

'Well, Mother, I have evidence of his sins – irrefutable evidence. So, I showed it to him. At first, he denied it, but I persisted. He eventually confessed – he had no alternative. It was then a straightforward matter to "persuade" him to join our cause.' The sister pointed to the letter that Gertrude Rankin still held in her hands.

The leader of the Rankinists folded up the letter and laid it down on the sofa next to her companion. 'What is the nature of this evidence, sister? Speak now!'

'Letters and photographs, Mother.'

'And where are they now?'

'Some of them I gave to Sir Templeton. Others are still in my possession, ready to be used as needs be.'

'And the other material?'

The sister smiled. 'Sir Templeton – Lord Hartley – thinks that he has the only copies, but he does not. I made sure duplicates were developed, and I know where the negatives are kept if required.'

'And who is implicated by this correspondence and these photographs, apart from Taylor?'

The sister looked down and shook her head.

'Please, you must tell me everything. The members of the sisterhood can have no secrets from each other.' Gertrude Rankin wagged her finger.

'Very well, Mother. The letters are to the Vicar of Hartley, the Reverend Dr Percy Banks, my husband.'

'Did Mann have to die?'

'There was no alternative. What else could we do?'

'Well, we could –'

'No, we could not, whatever it is you were trying to say. And you know it. Our plans would have been foiled. It would have become obvious what was happening. Charleton Mann is – was - the only person left who could make a clear identification. No amount of disguise on our part or misplaced memory on his would have prevented him from ruining our game. We agreed that we needed to be bold to see our plan through, and we have done so! Victory is ours!'

'You may say that and think that, but I am sad – so very sad – that Dr Mann had to be murdered. I always had a soft spot for him, and he for me. He was a kind old soul, and a fine organist in his day. He was such a delight when I started solo singing. He conducted my first *Messiah*.'

'There is no place for sentiment! Not now, not ever!'

'I know, but the killings must stop!'

'And they will. Come, do not be so down and disheartened. There will be no more "Organ Loft Murders", I promise you. Now we must get back to our work.'

'What should we do with the monkey?'

'Keep it as a pet and call it Tommy Burchill', came the reply.

Wright Watson looked at the body. Was there life after death? What would Thomas Burchill, Algernon Burford, Edward Smith, and Charleton Mann be doing now? Singing in some heavenly choir? Arguing about who should be in charge, more like. Mann was the oldest of the four victims and looked it, by a good margin. The white hair flowed from the centre parting down to each shoulder. Watson shivered as he touched the cold slab on which the cadaver had been placed. Leaning over the organist he noticed the bruising around the neck consistent with garrotting. The tongue stuck out and the eyes bulged. The Detective Chief Inspector next inspected the deceased's hands. How delicate they were – almost like a woman's! The long thin fingers were bruised and scraped where the victim had tried to wrest himself free from the hands that so brutally cut off his wind supply; just like when an organ is switched off, the bellows gradually empty until there is only the sound of silence and the stillness of motionless wood and metal, ivory, and ebony. Watson now knew how the instrument worked and found himself admiring the talent, skill, and expertise necessary to tame these great beasts, much as one needed considerable ingenuity to control a steam locomotive.

'Did the Rankinists do it, sir?'

'Hello, Sergeant. You gave me a fright there! I did not hear you enter!' Watson exhaled deeply.

'What is the matter?'

'Well, Harry, I do not think they did. I believe Gertrude Rankin when she says that she and "the sisterhood" knew nothing of these murders, just as I am convinced that "Mother" and her lady friends were behind the abduction of Sir Templeton Taylor.'

'Has he said anything more, sir?'

'Absolutely nothing, Harry. He swears that he was simply away on private business. Sir Templeton insists it is nothing to do with us as to where he was, and I cannot compel him to elaborate. There is no evidence to suggest that the Rankinists were involved, apart from Mother Gertrude's comments when we arrested her at the Town Hall.' Wright Watson paused for a moment. 'Nor have we found anything to incriminate the women when it comes to the organ loft murders.'

'Except one of them was a station platform murder, sir.'

Watson grimaced. 'But Edward Smith was an organist, like the other three, was he not?'

Makepeace nodded. 'And at Hartley Parish Church, until he got the sack.'

'Is that the connection, Harry? Person or persons unknown who wanted to discredit the Parish Church and its Vicar so that the decision about the new bishopric would go against Hartley.'

'Banks would also suffer if that were to happen, and we know he has gambled both career and reputation on becoming the Bishop of Hartley.'

'Wakefield and Halifax are the other contenders, I gather, but would they stoop so low as to have four people murdered? It seems incredible to think so.' Watson sighed. 'I had better ask the Chief Constable for permission to interview the Dean of Yorbridge. Someone needs to tell him about the murder of his Organist and Master of the Choristers in any case. I wonder who will apply for the job there!'

Makepeace shrugged his shoulders. 'Somebody who would kill for a salary of £400 per annum and a rich and healthy teaching practice, perhaps, sir?'

Ernest Snelgrove wondered if he would receive another visit from the mysterious shopper. The choir men had gossiped long into the night about Mann's murder. He purposely did not lock up until a full five minutes after closing time in case another advertisement was to be placed in the *Gazette and Argus*.

Snelgrove need not have delayed his supper. The Parish Church clock struck quarter past as he finally closed the shop and wearily trudged up the stairs to where his cold repast would be waiting.

At eleven o'clock, an envelope was pushed under the shop door. The shopkeeper knew what it was as soon as he opened for business the following morning.

CHAPTER 45

TWO PAIRS OF LOVERS ARE RECONCILED; MARTHA BURCHILL MAKES A DISCOVERY

Whiteley George listened to the peal of bells. The longcase clock in the hallway struck ten. There was still time to attend Mattins at the Parish Church, but the former Organ Trustee had lost much of his enthusiasm for worship ever since the near-debacle over the procurement of Grindrod's hydraulic machines. The land deal was secure, thanks to Burchill's death, tragic and unforeseen as that had been. George thought back to the arguments the two of them were always having and shook his head. TAB only ever agreed to participate in the town planning project to get the organ rebuild funded. The good doctor never wished for the money from all the concerts to be used for acquiring land. He had nevertheless gone along with it, until that final refusal to co-operate. It was just before the performance of Charleton Mann's *David and Goliath* at the end of September. TAB's smug face had said it all: his circumstances had changed and there was no need of the money from the land any more.

That had been it. The two men had parted. George had made Burchill promise to reconsider but the Organist and Choirmaster had never turned up to the meeting scheduled for the Monday afternoon. Whoever had murdered TAB had done George and the Organ Trustees a favour, sad as that seemed. Everything was now complete. Whiteley George smiled. There would be some very rich men in Hartley before the year was out.

Perhaps he would go to church after all. It would be good to cleanse his soul by listening to a first-class sermon from his fellow shareholder, the Reverend Dr Percy George Banks, soon-to-be the first Bishop of Hartley. It was a pity that Stanford would not be presiding at the organ, but there was still time for the boy to make good. At least he was alive, unlike other occupants of that unfortunate organ loft.

Whiteley George gripped the front door handle. As he did so he heard someone walking away from the house. He looked outside and saw a hooded and cloaked figure. 'Hello. Wait! Who are you? What are you doing here?' The figure picked up speed. 'No! Please! Stop!' George ran down the garden path. He soon caught up with his mystery visitor, who stopped, turned round, and pulled back the hood.

George gasped. 'You! I thought never to see you again!'

'It is over. Our secret is out.'

'Are you sure?'

'They had incontrovertible evidence.'

'What "evidence"?'

'Letters. My letters to you. And worse – some of our "art photographs".'

'Oh my God! I am ruined!'

'*You* are ruined? What about me? And stop damn well pacing up and down.'

Percy Banks and Templeton Taylor looked at each other across the Vicar's study.

'How can I give this sermon now?' The Vicar picked up his papers and threw them on the floor. 'How can I continue? What will become of me?'

Taylor walked over to Banks.

'Look at me, Percy. I will be in the House of Lords next week. I am a man of great power and influence already but from then on, there will be no stopping me. Our secret will not come out, I promise you! Here, take these.' Taylor handed over a large bunch of letters neatly tied up in a red ribbon.

'How did you get them?'

Taylor laughed. 'They were my "reward" for agreeing to support the Rankinists!'

253

'The Rankinists? My God, what have you done?'

'Only promised to do what I was going to do anyway, Percy. For all my faults, I believe in universal suffrage. I will be happy to lead on the push for votes for women when I am in government.'

Banks picked up the letters and caressed the ribbon. 'Who tied the bundle up like this, Templeton?'

'One of my captors. Why do you ask?'

'And it was their ribbon?'

'Yes, Percy. What of it?' Taylor sighed. 'Why is it so important?'

'You never found out who had kidnapped you, other than that they were Rankinists?'

Sir Templeton Taylor shook his head. 'No, Percy, they were careful to conceal their identity.'

'Where did they keep you?'

'How should I know? Somewhere in Hartley, not far from the town centre. Not far from here, in fact. At least I surmised that was the case.' Taylor looked out of the study windows. The Vicar's carriage driver was walking up the pathway.

'Come, Percy. You are safe; we are safe. Nothing ill will come of the episode. I promise you. Now gather up your papers and go to church. You have a sermon to give. Your congregation awaits. And your new Organist and Choirmaster, to boot!'

Banks smiled weakly at Taylor. 'Very well, Templeton. You go on ahead. I will join you shortly. I must compose myself a little first.'

'Very well, Vicar.'

Once Sir Templeton had closed the study door behind him, Percy Banks went back to his desk and opened the top right-hand drawer. Inside were bundles of letters to and from Rose; correspondence that the Vicar's wife had neatly organised, as she had done with all her husband's papers. He looked at the ribbons; the same colour and the same bows as the letters from Sir Templeton Taylor that he still held in his hand.

<hr />

'You remembered how I like my tea!'

'Of course I remember. How could I ever forget?'

'Whiteley! I am so sorry!' Gertrude Rankin put her hand on George's knee.

'What for?'

'For leaving you; you and Stanford.'

'You didn't leave us, Gertrude, you were arrested and imprisoned! In any case, you were not leaving us so much as abandoning your place in the home and denying your womanhood.'

'What do you mean "denying my womanhood", Whiteley?'

'I loved you, Gertrude. I hated what Wilson did to you, day in, day out. I would have done anything for you; I always will.'

Gertrude Rankin looked down at her half-drunk cup of tea. 'How is Stanford?'

'Stanford is well. He is not here at the moment.'

'Not here?'

'He is at the Parish Church. He is turning into a fine musician. He is one of the assistant organists there. I had hoped he would be Organist and Choirmaster after Burchill's death, but it was not to be. Stanford needs to gain more experience and additional qualifications before he is ready to take on a role as prestigious as that at Hartley.'

'I am sure you are right. It would be good to see him again. It has been a long time.'

'It has, Gertrude, and you will, as soon as he is home from the service. I am very proud of your son. Not a day passes but that I look at him and think of you.'

'My son, Whiteley? He is *our* son.'

'Our son, Gertrude? What do you mean?'

'You know full well what I mean, Whiteley George. I never let Wilson near me after I discovered what an utter brute he was. Stanford is your son; I assure you!'

Whiteley George wept. 'My son! *My son!*'

'Yes'. Gertrude Rankin took her brother-in-law in her arms and let him cry. When he was done, the two of them sat close to each other, holding hands.

'What happens next, Gertrude?'

'Nothing, Whiteley. Nothing can happen. Too much has happened for us to go back. I have my work and you have your reputation to think about.'

'My reputation?' George laughed.

'Yes, Whiteley. I know what you and your fellow Organ Trustees have been up to.'

'You do?'

Gertrude Rankin traced a finger over her former lover's lips. 'But I promise not to tell anyone.'

George's face reddened. 'Thank you. And your secret is safe with me.'

'What secret?'

'The one concerning Templeton Taylor and Percy Banks.'

'How do you know about that?' Gertrude tightened Whiteley George's bow tie.

'Ow. You are hurting me!'

'And I will hurt you some more if you do not tell me how you know about those two.'

'I saw them together once, at the Athenaeum club in London. I followed them afterwards. They went to a well-known haunt for men who engaged in the most unspeakable of crimes.'

'And what did you do about it?'

'Nothing, Gertrude. "Least said, soonest mended", as my mother used to say.'

'So how did you work out that I knew?'

Whiteley George looked away.

'Tell me, Whiteley! Now!'

'Because I was spying on Thomas Burchill! He was a partner in a land deal, but I did not trust him, so I had someone keep an eye on his comings and goings.'

'And what has that got to do with Banks and Taylor?'

'Annie, Burchill's maid.'

'What? But she is a sister! She is a Rankinist; a member of the Union!'

'Exactly.'

'She must have overheard the plans for Sir Templeton at our meetings at number 82 and told you what happened.'

Whiteley George nodded.

'Did Annie say how we knew about Banks and Taylor?'

Whiteley George shook his head.

'How could she betray me? How could she betray the movement?'

'Do not blame her, Gertrude. She does believe in your cause, I promise you. And your secrets are safe with me, my dearest. I promise you with all my heart.'

Rankin and George heard footsteps.

'That will be Stanford back from church. I think I should see him on my own first and tell him that his mother is here. Then I will call you in.'

Gertrude Rankin nodded. 'Very well, Whiteley.' She kissed him full on the lips as he went to greet their son.

———⋄⋄⋄———

Martha Burchill looked up at her father's portrait. She had lost both him and her fiancé in a matter of a few weeks. There she was all alone, except for a housemaid, at number 84, New Station Street. Would she stay there, or would she move elsewhere? There was nowhere else to go. Hartley was the only place she had ever known; she had rarely been outside Hartleydale and never ventured beyond Yorkshire. The sights and sounds of London were completely unknown to her.

She sat down at her father's desk and looked at the four drawers, two on either side of the central opening. She saw how the carpet was worn where her father had rubbed his shoes up and down in that impatient way of his. In two places there were burns where his cigar ash had fallen and scorched the flooring. She opened the upper left-hand drawer and took out its contents. Would she find any more incriminating material? Pray to God she had seen the last of those vile photographs. Martha Burchill breathed a sigh of relief as she worked her way through bills and receipts, then letters from publishers and music institutions. The second drawer on the left was devoted to papers concerning the College of Organists: past examination papers; meeting agendas, minutes, and related documents. Her father had been proud to become a Fellow and wore his academic dress with pride, whether it be his College hood or his Doctor of Music robes.

The right-hand drawers contained much the same sort of material, including a large envelope marked 'School for the Blind'. Martha spread the contents across the desk. Her attention was drawn to a photograph of staff and students. How young her father looked! Despite a slight tendency to chubbiness even then, he must have been an attractive man in his youth. She traced her finger along the rows of men and women whose graduation day had been so ably depicted in the photograph. One face stood out. She took out her father's magnifying glass from its box at the edge of the desk.

'I am sure I have seen that student on the front row before; but where?'

CHAPTER 46

A REWARDING DAY OUT FOR TWO POLICEMEN

'Sir. What do you make of this?'

The Detective Chief Inspector shook his head. 'I don't know what to think, Harry. I thought Sir Templeton's castle was grand enough, but this place takes the biscuit!'

Detective Sergeant Makepeace snorted. 'I have never seen anything like it! This is supposed to be the Dean's House – Palace more like!'

The two policemen surveyed the scene. The grand entrance hall was more like a cathedral than a home, its gothic arches stretching up to a sky-and-stars ceiling. All around, the walls were covered in serious-looking clerics, some in their religious robes, others in the best secular fashion of their day. Between the portraits were alcoves, each of which housed a marble bust. Laughter could be heard in the distance. Watson and Makepeace looked at each other as the great bell of Yorbridge Cathedral struck ten. Before the last knell of 'Great Richard', a pair of double doors opened at the far end of the hall. Out came a thin man dressed all in black. Watson nudged Makepeace as a way of drawing attention to the servant's gaiters and buckled shoes. The Detective Sergeant raised an eyebrow slightly in reply.

The servant looked at each of the detectives in turn, then sniffed. 'The Dean will see you now. You have fifteen minutes. Dr Kilbey is a very busy man. A very busy man indeed.'

'We understand. My Sergeant and I simply wish to talk to the Dean about the recent death – or rather murder – of Dr Mann.'

The servant said nothing, though both policemen later agreed that Kilbey's butler had reacted in a most queer way when the word 'murder' had been used.

The study was just as grand, in its own way, as the entrance hall. Dean Kilbey was a portly man, much given to imbibing port and other alcoholic beverages, judging by his ruddy complexion and gout-affected gait. 'Good morning, gentlemen. Do sit down, please. Chief Inspector Watson and Sergeant Makepeace, I presume. I do not believe I have ever had the pleasure of entertaining detectives before now. You will have to excuse me if I say little; I have an important meeting with the Chapter shortly to discuss Dr Mann's successor.'

'We understand fully, Dr Kilbey. We just have a few questions for you. In particular, we are keen to know if your Organist and Master of the Choristers had any enemies.'

'Any enemies?' Kilbey sniggered. 'What do you think, Chief Inspector? This is the Church of England! Mann had enemies; I can tell you. I can think of half a dozen people just here in the Cathedral Close who hated him.' The Dean pointed out of the french windows and across the lawn to the Georgian houses on the far side. 'Most of the Chapter, certainly.'

'Could we have their names, sir?' Sergeant Makepeace took out his notepad and pencil ready to write down the relevant details.

'No need for that, Sergeant. They might hate, but they would not kill, I can assure you!'

'Then who would want Dr Mann dead, Dr Kilbey?'

The Dean stroked his neatly shaved chin for several minutes, to the point where Watson and Makepeace wondered if the cleric was ever going to reply. Kilbey then cleared his throat. 'This is an organ loft matter, gentlemen. The competition for these posts is intense in the extreme. I could well imagine a man breaking the sixth commandment, especially if it meant he became Organist and Choirmaster at Hartley Parish Church.'

'Why Hartley in particular, sir?' Why not Yorbridge Cathedral or any other major church in England, for that matter?'

'Aha, Chief Inspector! There's the rub! Do you know what is so special about that place?'

Watson and Makepeace looked at each other, then at Dean Kilbey. 'No sir, we do not, other than that, thanks to Dr Burchill, it was the premier church choir in the land.'

'Indeed, it was, gentlemen. And for all my loyalty to this beloved cathedral of mine, I trust that it will continue to be so in the future. Most of the men in my choir are from Hartley, well trained by Burchill, I guarantee you! But that is not the reason why a man would kill for Burchill's position.'

'Then what, sir?'

'Hartley Parish Church is unusual – unique, in fact – in the Church of England, though very few know about the strange arrangement concerning the organ, and more pertinently in terms of your enquiries, gentlemen, the post of Organist and Choirmaster.'

'No-one has said anything to us before about this matter, Dr Kilbey.'

'I am not surprised, Watson. Banks and the Organ Trustees are sworn to the utmost secrecy and none - bar one - knows the details of the financial arrangements.'

'If that is the case, sir, why are you telling us now?'

'Because, Detective Chief Inspector, you need to know. It will explain much, I can assure you. But what I tell you I tell you in the strictest of confidences. You must inform no-one else, not even your Chief Constable.'

'That might be difficult, sir, if it came to an arrest and a trial.'

'Then, Detective Sergeant, I will not tell you if I do not have such an assurance; and please put that damn notepad and pencil of yours away, now!'

Makepeace looked down as he put his recording tools back into his waistcoat pocket. 'Sorry, Dr Kilbey.'

'We will give you such assurances, sir.' Watson sighed. 'I swear.'

'Very well, Inspector. I trust you.' Kilbey stood up and began to pace round the room, as if giving a supervision to his theology students. 'Back in the 18th century, a considerable amount of money was raised to pay for a grand organ in Hartley Parish Church. Dr Mann – a considerable expert in the history of that instrument – told me that when first constructed, the organ was the largest in the kingdom, and even had pedals.'

'And the import of this fact, sir?'

'I digress, Watson. My apologies. What is of relevance to your case – nay, central to its resolution – is the fact that the residue of the monies went to pay for the Organist and Choirmaster. The fund was set up not only to pay the postholder a most attractive salary, but also to buy land, whose ownership and rental income were to be vested in the incumbent of the organ loft at Hartley for the duration of his tenure of office. It was all to do with the politics of the age and the first Organist's commercial machinations. Since that time, the Organ Trustees have had oversight of the funds, though in practice, it was Burchill and his successors who are the sole financial beneficiaries of the arrangement and no-one, not least the Vicar of Hartley, can do anything about it.'

'And the value of this arrangement, Dr Kilbey?' Makepeace held his waistcoat pocket, feeling for his notepad.

'Only I and one other person, a Trustee, who shall remain nameless, know this fact. The value of the fund is £100,000 and the annual payment to the Organist and Choirmaster close to £3,000. As to the worth of the land, I leave that to your further calculation. That, gentleman, is why someone might commit murder in the organ loft.'

Watson and Makepeace stared ahead blankly. If they both worked for one hundred years, they would not have earned anywhere near the sum quoted by the Dean of Yorbridge. It was a different world, whose orbit was beyond their comprehension.

The door to Kilbey's study opened and the gaitered servant walked in and nodded at his master.

'I must go, gentlemen. It is time for the Chapter meeting. Remember what I have told you and stick to your word, for evermore!'

With those words, Dean Kilbey grabbed his papers and a small leather-bound notebook and rushed out of the room, his frock coat flapping as he did so. Watson and Makepeace saw the diminutive cleric walk across the cathedral close towards the Chapter House. At one point he stopped and took out his book and a pencil, then proceeded to draw lines across the page (or so it seemed to the detectives). Little did they know that the Dean of Yorbridge was crossing out names: Clarabella, Diapason, Hohlflute, and so on...

'What do you make of it all, Harry? Riches beyond compare. I cannot comprehend such a sum of money!'

'Neither can I, sir. But at least we have our motive. I would probably commit murder for that amount!'

'I fear that I would as well, though it pains me to say it!'

'Who is the Organ Trustee, I wonder?'

'I have my deep suspicions about Whiteley George. Remember the half-burnt document that we retrieved from his office? I still have it and think we should use it to help us force a confession from his lips.'

'Yes, sir, that seems the obvious course of action, especially when he – and Banks, for that matter – were pushing Stanford George as the next Organist and Choirmaster of the Parish Church.'

'At last, we are making headway in this case. And not before time!'

'What about Olivier Laverne, sir? Does he know what his remuneration will be? If so, might he not be implicated also? Perhaps he is in league with Banks and George?'

Watson nodded. 'You are right, Sergeant. We should interview Monsieur Laverne when our train gets back to Hartley. If only we did not have to wait for a connection when we get to Wakefield!'

Makepeace nodded. 'By the way, sir, the missus said I had to give you these bits of paper. She reads the *Almanac* and thought you should take a look.'

'What are they, Sergeant? I do not read sensationalist gossip!'

'I think you will be intrigued by these cuttings, sir!'

Makepeace handed over four small extracts from the *Almanac*. On the corner of each clipping someone – Watson presumed Mrs. Makepeace – had written the date. The Detective Chief Inspector read the material in silence, then rubbed his chin vigorously.

'Each one of these is a reference to an organ loft murder; all of them posted just after the killings took place.' Watson looked at his Sergeant.

Makepeace nodded. 'Is this our murderer taking great delight in advertising his handiwork? But why the reference to "thwarted organists everywhere"? Thwarted in their quest for riches, perhaps?'

The train pulled into Wakefield Kirkgate station. Watson and Makepeace waited for the connecting train to Hartley (via Halifax) in silence.

263

CHAPTER 47

LAVERNE REMAINS ELUSIVE AS NEW CLUES EMERGE

Watson and Makepeace determined to locate Olivier Laverne. The first stop was the Parish Church itself, in the hope (if not the expectation) that the newly-appointed Organist and Choirmaster would be practising. The building was open, but empty, save for the cleaning ladies. Makepeace squeezed Watson's arm and nodded ahead. The two men made their way towards the organ loft entrance.

Watson cleared his throat. 'Good morning, Mrs Grimshaw. How are you today?'

The woman took no notice and continued to polish the brass knob on the organ loft door.

'Mrs Grimshaw, may we have a word with you?'

The polishing became ever more vigorous.

'When I have done this and not before. And it is Miss Grimshaw, I will have you know!'

'Very well, **Miss** Grimshaw. We can wait. Will you be long?'

The cleaner chose not to reply. Watson and Makepeace sat in the north aisle pews nearest to the organ. The front pipe that had so grievously injured Algernon Burford was now back in place, though a close inspection of the lower sections revealed dents where the metal had come into contact with either the casework or the organist's head, or both. The extensive blood stains had been wiped away. A small vase of lilies stood next to the loft entrance as a memorial to the fallen organist.

Wright Watson was forced to admire the woodworker's craft as he looked up and down the two organ cases; the one facing across the chancel from north to south was the more ornate of the two, with its trumpeting angels atop long, majestic towers of pipes. Delicately carved foliage wove in and out of the metal. At the base of the case were verses from the scriptures; Watson remembered at least one of the quotations as coming from Psalm 150. The north aisle frontage was the plainer of the two sides, though there was something awe-inspiring about its plain grey pipes racked in order of size from large to small and then back to large. Where the rank dipped in the centre was what appeared to be a series of guns pointing to the back of the church.

'They must have called in the artillery, Harry.'

Makepeace nodded. 'They have the same arrangement at St David's, sir. I think once Burchill saw the set-up there, he had to have the same at St Martin's, only bigger!'

The two men smiled at each other.

'What are you laughing at?'

'Nothing, Miss Grimshaw. Nothing except those funny metal things up there!'

'Funny metal things? I'll have you know those are the pipes of the Tuba Mirabilis stop. It is the finest in the land. Dr Burchill was especially proud of it. That and the old Mounted Cornet immediately behind and above, up there in its own case.'

The old woman pointed to the top of the north aisle case. For the first time ever, the two policemen saw the cleaner's face in full perspective. There was a dainty prettiness about her visage that startled them, but before they could take in Gladys Grimshaw's surprising beauty, the cleaner had dropped her gaze and turned away.

'What do you two bobbies want, anyway?' The cleaner picked up her mop and bucket and began to walk back to the choir vestry where she kept her materials and equipment.

'We are looking for Mr Laverne.' Watson began to hurry after Miss Grimshaw.

'Well, he isn't here.'

'Hold on. Hold on, Miss! Why the hurry?'

'Because I have work to do, that's why. I don't have all day to "pursue my enquiries". Leave me alone, will you?'

'Where is Mr Laverne, then?'

'Try *The Station Hotel*. That is where he was staying when he first arrived.'

'And is he still there?' Makepeace asked.

'I don't know, do I? I am just a humble cleaner. Now be off with you!' With that Gladys Grimshaw scuttled through the door in the south aisle into the choir vestry.

Makepeace looked at Watson. 'She's a funny one, sir.'

Watson snorted in reply. 'You can say that again, Sergeant. **Miss** Grimshaw seems to be very knowledgeable about the organ to say she is only a cleaner; and a woman.'

Makepeace nodded. 'Perhaps Dr Burchill talked to her, sir. He seemed to be friendly with all sorts. And didn't she sing in the Parish Church Choir in the old days, along with Sarah Anne Smith and that other woman we saw in tow with them at the service the other week?'

'A good point, Sergeant. Once we have sorted Mr Laverne, then I think our cleaning lady over there deserves to be interviewed.'

The warmth generated by the Parish Church's newly-installed 'Otto' gas stoves contrasted sharply with the autumn cold. Watson and Makepeace wrapped up well as they headed towards Olivier Laverne's last place of lodging. *The Station Hotel* had seen better days. Competition from other establishments in the centre of Hartley, together with the spanking new building that formed the centrepiece of Hartley North Station, had meant that trade was not what it was when the railways first arrived in the town.

The two detectives entered *The Station Hotel* through the main door, complete with pillared portico. Nobody was on duty at the front desk. The lounge bar was empty. Makepeace sneezed as the smell of stale beer entered his nostrils. Watson hit the bell at reception hard enough to elicit both an echo and a response from the hotel office.

'Sorry, gentlemen. I was just doing my accounts for the month. Got to try and make a living somehow, eh?'

'Detective Chief Inspector Watson and Detective Sergeant Makepeace. And you are?'

The hotelier peered at Watson and Makepeace.

'I suppose you are here about the murders, an' all.'

'We are, in a manner of speaking. And who are you, sir?'

'Tomlinson, Inspector. Joseph Tomlinson. Proprietor of *The Station Hotel.*'

And why do you say we are here about the murders, Mr Tomlinson?' Makepeace took out his notepad and pencil.

'They were warned, you known, Sergeant. They were warned, alright.'

'How do you mean?' Watson leaned his arm on the counter.

'Letters.'

'Letters?'

'Let us pray!' Tomlinson burst out laughing. 'Sorry, sir. Just my little joke, though they could have done with some help from above, those men.'

'Come on, man. What are you saying?' Watson tapped his fingers on the desk.

'They all got letters.'

'Who got letters, Mr Tomlinson?' Makepeace began to write in his notepad.

'Them there organists. You know. The ones who came for the job down the road. All except one that is.'

'And who was the one who did not receive a letter?' Watson looked at Makepeace to make sure he was writing down every detail, then back at Tomlinson.

'The last one. What was his name?'

'Go on, man. Try to remember. We do not have all day!'

Tomlinson took down his signing in book and flicked through the pages. 'Here we are, Thursday, 9th October 1879. That's when the candidates came, the night before the auditions. They were all very nervous, apart from this chap.'

'Which chap?' Makepeace continued writing as he spoke.

'The one who did not get the letter.'

'And he was?' Wright Watson sighed.

'Hmmm. The last one. The one who never got to play.'

'Do you mean Mr George?'

'That's the one, Stanford George. His uncle has a share in this hotel; a finger in every pie in Hartley, that one!'

'You are sure Stanford George did not receive a letter, like the other candidates?'

'I am sure, Mr Watson. All neatly addressed on a piece of paper, they were, on one of those new-fangled machines. Then glued onto the front of the envelope. A funny smell there was with the letters too.'

'A new-fangled machine? What sort was that Mr Tomlinson?' Makepeace was now scribbling furiously.

'I don't know. One of those things that lets you duplicate the same writing.'

'Really? And have you seen one of those machines before?'

'I have.' A junior's voice could be heard in the background.

'Have you, Jim?' Joseph Tomlinson looked surprised to see his son.

'Yes, Dad. Dr Burchill used a machine like that to copy our music. It saved him a lot of time, or so he said.'

'Well, I never, gentlemen. That's a turn up for the books, I imagine! Is it one of these clues you policemen follow?'

Watson and Makepeace looked at Tomlinson and son. 'It could well be. I don't suppose you have any of those letters still, do you, by any chance?'

Tomlinson Senior pondered for a moment, looking at Junior for inspiration.

'There, Dad. Look! Behind you!'

The hotelier turned to the pigeonholes, most of which (as befitted a largely empty hotel) had their keys hanging limply. Box number thirteen was no exception, and Tomlinson Senior had difficulty seeing the envelope hiding behind the large piece of wood to which the key was hooked. The hotelier pulled the correspondence out and handed it to Watson, who opened it. Inside was a single, thick, folded piece of paper. Watson took it out, unfolded it, read it, then passed it to Makepeace, who pointed to the cut-out letters on the page.

'Who was this letter meant for, sir?'

'Dr Algernon Burford, Sergeant. His name is on the envelope. He was the only one who did not pick up the letter. Apart from Stanford George, who was not left a letter, it would seem. But then Burford had been murdered by the time it was George's turn to be auditioned. Is there a connection there, Harry?' Watson pursed his lips tightly.

'Is there such a thing as coincidence, sir?' Makepeace queried.

Watson shrugged his shoulders. 'I doubt it, Sergeant, but it was unfortunate that Dr Burford chose not to pick up the letter warning him to keep away from the auditions on pain of death! But that is for another day. There is something more pressing that we need to investigate in the meantime.' Watson turned back to Joseph Tomlinson. 'Tell me, sir, where might we find Mr Laverne?'

'No idea, Inspector. He checked out of the hotel some time ago'

CHAPTER 48

WRIGHT AND MAKEPEACE; VERNEY AND LAVERNE; DEAN AND BISHOP: ALL HAVE MUCH TO PONDER

Makepeace shook his head. 'What about Stanford George, sir? The only one not to receive a warning letter; was going to be auditioned last, after Burford; offered the job without further ado, no doubt because of his uncle's position. What is going on there?'

'And yet he had to eat humble pie and become Laverne's assistant alongside Charlie Verney! You know the choir refused to accept George as Burchill's successor?'

'I do. It has been the talk of the town, or at least the musical part of it, but you would know more about that than I do!'

'What? You mean the Glee Union?' Watson laughed. 'We are mere amateurs, Sergeant. We meet to get away from our lives, not talk about them. You are right though. There has been lots of tittle-tattle about what went on in the choir and who planned the 'rebellion'.'

'And who did plan it, then, sir?'

'Everybody's money – not that I am a betting man – is on Ernest Snelgrove and Warburton Sutcliffe. They are the leading lights after Burchill. What they say goes, according to my friends in the Union who sing in the Parish Church choir. Nothing gets past those two, apparently. If they don't want it to happen, then it doesn't happen. Only Burchill could control them.'

'The lead tenor and the choir administrator? Could they be the murderers?'

'I don't know, Harry. I can't help feeling that Mr Laverne is in danger though. If the others were killed because they were in Stanford George's way, does that mean the new Organist and Choirmaster is next in line?'

'There is so much more to these murders than meets the eye, sir.'

Wright Watson nodded. 'All the more reason to find Laverne, Sergeant. Even though he is blind!'

'How do you do that?'

'Practice makes perfect. I am sure that you could do as well as I.'

Charles Verney laughed. 'I have practised hard all my life, Mr Laverne, but I have never achieved anything really. I thought that I might be offered the post at Hartley.'

'It will be a pleasure and a privilege to teach you all that I know. You are well capable of gaining your Fellowship exam, and your Mus Bac, I can tell... Whatever is the matter? Why are you crying?'

'Nobody ever believed in me. No-one thought I was any good. Burchill constantly criticised me in front of the choir. I will never forget the visit of those American organists. TAB tore a strip off me in front of them all because I made a mistake; ONE mistake.'

Laverne laughed. 'Thomas Augustus Burchill was a very special person. He got results at any costs. You know that. And I know that. But he cared for you, Charles. He thought very highly of you.'

'Nonsense, Mr Laverne – I mean Olivier. The only person that old Tommy cared for was himself!'

'Not true; he rated you highly. He told me on many occasions.'

'Really? When did TAB tell you about me?'

Laverne fell silent.

'What is the matter? Have I said something wrong?'

'No, Charles. Nothing wrong at all. Tommy Burchill called himself "a funny one": he never let his guard down when it came to emotions. Did he ever praise you?'

Verney shook his head. 'No. Never. Not once in all the time I worked for him.'

'I understand your anger and your sadness. But don't take it personally, Charles. He cared for you. Believe me.'

'Well, he had a strange way of showing it; that's all I can say! Now what do you want to do about the music for next week's services?'

'I want those services to be the best ever heard in Hartley. I am going to choose the hardest music there is in the library and train the singers to be the top choir in the world.'

'You sound just like your predecessor! Except you don't talk in a broad Yorkshire accent. Come to think of it, Olivier, you don't speak with any accent. Why is that?'

'What a tragedy. Mrs Mann is inconsolable. The choir members are distraught. The Close has been shocked to the core by Charleton's demise. Who would have thought the Organist and Master of the Choristers of Yorbridge Cathedral would be murdered? This is all so very disturbing, coming on top of the other killings at Hartley.'

'Port, Kilbey? Help yourself.'

'I don't mind if I do, my Lord Bishop. Very kind of you.' The Dean of Yorbridge poured from an ornately decorated decanter on the sideboard. He filled a large glass almost to the brim. 'Hmmm. You always did have the best cellar in the Church of England, Herbert!'

'And you the second best, my dear Dean!'

'These "organ loft murders" have hit the national press, Kilbey. Questions are being asked in Parliament. What is so important about that damn post of Organist and Choirmaster?'

'I have no idea, my Lord. I cannot possibly imagine.'

'But why Mann? What has he got to do with Hartley?'

'Charleton was the advisor to Banks over the appointment of Burchill's successor. Perhaps whoever is behind these killings did not like Dr Mann's choice of candidate.'

'Algernon Burford? Was he not a former Assistant Organist here at Yorbridge?'

'He was, my Lord Bishop. A worthy second-in-command. He might have been our Organist and Master of the Choristers in due course.'

'But why kill Mann when Burford had already been murdered?'

'Perhaps Charleton knew something that the killer – or killers -- could not afford to have discovered. Something about Burchill, or the other candidates, or even who carried out the murders. Who can tell? That is for the police to find out, if they are able. Watson and Makepeace, those two detectives I mentioned to you, seem intelligent enough, though I doubt they will find everything that is to be discovered about Hartley Parish Church. You and I both know that some secrets have to be kept for all time, do they not, my Lord?'

The Bishop of Yorbridge looked at his dean, then nodded and smiled thinly. He got up, walked over to the study window, and looked out across the Cathedral Close. Saint Anne's was bathed in moonlight, the tall thin spire reaching up to the heavens, as its mediaeval designers had intended. It had looked much the same the first time he had stood there after his installation. How could he have fallen so far from grace in the few years following that wonderful service?

'What do we do about Banks? His position is well-nigh untenable at Hartley after the shenanigans of the last few weeks.'

'A very good question! I agree, Bishop. It is a pity. I had high hopes for Percy, but his "failings" have surfaced once again, so I fear strict measures will be required if we are to avoid a scandal in the diocese and beyond.' Dean Kilbey downed his glass of port in a single swig and poured himself a second. 'My Lord Bishop?'

'No thank you. One glass is sufficient for me these days. I must read my documents for meetings later in the week before I go to bed. The House will be in session from tomorrow for at least the next two weeks. I leave for London first thing in the morning.'

'I trust you will meet up with Sir Templeton?'

'Indeed, I will, Kilbey. I will be at the ennoblement of Lord Hartley, as he will be known, and then the reception in his honour. I have also arranged to meet him for dinner at The Athenaeum.'

'That will give you the ideal opportunity to talk about the future of our organisation.'

The Bishop of Yorbridge nodded, gravely. 'If it has a future, my dear Dean. Recent events have made many in the circle question whether or not we should continue our activities.'

'Perhaps we should – how can I put it – "lie low" for a while, if you see what I mean, my Lord. It would be a pity not to continue our work in any shape or form, would it not, after all we have achieved in recent years?'

'Very true, Mr Dean. Very true. And I think I shall have a word with Lambeth Palace. The See of Ayton-on-Hebble is soon to fall vacant, and I believe we have the ideal candidate to succeed him.'

'We do? What, for that backwater?'

'We do, Kilbey. It is the Reverend Dr Percy George Banks, lately Vicar of Hartley.'

CHAPTER 49

A WOMAN SAYS HER GOODBYES; A BODY BEGINS GIVING UP ITS SECRETS

'I am leaving Hartley in the morning. I cannot stay here.'

'I agree. It is too dangerous for you to remain in this town. Can you not leave now? There are times when I think the police are already onto us!'

'Well, they are very suspicious of me, I give you that. I dare not go back to the inn, for certain. I will surely be arrested if they find me there, or anywhere, for that matter! I am more than a little surprised I was allowed to go free after my last visit to the police station.'

'I presume it was Inspector Watson who interviewed you.'

Sarah Anne Smith nodded. 'I fed him just the correct amount of truth – or at least my truth -- to make him go off in a different direction; the Rankinists' march and their kidnapping of Lord Hartley came at just the right time: an absolute godsend. It bought me – us – time. Just enough time to finish our work and for me to plan my escape.'

Smith poured herself and her host a drink.

'I think Watson finds you – well -- finds you attractive!'

'All men find me attractive, my dear. That has always been the secret of my – well -- of my success! Long may it remain so, though there are times when I feel that our recent "adventures" have taken their toll on me. I begin to feel old – old beyond my years!'

'Nonsense, you are as beautiful today as you were when I first met you in that organ loft. You must go, now your – our – work is done. It will not be the same without you! And Ottie will miss you so very, very much, Sarah Anne!'

'I know. And I will miss her; very much. She has been like a daughter to me! But my little girl will be well looked after. I know you will see to that, my dearest friend. You do promise me, don't you?'

'Of course! But you underestimate Ottie! She is not a little girl any more: she is a grown woman, with so much talent and so much to give this town, if only people would let her; and they will now, thanks to you and me!'

'It would have been so different if she were my flesh and blood! She would have been given the best, the very best from the very beginning!'

'I know that Sarah Anne. But I must ask you this: why did you never have children of your own?'

Smith laughed. 'Edward was never capable! For all his ardour, nothing ever happened by way of offspring, even in the early days, when we were first together. You know what alcohol can do to a man, don't you?'

'I am not sure I do. But that is of no importance. What about your other suitors?'

Sarah Anne blushed. 'My other what?'

'You know what I mean; don't come the innocent with me, dearie! Your gentlemen friends, dotted all over Hartley. I may not be interested in men myself, but I know how they think and how they feel about women like you, especially the strait-laced ones. They are the most gullible, they are! They have served you and me both well, in their different ways, those *beaux.*'

'You are so right, my dearest friend. Men are such fools! So easily persuaded. They are the weaker sex! We are the strong ones!' Sarah Anne Smith clenched her fists as she burst out laughing.

'Where are you going to go?'

'America. My passage is already booked. I have friends over there. They have told me how wonderful it is! The money, the opportunities, the fame, the men! I will have more concert invitations in a week than I would get in Yorkshire in a year.'

'Opportunities for what?'

'For singing! What do you think I meant?'

The two women laughed raucously, raised their glasses, clinked them, then downed the stout in one large gulp. They slurped and wiped their lips as they smirked at each other.

'I will miss you too, Sarah Anne. I wish this could all have been done differently, I really do.'

'I don't believe you. You never liked Tommy Burchill. Not since he rejected you so. I shall always remember how he treated you; just like he did with poor Charlie, except only worse. Burford was just as bad when he was Assistant at Yorbridge. An awful specimen, with his airs and graces and his superior attitude; he would have made old TAB seem kindly in comparison if he had got the job at Hartley. Charleton is the only one I feel sad about.'

'You performed for him; I know that.'

Sarah Anne Smith nodded. 'Many times. Now I do wish it could have been different with Dr Mann. We both know that was not possible. He could so easily have given the whole game away; all because of that one visit to the Parish Church to wish Laverne well. We could not take the chance. He was the only one left who would have realised what had happened if he had met the new Organist and Choirmaster.'

'Do you have any regrets about Edward?'

'None. My love for that man was long gone. He had outlived his usefulness to us both once he had helped us do away with Burchill and Burford. Though I swear to you, as God is my witness, it was an accident; he lost his footing when he saw me and Wyn approaching him on the station platform.'

'And what about Wyn? You have not spoken of him of late.'

Sarah Anne Smith smiled. 'He and I are to be married once we have reached New York.'

'What! When did that happen?'

The Parish Church clock struck ten.

'Shhh! There is no time for explanations now. Just believe me that I love him, and he loves me. He would do anything for me – he has shown that, as you well know. Getting those men into the organ stop circle was just what we needed to do to compromise them. I am tired. I must rise early tomorrow morning if I am to catch the first boat train and begin my new life. Think of it! This is my last night ever in Hartley, and England!'

'What are you doing down here in the mortuary at midnight? Isn't it time you went home, sir?'

Wright Watson snorted. 'I could say the same for you, Sergeant. Still no sign of Mr Laverne?'

Harry Makepeace shook his head. 'I am afraid not. Not a single sighting. It is as if he is in hiding or, well, or worse. I begin to worry that he is yet another victim of the Organ Loft Murderer.'

'Don't say that, Harry. The Chief Constable will have me out of my job if anything happens to him. We must renew our efforts tomorrow. Laverne will have to appear soon if he is to take the next practices and play for the services that are coming up, though Verney said he and Stanford George might be doing more playing in the future. But if our murderer wants George as the Organist at Hartley Parish Church, then Laverne needs to be disposed of at some point.'

'Whiteley George has been asked to come to see you tomorrow morning, sir.'

'Thank you. That man still has a lot of explaining to do, as we have already discussed.'

Makepeace nodded. 'Why are you still looking at that body?'

'Because, Harry, I wanted one last look before it goes off to be buried. Something is troubling me about this corpse. Is it one of the Organ Loft Murderer's victims, or just a coincidence?'

'Other murders do occur in Hartley, sir, especially in the rougher parts of the town. Though this is the first man I have ever seen with his head cut off!'

'I agree. I have seen some ghastly sights in my time, Harry, but nothing like this.' Watson walked around the body as it lay on the slab in the centre of the mortuary. 'The doctor tells me our victim was decapitated after death rather than before.'

'Thank God for that, sir!'

'I agree, Harry. The doctor also said that it looked as if the man was strangled, like Dr Burchill.'

'A common method, sir. We have had a number of killings like that; especially men murdering their wives in a drunken rage on a Saturday night.'

'Sad to say you are right, Harry. But why cut off the head after death?'

'As a trophy? A sign? A fearful form of revenge?'

'I can think of only one explanation.'

'Really, sir; and what is that?'

'Simple: in order to hide the victim's identity.'

'I had wondered that, sir. But why? And who?'

'Because the true identity of the victim would cause problems for the murderer. If only we had some clue as to who this man was. I doubt if we will ever find the head, so we shall have to make do with what the body tells us, eh, Harry?'

'Yes, sir. Perhaps he was an organist.'

'What makes you say that? Just because the recent victims have been organists?'

'No, sir. Look at his hands. They are so like those of the others.'

CHAPTER 50

A TIME OF RECKONING FOR BOTH BANKS AND VERNEY

The Reverend Canon Percy George Banks, DD, got up from his knees, bowed to the high altar, turned round, walked down the chancel, admiring the ornate organ case as he did so, then turned into the south aisle and down to the Vicar's vestry. He sighed at the sight of the mop and bucket, left by the cleaners – yet again – at the top of the staircase. Once inside the inner sanctum, he sat down at the roll top desk, took out the envelope from his coat pocket and began to read the letter once more. As he did so, he hoped against hope that he had misunderstood the message from Lambeth Palace. Cantuar and Eboracum were in full and absolute agreement. There was now no possibility of Hartley being considered as the home of the new bishopric; it would be a straight contest between Halifax and Wakefield.

'My enemies have won! The organ loft murders must have been the final straw! We had the best choral establishment in the land, and it did us no good! I had friends in high places, and, ultimately, they were powerless to press my case to a successful conclusion. Why? Because malcontents in the choir, led by Snelgrove and Sutcliffe, prevented my appointment of Stanford George. His Uncle Whiteley will never support me financially or politically in the future! Why? Because the Organ Trustees dug in their heels and refused to change those ridiculous, arcane, financial arrangements. Why? Because my beloved wife betrayed me to the Rankinists! Sir Templeton will never trust me again, and rightly so! I have lost his affection, once and for all! For all his assurances, what will he say about me after he is ennobled?

'They were against me; every single one of them! Which of them hated me so much? What deranged madman would murder to thwart my ambitions? It was all of them! I can see it now. It was a conspiracy. Everyone here in this town hates me. I worked so very hard for Hartley. *I have been very jealous for the Lord; the Lord God of Hosts!* I would have been a good – no, a great – bishop. I would have given speeches in the House of Lords; the champion of anti-disestablishmentarianism; the defender of Anglicanism. What is my future now?

'I am undone.' Banks buried his head in his hands. He sat in silence for several minutes. He was stirred from his depressive musings by the sound of footsteps. Despite the heavy rain, the Vicar of Hartley could see clearly out of the vestry window. A statuesque lady was walking slowly and solemnly towards the south porch. Banks stood up and leaned over his desk to get a better view. He blushed as he realised who it was entering his church. 'What does she want, I wonder?'

Charles Verney was happier than he had been in years. At last, he felt cherished and respected by a great player. According to Laverne, even Tommy Burchill had thought something of his Assistant Organist! If only TAB had said so! Why did he have to be so critical all the time?

Verney wiped a tear from his cheek as he listened to the new Organist improvise on the hymns chosen for the following Sunday morning's service. How could someone be so brilliant without the power of sight? Olivier Laverne could! More than that: the blind man was a great teacher and an even greater choirmaster. Verney had learned more from the diminutive Laverne in a few short weeks than he had in 20 years and more working for Burchill; the choir was better than ever. There was something about the new Organist that made all under his direction want to give their very best. Even Snelgrove and Sutcliffe thought well of him! Laverne must be good if those two had given their seal of approval.

Verney had asked them what they thought of Laverne after his first services and practice, when the Frenchman charmed and entranced everyone so completely. 'He's the one for us; no doubt on't,' the two senior choirmen had said in tandem. 'Oliver could have been made for this place; who'd have thought it?'

All was well in Verney's world, but for one thing: he had aided and abetted the killing of Charleton Mann. It kept the Assistant Organist awake at night. Even when he drifted into fitful sleep there was no escape. There was the illustrious Master of the Choristers at Yorbridge Cathedral advancing towards him, pointing an accusatory finger as Verney turned and ran, but to no avail: there in front of him were Burchill, Burford, and Smith, all covered in blood, each laughing outrageously. Whichever way he turned the four organists were in his way: there was no escape. Every night since Mann had been killed, Verney had that dream. Sometimes, Burchill was the one who appeared first; other times it was Burford. One dream had them all in the organ loft, watching and listening as Verney sat at the console while Burchill told his Assistant to play faster and faster.

Why had he agreed to assist in the killing of Mann and the moving of his body from the Parish Church to Templeton Towers? Because there was nothing to lose and everything to gain. Laverne offered him hope and encouragement, a status, a future, perhaps even as a professional musician. Think of it! No more shifts in the mill; no more subservience; a chance to become a gentleman! Mann would have spoilt all that. The Organist of Yorbridge Cathedral would have realised the truth of the situation as soon as he entered Hartley Parish Church and learned of the new arrangements. Everything would have been in vain. There was no alternative. Charles Verney would have to live the rest of his life knowing that he was a murderer.

Laverne's masterly improvisation was coming to a climax; Verney could tell. He knew that the swell of sound and the brilliant combining of themes naturally and inevitably heralded the final statement of the opening melody. The very last chord was played on full organ, including the *en chamade* Tuba. It was enough to make the most cold-hearted human being's hair stand on end. Verney stood up and clapped heartily. He had thought he was the only listener, but another was applauding Laverne's performance. Verney turned round to see who else had been in the audience.

'You! What are you doing here? I thought never to see you again!'

CHAPTER 51

SURPRISES GALORE; A RESCUE MISSION IS MOUNTED; A SINGER DEPARTS FOR EVER

Percy Banks determined to go back to the Vicarage. He read the rejection letter a final time, then put the unwelcome correspondence into his document case. He looked round the vestry as he put on his coat. The organ music had stopped. For a moment he wondered if yet another organist had been murdered. He quickly dismissed the thought, on the assumption that, having got their way, his enemies in Halifax, Wakefield, Yorbridge, Lambeth and, most evil of all, Hartley itself, had no further need to blacken the Parish Church's reputation.

Whatever the Organ Loft Murders had done to dent plans and aspirations, there was no need to be concerned about the musical part of the service. Under Olivier Laverne, much to everyone's surprise and delight, the choir was performing to an even higher state of perfection than when Tommy Burchill had been in charge. Who needed a cathedral in Hartley when the Parish Church already had the best singers in the country?

Stanford George seemed happy enough to be a second Assistant Organist to Laverne and Verney. Now that Edward Smith was dead, there was considerable enthusiasm for a joint approach to music making between St Martin's and St David's. Sir Templeton had proposed the idea. Stanford George, Charles Verney and Olivier Laverne seemed attracted to the idea, given what would be a significant increase in remuneration for all three organists.

Whiteley George was, to date, surprisingly calm about the potential thwarting of his plans. Having repeatedly said 'no cathedral city, no Hartleyville estate', the former Organ Trustee suddenly declared his intention to proceed with the development of the land to the north of the town. The source of his considerable investment funds was a mystery. The work would begin after Whiteley had remarried. The identity of the second Mrs George was a highly guarded secret, though Banks had already acceded to Whiteley's request to conduct the ceremony. Stanford would be at the organ while Laverne conducted the choir.

Banks locked his vestry, double checked to ensure the key had fully engaged (not that he kept confidential papers in that room any longer), then walked down the south aisle. Much to his annoyance, the cleaner's bucket was still in sight, albeit now moved nearer to the chancel steps. The Vicar of Hartley looked across to the front of the nave where Verney was in conversation with a well-dressed woman, the one he had seen entering the church some moments earlier. It was obvious from the Assistant Organist's expression that he cared much for the visitor, hanging on her every word, and nodding firmly at each instruction. The couple were then joined by Olivier Laverne, who put a hand on Verney's shoulder before embracing the woman, kissing her on both cheeks in the French manner. The trio laughed.

Had Banks not felt so tired and careworn, he might have engaged the people in conversation. Engaging with staff, parishioners, and visitors and regaling them with his plans and ambitions had been a favourite pastime, but no more. He resolved to stick to his original decision and went out of the south porch into the cold autumn air. The Vicar of Hartley walked briskly back to his home, the top priority now being to speak candidly to his wife, for better or for worse.

⸭

'I wish you both well. If only things could have played out differently. I know that is impossible in this day and age. I shall miss you, Ottie – I mean Olivier.'

Charles Verney looked at Laverne and then at Sarah Anne Smith. 'Ottie? Who is Ottie?'

'A slip of the tongue, Charlie, nothing more. I meant Ollie – short for Olivier. I sang with him at some concerts when I was "in my pomp" as Sarah Anne Jessop. Dr Charleton Mann – poor soul – introduced us after I had sung for him at Yorbridge so successfully in his annual performances of *Messiah*. Everyone who got to know him well then called him Ollie, but I imagine you are too grand for that, now you are Organist and Choirmaster at Hartley Parish Church! Strange to say, Olivier here does remind me somewhat of the girl who studied at the Blind School with Mr Laverne and TAB as well, at least briefly, before he got the huff and told her she was no good. You didn't think that of her, did you, Olivier?'

'Not at all, Sarah Anne. She was the best organ student I ever had in all the time I taught there, or anywhere else, come to think of it.'

'Ottie – Ottavina – Badland came to the services here occasionally. You may have seen her with me and Gladys.'

'But what happened to Miss Badland? I never realised she was an organist.' Verney looked puzzled.

'She left for the United States of America, two weeks ago. And that is where I shall be living in the future. I sail from Liverpool this evening. My train departs from Hartley Central within the hour. I just wanted one last look round the Parish Church before I said goodbye to this place for ever. And to thank you for your recent help, Charlie. It was much appreciated. My affairs in Hartley could not have been brought to such a successful conclusion without you!'

Verney blushed. 'I am glad I could be of assistance.'

'I have no idea what you two are talking about!' Laverne interjected. 'However, I do not propose to enquire further.'

'That is for the best, Olivier, believe me.' Sarah Anne Smith and Charles Verney smiled at each other.

'Then I bid you farewell, Sarah Anne!' Laverne embraced Smith once more.

After a moment when time seemed to stand still, Smith pushed Laverne away and picked up her baggage. 'Enough! I must be away. God speed, Olivier Laverne. You are the best organist of them all. No-one will thwart you ever again!'

The Vicar of Hartley was just about to close the front garden gate when Wright Watson and Harry Makepeace ran towards him, shouting.

'Have you seen Mr Laverne, Vicar?'

'What is the matter, Sergeant?' Banks held the gate open, in case the two policemen wished to follow him into the Vicarage.

'We believe he is in grave danger.' Watson puffed.

'Laverne? Surely not!'

'Yes! Yes! Have you seen him?'

'I have, only a few moments ago.'

'Where? Tell us!'

'Of course, Inspector. Laverne is where I would expect him to be – at the Parish Church. I heard him practising.' Banks laughed. 'Then as I left the building, I saw that he was in conversation with Charles Verney and a woman.'

'A woman? Who was that?'

'Sarah Anne Smith, Sergeant.'

'And Laverne was well?'

'Of course, Watson, if his brilliant playing is anything to go by!'

'We have been searching for him for a while now, sir. Where has he been staying?'

'I have no idea, Watson, and I do not care either, as long as he turns up to services and practices. What he does with the rest of his life – subject to the rules of decorum befitting the standing and position of a senior church organist – is Mr Laverne's affair. If you require nothing else of me, gentlemen, I shall bid you good day. I have much to contemplate at the moment, so I intend to go *incommunicado* for a little while.'

'Of course, Dr Banks. Thank you. We shall leave you in peace.' Watson nodded and turned away; Makepeace followed behind.

'Just one thing, Inspector. You will let me know first if you find anything – well, anything "untoward" shall we say?'

Watson turned, nodded, and smiled thinly. 'Of course, Vicar. I understand perfectly.'

Banks watched the two detectives run all the way down the hill towards the Parish Church. It was just possible to see Watson and Makepeace walk through the enormous west gate before disappearing out of sight. Only then did the Vicar of Hartley walk up to the front door of the Vicarage and enter, to be greeted by his wife.

'I think we need to talk, Percy.'

'We do indeed, Rose. Shall we go into my study?'

Sarah Anne Smith hated waiting, especially when she had to be in Liverpool by six o'clock in the evening in order to begin the embarkation formalities. What a relief it was to be leaving Hartley -- grimy, cold, sooty, drab Hartley. She had lived in this place for the whole of her life: forty years. The furthest abroad she had ever been – until now – was Dublin, in the days when there was a real chance of success as a soloist, at least on the concert platform if not the opera stage (a career move Charleton Mann had advised against, much to her annoyance). Then Edward had come along and ruined what was left of her career after Burchill had started the rot. She could still remember – word-for-word – TAB's critical reviews of her performances. No-one deserved such vitriol! Burford's undermining of her role as principal soprano with the Yorbridge Choral Society had not helped either. The Carl Rosa Opera Company had beckoned until Burchill wrote an adverse reference about her.

That was all behind her. Good riddance to Burchill and Burford. Thank God there had been someone willing to commit murder for her, with Edward and then good old Charlie happy to help with the dirty work. Sarah Anne could not shed a tear for her useless husband: he had served his purpose and needed to be murdered once he knew too much, but before his drink-loosened tongue gave the game away. What a pity that Mann and Laverne had to die!

Enough! Sarah Anne Smith admonished herself for dwelling on the past. There would still be opportunities – genuine opportunities – to make a name for herself in the New World. Sarah Anne Jessop – a force to be reckoned with! There would be the accolades, the invitations, the premium fees, the glowing reviews! She had to get there first, though! The nerves were worse than any she had ever experienced on the concert platform. She went to the last carriage. A kind porter helped her with her luggage. He joked about the weight of her suitcase: 'got a dead body in here, Missus?

Haven't I seen you somewhere before? You're that singer, aren't you?' She smiled and said nothing, tipping the lad handsomely to get rid of him.

The whistle sounded shortly thereafter. Sarah Anne had selected the only empty compartment, but just as the boat train began to move, the carriage door opened and in sprang a tall figure dressed in black, the bowler hat pulled firmly down over his eyes. The man slammed the door shut and lowered the blind. Once the train was well out of Hartley, Sarah Anne's fellow traveller got up, turned away from her, took off his coat and hat, then turned back and sat down once more.

'My God! What are you doing here?'

CHAPTER 52

THE MURDERER IS REVEALED

On first entering, Watson and Makepeace assumed the Parish Church was deserted: all was quiet; no sign of life. Watson put his finger to his lips and signalled for Makepeace to go to the south of the church and walk up the far aisle while he did the same on the north or 'organ' side, as everyone called it. That way, Watson decided, the whole of the nave could be checked in the speediest manner possible.

Makepeace was the first to observe signs of life. Up in the chancel, right between the choirstalls, Charles Verney was talking to Olivier Laverne and an unknown third person clothed in a heavy black coat and hat. The Detective Sergeant motioned to Wright Watson, who tiptoed up to the west-facing organ case. Once in position, he peered through the chancel arch to see the trio in conversation.

'That is the end of the matter. I will be leaving Hartley myself shortly. Sarah Anne was right. But all is well, I assure you. There is just one last thing to attend to; one more act to commit.'

Upon hearing these words, Watson sprang into action, leaping up the chancel steps and tackling the criminal before Laverne could be attacked. Makepeace caught up with his commanding officer and attempted to help subdue the struggling assailant. Once the wrestling match was concluded, Watson and Makepeace turned the criminal over and pulled off the hat.

'You! What are you doing here?'

'Minding my own business, like you should be doing. Now get off me! Charlie – help me up!'

Verney helped Gladys Grimshaw get up from the chancel floor. The cleaner dusted herself down.

'Are you alright?' Laverne listened to the sound of her voice and the direction from which it came.

'She is just a little shaken up, by the looks of it, Olivier. Wouldn't you be if you had been felled like that?'

Watson looked firstly at Gladys Grimshaw then Olivier Laverne. 'We had reason to believe that Mr Laverne here was in danger; that he was to be the next victim of the Organ Loft Murderer. It looked as though he was about to be attacked. Mrs – sorry, Miss – Grimshaw was just taking something out of her pocket. I – we – assumed it was a weapon.'

Gladys Grimshaw laughed. 'And if your Sergeant will take his hands off me, I will show you what it was!'

Watson nodded to Makepeace, who released the woman's arms from his grip.

'Thank you!' Grimshaw took out a piece of paper from her coat pocket. 'This is for you, Laverne. Read it, please!'

Laverne held his hands out to the cleaning lady while Watson and Makepeace looked on.

'Read it to me if you will, Charles.'

Verney took out a pair of spectacles from his waistcoat pocket and looked at the document. 'It is a testimonial saying that one George Grimshaw attained the highest marks in the examinations for Fellowship of the College of Organists and that the same Mr Grimshaw was awarded the degree of Bachelor of Music in the University of Oxford with distinction.'

'A relation of yours, I presume, Miss Grimshaw?' Laverne enquired. Makepeace was now taking notes, as directed by Wright Watson. Verney smiled knowingly.

'I am George Grimshaw.'

'What? You are a man posing as a woman?' Makepeace stopped writing in his notepad.

'Don't be ridiculous, Sergeant. I am female and proud of it; a Rankinist, through and through! But in order to take the examinations, set, marked, and regulated by men, I had to pretend to be a man. How ridiculous is that? As a female organist I was spurned and ridiculed by such as Burchill and Burford, Smith, and Mann; but when I disguised myself as a man, they and their kind thought nothing of awarding me top marks. As a woman, I was refused entry to the club; as a man, I would have been welcomed with open arms. How ridiculous is that? Then there was the ignominy of being thrown out of the choir, just because we were women – me, Sarah Anne Smith, Ottavina Badland, and many others. There was nothing wrong with our singing; just our sex! Now that you have become Organist and Choirmaster at Hartley Parish Church, Olivier Laverne, I want you to fight the cause for all who encounter prejudice; you because of the lack of sight; me because of my sex! Admit it, you would never have been appointed here if it had been known you were blind that Sunday morning, would you? Yet when people heard you playing *without having seen you*, it was obvious you were the best person for the job, though I think the Reverend Canon Banks needed some persuading even then.'

Laverne nodded. 'I fear you tell the truth about the prejudice against blind people and women, or both! It is wrong; completely wrong!'

'Then I leave you to carry on the good work on behalf of thwarted organists everywhere, Ollie!'

Watson looked at Makepeace and then at Gladys Grimshaw. 'What did you say?'

'I said thwarted organists everywhere, Detective Chief Inspector. And before you ask, yes, I put those notices in the *Almanac,* just as I arranged for those four men to be murdered.'

'What!' Watson, Makepeace, and Laverne exhaled in chorus.

Verney shook his head vigorously. 'And I helped her, at least with Mann's death! I am proud of it too! Sick to death after all those years of being downtrodden.' The Assistant Organist turned to Laverne. 'I am sorry, Olivier, whatever you say about Tommy Burchill, and even if I took it the wrong way at times, he wronged me and so many others, with his high-handedness and his impossible standards. I could no longer bear his criticisms of me; you of all people know what he was like.'

Laverne shook his head. 'I understand how you both feel, but what you have done – it is so wrong. I should –'

'Don't say another word, Laverne. Be silent! The time for talking is over!' From her other pocket, Gladys Grimshaw took out a small pistol. 'I hoped that it would not come to this, but my secret is out; I will have to act. Charlie, get some rope from the cleaners' cupboard and tie these three up before we make our escape. It's what we used before; you know where I keep it.'

Verney nodded and ran off.

'Now kindly go up to the organ loft. You first Inspector, then your Sergeant, and lastly Mr Laverne.' Gladys Grimshaw motioned towards the loft door with her pistol. Once all four of them were by the organ console, the old cleaner looked down at the keys. 'I once dreamt of being Organist here; of playing triumphantly for glorious services. But it was not to be. I lived my dream through you, Olivier Laverne, when you surprised everyone with your brilliant playing the other Sunday. O how glorious it felt!'

Steps could be heard. Verney rushed up. 'Here you are', he said, breathlessly.

As the Assistant Organist entered the loft itself, Makepeace, seeing that Gladys Grimshaw was distracted for a moment, launched himself at her to wrest the gun out of the woman's hand. The cleaner was too quick for him; a shot was fired; the policeman fell to the floor, clutching his stomach.

'What have you done Gladys? Enough!'

'Stop it, Charlie! Whose side are you on?' Grimshaw pointed the pistol at Verney and then moved round in a half circle, waving the weapon at Watson and Laverne as Makepeace continued to writhe on the floor. 'Hands on your heads, all of you! You too, Charlie, if you will not help me!'

'No, I will not. I said no more killing. And look what has happened. Another body in the organ loft! It will never end, will it?'

'Very well,' Grimshaw said angrily. 'Take that, Verney, you weak little man!' The cleaner pointed her pistol at the Assistant Organist's foot and fired. He screamed in agony.

'Stop it now, Gladys Grimshaw. This has all gone far enough – too far, in fact!'

'No, I will not, Watson! Hands on heads, both of you. Right back against the console, now!'

Watson and Laverne did as they were told. Watson murmured to Makepeace. 'Don't worry, Harry, we will get out of this, I promise you.'

Gladys Grimshaw slowly walked backwards, pointing the gun at her captives as she did so. In her haste to escape, and her anxiety to ensure that Watson did not make a sudden move, Grimshaw did not see Harry

Makepeace inching along the organ loft floor, despite his wounds. As she stepped onto the top loft stair, the Detective Sergeant grabbed her by the ankles. Grimshaw toppled backwards and over the edge of the organ loft balcony. Unbeknown to anyone, Grindrod had been in the cellars working on the hydraulic engines. The inspection hatch below the loft and behind the north choirstalls had been left open. Grimshaw fell through and onto the blowing mechanism still revolving in all its industrial majesty. There was an agonising scream as the engines devoured the woman. Watson rushed to see what had befallen the assailant. Gladys Grimshaw was mincemeat! The engines groaned to a sickening, deathly halt. After a few moments, a head appeared from the hatch. 'What the hell is going on? Who has been playing silly buggers with my machinery?' It was Grindrod.

'Call the police, and a doctor, now! No questions. Just do it! There is a man up here badly injured, as well as someone in the cellar!' Having issued instructions, Watson turned back and knelt down in front of Makepeace. 'Harry! Harry, stay awake, Help has been summoned!' Watson did not notice Verney tiptoeing down the stairs, then walking briskly out of the church. Laverne could hear the steps perfectly well but decided not to inform the Inspector what was happening. Charles Verney deserved some happiness and escaping Hartley was one way of achieving it. Instead, Laverne reflected on the fact that there was no one now alive who really knew his secret. Nobody would ever find out.

CHAPTER 53

EVER THEREAFTER

There were no more Organ Loft Murders after the debacle of Thursday, October 30th, 1879. Hartley Parish Church never became a Cathedral. The new See went to Wakefield in a straight competition with Halifax.

Within three months of the last killing and Gladys Grimshaw's horrific death, Percy Banks had left Hartley to become Bishop of Ayton-on-Hebble. Rose Banks continued to look after the family, playing the part of a Bishop's wife to perfection. Much to Percy and Rose's surprise, she gave birth to a boy, Thomas Augustus Banks, shortly after leaving Hartley. She later took up the organ, having lessons from the Organist and Master of the Choristers, Stanford George. Stanford came to Ayton in 1889, having gained the degree of Mus Bac in 1882 and Mus Doc in 1887. Olivier Laverne was his teacher throughout this period.

Whiteley George and Gertrude Rankin married in a small ceremony at Hartley Parish Church. The Reverend Percy Banks officiated, in his last service before moving to Ayton-on-Hebble. Stanford George played the organ and Olivier Laverne conducted the choir.

Once ennobled as Lord Hartley, Sir Templeton Taylor was a vociferous and energetic campaigner for universal suffrage. In contrast, he remained silent on the continued and increasingly cruel outlawing of homosexuality.

Martha Burchill became an ardent campaigner for universal suffrage, along with her maid Annie. The two of them remained at number 84 for the rest of their lives. Martha never married, spending her time, energy, and money on leading the Rankinists after Gertrude stood down following her marriage.

Charles Verney escaped to South America. Gladys Grimshaw had deliberately missed when she aimed at the former Assistant Organist's foot. As a result, the police were tricked into thinking that Verney was incapable of evading capture and had not thought to restrain him in the wake of the struggle with Grimshaw.

Ernest Snelgrove and Warburton Sutcliffe set up in business together running a highly respectable photographic studio, using the equipment that Wyn Williams had given them before his departure to the United States. Snelgrove and Sutcliffe set out to create a photographic record of life in Hartley in the late 19th and early 20th centuries. They remained stalwart members of the Parish Church Choir.

Neither Wyn Williams nor Sarah Anne Smith were ever heard of again. Ottavina Badland also disappeared without trace. No record was found of any arrivals in America in late 1879 or early 1880.

Ishmael Monkhill retired in 1885. His son carried on the business into the 1920s, when the firm went bankrupt. The company proudly maintained their *magnum opus* at Hartley Parish Church until then. Grindrod's water engines continued to give reasonable – if at times erratic – service until being replaced shortly after the First World War, when an electricity supply was introduced. As the water engines were being taken out, a shrivelled head was discovered weighted down at the edge of the main supply tanks. The remains were too far gone to permit identification, though the widely accepted theory was that the skull belonged to the headless torso discovered in late 1879. As a result, the head was buried with the other parts of the corpse in Hartley Town's Municipal Cemetery.

Harry Makepeace made a full, if lengthy, recovery. He was promoted to Inspector and awarded a medal for his bravery. His son later joined the police, eventually becoming Chief Constable of Hartleydale.

Wright Watson was criticized by the authorities and the Chief Constable in particular for his handling of the Organ Loft Murders. He therefore retired to farm a small plot of five acres to the north of Hartley in 1880. In the 1891 Census he described himself as a 'gentleman farmer' with several employees and more land. His grandson sold the farm in 1947 to the local council to build a large estate of modern 'homes for heroes', with indoor bathrooms, hygienic kitchens and spacious living accommodation. The appalling slums were finally replaced.

Olivier Laverne had a long and distinguished career as Organist and Choirmaster at the Parish Church, maintaining and at times exceeding the standards set down by Dr Thomas Augustus Burchill, Mus Doc, FCO. Laverne became a much-loved figure in Hartley. He remained a bachelor all his life, his solitary companion being a pet monkey called Tommy.